THE DEVIL'S SNARE

Michael Donovan was born in Yorkshire and now lives in Cumbria. A consultant engineer by profession, his first novel *Behind Closed Doors* won the 2012 Northern Crime competition.

Praise for
THE DEVIL'S SNARE

'... good old-fashioned detective work. A slick, dynamic mystery...'
Kirkus Reviews Recommended Book

'... one of the best novels I have read this year. Brilliantly absorbing ...
escapism at its best.'
Postcard Reviews

'... complicated ... wonderful ... brilliant. I recommend anyone ... to try this
book. [It] will haunt your days and nights.'
Georgia Cuthbertson, Cuckoo Review

Praise for Michael Donovan

'At a time when there seems more competition than ever in the crime-
writing genre, Donovan's debut novel is a real winner...'
Lytham St Annes Express

'... a wonderful debut novel in a hugely competitive market ... an
enthralling novel ... deliciously complex ... make(s) the readers hair stand
on end. Donovan ... succeeds in breathing life into a host of warm, witty
and realistic characters.'
Cuckoo Review

'Eddie Flynn is part Philip Marlowe, part Eddie Gumshoe, a likeable
wisecracking guy but with a temper when roused ... humour ... violent
confrontations ... well recommended.'
eurocrime

'... a chilling thriller crafted with a fluid narrative style... always engaging ...
wild nightmarish scenes...'
Bookpleasures

www.michaeldonovancrime.com

THE DEVIL'S SNARE

MICHAEL DONOVAN

HOUSE ON THE HILL
Publishing

First Published 2015 by **House On The Hill.**

ISBN-10: 1 508569 90 8
ISBN-13: 978 1 508569 90 9

Cover design by **House On The Hill** from Shutterstock images.

p0005

Published by Human Vertex Publications, UK.

In memory of my parents
Harry and Monica

CHAPTER ONE
A swim in a shark tank

It was barely ten in the morning but Shaughnessy's office was already baking behind its drawn blinds. Beyond the windows London was in the grip of a heatwave, a mid-May freak that had arrived early and stayed long enough to turn suspect nostalgia for childhood summers into bad tempers and scandals about Tube ventilation. This side of the glass business was sweaty but otherwise normal in the sense that we could see trouble coming with every word from our prospective clients' mouths.

They were a fortyish married pair, and were enjoying neither the heat nor the novelty of explaining their problems to private detectives. The guy was doing the talking, and though his words were calm and assured his eyes were those of someone watching from behind barricades as his hands clenched and un-clenched round a secret he wasn't telling us. I was wondering what that secret was and how much of his story was true but mostly I was watching the woman. The blinds had softened her face but couldn't hide the bitterness she wore over it like yesterday's make-up, the cold intensity of her eyes as she watched her husband, like she was ready to pull the plug if he veered from script. I listened and watched and mused on how ordinary the two looked. If you didn't know it, you'd never guess they were the most hated couple in Britain.

Eventually the guy wound up and I glanced at Shaughnessy and caught a raised eyebrow. Stood and went to throw up the sash and let air in. Then I walked back to my chair, smiling reassuringly at our guests whilst I tried to figure what length of barge-pole was right for this one.

Shaughnessy was wondering the same thing. Sean and I are not exposure-hungry. The agency trades on its reputation for discretion. The people who hire us have never heard of us until they need to, and it works nicely that way. That's why the offer the guy had just pitched left us with a quandary. It's not often that fee-no-object jobs come up, but the job the man had just described sounded like a swim in a shark tank.

I silenced the warning bells. Focused on practicalities.

'Are the threats specific?' I said.

The guy opened a leather portfolio and passed some sheets across. Five pages. Computer-printed hate-mail. I flicked through them.

'Copies?'

'The first three. The police have those originals.'

I read the letters and slid them one by one across to Shaughnessy. As hate-mail went they were good. Seemed the writer disliked our visitors on a whole different level to the general public, who didn't like them much in the first place. The writer's theme was consistent: accusations; talk of retribution; threats. The tone was that of someone giving the subject plenty of thought. The couple had pencilled dates at the top of each letter, since the writer hadn't thought to include that detail. According to the annotations the first letter had arrived sixteen months ago, the two recent ones within the last few weeks. Not a regular correspondent.

'You get much of this?'

The man shrugged. 'Apart from this guy? Maybe a dozen a month.'

So, a steady market. Maybe Hallmark should do cards.

'Most of it's just idiots letting off steam,' the man said. 'It's this guy we're frightened of.'

'You sure he's the one?' Shaughnessy said.

'The letters tie in. Our car was wrecked after the first and Elaine was attacked following the third.'

I recalled a hit-and-run story from a few months back, the couple's claim that it was their hate-mail guy. I also recalled that not everyone shared that view.

'The police put it down to a drunk driver,' I noted.

The woman sat forward. Spoke for the first time. 'Forget the police,' she said. 'We're doing this our way now.'

She looked at me with fire in her eyes, something between hunter and hunted. Desperation, basically. The two of them – Stuart and Elaine Barber – were travelling a rocky road, and from what Stuart had just told us they'd been fighting uphill for a year.

'We want this lunatic stopped,' Elaine said. 'And we don't care how you do it.' Her eyes angled between me and Shaughnessy. 'We didn't invite any of these people into our lives. We're the ones who've lost everything. Do you know the worst of it?' – emotion cracked her voice – 'Everyone was on our side at first, even the police.'

Her husband worked up a smile that didn't touch his eyes. 'But you know how things went after that...'

Not much more than he'd briefed us. The Full English with Tabloid has never been my breakfast habit. Shaughnessy's neither. If we took this case we'd need to catch up. That was no problem, of course, since we knew someone who knew everything.

Shaughnessy's door burst open and an explosion of colour annihilated the shadows as Lucy backed in wearing pants in a screaming lime that were outdone only by her violet-streaked hair. She carried a drinks tray that was an obvious prop to get her in for a gander. Unlike Shaughnessy and me, Lucy kept her nose diligently in the tabloids. She'd spotted the Barbers the moment they'd walked through the door, despite the false name in the appointments book. Lucy would have their life history down to a pat when we needed it. Right now I looked at the coffee pot. Raised an eyebrow.

Lucy wrinkled her nose. 'It's hot, Eddie,' she said.

I took her word for it. Operating the filter machine was one of her tricks, like the owner of the vicious dog who can make it roll over. Lucy brought a number of talents to her front desk job. The main one was keeping the firm running on minimal budget and bad equipment. I smiled at our guests and offered refreshment. Stuart Barber accepted out of courtesy. His wife declined. Lucy poured the spare for me. I felt a momentary goodwill.

'Hang around, Luce,' I said. 'We may need copies.'

Lucy threw a grateful smile and went to prop herself against the wall in lieu of her usual perch on Shaughnessy's desk. It was that kind of meeting.

I took a breather. Re-read the letters. They all seemed to be the same guy. The tone was consistent and the greeting unvarying:

"To the Killer Couple..."

Reading the stuff it was easy to see why the Barbers wanted protection. The writer was not high on style but you couldn't fault his creative venom. And the tone escalated in the recent stuff – the letters that had brought the Barbers up our stairs. The latest promised imminent hurt, no more mistakes, maybe a reference to the hit-and-run failure. If you took the guy at his word we were dealing with someone teetering on the edge.

'If we did help,' Shaughnessy said, 'we'd need you to keep a low profile while we tracked the guy down.'

Stuart shook his head. 'That wouldn't be possible.'

I looked at him. 'My partner's right. We're not security specialists. We can't put a wall round you.'

'We've no intention of hiding,' Elaine said. 'The book is published tomorrow. We need to be out in the public eye.'

'Sure,' I said. 'Makes sense. But public appearances would be risky right now. Your campaign should probably go on hold for a while.'

'That's not possible,' Elaine repeated. 'We're committed to a schedule.'

An ambulance screamed its way across Paddington, homing in until the siren muted a block away. A false peace descended. I looked at Elaine Barber and wondered what drove her. I was about to speak when the siren kicked back in with a din that rattled the cups. I walked over and slammed the sash. Angled the blinds while I was there. Checked the street. A white Astra was loitering thirty yards down, squeezed into a too-tight spot that left it standing out from the line of parked vehicles. It had been there when we brought the Barbers in, which meant the driver had just sat for forty-five minutes with the windows tight and engine running for aircon. Interesting. Had me wondering if he was connected to our visitors. Had someone followed the couple here?

'Your book promotion's likely to stir things up,' I said. I was still watching the street. 'You're going to face hostility when you're out meeting people. Might make it difficult to spot the hate-mail guy if he makes his move.'

I turned. 'Is the book worth getting hurt over?'

'The book's everything,' Elaine said. 'People need to know the real story.'

I hadn't read the first edition of the Barbers' book but my understanding was that people had had plenty of opportunity to hear the real story. The Barbers had sold it all over the place. A serialisation in *The Sun* had been running for as long as I remembered. They had some kind of website and a Facebook page.

Plus the book – and now its new edition. The Barbers had been up there in the public eye for nearly two years, hate-mail or not. Their problem was that they hadn't convinced people. They were still the couple everyone loved to hate. That didn't stop everyone buying their book, of course, but then Margaret Thatcher's memoirs sold a million.

Now they planned to go out in public to flog the new edition with a vigilante running round just waiting for his opportunity. So they figured they needed protection. Pulled our name from the hat.

'Here's the problem,' Shaughnessy said. 'Even if we had the resources to put a wall round you it would defeat the purpose of a publicity campaign.'

'We don't want a wall,' Stuart said. 'Just enough visible security to deter this lunatic from a direct attack.'

'And in the meantime you want us to go after him?'

Elaine leaned forward. 'Not just that,' she said.

Stuart reached back into his portfolio and handed me a photo, which I looked at for precisely half a second thinking what in holy hell before the penny dropped and the lever fell and the cogs meshed and I finally knew why the Barbers were here.

The photo was a three-by-two, snapped on the quick, blurred and badly framed. At its centre was the out-of-focus figure of a little girl. The girl's face was way too blurred for identification but I recognised it the same as everyone. I placed the photo on Shaughnessy's desk. Shaughnessy looked at it and looked at me. A moment ago we had a tricky security job. Now the game had changed: now we were looking at an impossible detective job. Across the room Lucy's mouth opened, and I guess my own face wasn't too neutral as I looked at the Barbers.

'You want us to find her?'

The Barbers stared back with the vacant eyes of the true believer. To them the truth behind this photograph was beyond dispute. It was the basis of their existence. Shaughnessy fingered the photo and twirled it and slid it back. I picked it up again. The "Hoax Photo" to everyone but the couple in front of us.

To the Barbers the child in the picture was their three-year-old daughter, proof that she was alive and well.

But to everyone else it was either a hoax or clever showmanship.

Because their daughter was Christa Barber, and whatever had happened to her everyone knew that she was not coming back.

CHAPTER TWO
If she's faking, she's good.

'That's an interesting challenge,' I said.

I guess the couple had a radar for scepticism. Elaine glared at me.

'The photograph is Christa, Mr Flynn.'

Sure it was. It was something the two of them told themselves a million times a day. The mantra they'd stuck to with the desperation of people grasping the lifebuoy after the ship's funnels have gone. I kept quiet.

'We don't know who took it,' Elaine said, 'but it's Christa. It proves she's alive.'

Perhaps. Twelve months ago when the photo was taken. If the picture was their daughter in the first place, which no-one believed. When I looked at the snap all I saw was a blurred impression that could be any of a million kids.

'To be honest,' I said, 'it's hard to see a positive identification coming from this.'

The Barbers stayed impassive. I was preaching to the unconvertible.

Christa had gone missing from the couple's holiday caravan in the New Forest twenty-two months ago. She'd been two years old. They'd put their daughter to bed one night and left her alone in the caravan while they ran an errand. Somehow a door was left unlocked. When they got back Christa was gone. The disappearance and search had dominated the headlines for a month. The month became two then three and Christa stayed missing. Then the Barbers became the number one reality soap when the police announced that they were looking at the couple themselves. There were inconsistencies in their account of the disappearance, questions they couldn't answer. Eventually, the move that everyone was expecting: Stuart and Elaine were arrested on manslaughter charges. The tabloids had a field day. I remembered riots outside the magistrates' court, the Barbers looking guilty as sin as they were sneaked in through a back door. Everyone had a theory. Everyone could see the truth. Stuart and Elaine got themselves bail but might have been better off in detention than living as tabloid fugitives. But the two of them picked themselves up and started fighting. They got a campaign going, fought high-profile media skirmishes and eventually lashed up a best-seller. Then more dramatics: the couple got themselves a good lawyer and the police screwed up. The prosecution began to founder even as the trial date was set. Finally, just four months ago, the field day had become a circus when the CPS dropped the charges the day the trial was due to start. More riots. Camera footage of the Barbers being hustled out of court by their *Sun* minders. A chief superintendent penned behind microphones, choosing her words: the police weren't looking for anyone else but the case was still open. The police's problem was that they'd messed up and the Barbers had simply stuck to their story. Stalemate.

Soap operas are not my thing and I hadn't bought a ticket to any of the show but now here it was, knocking on our door. The Barbers needed investigators and protection, and they were inviting us in.

Elaine was watching me.

'Please don't doubt the photograph,' she said.

Her expression challenged me to disagree. I stared back, trying to judge the line between parental instinct and misguided fixation – or acting.

'We're not blind,' Stuart said. 'We know we're in the minority. But most people are starting from a different assumption.'

'The assumption that you killed Christa.'

He shot out a humourless laugh.

'That does condition people's view. Just like the police's. Look at them: they accuse us of the unthinkable and try to destroy us, pick every little hole they can in our account of what happened; put together a whole prosecution based on circumstantial evidence; but they've never answered the most obvious question about this photograph.'

I got it: 'If the girl in the picture is not your daughter then whose is she?'

Stuart's face shed some of its reticence. 'If the photo isn't Christa then that's someone else's little girl. So why has no-one come forward?'

Good point. Even an out-of-focus snap should trigger someone's memory.

'Let's be clear on this,' Elaine said. 'Christa is alive. That's her in the picture. If you're going to work with us we need you to focus on that.'

Elaine clearly hadn't focused on the fact that we hadn't yet agreed to work for them. And like all true believers she was confusing fact with faith. I spoke quietly: 'If we took a look at this,' I said, 'you'd also need to understand our position. The agency's approach is to assume nothing that isn't supported by facts. We could trace the girl in this photo but that doesn't mean we'd find your daughter.'

Stuart cut off his wife's reply. 'Just get to the photo. Believe me, you'll have found her.'

So that was the package. A protection detail in a circus ring; a hunt for a lunatic vigilante; and to top it off, a search for a little girl who didn't exist. Fees unlimited. When I came in today I'd been worrying about a knock in the engine. Shaughnessy and I looked at each other. Then we told the Barbers to sit tight and went with Lucy through to my office.

~~~~~

My office hasn't got Shaughnessy's style. Shaughnessy's wallpaper isn't peeling and the hole in the roof isn't over his ceiling. But then Sean doesn't get the view of the Great Western railway or the Westway. And he doesn't get the northerly aspect. In heatwaves northerly aspects are good. My room was ten degrees cooler, even if the lumpy club chairs made appreciating the fact a little difficult. Sean eased himself into one of them whilst Lucy found space on my roll-top. I sat behind the desk. Set the recline of my Herman Miller executive chair to *Think*. The Miller is my concession to yuppie culture. The chairs were all the rage in the nineties, the ergonomic must-haves for city up-and-comers. Comfortable as hell. They needed to be, considering that they set you back nearly a thousand quid. My Herman Miller wasn't quite as ergonomic as most, due to a missing arm, but then it hadn't cost me a grand.

I got my feet onto the desk, careful not to scuff Lucy's pants.

'When things come down to it,' I said, 'money-dependency is a pain.'

We looked at Lucy.

'The glass needs replacing in the front door,' she agreed. 'And the carpet's beginning to smell. Also, my computer keeps re-booting. And I've had to cancel the council direct debit. We're hanging in, Eddie, but we could do with a little mouth-to-mouth.'

My Miller creaked under its off-centre load. I gazed at the ceiling.

'The job might max us for two months,' I estimated. 'Commercial rates.'

'I like the sound, Eddie,' Shaughnessy said. 'Just not the smell.'

Like the carpet.

'Are the Barbers for real about their daughter?'

We looked at Lucy again.

'Everyone says they killed her,' she said. 'An accident of some kind.'

'But they couldn't get it to trial.'

'The case didn't hold up. One of the witnesses had told lies and the forensics fell apart – and they never found a body. You always told me it's hard to get a conviction without a body, Eddie.'

'Prosecution errors aside,' Shaughnessy recalled, 'things pointed their way.'

Lucy agreed: 'The police haven't been looking for an abductor for eighteen months.'

'Suppose they killed her,' I said, 'why would they hire us to find a non-existent child?'

Shaughnessy and I exchanged smiles. The answer was obvious. If the Barbers had killed Christa then their whole campaign to get her back was sham. And death-threats aside, the couple were doing pretty well living that fantasy. A high-profile search for Christa would go nicely with the sub-title of their book's new edition which was up on posters around town:

"The New Evidence"

The Barbers hadn't mentioned what their new evidence was, but being able to say they'd a team of investigators on their daughter's trail couldn't hurt their case. A costly smoke and mirrors if you considered Eagle Eye's commercial rates, but nothing that book royalties and the ongoing *Sun* serialisation wouldn't cover ten times over. The smell was getting stronger. Sure, the agency had a cash-dependency, but we were getting by. We were strong enough to walk away from circus acts. Searching for make-believe kids didn't interest me – Shaughnessy neither.

Of course, there was the flip side.

Believe Stuart and Elaine's account and you saw two lives shattered. If Christa really had been abducted, and if the Barbers saw her face every time they looked at that photo, then the torment of knowing that no-one was searching for her would be unimaginable.

The problem was that it's hard to sympathise with someone whilst you're trying to figure whether they're acting. We looked back at Lucy.

'I don't like her,' Lucy said. 'But she always seemed sincere. Elaine was totally broken at those news conferences. She nearly had a breakdown when the police called off the search. If she was faking, she was good.'

'Don't like her?'

Lucy kicked her heels. 'She's cold. Maybe vindictive. It comes out in the book, too. She's on a crusade against the world. Almost a religious thing, like the crusade's taken over from Christa.'

'Understandable,' I said, 'if a disbelieving world is the biggest obstacle to getting their daughter back.'

The thing had a fascination. If we did take this one it would not be for the money: the agency might be a little dusty behind our cracked front glass but we'd survived three years of recession. We'd turned down jobs before and we'd turn them down again. As turn-down candidates went this one was right out in front but it also had one thing going for it: the chance of some real detective work. I racked the Miller another ten degrees; scrutinised my shoes.

'Eddie,' said Lucy, 'it's all over your face.'

I snapped back. Gave her wide-eyed.

'Your *itching* look,' she said. 'Everyone says the child can't be found. You can't resist that kind of challenge.'

I kept my face straight, which told Lucy everything. Lucy and I had a thing once. It was a great thing but it was doomed from the start, mainly because of her mind-reading skills.

'You're like a cat watching kippers,' she said. 'If you want to know what happened, Eddie, read the tabloids like the rest of us.'

I threw her a smirk. Winding me up wasn't going to work. Even Lucy knew the difference between a tabloid front page and reality. She just didn't share my preference for fact over fiction.

Shaughnessy cleared his throat. 'The thing does sound kind of interesting,' he admitted.

My smile broadened.

'It would be nice to find out what happened to the kid,' he said. 'Even if what we found didn't suit the Barbers.'

My smirk hit full wattage. Beneath my instinct to chuck this one back into the pond I'd had the same idea. If the Barbers were looking for stooges in some kind of publicity stunt they'd come to the wrong agency. The photo – hoax or not – was real. Which meant that we could get to whoever took it and whichever child was in the picture. And along the way we could take a look at the whole thing. The police didn't go after the Barbers for nothing. There was a nice irony in the thought that the couple's own money might finance a trip back to court.

'There's also the security side,' Shaughnessy said.

I held the wattage. Now we'd hit my partner's bottom line: his special forces background. Sometimes he couldn't wait to get back into the firing line. There was no way that two of us could handle it, of course.

'We'd need Bernie in,' Shaughnessy said. 'That would free up the two of us plus Harry for the footwork.'

Lucy rolled here eyes and slid her backside off my desk; folded her arms. 'I don't know which of you is worse. You've already decided on this.'

Shaughnessy and I kept quiet. Lucy broke first.

'Who am I to argue? Look on the bright side: the money will come in handy. Maybe I'll even get paid.'

'I guarantee it Luce!' I said, jumping onto any argument. 'Your back-pay will be in the bank the moment the new carpet's down. Let's give the man a call.'

Lucy welded a smile to her face and went out to try to get hold of Bernie.

Bernie Locke was my old pal from the West Riding. We'd been mates since school, despite the fact that he couldn't wield a cricket bat to save his life and had once put me in hospital with a stupendously irresponsible googly in a Yorkshire schools. The month I joined the Metropolitan Police Bernie took his six-foot-six black backside off to terrorise the marines. Retired as a captain eight years ago and now ran an outward bound cum business seminar centre in Hampshire. The guy was a year ahead of me approaching forty but fitter than most twenty-year olds. He stepped in sometimes when things heated up. His fees were extortionate but the Barbers had a cash mountain to excavate. If Bernie was available we could cover it.

Harry Green was our part-timer, in the business for forty-plus years and fast approaching a retirement he couldn't afford. He'd be happy to put in the extra hours to handle the digging and to provide extra eyes. Shaughnessy and I put some figures together while Lucy was out.

Lucy came back in, cheeks flushed. Seemed she'd got through to Bernie. When it came to the girls the guy could still spin fast ones. I gave her disapproving. She returned haughty.

'He needs two days then he's in.'

A couple of days we could cover. The thing was on, if we wanted it.

Shaughnessy and I looked at each other. We both knew we shouldn't be touching this. But the temptation of real detective work and a solid security gig was hard to resist. The temptation of a full bank account was even harder to ignore.

And Lucy might be acting uppity but she'd give her hind teeth to get a look behind the Barbers' curtains.

'Let's talk to them,' I said.

We wound up and went back through. I smiled at the Barbers and pushed aside the question of whether we were about to sign up with child-killers; gave them the estimate of what the thing would cost. The figures didn't faze them. I picked up the photo again.

'If the photograph is traceable we'll get to it,' I said.

Elaine's mask dropped a little. Something of the misery Lucy had spotted in those TV appeals came through. She spoke softly: 'Take as long as you need. You can't imagine how it feels to know that no-one is looking.'

Sure I could imagine. It must hurt like hell, assuming the thing wasn't an act.

But I had to go along with Lucy. If Elaine Barber was acting she was good. Maybe she was simply a mother in torment, like they claimed.

Lucy brought the forms through and we all shook hands.

'Welcome to Eagle Eye,' I said.

CHAPTER THREE
Paranoia, maybe

I stood at the window while Lucy sorted the paperwork. Fingered the blinds. The Astra was still down the street, windows tight, engine idling. Gut feeling became certainty: the vehicle was connected to our visitors. Paranoia, maybe, but we'd just signed up to protect the couple and paranoia was our job. For all we knew this could be their vigilante. In a few minutes I'd find out.

Lucy printed the contract form and we walked the Barbers through it and explained what we were going to do.

First priority: security. We'd put someone with the couple twenty-four-seven. Secondly: we'd chase down the vigilante. Get him off the streets. Priority three: investigate the Christa Photo. Elaine stopped me to suggest that the photo be top priority. I overruled her. Repeated my one-two-three. If that was unacceptable we could shred the contract. I looked at her. Made sure we understood each other. Shaughnessy asked if there were any more questions. There weren't.

Lucy normally worked mornings only but she was happy to hang on to put an education pack together. She wasn't about to miss tabloid action. Shaughnessy had business to close off but he'd be free by the end of the day. I was free right now. I took first shift. Escorted the Barbers out.

A crowd was milling, down in the lobby. Elaine shied back but I coaxed her through. The mob was harmless. Clients of Rook and Lye, the personal injury lawyers who roosted below us as they rode the wave of the liability business. Everyone had a gripe worth money and Rook's commercials brought them in by the bus-load. Elaine needn't worry about recognition: Rook's crowd had eyes only for their own misfortunes and the cheques at the end of their rainbows. My judgement was sound. The Killer Couple squeezed by unnoticed.

Outside, the heat knocked you flat. More August than May. The air was a syrup that muffled traffic sounds and set dogs yowling. Pigeons squatted moodily on the roofs. I flipped my shades down, told the Barbers to hold still and walked down towards the Astra but it was already moving through a quiet three-point and rolling away towards the main road. The guy was sharp. But that hasty exit gave the game away. He was here for the Barbers. We wouldn't be meeting today but from now on we'd be looking out for him. I walked back.

Stuart opened their Galaxy to ventilate it while I went round to pick up the Frogeye.

When I reversed off the parking spot behind the building the car's shadow stayed put, a memorial to my previous Sprite that had burned up there during a job with complications. My replacement was a rebuilt Super Sprite, courtesy of a business we'd saved from getting hooked up with the wrong kind of contractors. The rebuild packed a modified Coventry Climax engine which outperformed the old one by a factor of three and made driving almost normal. For the first time in years I could overtake.

I followed the Barbers north out of London to the corner of a leafy junction near Elstree. Electric gates swung open and we drove onto a gravelled parking area fronting a red-brick house. I told Stuart and Elaine to go on in and took a walk round the grounds. The public boundary was a hawthorn hedge that bordered a side lane, interrupted only by a wooden gate. The gate was bolted on the inside but a little finger work would get you through in seconds. I opened it and went out, looked back from the lane. The half-dozen poplars backing the hedge looked nice, but the spring buds hid nothing. Anyone out here would have an unobstructed view of the house.

Back inside I followed a lawn inset with flower beds to a rear fence; hoisted myself up and looked over at an access path running behind the property – more opportunity for anyone watching the house. I completed my circuit along the dividing fence with the neighbouring property and came back to the front. Overall, the fencing and hedging worked nicely for a watcher. If someone wanted to get near the house there wasn't much we could do.

I made a second circuit and checked windows and doors. The house was a 1920's two storey building with steep slate roofs and leaded casement windows showing their age. An intruder in a hurry would have to choose between pushing the glass through and ringing the doorbell. Three-quarters of the way round I discovered that someone had already made that decision. A rear parlour window exhibited a mess of jemmy marks. The marks weren't new but the cracked paintwork said that the damage had been done after the last exterior painting. Say three months to three years ago. The Barbers had been in the house for four months.

I finished and went in.

The interior was twenties affluence designed for the upper strata of the Metroland expansion: high ceilings, ornate covings, broad stairs, generous floor spaces. Spoiled by tired decor, but I guessed the Barbers had had other things on their minds since they'd moved in.

The ground floor window casements had latches and stays but no locks. The latch of the jemmied window was badly seated where the screws had been forced back into the frame. Either a cheap repair or the intruder tidying up. I brought Stuart to look but he shook his head. Maybe the break-in was before their time.

We sat at a breakfast bar in the back kitchen. Elaine brewed coffee.

'Tell me about the Orchard Grove,' I said.

This was the New Forest caravan site where their daughter had disappeared.

'It's a small site near Lyndhurst,' Stuart said. 'Thirty static caravans.'

'Easy access?'

'No. There's just one track in through the woods, and a small river runs along the whole of one side. The other boundary's a hedge separating the site from a bridle path. There's no passing traffic.'

'People live there all year round?'

Stuart shook his head. 'Most units are holiday lets. There were four or five owner-occupiers like us but none stayed the year round.'

'How often did you go there?'

'Just spring and summer,' Elaine said. 'I took Christa for odd weeks from May onwards. Stuart would come down at weekends.'

'You knew the other owners?'

'Nodding terms only,' Stuart said. 'Nothing more.'

'What kind of people stayed there? Anyone who ever worried you?'

'No. It was mostly elderly couples. A few families in the holidays. The site felt safe.'

'How busy was it that week?'

'Most units were in use,' Elaine said. 'All older people. It was term time but the weather was good.'

'And nothing unusual? No suspicious characters around?'

'Nothing. It happened right out of the blue.' Elaine's eyes focused on the past.

'Go through it again,' I said.

Stuart took a breath.

'It was a stupid mistake,' he said.

'In retrospect,' I suggested.

He shook his head. 'From any point of view. We should never have left Christa alone in the caravan. We were utterly stupid and we paid the price.'

Elaine picked up the story.

'It was a Friday evening. Christa and I had come down the day before and Stuart had just arrived from London and driven out to do some shopping whilst I got Christa ready for bed. She was a little difficult that night. As the whole world now knows she was prone to tantrums. We'd had a long day and she was tired. Bath-time was a struggle. Christa was crying the whole way through. Eventually she calmed down and I got her into bed and when I started to read her a story she dropped off as if you'd thrown a switch. That was Christa: one moment wide awake and asking questions, the next fast asleep so a foghorn wouldn't wake her.'

'What time was this?'

'A little after seven. Twenty minutes before Stuart got back from the shopping.'

'Did you see Christa when you got in?' I asked him.

He shook his head. 'Elaine didn't want me to disturb her.'

This was the kid a foghorn wouldn't wake. I let it go.

'We ate dinner and watched TV,' Elaine continued, 'until around eight thirty.'

Her words hesitated as she reached the moment their lives had changed. Her eyes glazed. Stuart stepped back in.

'We decided to go out,' he said. 'We owed some money to a neighbour who'd settled a maintenance bill for us. I'd forgotten to pick up the cash whilst I was shopping so we decided to pop back into Lyndhurst.'

'Both of you?'

The two were silent. It was the question they'd been asked a million times.

'My card had been rejected in London. Elaine came along in case we needed to use hers.'

Elaine fixed me with a look that dared me to criticise. Criticism wasn't my business. I waited.

'Lyndhurst was only up the road,' Stuart explained. 'Christa was sound asleep and our neighbours were at home next door. We decided to risk a quick dash to the cash machine. Thought we'd be twenty minutes at the most.'

'Did you check Christa before you went out?'

'She was fast asleep,' Elaine said.

'What time was this?'

'A quarter to nine.'

'Tell me again about locking the caravan.'

'The caravan has front and rear doors. We went out of the front door and locked it.'

'And the rear one?'

Elaine's face was pale. 'We all know now. It wasn't locked.'

'And you didn't speak to your neighbours on your way out?'

'No,' Stuart said. 'We thought we'd only be a few minutes.'

'How long were you away?'

'We got back around twenty-five past nine.'

Forty minutes – a little longer than their estimate.

'And when you got back you decided to move the car.'

Stuart nodded. 'I dropped Elaine off and drove straight out.' For the first time bitterness crept into his voice: 'The famous Fiat,' he said.

'Parking's limited at the site,' Elaine explained. 'We already had the Galaxy there and the Panda would have been blocking the avenue so Stuart took it to a garden centre about a mile away rather than park on unlit lanes. They don't mind cars left overnight. Stuart parked the car there that evening and it never moved. All the theorising about it is nonsense.'

'What did you do once Stuart had gone?'

Elaine's face tightened. 'I went in to check on Christa. That was when I noticed that the rear door was slightly open. I was surprised that we'd missed it when we went out but the significance didn't hit me at first. Then I went into Christa's room and saw that her bed was empty.'

Her words dried up again. Two years, a hundred interviews, the

19

serialisations and the book, and still the moment defeated her.

'Go through it,' I said.

Elaine clenched her hands round her cup.

'I assumed she'd woken up and wandered into one of the other rooms. But the caravan was empty and that open door suddenly scared me, though it was hard to believe she'd gone out through it: I was sure the door was closed when we left and it tended to stick. Christa didn't have the strength to open it. But I rushed out and searched beneath the caravan and around the units nearby. Then I knocked on neighbours' doors and they came out to help. We checked the whole site but Christa was nowhere. Then I thought of the river. There's a fence all along the site to stop children wandering but if Christa had gone out onto the bridle path she could have reached the water further down. I raced down there but there was no sign of her.'

'That's when you raised the alarm?'

Elaine nodded. 'The site manager got everyone out. I was running around frantic, not rational at all. It felt like I was trapped in a nightmare.'

'When did you call the police?'

'I called them,' Stuart said. 'At ten p.m., as soon as I got back to the site. I'd phoned Elaine while I was walking back from the garden centre. She'd told me what had happened and I ran the rest of the way.'

'How quickly did the police get there?'

'A car from Lyndhurst was there inside ten minutes. Forty-five minutes later they had a full search up and running.'

I stood. Walked to the window. Watched the garden. The account tied in with the bare bones they'd given us back at Chase Street, but the two of them had still not mentioned the contentious issues. My memory was shaky on the subject but I did recall two things.

'You weren't at the site, Stuart, when the police arrived.'

The fact wasn't disputed – only the explanation.

'As soon as I'd called the police I went out to search for Christa,' Stuart said. 'It was Elaine who met the police.'

'Go back to nine thirty,' I said. 'The time Elaine discovered Christa missing. Am I right that the police view differs from yours at that point?'

Stuart shrugged. 'The police had all kinds of witness statements and sightings. Everything was confused in that first half-hour.'

'Let me get it right: you'd driven the Fiat to the garden centre unaware that Christa was missing. But witnesses later claimed to have seen you searching with Elaine *before* you drove out. Were they mistaken?'

'Yes. I didn't know there was any problem until I phoned Elaine on my way back from parking the car. If I'd been there when we discovered Christa missing the last thing on my mind would have been to go and park it.'

The logic made sense but why did witnesses insist that they saw him searching with Elaine around nine thirty that night? That discrepancy – and his absence when the police arrived – had been a major issue. An even bigger problem had been that the police hadn't known that Stuart and Elaine had *had* a second car in the area until three days later. The Barbers' failure to mention that detail hadn't looked good, retrospectively.

I walked back. Sat down to listen to the Barbers' description of a long night. The search party. Tramping the fields until dawn. The next day: divers in the river, police walking the banks, covering twenty miles downstream. But Christa never showed up.

Elaine stood and went to take my place at the window. She gazed into the distance, arms folded. That night twenty-two months ago had manacled the two of them. They were locked forever to the moment their daughter became inaccessible.

'Tell me about the photo,' I said. I avoided the popular term. "Hoax Photo" didn't fit well into the Barbers' world-view.

'It arrived in the post,' Stuart said, 'ten months after Christa disappeared. A photo and a message. The sender could take us to Christa but he wanted money.'

'What was your first reaction?'

Elaine spoke with her back to us. 'We knew it was her right away. We'd begun to lose hope before it arrived. Christa seemed to have been gone a lifetime and it was getting harder to tell ourselves that she was coming back. But the photo was like a light going back on. Finally we had proof that she was alive. It gave us a reason to live.'

'But the photo didn't convince everyone.'

'No,' Stuart said. 'It was the height of the media campaign against us. One fuzzy photograph wasn't going to turn the press round. There was no way that train was stopping.'

'As you say – fuzzy.'

This was gist of the problem. *Fuzzy* hardly covered the quality of the photograph. The picture's focus was further off than a drunk's balance. Sure, it was a young blonde girl, maybe three years old and maybe with a passing resemblance to photos I'd seen of Christa. But the snap might have been any of a million kids. The press published the picture, but once its entertainment value died down they declared it a fake, and most people went along. Only the Barbers never doubted it – or so they claimed.

Elaine turned.

'It's not something you can explain. We saw the picture and we knew it was her. It's her face, her energy. The way she's holding herself, watching for somebody's attention. Christa's a natural performer. When we saw the photograph we knew she was alive. And we've not changed our minds, despite everything.'

"Everything" including the police taking the view that Christa was dead by seven p.m. the night she disappeared and that every subsequent action by the Barbers was nothing more than an elaborate charade to cover that up. The eventual collapse of their prosecution was history now but the fact that the police weren't looking for anyone else told its own story.

'Any idea why the photo sender stopped communicating?'

Elaine came back over. Sat down. Rubbed her face.

'We've never understood that,' she said.

'They contacted us three times,' Stuart said, 'through the *Evening Standard* classifieds. They used a code – "Reunited". We replied the same way and said we were ready to co-operate. Pay their price if they could take us to Christa.'

'*Evening Standard* advertisers are traceable. Did the police go after the person who placed the ads?'

'Only as far as an East End pawnbroker who was placing the adverts for them. He claimed his customer just walked in and paid cash for the service. Claimed not to know him. The police didn't push their enquiry since they'd already decided that the photo was a hoax.'

'But then the communication stopped.'

'Yes. We had three exchanges and a price was named. Two hundred thousand. Then the ads stopped. We've continued checking the paper every damned day for the year since, but there was nothing until three weeks ago. That's when a new message appeared out of the blue telling us to be ready.'

A message the police and public didn't know about. The Barbers were no longer taking things outside the family. But it seemed our Christa Photo guy was active again, pursuing the show-and-tell. The puzzle was why he'd gone quiet for a year.

'There's no explanation,' Elaine said. 'It's as if it's some kind of game.'

'The photo is Christa,' Stuart said, 'and they want their money. So it's not a game.' He looked at me: 'We have to find out where the photo was taken,' he said, 'or pay this guy off. The photo's our route to Christa.'

I looked at them. Wondered whether this was true or whether the Barbers already knew that the photo was a dead end.

CHAPTER FOUR
If it smells like a turd...

A car horn sounded. I walked through and pressed the gate-release and a green Mondeo rolled in. The car coughed to a stop and Harry Green got out and pulled a bag from the back seat. He gave the house the evil eye.

'They want us to keep them safe here?'

I grinned. 'That's the easy bit.'

I took him in to meet our clients. He shook the Barbers' hands then I walked him back out for a tour, brought him up to speed. Not being a partner in the firm Harry could take an objective view of the job. He heard me out and gave me his analysis.

'Smells like a turd,' he said.

It's this breadth of expertise that gives our firm the edge.

Harry pushed and prodded at the break-in window.

'Old,' he confirmed. He ran his fingers along the join where a blade had been slid in to force the latch. Asked if our clients had been burgled.

'Nothing since they moved in four months ago. Maybe this was the previous owners.'

Harry grunted. We completed the circuit then went back in. He took a look at the windows from the inside, prodded and pushed and grunted some more. Then shook his head. Updated his assessment.

'A turd,' he said.

Now we knew it.

I briefed him on the threat-letters. Harry promised to take a look at them. He's our tech and forensics man.

The Barbers offered him a guest room but Harry opted for the couch in the drawing room; took his bag through. Elaine asked if he'd eaten lunch. Harry's face cracked into a smile.

'Lunch would be wonderful,' he said.

I left them to it and headed back to Paddington.

Connie had his tables out and was doing a roaring trade, rushing round and yelling at everyone, the way he did when profits were flowing. When he saw me the yells upped a few decibels. He grabbed me off the pavement. 'Whatcha want, Eddie? Whatcha want?' as if I was going to tell him I wanted to pay off my debts and feel good again. Instead I ordered a takeaway tuna baguette and mineral water which got us to the bottom line. 'You paying today?' he said.

Connie's a funny guy.

'Next week,' I promised. 'I'll surprise you.'

Connie's face stayed doubtful but he brought the sandwich and I flicked him a salute and walked to our building. Lucy was still in. She'd already put something together. My desk was covered in more paperwork than usual. Not my own paperwork because it was neat. A stack of printouts. A couple of books. Two copies of the same book, to be precise. The title stood out over a photo of the Barbers' lost child:

WAITING FOR CHRISTA

I looked at Lucy.

'Two copies? Are we on a spending spree?'

'One for here, one to take home,' she said. 'I've put it on the Barbers' sheet.'

'Good girl,' I said. It was funny to think of the Barbers funding the purchase of their own book. How did that work on their tax return?

Shaughnessy came through and flopped into one of my chairs. I made room on the roll-top for my lunch. Lucy made more room and perched herself next to it. Kicked her heels. 'What do they say?' she said.

'The same as this morning. A few more details. Sounds straightforward.' I got my jaw round the baguette. Clamped. Pulled.

'If you believe them.'

I spoke through mouthfuls of tuna. Summarised what the Barbers had told me about that night and what came after. The Christa Photo; the offer of information for money; then the photo-sender's puzzling silence before the recent communications. Once we'd got the Barbers secure we'd go looking for the guy. Figure out what that twelve month silence was about.

'Maybe the photo really was Christa,' Shaughnessy said, 'but then something happened to her.'

He looked at Lucy. 'How's your contact at the *Standard?* Maybe she can tell us who placed the new ads.'

'Angela. I'll talk to her,' Lucy promised.

I chewed baguette. Sipped water.

'The big question,' I said, 'is what really happened that night? We've got Stuart's and Elaine's story. Take us through it, Luce: what's the flip side?'

'The flip side is all the inconsistencies,' Lucy said. 'According to the police, Christa threw more than just a tantrum that night. She was screaming to wake the dead then suddenly went quiet. And Stuart and Elaine didn't leave the caravan at the time they claimed. They were seen there fifteen minutes later. So the abductor's window was shorter than they say. And when they got back the two of them were seen searching for Christa despite Stuart insisting that he went straight out to park the Fiat, unaware she'd been taken. Those are the main problems.'

I reclined the Miller. Got my feet onto the desk.

'So what's the police conclusion?'

'They say Elaine killed Christa whilst Stuart was out doing the shopping. She snapped during the tantrum and either hit her or shook her violently. Just a moment's lost control and Christa was dead. When Stuart got back they tried to revive her but she was gone. The two of them were in shock. They had a nightmare decision: call the police and own up and maybe Elaine would go to prison, or act quickly and cover it up. They went for the second option. Stuart put Christa's body into the Fiat's boot and they worked up their abduction story and drove to the cash machine to create the window of opportunity. When they got back to the site they pretended to discover Christa missing and started the search. That's where they messed up: they should have dumped the car before they raised the alarm. I guess they weren't thinking straight.'

'Understandable if you've just killed your child,' Shaughnessy said.

I agreed. 'What else do the police say?'

'They say that the reason Stuart wasn't there to talk to them when they arrived was because he was out ditching the Fiat. The real problem was that the police didn't know the Barbers had the Fiat with them until three days later, by which time they say Stuart and

Elaine had disposed of Christa's body.'

'Meantime, we had the search.'

'Yeah. Three days intensive hunt. Two hundred police and volunteers. Stuart and Elaine were in the thick of it but the police say it was just an act. And part of the act was their story about seeing a suspicious woman near the site that evening. The police gave out a description but no-one ever identified her. Meantime, Stuart and Elaine played the distraught parents. They were out with the search parties that first night until Elaine collapsed and had to be taken back to their caravan. The second night was another puzzle: Stuart claims he was out searching but no-one recalled seeing him. The police say that's when he disposed of Christa's body.'

Shaughnessy cracked his knuckles. 'They did that TV appeal,' he recalled.

I dug into my own memory, saw Stuart and Elaine, white-faced behind a bank of microphones, pleading with whoever had their child.

'It fooled me,' Lucy said. 'Elaine seemed devastated. And Stuart couldn't even talk.'

'They'd just lost their child,' Shaughnessy said. 'However it happened, it didn't need much acting.'

'Elaine wasn't just upset,' Lucy said. 'She was distraught. Didn't want the search to be run down. If she'd been pleading for her life it couldn't have been better. I've just watched it again. If that was acting Elaine deserves an Oscar.'

She snapped a memory stick onto my desk. I strained my abs. Pocketed it.

'All the TV appearances are on there,' Lucy said. 'And I've printed the main newspaper stuff.'

I strained again. Riffled the paperwork. Lucy had printed out copies of the entire tabloid coverage. Two rags in particular. The Barbers had done a deal with *The Sun,* who ran their tragedy blow-by-blow before realising they'd signed up with the wrong party: by the time the evidence began to stack up against the Barbers the paper was committed to a crusade they were probably regretting. To their credit, they'd stuck with it through twenty-two months, but then *The Sun* had stayed with the Tories all through the nineties. I skimmed a stack of pun-free headlines that were a measure of how seriously the paper had taken the campaign.

The other prints were extracts from *The Nation*. That paper had started at the same end as the rest – everyone loves a bleeding heart story – but since they'd been pipped for the Barber exclusive they looked for a new angle. When the tide turned against Stuart and Elaine *The Nation* popped the champagne corks and got down to their own speciality. Demolition. Their anti-Barber campaign had been strong enough to put them in court twice. It was *The Nation* who'd coined the term "Killer Couple", which technically was a little loose since no-one had implicated Stuart in Christa's death. But I guess "Killer Person" doesn't have the same ring. I skimmed twenty-two months of the stuff, right up to the present. *The Nation's* enthusiasm for the story hadn't waned in all that time. A front page a week ago gave us a considered comment on the Barbers' updated book: "Killer Couple's Best-Seller Shame" summed it up nicely, even if the new book hadn't yet made a single sale.

But hostile tabloids weren't our immediate worry. The hate-mail vigilante was. Maybe this was a guy with grievances stirred up by the tabloids. We all feel entitled to take other people's affairs personally nowadays. Our first priority was to keep the couple safe, guilty or innocent.

I reported that Harry was with the Barbers. Gave them his appraisal of the job. His exact words.

Shaughnessy grinned. 'It's away from the house that's going to be fun,' he said.

Tomorrow, when the Barbers' book promotion kicked off. That's when the job would start.

'I'll have my desk clear by the end of today,' Shaughnessy said. It was more than I would. But that was Shaughnessy: a neat freak.

He heaved himself from the chair and went back to his office. Lucy followed him out. I started on her information pack, catching up on twenty-two months of minding my own business. I sifted through *The Sun* and *Nation* stuff first. Not in the hope of truth but on the basis that the average of two extremes might put me near centre. After two hours I knew better. You can't average extremes. The two papers delivered mutually exclusive views of the universe, both of them convincing in their partisan hysterias. Maybe I'd get a better sense of the thing when I read the Barbers' book. At five thirty I shoved a copy, along with the paperwork, into a bin bag and headed out.

CHAPTER FIVE
And you swallowed it?

Home is the top floor and loft in a Victorian terrace a stone's throw from Battersea Park. I lived alone but a girl called Arabel Mackie had the keys to my door and an open invitation. Some nights the invitation delivered a bonus in the form of home cooking aromas waiting when I came up the stairs. Tonight was one of those nights. Tonight my door was sweating. Home cooking with chillies.

I went in and Arabel turned from the stove.

'Babe, you're early!'

I looked at her. It was the first time she'd ever said that to me. It was like she was talking dirty. I threw down the bin bag and moved in to try a few dirty moves of my own but she fended me off.

'Quit that, babe, we're eating in ten minutes.'

'Ten minutes? I thought I was early.'

She shook her head. 'You're twenty minutes behind, Flynn. I just thought you'd be later.'

I grinned. Now I was late, even if I was early. I might have argued the point but the aroma of the cooking had my senses in a half nelson. My world had closed down to a vision of a dinner plate. I was showered and changed in eight minutes and got to the table just as Arabel was pulling something off the flames that would have had Lucifer sprinting for the extinguisher. Crayfish, Caribbean style. Grolschs to keep the fire under control. I heard somewhere that bread damps heavy spices better than beer but how do you get bread into your mug? Arabel spotted my bin bag.

'Work, babe?'

I told her about our new clients. Her eyes widened.

'You're working for the Killer Couple?'

'We don't know if they killed anyone, 'Bel. That's just hype. The Barbers say they're innocent. They say their daughter's alive.'

She grinned sweetly. 'And you swallowed it?'

'I swallowed nothing. This thing may be some kind of reality show to most people, all about sides, but we shouldn't forget the person at the centre of it. Personally, I'd like to know what happened to

Christa.'

'And you'll find out,' Arabel said.

'Yeah, I'll find out.'

Arabel finished eating ahead of me on account of her serving herself a smaller portion. She made a move and was suddenly perched on my knee. Now it was my turn to fend her off. Balancing beer whilst forking crayfish is tricky enough as it is.

She returned to her chair and planted her arms on the table. 'Before you get too far into bed with your Killer Couple,' she said, 'just remember the weekend.'

We were due out of town, Saturday.

'Is that likely to get messed up?' she asked.

'Absolutely not,' I assured her.

'Promise me, babe.'

'Pass the chilli sauce,' I said.

~~~~~

We liked to go out after dinner but tonight Arabel was jet-lagged from a change of shifts so we settled down to watch a movie. Quit when her eyes started drooping. It was nine thirty and she was on earlies tomorrow. She headed for bed. I said I'd be right along. Opened the Barbers' book, *Waiting For Christa*, dedicated to "the daughter we love more than life". There was also a dedication to a guy called Owen Jagger who'd "guided them through their darkest days". Maybe their preacher or their lawyer. I grabbed Arabel's iPad and trawled the internet. Found that Owen Jagger was their publicist. Why didn't I guess?

I turned the pages and immersed myself in the nightmare that started at nine p.m. on a summer's evening twenty-two months back. Read pretty much what I'd read this afternoon in Lucy's *Sun* extracts but presented with a little more literary flair. The story gave the world Elaine's viewpoint. If she had a ghost-writer he wasn't named. Maybe this came straight from her. I told myself I'd give it an hour. By midnight I was half way through and not much enlightened.

If I believed Elaine's story they were living a nightmare. If she was fibbing then the book was an impressive novel. Was it possible to work up 500 pages of phoney anguish and make it stick? I didn't know.

When you took the book at face value the Barbers had had it rough. Starting with an earlier tragedy when their first child, Grace, had died, the victim of infant cot death syndrome. A tragedy that was thrown into a different light after the disappearance of their second child. No-one accused the Barbers outright but *The Nation* for one started working the limits with questions that left their readers in no doubt they were looking at double killers, a proposition that eventually landed them in court. The paper settled and the Barbers got wealthier but the accusation stuck. None of it mattered, according to Elaine. It was all just noise around their one focus in life: getting Christa back.

The book described the night Christa disappeared in minute detail. The narrative tied in with what they'd told me today: the quick trip for cash; the open caravan door; Christa's empty bed.

No-one at the site had noticed anything. The only hint of something untoward had been the Barbers' own sighting of a woman standing by the road at the top of the bridle path that ran back to the site. It had been barely a glimpse as they passed, but the significance of her standing there alone would come back later. The woman had become the "Mystery Woman" in the tabloid pages. Who was she? Why was she waiting there? Elaine dwelled on the mystery in endless "what-if?" detail and threw in a computer generated impression of a pretty, dark-haired woman, described as of medium height, around twenty years old.

Meanwhile, the search for their daughter was painted as a slow drowning in despair as time took Christa further from them. The first black night; the first twenty-four hours; the first week then month; the world round them darkening all the time. Their daughter's disappearance swallowed the Barbers' lives whole, regurgitated it as media headlines and hype, endless speculation, countless chases after shadows. Christa look-alikes popped up all over the country. The police followed up but drew a blank on every one. Meanwhile the Barbers gained a tail of hangers-on, press, cranks and psychics, all with their theories.

The search for Christa wound down. The search for the Mystery Woman continued. Nothing turned up.

Then the turning point. The police focus switching to the Barbers themselves. The Mystery Woman forgotten. Elaine's bitterness radiated from the pages. Her narrative didn't shirk from the police theory, but her attacks on their case were caustic, even if her arguments were more emotion than evidence. It's easy to fake emotion on the page, of course, though when Elaine blamed herself for abandoning Christa that evening the emotion seemed credible. But neglect your child or kill it, I guess there's room for regret either way. I remembered Lucy's memory stick. Slotted it into my computer.

The Barbers' appeal, two days after Christa disappeared, was a tear-jerker. The two of them sat pale behind a bank of microphones, talking through a storm of motor drives and flashes. A senior policeman sat at Stuart's side. Elaine's sister, Sharon, at hers. Elaine spoke in a hoarse whisper. Stuart sat with glazed eyes; said nothing. Lucy was right: they were convincing. Elaine looked every bit the broken woman as she begged whoever had Christa to bring her back. It was hard to see the acting, just a woman suffering the agony of not being able to reach her child. I watched and wondered.

One a.m.

I went back to the book; waded through the morass that followed the change in direction of the police enquiry. Hampshire police pulled the Barbers down to Winchester eleven times to go over inconsistencies of timing and sightings. Elaine took us through their accusations point by point but stayed consistent with her rebuffs. Wrote about unreliable witnesses, mistaken sightings and manipulated memories.

But the thing that interested me was the car. Their Fiat Punto.

Elaine rebutted the police theory on that too. Enlightened her readers on why they hadn't told the police that they had a second car parked out of sight that night. Simple: they'd been focused on the fact that Christa was missing. If the police wrongly assumed that their Ford Galaxy, parked by the caravan, was their only car it had gone over their heads. Elaine's account hadn't yet touched on why the police became so interested in the Fiat, but that one I already knew. By two a.m. my eyelids were calling time and my stomach had had its fill of the nightmare.

I called Harry. All quiet at the Barber house. He was kipping on the couch where an opening window or ringing doorbell would wake him. I told him I'd see him tomorrow. Went up and showered and slid into bed beside Arabel. Once I was horizontal my eyelids revived. Like those girls' dolls but wired the wrong way round. Elaine Barber's TV appeal re-ran in endless loops as I tried to separate real from acting.

It had been the car, finally. The Barbers' black Fiat, standing unnoticed on that garden centre car park a mile from the action. No-one disputed that there was a legitimate reason it was parked there – only whether Stuart had moved it from the caravan site before or after they'd discovered Christa missing. And the whole thing might have been inconsequential anyway if the police hadn't later turned up indications that at some point the Barbers had had a dead body stashed inside it.

CHAPTER SIX
Armani and spit-shiny

Stuart drove us in in the Galaxy. He navigated the morning rush hour into Wapping, crossed the bridge onto Canary Wharf and pulled into the drop-off zone outside a thirty storey tower fronted by massive marble planters. One of the planters was fronted by a Yamaha FJR racked up on the pavement. Beside it, Shaughnessy watched the inflow, helmet in hand.

A valet took the car keys and we were turning to go into the building when a Merc E-Class darted into the drop-off and almost rear-ended the Galaxy. Its back door opened and a dumpy guy in a double-breasted white Armani suit, spit-shiny white shoes and a coifed black frizz jumped out. He did a pirouette, palms up, looking for something that wasn't there, then came over and yelled at the Barbers.

'This is it? I'm on the blower all day and this is it?' He looked round, looked up, searched window reflections. 'All friggin' day and the bastards are still in bed! Why the hell do we bother?'

His hands floated down.

'Elaine! Stuart! How are you this morning? Who are these?'

He swept a finger at me and Shaughnessy. Elaine filled him in.

'Owen, meet Mr Flynn and Mr Shaughnessy from the detective agency.'

Owen's head turned to track his finger. He took a moment, decided we were real and threw up his hands.

'Finally! We're doing the private investigation thing! How long have I been telling you Elaine? Gentlemen!'

He thrust a hand at me. 'Owen Jagger! Working with the family. I've been begging them to bring the investigators in for six months. Who else is gonna find their baby? The police? Hey? The *police?*'

He shook my hand for a quarter of a second then turned to Shaughnessy, turned away even quicker when he saw that Shaughnessy's hand wasn't coming up. The guy learned fast.

'Owen's our publicist,' said Stuart. 'He's worked with Kestrel on the promotion schedule.'

'Worked with them?' Jagger yelled. 'Holy mother! I've run myself into the ground whilst Kestrel have sat on their arses. If it was up to them we'd be launching with a press release and a book signing at Dogshit Discount! I'm the only reason we get noticed in this town!'

He turned to yell at me and Shaughnessy above the traffic. 'Christa's coming back and we're gonna be in people's faces until that happens! We're gonna make them open their goddamn eyes. Pay attention. This tragedy's gone on long enough.'

My clients said nothing. I guess they were used to this. When the Barbers' story first looked saleable they'd been dropped on by all manner of heavyweights keen to get in on the deals. Jagger either showed up first or shouted loudest because he'd directed their activities ever since.

He flapped his hands again. Herded us towards the foyer.

'Let's go, people. I'm melting out here.'

We took the lift to the eighth floor where the Barbers' publisher, Kestrel, lived. We had a nine a.m. press conference. It sounded straightforward. An audience of news people – if any turned up – on the publisher's home turf. The Barbers might draw a few unfriendly questions but I didn't see their vigilante busting in.

Kestrel's Director of Communications met us and took us through to the press room. Shaughnessy positioned himself at the door and I went in with the party and found that the news people had turned up, maybe twenty of them including photographers and a couple of cameramen for the local stations. No personalities though. Unless the Barbers came up with something spectacular the book launch would be a filler on the local channels. People were still interested in the Barbers' story, but it wasn't prime time any more. The room had seating but the press had opted to crowd the dais at the front.

Jagger got behind the lectern and went through a warm-up, which included an admonition to the press that they needed to stay sharp, by which he meant they should turn up in droves when he put the Barbers on show. The press stayed quiet. They wanted to hear what the Barbers had to say.

What the Barbers had to say didn't amount to much. Stuart did his best to hype up the material that actually was *new* in their book but most of what he discussed was a mish-mash of dubious sightings and inconclusive theories. *The New Evidence* was the brainchild of

Kestrel and Jagger, a padding on the story everyone had already heard, polished up to draw the limelight back in and send another half million books out of the door. Stuart trawled through a list of reported sightings of Christa in places as far away as Stornoway and Dublin but it didn't add up to much. If any of the sightings might be Christa it was equally obvious that none might be. Then Elaine took us through the only real *new* item – the private investigation into Christa's whereabouts. Her "detective team" sounded impressive. Maybe Shaughnessy and I would be like that team once we'd recovered from the shock of being shanghaied.

When Elaine wrapped up Jagger opened things to the floor and a half-dozen questions were lobbed in on the old issues of the realistic chances of Christa being found, and why the rest of the world should believe she was still alive, a few stabs at the Barbers' unshakeable certitude.

Stuart and Elaine batted back with the practised ease they'd cultivated since the night they left their caravan door open. Then a guy piped up and asked Elaine to explain which material in the new edition answered the questions they'd dodged in the old one.

He was a short guy. Shapeless jeans. Brown leather jacket. Mottled face topped by a rag of brown hair. Owen jumped forward and started yelling foul before he'd even finished his question but Elaine held up her hand and answered.

'No comment for *The Nation*.'

She swivelled her gaze for the next question but the pack held back, happy to let the bruiser work. They needed a few sparks.

'Does this' – the guy held up a copy of the book – 'have anything new? Or should we review it on our fiction page?'

'Get out of here!' Jagger yelled. He moved in front of the lectern. 'We've heard all this before, Archie! You're out of bounds.'

But the guy persisted. He directed his voice round Jagger. *'The Nation's* readers want their questions answered,' he declared. 'Talk to me, Elaine!'

The Nation was the tabloid chasing the Barbers, which made the short guy Archie Hackett, their investigative lead. A photographer was snapping away beside him.

'C'mon, c'mon. Play it fair!' Jagger was still blocking Hackett's attempts to badger Elaine. Then Stuart stepped round the publicist and into Hackett's face. His fists were clenched. 'We've nothing to say to you, Hackett,' he growled. The press growled back. This was what they wanted. For a moment I wondered if we were about to see fisticuffs, which would be interesting. We were here for the vigilante. It wasn't clear whether protecting reporters from the Barbers was part of our remit.

'You never did say anything,' Hackett retorted. He stood his ground, nose to chest with Stuart. But the one he was after was Elaine. He stepped suddenly to the side and got in another thrust.

'Elaine,' he called. 'Simple question: does your book give us the missing explanation for what happened whilst your husband was out shopping that night?'

'Get out of here, Archie,' Jagger yelled, 'or ask sensible questions. This behaviour's unnecessary.'

'Necessary?' Hackett yelled back. 'I think it's necessary for the public to know the truth about your clients, Owen!'

'Hackett,' Stuart said, 'we've nothing to say to you. Step back.' His fists were still bunched.

But Hackett stood his ground. 'Give me a response,' he persisted, 'How does it feel to be exploiting the death of your daughter?'

Stuart's face coloured but Jagger grabbed his arm. 'Out of order!' he yelled. His white suit was blinding in the camera flashes as he held Stuart back. 'Come on, Archie, you know the rules. Ask relevant questions or leave the family alone.'

'Okay,' Hackett yelled back. 'Here's relevant, Owen: how much money have you personally pocketed this year from this circus?'

At that point the Kestrel communications guy stepped up to stem the debate. He threw up his hands for order and told Hackett to let someone else in. Hackett wasn't brushed off so easily but he got nothing from his further questions except a threat from the communications guy to call security. He looked in my direction as he said it. I looked away sharpish. Spotted Shaughnessy poking his head in the door. His face gave nothing but we both knew. This was why we should have been out chasing HP defaulters and straying husbands. Celeb-minding wasn't Eagle Eye's game. There are firms who specialise in that kind of thing, goons for hire with wrap-around shades and buds in their ears, good at looking mean for the cameras. I didn't own any wrap-arounds. If I did I'd go home and fetch them.

Maybe this circus would be over when I got back.

Luckily, Hackett finally shut up and we got back to less inflammatory questions. When the party broke up the *Nation* reporter was first out. He pushed past Shaughnessy along with his photographer and a blonde woman who'd thrown in a few barbs of her own.

Jagger followed the hacks out, yelling that this cause needed their full support. When he came back he gave Kestrel the same treatment. When their editor had taken all she could about cash infusions and upping the Barbers' profile and enhancing their USP she disappeared on urgent business and the party broke up.

Down on the street we waited for the Galaxy to be brought round. Jagger went straight for his Merc. As far as I could see it hadn't moved.

Shaughnessy gave a nod. 'Catch up.' He walked to the Yamaha.

The Galaxy was delivered and we climbed in and Stuart drove us out.

'That bastard,' Elaine said. 'He gets worse.'

Stuart filtered right for the tunnel. 'When we get Christa back I'm going to ram a copy of the book down the guy's throat,' he said.

I kept quiet. Watched the traffic.

CHAPTER SEVEN
Do you believe in God?

The Barbers' schedule shoe-horned a lunchtime radio interview in Kensington then took us across the river to London City Hall for the book launch. Tickets-only. Press invitations limited to the arts desks, if any showed up. We rode a lift to the LLR room and admired the view of Tower Bridge beyond two larger than life images of Christa watching us from either side of a low dais. Two hundred seats faced the dais, already half-occupied.

We waited in a screened off area while the audience finished drifting in. The stair doors were locked. Emergency egress only. The lift was the only way up and the ticket holders trickled out past Shaughnessy's gimlet eye.

Apart from some invited industry people the tickets had gone on sale to the public so we weren't looking at a tame audience. I stepped out to watch the seats filling with people who felt the need to get closer to the Barber tragedy.

At three the Barbers came out and Kestrel's editor-in-chief took the podium to introduce Jagger. Somewhere in the trip from Canary Wharf Jagger's suit had changed to cerulean blue over a navy shirt, both eclipsed by a sun-yellow tie whose width had gone out of fashion a couple of decades back. Jagger spieled for twenty minutes about the whole tragic thing, and the audience soaked it up with awed silence. When he quit Elaine Barber stood to give a ten minute talk on Hope. She wrapped up with a tear-jerker.

'Our daughter's somewhere out there. We can't see her and we can't touch her but she's with us every moment of every day. And one day soon she's coming home. One day someone will recognise her face or will have the courage to report their suspicions about a friend or loved one and her journey back will have begun. Wherever she is, Christa is still our baby. And we won't stop searching until she's back in our arms.'

It sounded good. Elaine exuded the sincerity of the seasoned politician. Maybe it was because she *was* sincere. You could put yourself in her shoes; feel the pain; imagine the torment of having to perform in this kind of circus every day. Then I imagined what it would be like if the whole thing was a sham and you still had to perform. That seemed somehow worse. A torment either way. And love or hate the Barbers, this was why everyone stayed interested: the fact that no-one knew. Christa alive or Christa dead? The Barbers innocent or guilty?

The show wrapped up with some Q&A's which Elaine fielded with stock answers she'd given a thousand times, side-stepping the hostile ones she'd heard just as often. The book was declared launched, and the Barbers stepped down to mix with the crowd before heading to the signing table. Jagger bee-lined for the industry people. Things seemed to be going smoothly. That should have warned me.

Elaine and Stuart were relaxed, chatting with the reading public. I stayed close through some lively conversations and a few argumentative thrusts but the Barbers dodged the unfriendly stuff and things rolled on fine for fifteen minutes. Then I spotted a tall woman with spiky blonde hair waiting for her moment. When the crowd shifted she stopped in front of the Barbers and when she asked her question it wasn't so friendly.

'Elaine,' she said, 'do you believe in God?'

The atmosphere changed. Elaine's eyes sharpened. That's when I spotted something I didn't like. A movement behind the throng. Suddenly people were moving out of the way and a bearded guy came barging through yelling 'Baby-Killers!'

His arm swung.

Something struck Elaine's thigh and exploded with a white burst. I moved to block the guy, hoping to God it was just a flour bomb. Then I spotted the *Nation's* photographer from this morning. The bastard had materialised from nowhere. No way was he in the room when we started. He raised his camera and flashes were going off right in my face and then the blonde spiky woman lurched forward into Elaine. Elaine reacted instinctively, handed her off with a push to her face and in a second it was a riot, hands pushing, yelling and screaming. I grabbed Elaine's arm and the bearded guy swung again. Something hit me on the shoulder and buried me in a cloud of sticky white. I hustled Stuart and Elaine backwards towards the screened area as the attacker barged forward again but his barging was terminated this time by his running smack into Shaughnessy. We kept moving through the angry faces. The Beard and Ms Spike weren't my worry. They weren't our vigilantes. I was watching for someone moving through the crowd with more than flour bombs. Somebody went down heavily behind me then Shaughnessy caught up and we shepherded the Barbers back behind the screens. Elaine's trouser suit and my shoulder and head were spattered. Flour, but the damn stuff was mixed with egg.

It wasn't the moment to say *told you so* but I didn't need to. For the first time I saw tears in Elaine's eyes. Stuart was cursing.

I tried to get the flour out of my hair but when there's egg it can't be shifted.

'Hackett,' Stuart snarled. He had his arm round Elaine.

I quit with the flour.

'Who was the woman?' I said.

'Meg O'Connor. Director of Child-Reach. She's dogged us for the last twelve months with her damned accusations. She's never physically attacked us before though.'

Not this time either. Meg O'Connor had been as surprised as Elaine when they'd come face to face. Her surprise was on account of the hefty shove from behind that had propelled her forward just as the flour thing happened. The fracas had been a set up, with Hackett's photographer right there to record it. But how the hell had we missed the photographer and the guy with the flour bombs? I looked at Shaughnessy.

'The stairs,' he said.

I'd checked the doors myself. They were protected by a keypad security lock. And Shaughnessy had watched the only way in to make sure no unwelcome guests stepped out of the lift. The Beard and Hackett's guy weren't in the crowd when we started. Someone with the code had let them in through the emergency doors and suddenly we were one-nil down on the day. I kept reminding myself that we weren't here to protect the Barbers against the hecklers and press mavericks, but these people had just shown us how easy it was to get through. The venues weren't secure. If the flour guy had brought something nastier or if the Child-Reach woman had carried a knife we'd have had a situation. It was like we'd told the Barbers: they either needed a full protection squad or they needed to keep out of sight.

Jagger came bouncing in. His tie was off-kilter and his coif was throwing hairs.

'Jesus Christ!' he yelled. 'Those friggin' journos want stringing up!' His arms windmilled. 'I'm gonna talk to Natasha.' He saw me looking at him; gave me wide eyes: 'Natasha Best! Runs *The Nation's* investigative team. She's either gonna rein her guys in or we're gonna be back in court.'

I threw him a sneer. He was just spouting. Jagger was in the same game. Knew the score. If it sells it's good. Reining-in didn't come into it.

'Okay, people, we're through,' Jagger declared. 'Let's get out of here before I get a stroke. Tomorrow's gonna be better. Tomorrow will be fine.'

He turned to the Barbers. 'Look on the good side,' he said. 'We moved a hundred copies.'

Stuart and Elaine glared at him.

'Okay,' Jagger yelled. 'Cancel that! Who's counting? The main thing is we're up and running and we're getting the exposure. We're in the public eye and the book's gonna sell. Christa's gonna be back in people's prayers.' He was dusting his suit, though he hadn't been within ten feet of the flour. 'We're gonna move forward,' he told us. He took Elaine's hand. 'We're gonna get your baby back. Remember that, sweetheart.'

He turned to look at me and Shaughnessy.

'That's why you boys need to get to the photo. I hear you got the highest recommendations. Well you'd better have, because we need results.'

He glared at us to make sure we were listening. I glared back to let him know I recognised a huckster when I saw one. Then I turned to leave.

What Jagger wasn't saying was that if Christa Barber ever came home then that would be the end of his milch-cow. No missing child, no circus, no cashflow. But I guess Jagger had other celebs on his books. When the Barber limelight sputtered he'd move on.

I went out and brought the Galaxy round to the parking area, trying to keep flour and egg off the seat. I handed the keys to Stuart and we all piled in and headed across Tower Bridge through rush hour traffic. Stuart and Elaine sat quietly in the front. I sat in the back and watched the road behind where a white Astra was following five cars back. Further back still, Shaughnessy's head weaved through the traffic as he tailed us on his Yamaha. The Astra stayed with us most of the way to Elstree then suddenly turned off and left us to it. Shaughnessy let it go; rode in through the gates behind us.

Elaine's eyes were still glistening as we climbed out of the Galaxy. The flour and egg had dried solid on my neck.

CHAPTER EIGHT
He's on our doorstep

Shaughnessy flicked the Yamaha out of gear and pushed up his visor. Looked at my jacket.

'It's fine,' I said. 'You get the number?'

He nodded. 'I'll get Harry on it.'

'Tomorrow.'

The visor dropped and Shaughnessy manoeuvred the bike back onto the road. I went in to join the Barbers. They were in the kitchen. Grim faces all round. Elaine got busy making drinks.

'That went well,' I said.

'Hackett!' Stuart said. 'He set it up.'

I'd already figured that. *The Nation* would have an interesting front page tomorrow. But Hackett wasn't our problem. Our problem was the vigilante. Chaos like this afternoon's was what we needed to avoid. It's hard to watch for trouble in the middle of a riot. All we had on our side was a presumption that the vigilante wouldn't make his move in a public situation. But that was assuming the guy was rational.

'This is a bad time to be doing public events,' I reiterated.

'The answer's the same, Eddie,' Elaine said. 'We've no choice. The book's our way of fighting back.'

A car horn sounded. I went out to let Harry in. He eyed my jacket and beckoned me into the drawing room. We sat at a table and he pulled paperwork from his hold-all.

'A couple of bonuses,' he said. He fanned envelopes. 'Stuart gave me these last night.'

I raised my eyebrows: 'The police didn't keep the envelopes?'

'Apparently they didn't ask for them and the Barbers never handed them over.'

'Postmarks?'

'Kinda interesting.' He laid the letters and envelopes out and sat back; clasped his hands behind his head. 'Better get the jacket sorted, Eddie. Those chemicals ruin leather.'

'Tell me about the letters.'

'The five look like the same guy but we've got differences, including printer. The first four are inkjet. The last is laser. Superficially similar – same typeface and layout – but we're looking at two machines. Might mean a different sender, might not. I've three printers myself, though I don't use shit like this. If I was sending poisoned-pen letters I'd do them quality. Maybe embossed paper.'

'Embossed?' I gave him what-the-hell?

'The wife: she likes fancy touches. She's the only one I'd be writing to.'

Harry and his wife were famous for their love-hate thing, but it was a love-hate that had lasted four decades. And Harry wasn't the romantic type. His wife would be in a swoon over any kind of letter. He got back to the point.

'Content and style say they're the same person. But style can be copied. Did these ever go public?'

'No. Only the Barbers and the police have read them.'

'So maybe a single writer. But the last one feels different. A jump in tone. Could be just the guy's mood but it makes me wonder. I'd say fifty-fifty we've got two writers. The thing in common is they're all a single page. Shows restraint. Someone has a rage burning, but they're keeping it under control.'

I read the letters again. The first two set the tone. They'd arrived over a year ago, soon after things turned against the Barbers. Maybe the writer had been cranked up by *The Nation's* campaign which had just been warming up. Hate-mail was coming in steadily and this guy's appeared amongst it. His message was clear from the start:

> *You're going to HELL, bitch. That's where I'm sending you. I'm just watching and waiting.*

and

> *You think you're so clever, fooling everyone. But you've not fooled ME. I know what cold-blooded MONSTERS you are.*

The first of the two had arrived with a warning:

> *Enjoy the SURPRISE that's coming.*

A couple of days after that one arrived the Barbers' car was written-off by an artist with paint stripper and a hammer. Then a lull: the writer cooled off after the second letter until the collapse of the Barber prosecution stirred him to fire up his word processor again three months ago:

To the KILLER COUPLE.

You think you've got away free to count your MILLIONS made from an innocent's death. But enjoy it WHILE YOU CAN. The courts may be blind and stupid but I'll bring JUSTICE. I was close today. Did you sense it? I'm here. I'll take ELAINE FIRST.

That one had stirred interest after it was followed by the failed hit and run. A car driven at Elaine on a dark street. The car was never identified, just something light and fast that missed Elaine by inches, clipped a few wing mirrors and sped off into the night. The police decided that it was a drunk driver. The Barbers had a different view. The letter-writer concurred in his follow-up:

Take your lucky escape as a warning. Next time I won't fail. Your time has come, Killers.

And the latest letter:

Justice means a life for a life! You first Elaine, because it was you who killed the baby! And I'll make it painful. You'll scream for your last breath, bitch! And when you're in the ground I'll send your scheming husband to join you.

Harry was right. The invective was racked up in that last one. Maybe the writer was having a creative day. Or maybe it was someone else. But how could they copy a style that hadn't been made public?

If the hit and run thing was real it showed that this guy was serious. Not exactly expert but if he or she kept trying then someone was going to get hurt.

Harry pushed the envelopes across. Pointed out the postmarks.

'The first one's Dartford then we've a couple with Mount Pleasant marks. The fourth's Gatwick and the last Jubilee.'

'How wide is that area?'

'Potentially big. The Jubilee centre is Hounslow. That catches mail posted way out west, maybe even in Guildford or Camberley. That gives us a fifty mile east-west spread from the Dartford letter. And Gatwick covers down to the coast so that's a fifty mile north-south spread from the Mount Pleasant postings.'

'They're travelling around, covering their tracks.'

'Maybe. But the area might not be as big as it looks. Jubilee and Gatwick overlap in the central London area. You could get all these postmarks except Dartford if you posted within four miles of Streatham. Go six miles east and you catch Dartford too.'

'So if our vigilante is posting close to home, he's somewhere south of Greenwich. Or if he's travelling to cover his tracks he could be anywhere within the fifty mile dispersion.'

'But not outside the wider area.'

I got the point. 'If you lived in Birmingham you might be cautious enough to drive to London to post the letters, but would you go for different postal locations each time? Why not pop the letters into the same box? As long as they're not Birmingham they're not going to point back to you.'

'Yeah,' Harry said. 'You only spread them around when you're posting close to home. This guy's on our doorstep.'

~~~~~

I drove back into town. Picked up a call from Arabel. She reminded me that it was my turn to cook. I stopped at a Waitrose and picked up supplies and a few funny looks.

Back home I dropped my jacket into the dry cleaners' bag, showered flour from my hair and flopped onto the sofa to wade through the last of the Barbers' book. A year on. The search is mired. No trace of Christa, and the police effort is focused on the Barbers. Elaine had written *Waiting For Christa* in a desperate attempt to get things moving again, but like a badly conceived novel the ending fizzled: when the anguish and drama had played itself out we were left hanging – until the last chapter. That's where the fuse was re-lit with the spark that had changed the Barbers' lives. The book had been ready for the printer's when the Christa Photo turned up and spawned a new ending. A revised final chapter was hacked together in a week and shoe-horned between redesigned covers featuring a blurred photo of a three-year-old. The book sold like hotcakes.

Arabel arrived. I ditched the book and went to cobble together a shepherd's pie. When we sat down to eat she asked how my day had been. I gave her the executive summary.

Her eyes opened. 'Your celebs giving you headaches, babe?'

'Not them. Just the nutcases they're attracting.'

I told her about our day in the world of publishing. The Barbers had wanted publicity and they'd got it. And Day One had told us that our instinct to keep clear of this thing had been on the mark.

Arabel finished her meal double quick then apologised and got ready to head out to something she had on with St Mungo's, an organisation that looks after the homeless around London. Arabel was one of their "Move-On" advisors, helping their clients find the next step on the ladder. She also covered at their Islington hostel from time to time. Tonight they'd sent out an SOS. She planted a kiss and said she'd see me. Reminded me that we had a theatre date on Thursday night. I hadn't forgotten the date. We were due at some kind of new wave existential music thing one of her weirder friends was involved with. The event was being unleashed at the *Anglican*, a disused gothic church in Finsbury Park that had been taken over by the obscure arts in the eighties. I'd been before. Discovered the new meaning of *new wave* which was basically music to fry the brain. The last performance had been some kind of John Cage throwback that had the punters sprinting for the bar at the interval. If the performers ever learned to play their instruments maybe we'd get their message. None of it was Arabel's scene but she hadn't the heart to tell her friend, and she figured I could tough it out a second time. My tough smile followed her to the door. I wasn't going to fret. We might get hit by an asteroid before Thursday.

I sat down and picked up the book. Returned to the heart of the police suspicions, the fork in the road where suspicion evolved into an all-out attack. A month after Christa disappeared the police were no longer swallowing the Barbers' story. There were too many inconsistencies and no hint of an abductor. The case had stagnated in the public view but behind the scenes the team had been busy. They'd impounded the Barbers' Fiat and brought in cadaver dogs. These are the ones that specialise in locating human remains or residual traces through the whiff of decomposition.

Waiting For Christa glossed over the marvels of canine noses. Presented the bare facts, which were that a month after Christa disappeared, on yet another routine trip to Winchester, Stuart and Elaine had been put through separate six-hour grillings and then hit with a *Gotcha!* The Fiat they'd stashed at the garden centre that night had thrown up an oddity: the cadaver dogs had signalled a hit. Seemed one of the car's recent passengers hadn't been breathing. The Barbers were asked to explain but couldn't, and Elaine's narrative didn't offer any reason why they should. She concentrated instead on endless anecdotal incidents of false sniffer dog findings. She had a point: no forensic evidence was ever lifted from the Fiat and when the canine examination was repeated after the Barbers' lawyer launched a pre-emptive challenge it came up blank. That, according to Elaine, was that: overstated canine powers; no forensics; no case.

It wasn't the end of it, of course, but without forensic evidence all the police had were the circumstantial discrepancies between the Barbers' story and witness accounts.

I picked up Lucy's press clippings. The story had broken nationally two days after Christa's disappearance with a Mystery Woman photofit. The image was so rough as to be hardly recognisable against the version that got into the book. A rush job, flat, all angles, eyes insanely intense, a subtly different shape to the face. Hard to imagine it was the same person as the one depicted in Elaine's book.

The clippings filled in where the book left off. After the sniffer dog thing the situation had taken another downturn when a witness turned up who claimed to have seen the Barbers lifting something into their Fiat the evening Christa disappeared. The CPS decided finally that they had enough for a prosecution. They were wrong. A week before the trial the Barbers' defence team produced evidence that the lifting-something witness hadn't been near the site at the time. The testimony was junked the morning the trial was due to start and the CPS reviewed things *in camera* and agreed with the judge that they had no credible evidence to suggest how and where the Barbers had disposed of their daughter's body. A few discrepancies in the couple's timings that night weren't going to cut it. The CPS withdrew its prosecution in a spectacular meltdown.

For the Barbers the nightmare went on – press lynchings, the hate-mail campaign, the move from the family home to a secluded house in Elstree – a more expensive house, as *The Nation* informed us, financed by their new-found celebrity status.

Elaine's book had taken us through the trauma of their status-shift from victims to presumed killers. The tabloids focused on the killers-who-slipped-the-net angle, which was better copy. Meanwhile the Barbers' website blogged their attempts to dodge the barrage and keep the search for their daughter alive. Long before the trial they'd offered a £100,000 reward to anyone with information, which had drawn out the lunatic element and an inundation of sightings and theories, astral projections and soothsayer premonitions. They got forty-two confirmed sightings from abroad. A guy in Bengal had Christa kidnapped by a travelling circus working its way across India and another reliable source put her in a village in Peru. You'd have pitied the poor bastards chasing down the reports if anyone *had* been chasing, but the police weren't looking for anyone outside the family. But the hundred K carrot eventually delivered a hit: three months after the reward was posted, the Christa Photo dropped through the Barbers' letter box.

When it arrived the ripped proofs of *Waiting For Christa* were already with the publisher. Stuart and Elaine squeezed Kestrel to hold up production and get the photo in. The photo made it onto the jacket, and a lashed-up final chapter delivered a rambling essay on the subject of renewed hope. The book signed off with a reminder of their reward offer but what it didn't mention was that the photo sender had already opened negotiations of his own, with a demand for a somewhat larger payoff. The Barbers went to the police but the police weren't interested in a photo scam, leaving the Barbers alone in their faith that they were looking at their daughter in the picture. What they hadn't known was that the photo was about to steer them into a dead end.

Its sender had communicated through the *Evening Standard's* classifieds for a month, named a two hundred K fee as the price for information, then stopped talking. No payoff. No explanation. He just stopped talking for nearly a year.

Until a month ago.

That's when he inserted a new advert and reopened communications. The Barbers had hope again. But certainly not trust.

Our job was to figure out the photo guy's game and get to the truth behind the snap, find out if it was Christa. But that long silence didn't sound like a guy chasing a cash windfall. Didn't point to the photo being authentic.

Maybe someone was just playing games with the Barbers.

CHAPTER NINE
Only part of him had been in the elevator

I was out at dawn. Ran three circuits of the park in thirty-five. Not good, not bad. I crossed back over the main road and diverted to a rack outside a newsagents. *The Times* and *Observer* were fixated on world recession and Iraq. The tabloids were more on target. *The Nation* had a photo of the Child-Reach woman with Elaine Barber's fist in her face. The headline and caption said:

THEIR TRUE COLOURS

Elaine Barber's answer to
Child-Reach delegate's plea for truth

I grabbed a copy. Stuck my nose into the shop doorway and promised to pay later. Jogged away before the shopkeeper could review my offer. Back home I opened a carton of orange juice and read the story.

Hackett had set it up beautifully. My guess said he'd persuaded Meg O'Connor, the Child-Reach woman, to throw in a question for good copy. What he didn't warn her about was his planned flour attack and the shove in her back that would put her right in Elaine's face. The picture caught the moment in digital perfection. You'd have to be looking closely to spot the dust cloud or the hand that had just launched her. The players came together in a beautiful misdirection. All the rag's readers would see was Elaine's snarling attack on O'Connor. And the "delegate" touch was nice. Made it sound like the Barbers were gate-crashing a Child-Reach conference rather than being ambushed at their own event. The copy below the headline revealed that delegate O'Connor had been "making an appeal" to the Barbers, coaxing them to come forward with the truth, to put Christa's memory to rest. The Barbers' response spoke for itself.

It made me wonder about the rest of the *Nation's* campaign. If the

Barbers were guilty how come it needed set-ups? I jammed the newspaper into the bin and called Shaughnessy. The Barber schedule was rolling on today but I'd other things to cover. Shaughnessy would be on his own. Not ideal after yesterday's fiasco but Sean would stay close and look mean. Even the most deranged vigilante would think twice before taking that on.

I grabbed a shower and went out into the rush hour.

~~~~~

It was only eight thirty but the temperature was already touching twenty-five. The weather man was LBC's celeb. of the moment, dispensing the feel-good jargon of high pressures and jetstream waves, long hot summers. Not even a nod to the fact that the heat was a freak and that people were sick of being fried, that once the weather broke we'd be back to the cold, wet summers we loved.

I found Sharon Larkin's business in a commercial street off the main drag in Twickenham. A high-gloss navy door set between a flower boutique and a hair stylist opened onto a staircase structured in glass and chrome that brought me to a bright open-plan upper floor backed by wall-to-ceiling plate glass that gave a rooftop air. A receptionist who might have modelled for *Vogue* lifted a phone and announced my arrival.

Sharon came out. She wore a pink blazer over a floral top, a short white skirt that showed lots of brown leg. Her perfume was one I'd once bought for Arabel after misreading the price.

Sharon was five years younger than her sister Elaine, and her smile had a lifetime's less wear. Her hand was cool as she gripped mine for a few seconds too long. When I'd recovered it we went through to her office. More plate glass with views over the town; chrome and glass furniture; a contrasting sofa with throw-cushions in bright pastels. The interior walls were a collage of agency posters and photos of Sharon sitting alongside catwalks with people I should probably have known.

'Nice,' I said.

'You don't skimp on style when you're in the image business,' Sharon said. 'We had the floor opened up and the glass put in when we moved in. It gives a sense of space.'

She gestured to a chair and folded herself into the one beside it. Fixed her cute smile on me.

'My sister knows how to pick her detectives,' she said.

I smiled back, wondering if flirting was her normal business mode or was reserved for discussing family tragedies. She watched me, amused.

'We were probably just a random selection,' I speculated.

She laughed. 'Random, hell! You've me to thank for this job, Eddie.'

That caught me. I resisted the temptation to explain just how thankful I was. Kept smiling.

'A friend of a friend,' she said. 'They'd heard about one of your cases. Something to do with camomile tea.' She raised an eyebrow.

I held the smile. We get tea cases.

'Paraquat,' she clarified. 'The transvestite in the elevator.'

The paraquat and transvestite narrowed it down and suggested that the friend of a friend wasn't entirely to be trusted with their recommendations. The transvestite in question was a guy called Lewis Wright and the last I'd heard he was still dead. And technically only part of him had been in the elevator. Lewis had been our client for only forty-eight hours but Eagle Eye had been on the case for three months afterwards, chasing his killer. And I'd not drunk camomile since.

'Did Elaine talk to you?' I said.

Sharon held her amused look.

'She did, though I don't see how the family background relates to Christa's disappearance.'

'We don't know what's relevant. That's why I need to ask.'

'Do you think you'll find Christa?'

'Do you think we won't?'

Sharon clamped her lips. Unfolded herself from her chair. Asked if I'd like a drink. I said juice would be fine. She stuck her head out of the door and passed on the order.

Maybe family background wasn't relevant. If we were looking at a stranger-abduction then I was wasting my time. But since I didn't know what had happened to Christa I didn't know what was relevant. And after the Barbers themselves Sharon probably had the clearest thoughts on the subject. Her name was peppered throughout the pages of *Waiting For Christa* and she'd sat beside Elaine at the first TV appeal, was constantly at her side over the following year. Sharon had been close to the events, but maybe she'd have a little more distance than Stuart or Elaine.

She stayed standing. Leaned against her desk. Arms folded, legs long. I redirected my attention. Caught an amused smile.

'That was an interesting episode yesterday,' she said. 'Some bodyguards!'

The smile was sugar coating around criticism. Air conditioning flicked her hair. She slipped her blazer off, hung it, came to sit back down.

'No-one got hurt,' I pointed out. 'That's the main thing.'

'But someone might have.' She folded a leg beneath her, rested her arm on the chair-back and rested her chin on her arm. Locked eyes. 'Forgive me for saying it, Eddie, but things didn't look very secure back there.'

'We're not there to handle press stunts,' I said. 'You were about to tell me whether you thought Christa was findable.'

Her eyes continued to bore into mine.

'I ask myself the same thing every day,' she said.

'And what's the answer?'

She broke the stare. Looked out through the glass wall.

'You think Christa's a lost cause?' I said.

She looked back.

'Eddie,' she said, 'whatever Christa is she's not a lost cause to us.'

'Bad phrasing. So what do you think?'

'The truth? I don't know.'

'Elaine says they had no enemies. No-one who might have targeted them. Is that your understanding?'

'Yes. Christa was taken by an opportunist. Someone they'd never met.'

'And you're not convinced she's findable?'

Sharon's receptionist came in and handed me a glass of juice and Sharon a glass of wine. Sharon took a sip and chose her words.

'Elaine is doing what she believes best. I want Christa back as much as she does, but I'm realistic enough to recognise that it's been twenty-two months.'

'What's your take on the photo?'

Sharon frowned. Shook her head.

'I've never been entirely sure. The photograph could be Christa but the quality is not good.'

'So you don't think it's her?'

'Elaine thinks it's her, so I'll at least consider the possibility.'

'Any thoughts on who might have sent it?'

'An opportunist who happened to snap a picture that fitted the bill and thought he could prey on my sister.'

'Why did he go quiet? Why didn't he collect?'

'That's the mystery,' Sharon said. 'Elaine and Stuart were willing to pay. They were desperate to know about the photo. So maybe whoever sent it got cold feet. Two hundred thousand is a lot of money. You'd do time for that kind of fraud.'

'If the photo was a hoax.'

Sharon's eyes burned into me.

'If it's a hoax I want to see them strung up. Elaine's whole existence is centred on the photograph. It frightens me to think how she'll react if it's exposed as a fake.'

'She's hired us to track it down. It's a risk she's taking.'

Sharon nodded. 'But how could they not look? If there's a chance in a thousand that the photo *is* Christa then they can't ignore it. And it's better to find out the truth than live with the torture of not knowing. I'm just praying for a miracle.'

Her mood had cooled. She looked at me with a wistfulness that might have been sincere. If the Barbers were playing a game it had fooled Elaine's sister.

'Are you and Elaine close?'

'We didn't used to be. We had our own lives. But Christa's disappearance has brought us together.'

'You've never had fallouts?'

'No. We're just average sisters. Little in common apart from the fact that we both love Christa. Why do you ask?'

'Elaine has a reputation for a cold temperament. Do you see that side?'

Sharon's foot tapped air.

'Why are you so interested in Elaine?' she said.

'Christa's trail is cold,' I said. 'And I wasn't there at the start. So I need to look at everything – family, friends, places, anything that might be relevant. Such as Elaine's actions and state of mind when Christa disappeared. I don't want to be blind to any possibility.'

'Including the possibility that she killed Christa?'

I finished my juice. Sharon stood again and paced the room.

'No,' she said. 'I don't see a cold side. Elaine's enemies see that but it's just her defence mechanism. She's lost her daughter. That should have been the worst thing that could happen to her. But then something else happened: instead of being helped Elaine has been persecuted.'

She stopped in front of me. Her smile was back but tension took away its cuteness. I kept quiet. Waited to hear what was on her mind. Then the smile relaxed. She shrugged and dropped back into the chair; laid two long fingers on my arm.

'You need to understand, Eddie. Elaine's headstrong. She can be formidable when she's fighting for what she believes in. But she's the most loving mother any child could want. She was no more likely to harm Christa than to kick an old lady. But the police never took that into account. Human nature doesn't register as a circumstantial evidence category. If something isn't tangible, they don't recognise it.'

I stood up and walked to the glass. I'd been a detective for nearly twenty years and every day told the same story, which is that you can place an awful lot of faith in facts and very little in human nature. Sharon thought she knew her sister but maybe there were things she didn't see, didn't *want* to see. I watched the Twickenham skyline.

'How did Elaine cope when she lost her first child?' I asked.

'She was devastated. Cot death syndrome is all the worse because there's no warning. Elaine was convinced she'd done something wrong. Put Grace to bed the wrong way or fed her badly or ignored signs of distress. Elaine knows more about children than I ever will but when Grace died she abandoned rationality. Someone had to be blamed and she selected herself. It nearly broke her. They'd tried for so long for a child. They lost everything when Grace went.'

'I read that you helped her out.'

'As best I could. She was deeply depressed. I stayed with her for a few weeks to take some of the burden off Stuart but I had my business to run. Eventually I had to go back to work.'

'What happened then?'

'Just what you've read in the book. Elaine is open about her struggle. We were all wondering if they'd try for another child – maybe that would help heal the pain – but Elaine had lost interest. Her depression ground her down. It was frightening to see her sometimes. But then after eighteen months we had the miracle. Christa came along and Elaine snapped out of it. How could she not? She loved Christa as much as a mother has ever loved a child.'

Sharon got up and walked over. Hugged herself. 'You can hardly imagine the hell Elaine went through when it happened a second time,' she said. 'But Christa's disappearance was just fodder for the tabloids. They played it like Christa was Stuart and Elaine's second victim. Serial killers sell more newspapers.'

Something of Elaine's bitterness had come into Sharon's voice. Her phone rang. She walked to her desk and hit a button.

'No calls, Kirsty.'

She returned to stand with me at the glass, still hugging herself. 'Hell, Eddie,' she said, 'these are bad memories.' She checked her watch.

'The guy who tried to run your sister down,' I said. 'Any ideas?'

She shook her head. 'Just a sick crackpot. We haven't a clue who.'

I came back to my earlier point, different context. 'You say your sister has no enemies. Are you absolutely sure there's no-one who'd might use the vigilante line as a cover to harm her?'

'I'm sure. And it would be a complicated way to attack them, sending all that hate-mail as a decoy.'

I switched tack. 'You were with Stuart and Elaine the morning after Christa disappeared.'

'Elaine called me first thing. I drove straight down. The site was swarming with police and press. Even our brother Damien turned up. A real family reunion.'

The contempt was hard to miss.

'Families do pull together in tragedy.'

Sharon laughed.

'Not our family. Not our brother. Damien's not someone you'd want around in a crisis. We asked him to stay with Elaine that afternoon in the caravan while we were out with the search parties but he couldn't manage even that. Drank himself into a stupor. Elaine was pretty much out if it by then, probably didn't care what state Damien was in.'

Damien's name had appeared in Elaine's book but it was nothing more than a bare mention. Something for the record. No description of him helping. Now I knew the reason.

Sharon shrugged. Her shoulder touched mine.

'Damien's one of life's failures,' she said. 'He stays in contact with Elaine to sponge off her but he knows better than to come near me.'

'He has financial difficulties? I understood your family were reasonably wealthy.'

'Not Damien. He's always been too easily tempted by fast money. Started businesses that failed through stupidity and sloth.'

'But he was provisioned for in your parents' will?'

'Well provisioned, but not in a way he appreciated. Our father never thought much of Damien. Saw him for what he was. But he was too honourable to cut him out. He actually gave him the biggest share of the estate.'

'He didn't like him, so he gave him the biggest slice?'

Sharon turned. Smiled.

'Our father knew how to handle Damien. We had a big family home in Devizes. Thirty acres. It used to be a stud farm. My father had inherited it from his father and he was determined that the place should stay in the family. But it wasn't practical to carve it up so he left Elaine and me his cash – half-a-million each – and Damien got the house and land. By far the biggest share but not one that could be converted into liquid assets.'

'He couldn't sell?'

'It was strictly prohibited in the terms of the will. On Damien's death or if he vacated the property it would revert to the first grandchild. That might have been Damien's if he'd settled down but in the event it became Christa. So Damien owns one of the most desirable small estates in Wiltshire and is penniless.'

'What does he do?'

'He runs a half-cocked camper van dealership. Barely solvent. And his gambling habit pisses away any profit he does make.'

Sharon walked back to her desk. Smiled.

'Eddie,' she said, 'it would be a pleasure to chat all day. Maybe we should do that sometime. But right now I've a client due.'

I left the window. Asked one more question.

'When you went to the caravan site that morning, did Stuart or Elaine have any theories about what had happened?'

Sharon collected her blazer and we walked to the door. 'They believed that the woman had taken her – the one they saw as they drove out to get the cash. Elaine assumed she'd been watching them. The first time they'd ever left Christa, the one time they'd left the door unlocked, and someone was waiting.' She shook her head, dabbed at a sudden moisture in her eyes. 'Just like that. Christa was gone. It tore Elaine apart that they hadn't checked that stupid door.'

She stood close. Looked earnestly into my face with her moist eyes. Her perfume was heady.

'Elaine wasn't acting that day,' she said. 'She hadn't rehearsed any script. She was absolutely broken. So forget all the accusations. There was no way on earth that my sister killed her daughter.'

CHAPTER TEN
Not Claridges' kind of thing

Back at Paddington Lucy was behind her desk stacking Post-its. Prospective business passing us by. Like the buses, jobs all come at once. I went through to my office. Lifted the sash.

Lucy followed me in to drop another item onto my Barber paperwork. A copy of the new edition of the book, the one all the fighting was about yesterday.

Waiting for Christa
The New Evidence

I could have picked up a complimentary copy yesterday but today they were on sale in every bookshop. We were billing the Barbers so nothing lost. Lucy had probably picked this one up at the same shop that had sold her the old edition two days ago.

I'd already asked Stuart about the new sightings they were publicising. He'd handed me twenty reports from across the UK: people seen with unexplained children; kids resembling Christa; kids named Christa or Christine or Chrissy. All duly delivered to the police without any obvious sign of interest. I filed the sheets. If nothing turned up from our own investigations we'd take a look.

The new book jacket promised *New Evidence* but I suspected I'd heard it all yesterday. It sounded a little like the *Old Evidence* between new covers. Bottom line, a promotion gimmick. I asked Lucy to read the thing anyway, see if anything other than smoke came out: impressions; inconsistencies; maybe things the Barbers weren't *intending* to say. I left her to it and went back out.

~~~~~

I caught up with the Barbers in the Drawing Room at Claridges. Jagger had scheduled an up-market luncheon for industry and media elite and a couple of organisations that were still behind the couple.

Invitation-only. Heckle-free. Little risk that my dry cleaners would be pulling pistachios and wine from my jacket tomorrow.

Shaughnessy was waiting with two of the hotel's security people. He introduced us and I went into the room to take a gander. Found fifty people milling around a monster buffet and looking mostly harmless. I walked the service corridor behind the room. Nodded to another of the hotel's security guys. Claridges had got the whisper about yesterday's City Hall fracas and were out in force to make sure we didn't get a repeat. It wasn't their kind of thing.

The affair went smoothly. By mid afternoon the luncheon had started to break up and people were checking their watches and the trickle of tipsy cognoscenti heading home became a steady flow. I stood by the door with Shaughnessy and smiled goodbyes. Just after four Jagger came out, jollying the stragglers in a too-loud voice that you might mistake for drunk.

The Barbers and their Kestrel editor were the last out. We walked down to an art deco foyer impressive enough to have everyone except Jagger whispering. The place was swarming with uniformed staff and afternoon shoppers coming in. Jagger and the Barbers were drifting doorwards and I'd just given the nod to the security guys when Elaine cursed and a familiar face popped out of the crowd.

Archie Hackett.

We tried to step round him but his camera guy snapped off a couple of flashes before the Barbers could react. The camera didn't need flash in the bright foyer so I guess the illumination was for effect. The effect worked. Heads turned and Hackett launched into his litany:

'Stuart! Elaine! A couple of questions.'

The Barbers knew all about Hackett's questions. They pushed through and headed for the door as Hackett's voice raised a notch.

'What's your message for Child-Reach this afternoon?'

He'd skipped along to block us, with his photographer sprinting off to the side. The Barbers stepped round him a second time, heads down.

Owen Jagger didn't do heads down. 'Back off, Archie!' he yelled. 'Come talk to me in my office. I'll give you what you need to know.'

Hackett wasn't interested in offices. He thrust his Dictaphone in the Barbers' faces and stepped up his badgering. The Barbers continued moving towards the door and this time when he tried to intercept them I blocked him. Shaughnessy stayed clear, watching the street. It was moments like this a vigilante prayed for.

Today's front page hadn't endeared me to *The Nation*. Each time Hackett tried to get past he met my shoulder. After three tries he locked his sights on me.

'Hey! This is a public place! Get the hell out of my way!'

'Let them out, Archie,' I said. 'They're not going to talk to you.'

'The hell they aren't. What are you? Their lawyer? Take your damned hands off me!'

My hands were at my side. I guess the comment was rhetorical. But the Barbers were disappearing fast through the revolving door whilst Hackett and I did our dance in front of Claridges' astonished customers. Once they were out I hopped past Shaughnessy and followed onto the street. Hackett dashed into the revolving segment behind me and I heard a thump. Turned to see Hackett's nose flat on the glass. He shook himself and pushed furiously but the door was stuck, mainly on account of Shaughnessy holding it fast. I heard muffled curses and hammering but those doors are tough. The valet handed us the keys and we climbed into the Galaxy. Stuart put us in gear and turned towards Oxford Street leaving Hackett hammering away at the glass like a lobster in a jar. He'd better pray that Shaughnessy had somewhere to go tonight.

We merged into traffic. Another successful day in our quest to keep the Barbers out of harm's way. Maybe tomorrow we could do Iraq. They must have bookstores.

We crawled along with the log-jam. Once we got over Oxford Street I swivelled in my seat and spotted the white Astra following like a faithful dog. Its plate was already with our DVLA contact but meantime there was a little checking of our own we could do. The car tailed us out to Elstree but when it sloped off from there it picked up a tail of its own, a dark green Mondeo. Harry would get the guy's address and keep an eye on him whilst we waited for ID.

Any of a number of people might be interested in keeping tabs on the Barbers but I had a feeling about this. The car that had attempted to run Elaine down three months ago had been a light colour. Was this the same guy, watching and biding his time?

~~~~~

Elaine went through to the kitchen to begin dinner. I asked Stuart for a moment. Pulled out a copy of the Christa Photo. Held it up.

'The background: we've got trees or high bushes; streaks of white in front of the greenery. I'm thinking some kind of fencing. Does it mean anything?'

Stuart shook his head. 'Eddie, I've looked at this a million times. We've no idea of the location.'

'Any idea what this might be?'

I pointed out a formless smudge of colour in the foreground. Bright primaries, blue and red; could be a sunshade, but why was it on the ground? And was there someone off-frame to the left? The girl was looking in that direction as if her name had been called.

Stuart shook his head again. 'It's all just a jumble,' he said. 'There's nothing we recognise in the picture except Christa. The location could be anywhere.'

A horn sounded outside. Stuart went through to release the gate and a matt olive Land Rover rolled to a stop. The engine died and a six-six black guy built like a tank climbed out. He was wearing cotton slacks and army boots, a white tee shirt stretched to tearing point across muscle. He gave the house the once-over and came across.

'Eddie, me old pal!' he said. He grinned at full wattage while he crushed my hand. I grinned back and kept a straight face. It was an old game. The guy pretended he didn't know he was crushing my bones and I pretended I wasn't about to faint.

'Glad you could make it, Bernie', I said. I introduced Stuart. 'Stuart and his wife are the people the vigilante is trying to hurt.'

Bernie shook Stuart's hand and probably had him wondering if the vigilante could hurt him more than this. When he got his hand back Stuart took Bernie through to introduce him to Elaine. Bernie would cover nights and the Barbers' road trips.

Elaine asked if he was eating with them and Bernie said he'd be delighted. I wondered how many Elaine had catered for. Bernie rarely consumed less than three meals at a time. I took him on a tour before the dinner gong; brought him up to date on the Barber story and on what had happened in our first two days. Turned out Bernie was already up to speed.

'Saw the pics,' he said. 'That flour looked nasty, chum.' He wrapped a consoling arm round my shoulder. 'I've got a mate in Newbury runs a dry cleaning place. If I sweet-talk him he'll cover you for the whole assignment; fixed price. Cotton, wool, synthetics. He'll get them good as new.' A thought stopped him. 'You don't wear silk do you?'

I gave him the evil eye. 'Dry cleaning's the least of my worries, Bernie. What scares me is trying to fend off the real lunatic whilst the Barbers are parading in a shooting gallery. Their vigilante only needs one opportunity.'

'That wouldn't be good, pal,' Bernie agreed. 'I can see it now: "Killer Couple Slain. Millions Helping With Enquiries".'

I held the evil eye. Wondered what went on in those business seminars of Bernie's. Wouldn't be surprised if the bastard was turning out banking magnates.

'Think you'll find their kid?' Bernie said.

'We'll do our best,' I told him.

His hand wrenched chummily at my shoulder.

'And I reckon you'll do it, pal. I only hope the girl's in a condition to appreciate being found.'

'Me too,' I said.

CHAPTER ELEVEN
Creative rage

I drove to Paddington with the hood stowed, fending off the early morning sun with a black fisherman's cap Arabel had given me. LBC were sticking to their forecast: stock up on sun lotion; the heat was here to stay.

A call came in as I rounded the Palace gardens. Bernie.

'They've got another letter, pal.'

'The vigilante?'

'Looks like it.'

I diverted at Marble Arch and headed up the Edgware Road. Drove against the rush hour. Hit Elstree in thirty-five minutes. Bernie opened the door and took me through.

The Barbers were at the breakfast counter. Elaine was dressed in a linen jacket and skirt, fresh for the road, but her eyes already had the five o'clock look, the effect of an early morning dose of hate. With Bernie around, the Barbers had nothing to fear bar a nuclear strike but the psyche can't be shielded so easily. She handed me the letter. The thing was not just a reminder that there was a hostile world beyond the breakfast table, it was a reminder that this wasn't the world the Barbers wanted at all. I guess they dreamed about a parallel universe where they were still living in quiet obscurity, taking weekend breaks at their caravan.

The letter was a single page, standard opening:

"To the Killer Couple..."

The message was as short and as vicious as the previous one, which had been the worst so far. A writer feeding on his own hate? Made you wonder if the guy was psyching up for his promised attack. The letter screamed at the Barbers that they were going to die soon. The "die" and "soon" were triple-underlined with angry slashes of red felt-tip. The embellishment was worrying. Suggested more than just invective. You'd write the hate stuff in a creative rage but this guy was standing back with his copy and still feeling the urge to add colour. This was all about *die* and *soon*.

'Mind if I take it?' I said.

Elaine shrugged. The thing had achieved its purpose. They weren't going to frame it.

Bernie was hanging on for Shaughnessy to take over and shepherd Stuart and Elaine through a couple of events in town. I left him to it. Drove back in.

~~~~~

I pushed in past a group of Rook and Lye's clients blocking the vestibule. The firm was running morning and evening clinics to handle a case they'd recently worked up against the local education authorities for the damage caused by corporal punishment in the sixties and seventies. A psychologist had turned up statistics to show that the regular canings of the era had knocked kids' development back by 8.5% and retarded their adult employment prospects pro rata. The 8.5% could be converted into a loss of earnings via a complex formula known only to Rook and Lye, and had drawn an army of back-of-the-class forty-somethings to their door looking for compensation for not making company director. I'd almost signed up myself: I'd barely caught the tail end of the corporal punishment era but I'd caught it hard. By Rook and Lye's algorithm I should have been prime minister.

Upstairs there was no crowd waiting. Just Lucy manning reception and Harry working in the front office. I planted the letter in front of him and went to see if the coffee aroma meant anything.

I returned with a brew and Lucy in tow. She perched herself on Harry's desk. I went to the window and angled the blinds; watched the street.

'He's getting madder,' Harry said.

I didn't dispute it. I hadn't come across invective like this since my school reports.

Lucy read the letter. 'He's not mincing his words,' she agreed. 'Listen to this.'

I exchanged a look with Harry. We'd both just read the thing but Lucy wanted to take us beyond the mere visual:

'When you're facing the cameras I'm staring right back.

'I'll make you suffer, Baby Killers. The child will be avenged.
*You're going to **die**. Picture it!!! Sliced open. Beaten until every*
bone is shattered. Or burned. I think burned. I imagine your
screams. I imagine your flesh on fire as you preen for the cameras.
*Think of me, watching. Think of the PAIN. Coming **SOON**.'*

Lucy has a great reading voice. By the time she was through Harry
and I were both eyeing the door.

Harry snapped back. Picked up the envelope. 'Jubilee postmark,'
he said. 'That's two in a row. We're staying west. It's also another
laser.'

That gave us two recent letters with the laser printer, more
extreme style and postmarks that hinted at a west-London – or out-
of-London – origin.

'Remind me,' Harry said. 'Who's seen the letters?'

'The Barbers. The police. Us. These last ones only the Barbers and
us.'

'So if it's two different people it's a puzzle how the copycat knew
how to copy. But that's what I'm seeing: two writers. The Barbers
need to think again about who might have seen this stuff.'

'We could be looking at a police leak. They've not been coy about
sharing information with the tabloids. But the first writer's our
priority, not the copycat. He's the real vigilante. You get anywhere
with the Astra?'

'I followed it home,' Harry said. 'Wembley. Driver's a big guy.
Dodgy type. I've a message in for Roger.'

Roger Daley was our DVLA contact. He pulled snippets from the
system from time to time and we gave him occasional help rooting
out illegal vehicles. The way it works, if you drive without tax or
insurance your car's in the crusher – once the police find it. Problem
is that some cars are tricky to find and are worth bugger-all anyway.
Cheaper for the owner to crush and buy again than to pay road tax
as long as he doesn't get caught too often. And the smart way to
avoid getting caught is to drive behind a cloned registration.

Investigating the smart felon is expensive. Alternatively, if the suspect is in the South East, Roger can call us. If his guy *is* driving an unregistered car we track it down for a fixed price and the tow truck rolls up.

'Roger's out today,' Harry said. 'I'll talk to him tomorrow. Get our ID. You think this guy's our vigilante?'

'Hard to see an innocent explanation for tailing the Barbers all over town.' I switched tack. 'You get the ad in?' I asked Lucy.

She pushed a copy of yesterday's *Evening Standard* across the desk. I picked it up and fingered a classifieds message under the *Reunited* callsign. Short and simple:

REUNITED

Essential contact.
Funds in hand.
Cannot hold.

It was a long shot but we needed to stoke things up. The year's silence from the Christa Photo guy prior to his recent message was a puzzle. Someone after two hundred K should have been pushing like hell. Now that he was talking again we needed to keep the line jiggling. Maybe he'd respond to pressure.

'You speak to Angela?' This was Lucy's friend in the *Evening Standard* sales department. If our *Reunited* guy responded we needed his details.

'She's on shift tomorrow evening,' Lucy said. 'She'll check the records then.'

She pushed a second newspaper over. *The Nation.* Another Barber story on its front page. Today's offering was a headline about "Barber Thugs" under Archie Hackett's by-line. I read a piece that reported a version of the Claridges affair filed from a parallel universe. The players were right but the action was a fantasy in which the Barbers' "bully-boys" had created mayhem in the venerable hotel lobby, "swatting aside" members of the public who got in the way. The only member of the public I recalled was Hackett. I guess he'd taken offence at that revolving door thing.

Shaughnessy had missed a trick, though. Should have nailed the door shut and let the bastard file copy by semaphore. I skip-read the overflow on the inside pages and got the story that there was no story. The only thing worthwhile was Hackett's sketch of Shaughnessy as a "sixteen stone gorilla with a Brillo hairstyle". That was good. I'd root out Lucy's scissors later.

Hackett ended his non-story like all good journalists with a carrot: *The Nation's* readers were admonished to put the tabloid on order each morning or risk missing a "shocking revelation". Obviously the revelation was not shocking enough to include in today's issue, but what's a soap without cliff-hangers? I searched the copy for clues but got nothing.

Harry asked about Sharon Larkin.

'She's adamant that her sister didn't kill Christa. Has a convincing line.'

'The book says the same thing,' Lucy said, 'Elaine's a cold one but when you read her story you don't see her losing her rag over a tantrum.'

Harry swivelled his chair. 'You've gotta see the other points too, Luce,' he said. 'The fact that the Barbers' account of that night is full of holes. And the story about a dead body hitching a ride in their car. If our clients are innocent they need to explain a few more things.'

Lucy thought about it. 'Something happened that they're not telling us.'

I grinned. 'Luce,' I said, 'you've almost solved the case.'

'That's your job, Eddie. It can't be so hard. They either did it or they didn't.'

I locked the grin. 'Well here's something that wasn't in your damn book. Black sheep Damien.'

'His name's in there,' Lucy said. 'Nothing more. What did Sharon say?'

'He's the archetypal family pariah. Been sponging off Elaine for I don't know how long. Lives in a financial cuckoo-land. Inherited the family estate but can't liquidate it.'

I gave them the details. When I got to the provisions in the will for the estate to revert to the eldest grandchild Lucy's mouth made an "O". Even Harry looked interested. The thing might be something or nothing but a dodgy family member who'd been kept out of the

71

Barbers' story was worth a gander. The police would have sweated the guy two years ago, of course, though they'd not shared their conclusions with the public. Damien Larkin was high on my talk-to list.

Lucy had put her finger on it though. Either they did it or they didn't. And we weren't going to get the answer in Elaine's book or the tabloids. Victims or killers: the route to the truth started at the place where Christa disappeared. That's where I needed to go.

CHAPTER TWELVE
They'd been there and wished they hadn't

Christa Barber disappeared from a caravan site in the New Forest twenty-two months before Stuart and Elaine climbed our stairs. In an instant shrouded in mystery the two-year-old had gone from being just one of a million toddlers to the centre of a circus of speculation and accusations. With missing kids, as with fresh bodies, you need to make headway in the first twenty-four hours. By two days you're playing a losing hand. I drove out of London pondering on where two years left us.

I followed the motorway past Southampton then steered the Frogeye down roads that narrowed and snaked through the once-wilderness that was the New Forest. South of Lyndhurst the trees closed in. I flipped up my shades and scanned the gloom. Spotted a sign and turned onto a shale track at a rotting barrier which had been erected when Christa's disappearance had put the Orchard Grove Holiday Park under siege. Twenty-two months later the site had dropped back into obscurity and the barrier was a chained up relic. I followed the track until the trees opened onto a blaze of dust at a wooden bridge. I crossed a stream and turned beneath a wrought iron arch to park by the site office. I took my cap off and went in.

A guy in a faded cord shirt and khaki shorts was expecting me. His badge identified him as Bob Bowland, site manager. He handed me the keys to the Barber caravan and walked me out to point the way.

The site was small, thirty static caravans on a cleared space inside a river bend. The office and a tiny shop were the only facilities. Two avenues branched off. I took the left and walked scalding concrete between lines of identical units. The paint on the decks varied but the satellite dishes all pointed the same way. Old folk lounged in garden chairs, killing time until lunch. The place was term-time quiet. I was the only thing moving. I checked pitch numbers but didn't need to. Down at the end, the Barber unit stood out a mile. It was identical to the others but had a miasma you could taste, an echo of its virulent history. It sat abandoned, hunched down behind its

73

splitting woodwork and ruined planters, staring out from blank windows. You sensed darkness behind its net curtains and if you were easily spooked you'd feel the chill.

Five days after Christa disappeared, when the search was wound down, the Barbers moved out and never came back. They didn't rent the unit and didn't sell. Stuart couldn't explain why. If they ever got Christa back this was the last place they'd come. I reached the caravan. Stood under the trees and looked back up the avenue. Fanned my face with my fisherman's. Pictured it as it had been that week: patrol cars and police vans, uniforms, high-vis. vests. Dog handlers coming in from the fields.

The Barber unit was on my right as I looked up the avenue. Which made the one to my left Irene Keenan's. She was the neighbour whose testimony nearly sank the Barbers' story. One up from Irene's was the Smiths' caravan – more witnesses who'd contradicted the Barbers' version of events. An elderly couple were reclining in camp-chairs in front of it. They watched me as I walked over.

'I'm looking for Reg and Pauline,' I said.

The man nodded. 'That's us.'

They were a matched set, stocky conservatives ten years into retirement with identical round faces and snow-white hair. I gave them the Barbers' regards. The woman blinked behind her tinted spectacles and asked how Stuart and Elaine were doing.

I said they were getting by, considering. Still looking for their daughter.

The Smiths' dead end imaginations dug up no replies. They'd been through the saga a million times, followed the tabloids back home in Bromsgrove as the story trickled its way down the months and years. I explained that I was taking another look and we all gazed across at the Barber unit. The Smiths were watching me when I turned back, wondering if the thing was coming back to blight them again. They might still be fascinated by the Christa Barber saga but a ringside seat they could do without. I took them back to the night it happened, watched them struggle with an ingrained politeness that prevented them from telling me to get lost.

The Smiths had been here and wished they hadn't. A quiet fortnight in the New Forest had turned into a media whirlwind with them trapped at the centre. The prosecution had labelled them key witnesses and their story had come close to destroying the Barbers' credibility. It wasn't something they were happy about.

'They were just your everyday couple,' Reg said. 'We'd got to know them a bit.'

'Christa was always dashing around the place,' his wife said. 'She was a lovely child.'

'Did you talk to them much?'

'Just Elaine occasionally, when she was down on her own.'

'There was nothing at all about them?' I was looking for impressions. Something outside the bubble blown by the family.

'Not as we ever noticed,' Reg said. 'We never thought all that would happen.'

I guess if people knew what was going to happen it would save a lot of bother. And investigators wouldn't need to dig for memories that had seemed inconsequential before the event. The problem with memory is you need to separate the real ones from the ones influenced by those events. I was fishing for any dark impressions the Smiths might have about the Barbers, but if they did have any I'd take them with a pinch of salt. In the event, the Smiths had nothing. Their main memories had been facts, not impressions. Facts that had nearly debunked the Barbers' version of that night. I asked the couple about the timings that didn't match and Reg went through it on rote.

'We got back here a few minutes after nine thirty,' he said. 'I don't know where the Barbers got their story that Stuart had gone off with the car, because he was still right here. They were out in the woods.' He pointed. 'The two of them were rushing up and down and then Elaine came out of the trees in a panic.'

'She told us Christa was missing,' Pauline said. 'I nearly died. The thought of her wandering about by the river...'

'What did you do?'

'We went to help, searched right to the end of the path. Elaine was frantic.'

'Did you talk to Stuart?'

'We didn't see him after that first glimpse,' Pauline said. 'We were ten minutes out on the path. When we got back he was gone. We didn't see him again until the search was in full swing.'

'That's a critical point,' I noted. 'You saw Stuart in the woods, right

</an

after you arrived back. I guess it must have been getting dark under those trees.'

'It were, but he was barely in 'em,' Reg said. 'I saw him clear as day.'

'Searching for Christa?'

'What else?'

The two looked at me for enlightenment. Enlightenment was in short supply. If Stuart was at the site searching for Christa immediately after her disappearance then the Barbers' story was hokum. The veracity of their account was locked into their claim that Stuart had driven out before they knew Christa was missing. It was the only way Stuart could legitimately have taken the vehicle out to park it. Hard to explain how moving the car would have been a priority if he'd known his daughter was missing.

The police story was that the Barbers didn't think it through. They'd started their phoney search with Christa's body warm in the car boot before Stuart realised that he needed to get the evidence off the site. So he'd quit and driven out. Dumped the car at the garden centre a mile away then hoofed it back and concocted the story that he hadn't known Christa was missing. With the Smiths' contradicting account it was no big surprise that the police were sceptical. I'd seen it a million times: guilty parties concocting stories in a panic, failing to spot the discrepancies within them, later caught out by witnesses who see something they hadn't allowed for.

The sun was burning. I fanned my face with my cap. The Smiths sat like people inured to discomfort. Pauline's face was placid behind her lenses.

'We don't know where they got their story,' she repeated. 'But we saw Stuart here.'

But they hadn't talked to him. They'd spotted him inside the trees at dusk. That was the extent of it.

I went on to their other sighting. This one was an oddity that fitted neither the Barbers' story nor the police version.

'An hour earlier,' Reg said. 'Eight fifteen. We were having dinner in the pub down the road. The Saracen. I looked up and there was Stuart poking his head in the door, looking for someone.'

'You were sure it was Stuart?'

'At the time I was. I got to thinking later that I might have been mistaken. It was only a flash and I wasn't really paying attention. But at the time I told Pauline I'd just seen him.'

'Eight fifteen. The Barbers say they were eating dinner in their caravan at that time.'

'Yes.'

'And the police didn't dispute it.'

Reg withdrew behind an old perplexity. His Saracen sighting fitted no-one's story. The sighting of Stuart searching at the Orchard Grove an hour later though fitted nicely with the police theory so they'd grabbed that one and discarded the unexplained thing. I wondered about it. Decided there was no reason to ignore either.

'They were absolutely frantic,' Pauline said.

I looked at her.

'That night. Stuart and Elaine were out the whole night. We did four hours ourselves. Covered from the road right down past the farm at the far end of the bridle. Stuart was sure Christa was around somewhere. He was rushing up and down like a madman; had us looking under every tree and bush; had the police in the farm buildings. It got so we believed him. We thought we'd find Christa any moment. But eventually we realised she was gone. My heart was breaking for them.'

'The Barbers were sure that Christa was nearby?'

'They sounded certain,' Pauline said. 'Of course, the police said it was an act. I was sick when I heard that.' Her tinted lenses sparkled in the sun. 'You'd never have guessed it.'

'You think they killed her?'

'They did somethin',' Reg said. 'Their story's up the creek, no doubt.'

I grinned at him. Stories that are up the creek: the trusty signposts to guilt. I'd cleared forty-two murders in the job. Thirty-two were simple stupidity, where solving the case depended mostly on my ability to suspend disbelief that people and their stories could be so stupid. The other ten killers were smarter, calculating. But five of those had stories with tiny inconsistencies that might not have mattered except that there had to be reasons for the lies. The longest it took to clear any of those was two weeks. I've a fondness for stories that are up the creek – just not from my own clients.

'What's up they've got investigators working for them?' Reg asked.

His conservative face radiated dismay that he was being nosey but he couldn't resist. The two of them watched me.

'They still believe Christa's alive,' I said.

The Smith's faces stayed impassive.

'I guess someone has to look for her,' I said.

Pauline's mouth opened then closed. Reg's mouth stayed clamped. Then he shook his head.

'I don't see it,' he said. 'Somethin' 'appened and the kiddy's dead. What's there to find?'

Maybe just that. Proof that she was dead. And the reason.

I asked them if Irene Keenan was in residence.

'Due tomorrow,' said Pauline.

I thanked them. Flipped my cap back on. Felt their blank expressions follow me as I walked towards the Barber caravan.

CHAPTER THIRTEEN
You're two years too late

I climbed wooden steps to the caravan's decking and walked past the rear door – the famous unlocked door, now safely secured – to open the front one.

A wash of baked synthetics hit me as I stepped inside onto a carpet covered by polythene sheeting. The unit's lounge area was sparsely furnished, dominated by a striped sofa and armchair, both oversized for the caravan's lightweight feel. I pushed the door wide to let air in.

The lounge gave onto a kitchen-diner clad in DIY beech veneer. Sterile as the moon, stinking of plastic and bleach. Work surfaces too hot to touch. I opened a sliding door and passed a tiny bathroom and arrived at the rear door. I unlocked it and swung it out.

I walked on into the main bedroom, found a double bed jammed between fitted units. Its bare mattress was dulled by two years' worth of dust. I backtracked and found Christa's room.

It was a tiny space, clad in white tongue-and-groove. Two children's beds a foot apart either side of a white locker. Two dusty mattresses. No way to tell which bed was Christa's. My guess was that she slept beneath the window from which a shaft of blinding light cut through the net curtains, heating the room to a dead fug. The units and shelves were empty. Nothing of the child remained.

I squatted and ran my finger over the locker; picked up the remnants of carbon powder. Undisturbed two years on. A forensic dead end. The fingerprinting had pointed to no-one. The rest of the bedroom, like the rest of the caravan, had been cleared of everything that had ever been linked to the Barbers.

I stayed down, pictured Christa asleep. Or maybe stirring. I craned my neck and looked out of the bedroom door from her viewpoint. Imagined the scratching and creaking of someone moving about the caravan. Pictured a silhouette in the doorway. Or was that fantasy? Was it all over by the time the Barbers went out for their cash? No stranger's hand on the unlocked door?

Or had Christa simply woken up and taken a walk?

I stood. Went back to the rear door and pulled it closed. Squatted and tested the handle from a child's height. It was as the book said: stiff as hell. No way a two-year-old could turn it. Not unless she grabbed it two-handed and put her weight on it, but that wasn't a credible picture. Two-year-olds don't force jammed doors.

I opened the door again and pulled it closed until the latch caught. The door looked secure but it wasn't fully closed. Was it possible that the Barbers failed to latch it properly? I tried the handle again. This time it turned without resistance.

The Barbers' memory was that the door was closed when they went out but would they notice if it was only partly latched? Did Christa wake up and wander? Pull on the handle?

I re-locked the door. Walked back to the front lounge. My footsteps echoed on the hollow underframe. I took off my cap and dabbed sweat; looked down the length of the caravan. Pictured it two years ago, furnished and occupied and the Barbers moving around that evening; the sound of Christa's tantrum, Elaine cajoling her, the screams deafening within the confines of the unit. Easy to imagine but impossible to get a sense of what was real because there was nothing of them left. Just a heaviness about the place like an invisible shadow. I went out and flipped my cap back on then locked up and stepped down off the deck.

The Barber pitch was the last in the avenue. Beyond it a shale track angled into the trees. Twenty yards along, the track ended at stone posts opening onto the bridle path. I followed the path towards the road under the shade of the trees. Fifty yards up, the river swept in in a fierce glitter. A wandering two-year-old could have been here in two minutes. The river ran narrow, a couple of feet deep from the recent spring rain, exposing surface rocks amongst the sprays and eddies. Two years back it had been higher, running fast – perhaps powerful enough to have swept a child away. But if the river did take Christa it didn't snag her anywhere in the twenty miles of twists and turns to the coast. I continued along the bridle way until I hit the road at a small birch-enclosed lay-by. I stood on the cool tarmac and watched occasional traffic pass on the other side of the trees. Of all the drivers who passed that night only the Barbers had spotted their Mystery Woman standing here.

I turned and walked back to the site. Peered between the stone posts at the track that ran in. The summer foliage would make it tricky but you could watch the Barbers' caravan from here.

Was the Mystery Woman waiting up at the road as the Barbers drove out? Would she know that they'd left a child behind in the caravan? What else might have motivated her to walk down and try their door? I went back in and arrived at the Barbers' unit without coming in sight of any caravans except Irene's and the Smiths'. The Smiths had been at the pub. Irene had been watching TV. There'd been no-one around to spot anyone climbing the steps to the Barber unit.

Read the police view and there was no Mystery Woman. By the time the Barbers drove out to Lyndhurst Christa had been dead for two hours and her body was in the boot of their Fiat, the unlocked door staged to divert attention towards an abductor. I walked out onto the concrete avenue. Pictured the Fiat driving away but couldn't see what was under the hatch. Out in the open the heat took on a new oppression. I turned for a last look at the caravan. It sat there quietly, emanating a malign sense of something that couldn't be undone.

I went up to the office and handed Bob Bowland the Barbers' keys.

'Get what you want?' His head tipped towards the bottom of the site. Curious rather than helpful.

'Just impressions. It helps to get a sense of the place.'

The guy grunted, waited. He was not rushing off. The Barber tragedy was still the biggest thing that had happened around here and he was still interested.

'How are they shaping up?' he asked.

'They're not exactly living their own lives,' I said.

He nodded, dropped the keys into a post-slot behind the desk.

'And they've got you looking for her?'

'We're looking for anything that was missed. Something to point towards whoever took her.'

Bowland shook his head. 'She's dead,' he said. 'I wish to God it wasn't true but I can't see it any other way. Probably an accident. They should have come clean about it.'

'You've always thought Elaine did it?'

Another shake. 'At the start it never crossed my mind.'

'When did you first know that something had happened?'

'Nine forty-five that night. One of the residents ran in and told me they were out looking for a child. I went down and we searched the whole site, checked under all the caravans. Opened the buildings. Elaine was out of her mind.'

'Where was Stuart?'

'By the time I went down I heard he was out with the car.'

'Did Elaine go down to the river?'

'Right after I got there. Then she ran all the way up to the road then back the other way towards the farm. We helped her check the fields the other side of the path but a two-year-old couldn't have got over the stile. I explained it but Elaine wasn't thinking straight. We even searched an old byre on the top field, as if a little kid could have got that far. Then Elaine phoned Stuart and he called the police.'

'Elaine met the police?'

'Yes. They talked to her for twenty minutes while they called up reinforcements then went back to the river but Elaine was fixated on searching further along the bridle path, looking for places a child might be hidden – the fields, woods, buildings. Stuart showed up sometime after ten, just as it was going dark.'

'You'd no sense that Stuart and Elaine were hiding anything?'

'None. It's easy to be wise after the event but they fooled me at the time.'

'They mentioned an abductor?'

'Stuart did. They'd noticed a woman up on the road when they drove out for their cash. He was convinced she'd walked down the path and gone into their caravan. He didn't accept that Christa could have got out by herself.'

'So the Barbers brought up the abduction theory whilst they were out with the search party.'

'Yes. Seems odd now. They were convinced that Christa had been abducted but were fixated on searching right here.'

'You think there was no abductor?'

Bowman shrugged; slid a ledger across the desk.

'Not for me to say,' he said. 'It's the saddest thing I ever heard, but the circus they're running now doesn't help the poor kid.'

'Assuming she's dead.'

He grabbed a pen. Scribbled in the ledger.

'She *is* dead,' he said. 'You're two years too late.'

I left him to it.

Two years late. I didn't need Bowland to tell me that. The Barber caravan had screamed it in every dust mote and powder speck. Alive or dead, we were a long way from Christa.

~~~~~

There was a small shop next to the office. I bought a mineral water and sat at a tiny table under an awning. Popped the tab and watched the site as I slaked my thirst. Then I drove out and followed the road towards Lyndhurst. I passed the bridle path lay-by where I'd stood an hour before. There was no-one there, nothing parked, but you had to look hard to be sure.

Half a mile on I turned into a side lane by the Saracen – the pub the Smiths had mentioned. The lane cut across to the main road three hundred yards up where a hoarding advertised the entrance to the Glades Garden Centre. A car park sized for two hundred vehicles ran round the buildings. Three cars were parked.

I drove across the asphalt in a cloud of dust and swung round under the shade of budding trees; killed the engine; hopped out and perched myself against the wing. Tried to see it.

Nine thirty on a July evening: the sun has just set to my left but the sky is still bright. A few cars are parked up near the entrance, but none down at this end. The garden centre is closed. It's just walkers' cars, maybe a few vacationers' vehicles parked overnight. Stuart's Fiat drives in and crawls towards me, swings round, backs up against the trees. Stuart locks up and heads back to the caravan site. Only a twenty minute walk but it's a hell of a distance to park the car, even if you're not planning on using it for a few days. Did Stuart glance back at the Fiat as he walked out? Was he walking back innocently, unaware that Christa's bed was empty? If I saw his face would it tell me anything?

The police didn't know the Barbers had the Fiat with them until three days later. When they did find out they got here pretty quick, checked the car over, found nothing.

They asked some hard questions but the Barbers stuck to the story that they simply hadn't thought to mention the car. The Fiat was a cock-up, though: the police's priority was the search for the girl and abductor but there was too little checking of the Barber timeline. Three days was a long time to wait to find that the Barbers had a second car with them that weekend and that Stuart's story didn't match the witnesses' statements. They should have pinned Stuart's movements down within a day of coming on the case. Then the police let things slide a few more weeks, lost more ground. It was a month before their theory shifted towards the possibility that Stuart had hidden the body of his daughter in the Fiat.

Two mistakes in a list of mistakes that ultimately toppled the CPS case. I was going with the theory that my clients were innocent, but a case that flops due to technical errors isn't the same as no case. And after three days of Barber boot camp it was hard to ignore the oddities behind my clients' story.

Maybe the guy running the police enquiry would have an opinion.

CHAPTER FOURTEEN
Aspirations are what we do

Hampshire police HQ was an antennae-capped sixties edifice a stone's throw from the centre of Winchester. It's gloomy lobby was curated by a uniformed sergeant who planted his fists on the counter to consider my query about whether a policeman called Barry Bedford lived there. Bedford was the detective who'd taken over the Barber team after the CPS fiasco, tasked with salvaging something from the mess. He lived either here or in the new building in Southampton. The desk sergeant wasn't inclined to tell me either way until the mention of Christa Barber sharpened him up. He told me to sit. I perched on a row of plastic chairs and sweated in my blazer, watching people going in and out until a heavyset guy in a creased tan suit stepped out of the lift. The guy had the gait of the active type, but the florid sheen across his face signalled problems ahead. He came across and asked if I was Flynn. Took me to a cubbyhole off the lobby and sat me at a small table under a spitting fluorescent. I explained that I was working for the Barbers; handed him a card.

Bedford scanned it and flicked it into his jacket. Lowered himself into a chair opposite.

'Why are you here?' he said.

'Just a chat. The Barbers have asked us to take another look at Christa's disappearance. I'm looking for direction.'

Bedford sat back. *Way* back. Gave me eyes of jaundiced diamond.

'You're aware, of course, that the police don't do "chats". We're not here at civilians' beck and call.'

'I'm just begging a few minutes. The Barbers want their daughter found and so do you. We're on different sides of the fence but there's probably common ground between us.'

'Highly unlikely,' Bedford said. 'Our position is quite clear on Christa Barber. If you're running round hoping to find her safe and well then you're on a fool's errand – though I'm sure you charge nice rates – but your activities have nothing in common with the police investigation.'

'I don't do fool's errands,' I said. 'If there's something to be found we'll find it. Whichever way it falls.'

Bedford's mouth twitched. 'And if it falls the wrong way?' His eyes fixed me. 'Are you going to bring your clients through my door?'

'We don't bury illegalities under a confidentiality gripe, if that's what you mean.'

Bedford's brows raised. 'You don't respect client confidentiality? Hide their nasty little secrets?'

'The Barbers are paying us to look for Christa. We'll go wherever the signs point.'

'Meaning what?'

'If girl in the photograph is Christa we'll chase her down and your view of the Barbers will have to change. If it's not her then we'll see what turns up.'

'The photo's not Christa. So let's quit with those aspirations.'

I forced a grin. 'Aspirations are what we do, Chief Inspector. We've told the Barbers we'll get Christa back if she's reachable. But we'll find out what happened either way. If a genie pops out of the bottle we're not going to re-cork it.'

'So you'll bring it all to us?' Bedford asked. His smile was nailed on.

'We'll do what's right for Christa.'

'Well your clients could be in for a nasty shock – and I don't mean finding out that the photo isn't Christa because they already know that. But they're not sweating, Flynn. You won't find anything they don't want you to find. There's either nothing left to find or your outfit's not up to handling their tricks. Probably both.'

My own grin held steady. 'Don't worry,' I said. 'My outfit's up to it. If there's anything you guys didn't catch then let's call this a second chance.'

'Anything we didn't catch?' Bedford's smile faded. 'Anything we screwed up? Yes, it's possible. But I took a good look when I took over and I didn't see anything bar the technical issues that damaged the prosecution. Nothing that pointed away from your clients. But good luck anyway, Flynn. As long I don't see you again I'm happy.'

'I won't be in your hair,' I promised.

'There was never a truer word spoken.'

'I'm just looking for a pointer. The puzzle is the timeline that night.'

Bedford eased forward. 'Is this what you mean by not getting in my hair?' he said.

I held up my hands. 'Can't blame me for trying. The whole thing's in the public domain anyway. Most of it unofficially, which I don't like. I'm intrigued by the police version of events. Wondering how much of what I read is accurate.'

Bedford looked at me. I'd just got to thinking he'd clammed up when he spoke.

'You're right: our timings for what happened that night weren't released via official channels. I can't explain how the information got out but those timings are on the button. If you've read the press accounts then you've got our viewpoint. The Barbers didn't leave their caravan until fifteen minutes after they said they did. So we've got two problems. One: their supposed abductor had a rather shorter window than they claimed. Two: the Barbers were telling lies. And they were also telling lies when they said that Stuart Barber went to park their car *before* they discovered Christa missing. He didn't. When people lie there's a reason. Save yourself some time, Flynn: go with our timeline and find out why your clients' version differs.'

I said nothing.

Bedford stared me out a moment longer then pushed himself out of his chair. Our chin-wag was over. I stood. Tossed one last ball.

'I guess you took a look at the cadaver dog findings when you took over.'

Bedford's florid face hid any reaction. 'That, Flynn, is one of many subjects I'm not going to talk about,' he said.

'It just seemed,' I persisted, 'that it was your strongest evidence against the Barbers.'

That got a smile. 'Finding signs of a dead body in a suspect's car does cast doubt on their plea of innocence. But like I said, it's not something I'm going to discuss.'

'The findings didn't hold up for the CPS though.'

But Bedford wasn't biting. He clamped his lips and held the door. I went out. Turned.

'I've been in the job,' I said. 'I've seen irrefutable evidence. Evidence that's so irrefutable you end up looking for whatever's hiding behind it. But you know all about that, Chief Inspector.'

If Bedford was tempted to discuss the finer points of criminology he suppressed the urge. He closed the door behind us and walked me to the foyer.

'When you find something that helps the police enquiry,' he said, 'don't hesitate to get in touch.'

He stood in the foyer and watched me go out. No handshake. And the guy didn't look better for seeing me. The Christa Barber failure still sat heavily on his shoulders.

CHAPTER FIFTEEN
Dead bodies and innocent explanations

I drove back to the New Forest. Ten minutes past the Orchard Grove I hit a crossroads with a sign that told me I was at Lockhurst Well, a name with no place. The only habitation in sight was a seventeenth century coaching inn called the Black Bull that stood off to one side at an angle that matched none of the roads. The interior was cool and empty. A guy in a striped shirt quit polishing taps to come and serve me.

I ordered a bitter shandy. Asked if he had a regular by the name of Starr.

'Friend of yours?'

'Professional interest.' I slid a card across. 'I could do with a chat. You happen to know his whereabouts?'

'Perhaps,' the guy said. But he wasn't about to divulge the information.

'Is he in often?'

'Off and on.'

'Be good if the card reached him,' I said. 'I need to talk to him urgently.'

The guy said he'd see Starr got the card but showed no sign of having heard the "urgent" bit.

Peter Starr was the dog handler who'd checked out the Barbers' car. He'd been based at Netley until he retired a year ago. Harry had fished out the information that he'd relocated to this area – barely ten minutes from where it all happened. If our landlord put my card in Starr's hands he'd either call back or not. If not, I'd be forced to track him down which would cost a couple of days. But the detail of the dead body in their car was the darkest of the clouds over the Barbers' version of events. I needed to understand if there was anything behind the story. Dead bodies and innocent explanations rarely meet. The fact that no forensic traces were recovered and that the sniffer dog findings couldn't be repeated had put the kibosh on the CPS case but I wasn't about to let it go without a closer look. Maybe Starr was a bumbler who'd distracted the police with a false lead. Maybe he wasn't.

The Bull did bed and breakfast. I stashed my crash-bag in a crooked room with creaking floorboards and went to chill in the bar with the new edition of the Barbers' book. Re-read the events of that night with newly educated eyes. The afternoon ticked by. The bar stayed quiet and cool. At five I called Arabel and told her I wasn't going to make it to her *Anglican* music-meltdown. If she detected relief in my voice she didn't mention it. Asked if we were still on for the weekend. I said sure, the weekend was safe.

I headed out for a walk.

The sun was low but the heat was still stultifying. I gave it forty-five minutes then went back in for a pub dinner and more reading. By last orders I'd finished the *New Edition* and picked up nothing new.

I climbed up to my room thinking of Christa Barber and irrefutable evidence, all the tomorrows that hadn't arrived for the kid. Couldn't shift the thought that after twenty-two months things didn't look good for her.

~~~~~

The sun woke me at five. I pulled on running kit and found a side door that let me out of the building, jumped a stile and did forty-five minutes along forestry tracks, dodging machinery and death's head warnings. The tracks' gradients induced a pain that gave the warnings real meaning. I hit a tarmac road and stepped up the pace. Blitzed the last mile back to the Bull. Took a long shower and lay on the bed. Keyed my phone.

Shaughnessy was on his way to Elstree to take over from Bernie for an out of town gig – a ten a.m. radio interview in Bristol then a couple of bookshop events in the area. A single pair of eyes was still not ideal, but if someone made a move on the Barbers they'd have to be quick to beat the tornado that would zero in within milliseconds. With the element of surprise on their side I'd give an assailant a ten per cent chance – though that was ten per cent more than I was happy with.

Harry was parked outside the Astra guy's address in Wembley. He'd watch the guy whilst we waited for ID. By tomorrow we'd know who was tailing the Barbers, maybe even why.

I went down and balanced the benefits of my run with a full English then drove the four miles back to the Orchard Grove. Parked outside the site office and walked down to see if Irene Keenan had arrived.

I spotted people milling about at the bottom of the site, gathered round the deck of the Barber caravan. I walked down. Found Bob Bowland there looking unhappy.

Up close the caravan was different. Something about the windows. Yesterday they'd been blanked by net curtains. Today the curtains seemed to be torn. Then I saw it. The curtains weren't torn but streaked with something that had soaked in and dried. Bowland turned to me, perplexed. This was a million miles beyond his experience as site manager. It was like a bomb had gone off; like a plane had come down on his park.

Because the inside of the caravan seemed to be dripping with blood.

CHAPTER SIXTEEN
I'm the guy who nailed your clients

I walked round the caravan. Every window was covered in the same dark red smears. It was like there'd been a massacre inside.

I met Bowland back at the steps.

'We found it ten minutes ago,' he said.

'Has anyone been in?'

He shook his head. 'I'm not sure I'd want to be first.'

'No-one saw anything?'

'Nothing.'

I stepped up onto the deck. The rear door was opened out flat against the caravan side. It had been jemmied. I signalled Bowland up and showed him the damage. The crowd closed in below the steps.

I went in through the open door and came into the space between the bedrooms and shower stall. Every wall had the same streaks of red. Bowland started to come in but I waved him back. The air was barely breathable.

I touched the wall. The stuff was dry but the acetone fumes were at knockout strength. I scraped a sample off and went out into the light. Rubbed the scraping between my fingers. The film broke up. Bowland was watching.

'Paint,' I confirmed. 'Stay here while I make sure that's all we've got.'

Bowland didn't argue.

I followed the dogleg corridor towards the front of the caravan. Saw the tail end of a sprayed-on message. Walked through to read it:

Child-Killers Burn in Hell !!!

I checked each room. The paint was everywhere – walls, furniture, windows. I opened the net curtains in the main bedroom to let in more light but it didn't make much difference. The glass was almost obscured by the blood-like smears. The double bed's bare mattress was stained with the simulacrum of a dried pool of blood convincing enough to have the hairs standing on my neck. Someone had taken time over this. Rendering blood-smears on the veneer surfaces had taken time. Getting that uniform thick coating, striated with semi-transparent smears and runnels, took a certain skill.

I walked into Christa's bedroom. The two single mattresses were likewise saturated, facsimiles of butchery. More artwork rendered the white tongue-and-groove a gory Rorschach with just one area kept clear for another message. This time my skin crawled:

Why, Mummy?

The intruder had worked through the whole caravan with the blood effect. Spray can vandalism was better than what I'd been imagining from outside but the effect was still chilling. It would be the Barbers' call whether they brought the police in. My interest was in what the work might tell me about whoever was chasing them. Maybe this was our vigilante.

I went out and begged a flashlight; worked through corners and crevices from front to back, looking for anything that the intruder had left behind. Came up blank.

Bowland was waiting outside.

'Just vandals,' I said. 'You might want to check with the Barbers. They'll need the door fixing.'

Bowland walked off to his office. The onlookers started to disperse. Vandalism lacked the drawing-power of axe murder.

I checked the doorframe. A small jemmy. One-point-five centimetre head. Sold by the million. I squatted and checked the decking. The wood was heating fast. I ignored a flattened cigarette butt. Too old, and I didn't see our spray painter getting out alive with fag breaks. I spotted nothing else. I descended the steps and checked the grass round the unit then ducked under the deck with the flashlight; crawled around in the shadows. The shadow prevented weed growth and the Barbers hadn't accumulated junk so it was clean. I started at the front and made my way back. Collected a comb, two empty beer bottles, a couple of coins and a scrap of paper. Then right under the rear door I found the top off a spray can.

I crawled back out. Sat on the steps. The paper scrap was nothing – an old notepad page, degraded by the elements. Likewise the comb and beer bottles – years old. The can top was what mattered. The top was new.

An attached sticker had a price and shop logo: "Penny's". Couldn't be too many hardware shops with that name. The top's colour was burnt umber which would be a good generic match for the rusty red paint inside the caravan. Other than the top our intruder had left the place clean. I pictured them coming out, half-asphyxiated in the dark, a top popping off a can and rolling under the caravan. Crawling after it would not have appealed. More chance of leaving extra evidence than clearing up. Maybe they'd decided to cut their losses. Maybe they didn't notice they'd lost the top.

I called Lucy. Got her searching the directories for hardware stores. Then I walked across to the unit opposite the Barbers' where an elderly woman in white slacks was sitting reading a magazine. Irene Keenan. I ducked under her awning and introduced myself. Irene lowered the magazine and gave me a hesitant smile.

'The Smiths said you'd be by. Who on earth did that?' She gestured to the Barbers' caravan.

'Beats me. Someone trying to stir things up.'

She pointed to a spare camp chair and I sat next to her in the shade. Irene was the star witness in the Barber prosecution case, though it had never been her wish. But her story had been central. She'd heard Christa screaming that night and she'd seen something the Barbers had never explained.

'It's hard to imagine Stuart and Elaine still in the middle of it after all this time,' she said. 'It was so sad. They were just a normal couple. Christa was such a bright little girl. Who'd ever imagine something like that happening?'

'How well did you know them?'

'Reasonably. I've spent summers here since my husband died, and Elaine and Christa were regulars that year. Christa would bring things over to show me. Elaine and I would natter.'

'And Stuart?'

Irene's face clouded. She looked back at the Barber caravan.

'He was here weekends sometimes. Most of the time it was just

94

Elaine and Christa.'

I followed Irene's gaze. The blood effect didn't look any better from here. Bowland needed to get that sorted. I wondered about the hesitation in Irene's answer. Why did she need to think about Stuart?

'How long had they been coming here?' I asked.

'They bought the caravan the summer my husband died. That was two years before Christa was born, although I didn't see them much in the second year.'

'The year after they lost their first daughter, Grace?'

Irene nodded.

'Did Elaine ever talk about that?'

'No. We were only occasional neighbours. She just talked about Christa.'

'What was Christa like?'

'Carefree. Independent, for a two-year-old. When she had something she wanted to show me she'd come running right over.'

'Did you ever see her tantrums?'

Irene shook her head.

'That's not how it was,' she said. 'The way they blew it up it sounded like Elaine couldn't control Christa. But I never saw anything like that. Christa was like any two-year-old. Sometimes she'd be fine and sometimes she'd have her rages. Perhaps she was a little more prone than most but some are like that. They grow out of it.'

'But your story was critical – about Christa screaming that night.'

'Yes, she threw a tantrum. I heard it from my kitchen. She was in a right old rage. But I wouldn't have read anything into it if it hadn't been for what happened.'

'This was early in the evening?'

'A little after six thirty. She was in a palaver for a good twenty minutes. Then it stopped and that was that. One of those dreadful papers described it as an uncontrollable rage but I said no such thing. A tantrum's a tantrum. It was as bad as any but no worse. When it all went quiet I assumed Elaine had managed to calm Christa down.' Irene shook her head: 'I never said "uncontrollable".'

'Is it possible that Elaine hurt Christa?'

Irene didn't answer. She was still watching the vandalised caravan. I waited until she came out of it.

95

'It was so awful. They were just an ordinary family. Then without any warning Christa was gone.' She touched a finger to her eye. 'I didn't come back here for a year. I couldn't get it out of my mind how easily they'd lost her. Like you'd lose a purse.'

The sun was moving round. I shuffled my chair to gain the shade.

'What do you think happened?'

Irene looked at me as if the question had never occurred to her. But it had. A thousand times. She just hadn't worked out any answer. Not one she wanted to believe. She sighed.

'Christa was such a happy child. Elaine could never have hurt her.'

She stood and went into the caravan. Came back out with a sheet of paper smudged with Blu Tack. A child's drawing, pulled from her wall. Bold slashes of crayon – brown, blue, green. A happy blue sun. A stick-family drawn into the landscape. Mother, father, child, holding hands. The child had a happy face. I sensed the guiding hand of an adult, but the drawing was still impressive for a two-year-old.

'That's how I remember her,' Irene said. 'So intelligent. She gave me that two days before it happened. It still makes me cry.'

I looked at the drawing. Said: 'It was a funny thing about the car.'

Irene gazed into the distance, covering feelings she didn't want to show. Her evidence about Christa's tantrum might have meant something or nothing but her memory of seeing the Barbers' black Fiat parked by their caravan that night was a discrepancy that had almost sunk Stuart and Elaine. Their story was that they'd driven out to Lyndhurst to hunt for cash fifteen minutes before nine. Irene's testimony had their car still outside the caravan at nine – smack in the centre of the supposed abductor's time window.

Irene tried to swallow something indigestible.

'It's what I saw,' she said. 'I'd just made a drink before sitting down to watch TV at nine. That's how I knew the time. I looked out of my window and their car was right there. I thought nothing of it until the police started asking about it a few days later. And I could only tell them what I saw: their car was parked by their door on the dot of nine.' She looked at me helplessly. 'It was awful to contradict them, but they must have been mistaken. At nine o'clock Stuart and Elaine were still here.'

I smiled. Watched the site. "Mistaken" didn't quite cover it. The Barbers' claim that they were already on their way to Lyndhurst at nine was fundamental to their abduction scenario. They'd given that timing right at the start, of course, before they knew about Irene's inconvenient sighting. Stuart and Elaine hadn't called Irene a liar but they hadn't explained the discrepancy either. Just insisted that the old lady was mistaken. Easy to say, but you can't beat TV schedules as a way of clocking the time. That's why Irene's evidence had done so much damage.

I handed Christa's drawing back to her; she tried to find meaning in the stick-figures.

'I don't know what to think,' she said. 'Elaine couldn't have hurt Christa.'

She looked at me for enlightenment. I looked at the caravan.

~~~~~

I was getting into the car when my phone rang. A voice I didn't recognise.

'Flynn? You want to talk about the Barbers? Bedford tells me you're some kind of hired lackey and I should tell you to piss off. I probably will, but I'd like to do it face to face.'

'Sure,' I said. 'You can do that. Once I know who I'm talking to.'

There was a pause. Second thoughts. Then a decision.

'I'm Starr,' he said. 'I'm the one who nailed your clients with a dead body they couldn't explain.'

CHAPTER SEVENTEEN
Boy that was popular delivery!

He was sitting at a bench table in front of the Black Bull. I joined him. Offered my hand and got a handshake shorter than a bookie's.

Peter Starr was a lean guy in his early sixties with sun-cured skin and a mess of hair to have Boris Johnson offering a comb. Starr asked for ID. I pushed over a card and my driver's licence.

'That's a nice bandwagon the Barbers have going. Lawyers, publicists, detectives. Employment opportunities all round.'

I leaned on the table.

'We're just here to do a job,' I said.

'Yeah. You're going to find their girl. Unless you're just covering the thuggery part.'

'You're reading too many tabloids,' I said.

'So it wasn't you guys attacked the journalists?'

'You saying you believe what you read in the rags?'

Starr pulled up a slow smile. 'Touché,' he said. 'But something happened at that hotel.'

'That's another story. We're trying to keep the Barbers safe but we're not muscle for hire. We do what's needed. The press makes what they want of it.'

'Doesn't change the fact that you've hired on to a circus.'

'We've hired on to do a job. The moment the job looks bogus we're out of there.'

'They've got you looking for Christa. That's bogus.'

'I'll decide on that when I've seen the evidence.'

'Including the cadaver evidence? The Barbers want you to look at that?' Starr raised his eyebrows.

'They've asked us to track down the Christa Photo. That means looking at all the circumstances around her disappearance. They don't tell us where to look.'

Starr nodded. 'Then good luck, Flynn! They'll certainly tell you to pull your nose out if you turn up something hot.'

I said nothing.

'Ex-copper,' he mused. 'Always depresses me to see them working the other side of the fence.'

'I know which side of the fence I work. It hasn't changed.'

Starr watched me.

'I didn't hear the reason for your early retirement from the Met,' he said.

'And you're not going to.'

He grinned.

'So what are you really after?'

'The truth. If the child is out there we want her back.'

'And if she's dead?'

'We'll still get to her.'

Starr smiled. 'Confidence! That's good. As long as it's not based on ignorance.'

I said nothing.

'So you're going to get where the task force couldn't? You must be better than the rest.'

'This used to be my job,' I said. 'And I was.'

'Confidence,' Starr repeated. He gave it a moment. 'What do you want from me?'

'I need to know if the Barbers had a dead body in their car.'

Starr thought about it.

'No traces were ever recovered,' he said, 'above what you'd expect in a family car. And sniffer dog indications do not constitute evidence, as you know.'

'I know the legalities. I'm interested in the truth.'

Starr pulled a faint smile onto his face. 'You heard about the dog that found the traces?' he said. 'She got her photo in their book.'

'Miss Marple.'

Starr nodded. 'A springer spaniel cross. I've been training dogs for thirty years, Flynn, and she was the best HRD I've ever worked with.'

'And you used her to check the Barber car three weeks after Christa disappeared.'

Starr nodded. 'The team were looking at Stuart and Elaine by then. They called us in to see what we could find.'

He leaned forward. 'There were a shed-load of inconsistencies in their account of what happened that night but the Fiat was the biggie. Shifting it away from the scene right after their daughter disappeared was kind of odd, don't you think? What the hell was Stuart Barber doing parking the car when he should have been out searching for his daughter?'

'Depends on which timing you believe. The Barbers say he moved the Fiat before he knew that Christa was missing.'

'But the more probable story is that he moved it to get his daughter's body out of the way until they could figure how to dispose of it.'

'I know the other side of the story.'

Starr pursed his lips.

'So they brought us in. Three weeks is late to find traces once a body's been moved. But it's within the capability of a good dog. I guess you know this, Flynn?'

I said nothing.

'And you also know the problem with dogs.' He waited.

'Dogs can be led on,' I said, 'to show whatever the handler wants. So-called blind tests can be influenced more by the handler's desire to turn up a result than the dog's talent.'

Starr nodded. 'Except I didn't make that mistake. The search was a true blind. We put ten cars on a yard. Six were black Fiats. I didn't know which was the Barbers' vehicle. I just brought Miss Marple in and we walked the whole line. Checked each car, inside and out. Average check fifteen minutes. A fifteen minute break after each set of three. And Miss Marple went down the line and didn't give even the faintest signal until we got to the Barbers' car.'

A tractor roared round the bend and turned at the crossroads releasing a convoy of cars. Starr waited for the dust to clear.

'My procedure was to cover the interior first, then open up the boot or hatch. Miss Marple knew the routine but at the Barber vehicle she tried to divert straight to the hatch. I had to pull her back. They're trained to focus where we point them, stay with the routine, but sometimes it's hard to keep a dog back. They want to show how smart they are. So Miss Marple went through the inside of the vehicle, but lightning fast, like we were wasting time. After a couple of minutes I quit. Took her round to the back of the car. That's where she started signalling like crazy. She jumped into the hatch and poked her nose in the cracks like she couldn't get enough. Then sat on the floor and gave me the signal. A good, solid, hit.

There'd been a dead body in that car, Flynn.'

'But the story was that she got it wrong.'

Starr concurred. 'Forensics couldn't isolate any traces despite the signal. In the end all we had was Miss Marple's indication. And when we were challenged a week later I couldn't repeat the findings with another dog. So the Barber team claimed that Miss Marple had simply got it wrong. And she never got the chance to repeat her performance. She'd been diagnosed with leukaemia. I retired her the week of the Barber check. She was dead within a month.'

Starr leaned and planted his elbows.

'Let me tell you about another of Miss Marple's mistakes.'

Two vans raced past, threw up more dust. We waited.

'In '03 we got a call-out to Andover. They'd found a body on the edge of Harewood Forest. Not much of a body. The woman who spotted it initially thought it was a pig carcass, except that pigs don't wear shirts and neckties. What she'd found was a man's torso. There were no other remains nearby but the killer was sloppy. Left a business card in the shirt pocket that ID'd the victim. It was a guy who owned a couple of clubs in Andover and had connections to villains in Bristol. Rumour had him falling out with the Bristol gang. Two of the gang had been spotted at one of his clubs the night he disappeared. Whispers had them frog-marching him out to a waiting car. But there was a second whisper that said that the guy had been offed right there at the club and moved after the place closed for the night. So I was called in to check for any sign there'd been a body on the premises. This was four weeks after the guy disappeared, which is marginal for transient contact. I took Miss Marple along.'

I flicked my shades down; watched Starr's silhouette.

'We went over the dead guy's office inch by inch. Miss Marple gave it her best shot. Nothing. We tried the back rooms at the club, the private ones where the guy ran card games and provided hospitality for clients looking for romance. We were in there two hours. Got nothing. No sign the guy had been killed there.

'Then I checked the back yard for form's sake. Didn't expect anything. But Miss Marple took an interest in the fence between the club and the restaurant yard next door. The fence was rotted and Miss Marple got a fixation on one spot. Started signalling.

'There was nothing our side of the fence so we went round to the restaurant yard and found a small refuse skip. The thing stunk to high heaven. But Miss Marple went right over to it and sniffed around like crazy. I lifted her in and let her crawl around in all the crap whilst I tried not to breathe. How the hell she could get a cadaver trace through that was beyond me but I'd learned to trust her. When she gave me the signal I knew we had something.'

'You brought in forensics?'

Starr laughed. 'Hell, no! We lifted out the skip. Took the whole shit-load to the lab. Boy that was a popular delivery! The tech people practically lined up to cheer us in! But they cleared out the refuse sacks and started checking them and Miss Marple got a pig's ear as her reward. That dog would have gone after Dracula's corpse for one of those.'

'They find anything?'

Starr shook his head. 'No.'

I gave him surprised.

'The lab had only finished about half the sacks when we got a call. There'd been a tip-off that led the team to a property connected to the Bristol gang and they'd uncovered evidence that the guy had been killed right there. They eventually dug up most of his remains at the site. The theory about him being killed at his club was wrong. So we carted the skip back to the restaurant and apologised for the inconvenience. That was Miss Marple's only recorded mistake.'

I watched him. It was a nice story. But a nice story about a screw-up wasn't the thing to persuade me that the mutt had been right about the Barbers' car. I pushed my shades up to see where Starr was going.

'Yeah,' he said. 'We went home with our tails between our legs. At least I did. Miss Marple had already eaten her pig's ear so she was happy.'

I waited for him to get to the point.

'Three days later I got a call from local CID. They'd heard about Miss Marple's false alarm. Turned out they'd been pulled in a fortnight earlier on a funny story about that restaurant. The place was owned by two Lebanese brothers, Farid and Kassin. Farid's wife had reported him missing, with a tale about a business dispute. Apparently he'd gone to confront his brother and never come back. Brother Kassin claimed that Farid had done a runner on his wife and headed back to the greener grass of Lebanon. When CID checked, Immigration confirmed that Farid had indeed flown out of Heathrow seventeen days before, heading for Paris and a presumed connection to his native land. The guy had done a runner just as his brother claimed. Case closed. CID wasn't about to argue with Immigration. But their noses told them that something was wrong. They'd never liked the casual way Kassin told his story or the fact that Farid's absence put the business in Kassin's hands. So when they heard about Miss Marple's findings they perked up and carted the skip right back to the lab.'

The Bull's door opened and the landlord pegged it back; looked surprised to see two of us chin-wagging. He went back in. The shadows inside looked good.

'The lab got a hit,' I guessed.

Starr sat back, folded his arms.

'Under all that shit they found part of a shirt with what looked like a small piece of flesh attached. We extracted some DNA. Degraded, but good enough to try for a match. Brother Kassin declined to help with a comparative sample but Farid's wife managed to get their mother flown in from Lebanon to provide one. Seems Farid had never shown up back home. When they processed the mother's DNA the match was sufficient to give a high probability the traces were Farid's. Good enough to turn up the heat on brother Kassin. They went right through his business affairs, found he'd been raking half the profits into an offshore account for years. They squeezed the guy hard and eventually he gave it up. He'd killed his brother in a business dispute. Dismembered the body and dropped the remains into the skip to let the contractors recycle his problem. Then Kassin took a trip to Paris using his brother's passport and returned under his own to make it look like Farid had left the country. It was just Kassin's bad luck that the shenanigans at the club next door brought Miss Marple sniffing around at his fence. So it turned out that her big mistake was no mistake at all. Traces four weeks old under restaurant refuse and she picked it up from next door.'

Starr sat forward again. 'Like I said, the dog was the best I ever had. She wasn't mistaken then and she wasn't mistaken when she found the traces in the Barbers' car.'

He stood. Grabbed his keys.

'The Barbers put their daughter's body in the Fiat,' he said. 'Then Stuart moved the car out of the way of the police search until he could dispose of it. The sooner you accept that, Flynn, the sooner you'll get to the truth about your clients.'

He walked off. Drove away in a cloud of dust.

CHAPTER EIGHTEEN
Massacre Red

My phone rang as I walked to the Frogeye. Lucy, about the paint can.

'There's a Penny's hardware store in Salisbury,' she reported. She read off an address. 'Is this guy the vigilante, Eddie?'

'The language fits.'

'So he's from out of town?'

'Salisbury's a long way to drive to pick up paint,' I said. I asked about the tabloids.

'*The Nation's* the only one running the Barber story. Mostly rehash. I dunno where their "new revelations" went.'

'They're coming. The bastards are just stringing the punters. How's our classifieds?'

'Out in two hours. I'll call you.'

I pulled my fisherman's low and took a B-road that promised a short cut to the A36 but led me into a convoy of tractors and tempers. When I hit the A-road things got worse. Roadworks clogged the route: heavy machinery and grey-vested navvies vying for still-life perfection behind battalions of cones. I breathed dust and diesel fumes for forty minutes. Reached Salisbury with blood-oxygen on critical. When I recovered I asked directions.

Penny's Hardware and Builders' Merchants was tucked down a side street off the centre. I went in and found the spray-can rack. Matched my top to a can and pulled it out. Went to talk to a tubby guy in brown overalls at the counter. I explained about the vandalism; asked how many cans it would take to coat the inside of a static caravan.

'The whole thing?' he said. 'That would take a week.'

'The guy worked fast. Covered quarter of the surface area.'

He took the can. Squinted at the label.

'These are four square metre coverage,' he said. 'What are those statics? Twenty by three? We'd be talking one-fifty-plus square metres of wall including the internals. You'd cover a quarter with ten cans but you'd asphyxiate yourself before you were through.'

I explained about the open door. 'Have you sold a batch of this colour recently?'

'The batch couldn't be more than five,' he said. 'That's the most we stock in any colour.'

'If you'd sold more than usual of this colour would it show in the sales?'

'It would show in the re-orders.' He came out from the counter and we went to check the rack. I'd already checked: there'd been just a single can of Massacre Red left – the one on his counter.

He came back and tapped at the computer.

'Okay,' he said. 'We've had two deliveries of those reds in the last fortnight. Looks like we've sold a few. Maybe most of your vandal's supply.' He gave the computer a final tap. 'You can get this stuff anywhere, of course.'

But the label on my can top said that our artist had got his supplies right here. The Barbers' vigilante had been in Salisbury recently. And with the hate-mail postal areas migrating west we had a guy either misdirecting us or getting lazy, leading us out of town towards where he lived.

I thanked the Penny's guy. Left the can on his counter. Went to see Damien Larkin.

~~~~~

Larkin lived in an eighteenth century limestone house at the head of a steep climb south of Devizes. The building stood right on the road, it's former affluence blighted by peeling paintwork and mossed slating. I swung into a cobbled courtyard and parked in the shade of a two storey coach house. Walked across and knocked on the house door.

No response.

I took a look around. The coach house had the potential for conversion to a small cottage but had degraded into a workshop full of junk with ominous glimpses of sky behind the upper windows. At the rear of the buildings a line of dogwood guarded a neglected half acre lawn and derelict tennis court. I walked across them to a summer house and a gate in a stone wall that let me out onto a paddock sloping towards the Downs. The view probably added a million to the property value. Damien might have been tied to the place but he'd got the plum of the inheritance. Elaine's and Sharon's half mills didn't compare.

The paddock was five acres, rough and ungrazed, dropping to a shaded corner. I walked down to where a stream chuckled deep in the trees. Stood a while in the cool shadows then went back up. The house was still dead.

I headed back to London. Doglegged onto the Orbital and cruised north in a hiss of scorched tyres and overheated tempers, horns going off like everyone was a cabby. I turned Elkie Brooke up on my 'phones and drowned the racket but couldn't tune out Peter Starr's words which bounced around in my head, taunting me with the thought that the agency was working for killers.

CHAPTER NINETEEN
Boycott could give you a quote

Back at Chase Street the sign said "Closed" but I heard a racket through the door. I went in and found Shaughnessy's office open and his chair occupied.

The occupier had her feet on his desk and his keyboard across her legs as her fingers bashed it to pieces to the cacophony of a shoot-'em-up. You'd sense that the girl was tall. You'd sense a cute face behind the sweep of hair that flopped over it. And you'd be right on both counts. I couldn't rightly say whether Shaughnessy's daughter was a girl or a woman but the Martians fighting their corner inside his computer would know for sure what they were up against.

'Hi, Eddie,' she said. She continued zapping the aliens or whoever they were. I hear the enemy nowadays are blood-sucking neo-nazi auto thieves, but who's to say they're not all Martians inside?

'How's it going Jazz-Man?'

'Cool.'

'This a social call or are you looking for an investigator to figure what happened to your school grades?'

Armageddon hit a lull. She slid the keyboard onto the desk.

'Has Dad been complaining?'

'Only when he opens his mouth.'

She grinned. 'It's cool, Eddie. I dropped a couple of marks in maths and music. It's a statistical anomaly. One standard deviation. I'll be back on the norm next year.'

'I haven't a clue what you're talking about Jazz,' I said, 'but I know you're smarter than to get on the wrong side of your father.'

'Damn right there,' she said. 'So how's business?'

'Business is interesting, as you well know.'

I perched on Harry's half of the desk. Jasmine's grin went impish. 'I saw you in the paper, Eddie. When that flour-freak got you? Cool! I think dad was laughing.'

I'll bet. Wait till someone messed with his bike.

'Hazard of the job, Jazz-Man. I've had worse thrown at me.'

'Like what?'

'Well, one time we were serving notice at a riding stables. That wasn't nice. And one time in the Met I had an angry wife come after me with a pan of cooking oil.'

'Wow. Was it hot?'

'No, but it was sticky. Took me a week to get it out of my hair.'

'Did you arrest her?'

'Are you crazy? I ran like hell. I'd enough on my hands trying to take her husband down. I wasn't being paid to sort out dysfunctional families.'

Jasmine swung her feet off the desk and came to sit on Harry's side beside me.

'He's gonna be a while, Jazz,' I said. 'Out with our clients.'

Her smile broadened. Shaughnessy's little girl had become a head-turner, and the guy was paranoid about the boys he didn't trust, which was all of them. He and Jasmine got on great but the guy was missing the calming influence of a wife to remind him how smart his daughter was.

'Damn,' Jasmine said. 'I thought I'd get a ride home.' She grinned at me. 'So what are they like? Elaine looks kinda weird.'

Weird. Maybe that lined up with Lucy's "cold". But it's hard to judge people's character when you've only known them post-disaster.

'They're probably the same as you and me, Jazz. Any of us would be a little weird after two years performing in a public circus.'

'Is Elaine as boss as she seems?'

'She's the one in charge. Maybe she's the one hurting most.'

'Like as if she'd killed Christa?'

'Are you digging for dirt?'

'Did she?'

I grinned. Jasmine would get nothing out of Shaughnessy. The two were close but he kept her out of his business. So she was squeezing me instead.

'Haven't a clue,' I said. 'But there are things need explaining.'

'The witnesses tore their story apart. Have they explained that yet?'

'They claim the witnesses were mistaken.'

'Would you have swallowed that when you were a cop? A suspect's word against witnesses?'

'I'd have taken a hard look,' I said. 'Figured out which stories held up. Witnesses can be wrong. Times, model of car, whether a person wore spectacles.'

'So why didn't the police figure it out?'

'They say they did. Just made technical mistakes that hurt the prosecution. Stuart and Elaine stuck to their story and with no hard evidence the case collapsed. You need a body for a murder conviction.'

'There's that guy from Elgin. They've never found his wife's body.'

'That was smart police work, Jazz. Sure, you get cases with no body but they're hard to bring to trial.'

'So – bottom line: did they do it?'

This was what was bugging her – the same as everyone. Most people had opted for "guilty" since lynchings make better entertainment than presumptions of innocence.

'Jazz-Man,' I said, 'I'm in the dark the same as you.'

Jasmine slipped off the desk and leaned casually to lift her bag. Pulled something out.

I stared in amazement. Looked at her. Not even the faintest flush in her cheeks.

'Think they'll sign it?' she said.

It was the book. *The New Evidence.* The kid had come here fishing for autographs. If I wasn't seeing it with my own eyes I'd not have believed it. If I knew anything about Shaughnessy's girl it was that she was no sensation-seeker.

'Jazz,' I said, 'since when did you start celeb-chasing?'

She jabbed the book at me.

'Since never, Eddie! The whole thing sucks. I just want a signed copy as a wind up for Dad's birthday.'

I laughed. Long and loud. Shaughnessy would be wound up all right! And the best part was that he'd never be able to admit it to Jasmine. He'd come bitching to me but would keep shtum in front of his daughter. I snatched the book.

'Don't say I helped,' I said.

She zipped her lips. 'Mum's the word. And remind Dad about the weekend.'

Shaughnessy was taking Jasmine out sailing. He had a boat at Portsmouth that had become his refuge after his world capsized ten years ago, but the time he needed alone had been time away from his daughter. When Jasmine turned six he'd solved the conflict by shanghaiing her into life at sea which she'd taken to like a duck to hoisin. Nowadays she spent her weekends sailing dinghies off Southend; was showing Olympic promise.

Shaughnessy had invited me to sample life on the high seas but I get seasick. Sean waved the excuse off; explained that Nelson got sick every voyage. I wasn't sure what the hell that was supposed to mean. As far as I remembered, Nelson's love of the sea cost him an arm and an eye before he turned forty, which didn't appeal any more than seasickness.

Jasmine leaned and planted a kiss and left me with the book.

~~~~~

I plugged in the coffee machine. Got a juicy spark, but the machine's light came on. I opened a new pack of Buckaroo and heaped the filter. Flicked the switch. Went through to my office.

I lifted the sash and swivelled the Miller to get my feet onto the sill. Something was flapping high up on a tower across the Westway. Fifteen or sixteenth floor. A flag or a banner, waving to and fro from a tiny balcony like a semaphore. A blue stripe across orange. What was that? The Armenian flag? The signal continued, silent and rhythmic. Maybe a code. I watched. Pondered the Barber case.

Heated voices floated up from below. Rook and Lye's people, arguing over whether forty-nine or fifty-one per cent was the lawyer's ethical share in compensation payouts. They'd probably conclude that the lawyers deserved the bigger slice since they did all the work. Apart from the litigation babble the building was quiet. The outer office was quiet too. No aroma of Buckaroo. I pulled my feet off the sill and went out. The coffee was dry in the filter. I fired up the kettle and poured boiling water straight into the cone. Instant filter coffee. I poured a cup and got back to my windowsill. Across the Westway the semaphore was still signalling. Maybe some new callisthenics thing with flags.

The outer door opened. Someone came in and stooged around looking for a receptionist. Our receptionist was at her afternoon job – the one that paid – so I yelled out for our visitor to come through and the last face I wanted to see appeared in the doorway.

I pulled my feet off the sill.

Same sagging jeans; leather jacket old enough for the cracks to flake; white tee shirt soiled to the stage that would wipe the smile off the brightest of detergent-ad girls; brown loafers older than my carpet. The sartorial elegance of the free world press.

If my face reflected my thoughts Archie Hackett didn't notice. He was looking round the room; let his eyes linger on the ceiling patch. The patch had taken a hammering this spring. The tide-mark had expanded three inches. Hackett gave it serious consideration before offering his conclusion.

'What a shit-hole,' he said

Which was the kind of cheek Hackett's breed was prone to since they'd shifted from their Fleet Street ghettos to the greener fields of Wapping. But no-one does hypocrisy like the tabloids.

'At least you'll be able to re-decorate once you've shafted your clients,' Hackett said. He flopped into a chair.

'What do you want?' I said.

Hackett shoved a wad of gum into his mouth. Checked the room from his new perspective. I guess it didn't look any better.

'How about a quote?' he said. 'Your perspective on the Barber situation. Who's your man?'

He was nodding at the poster beside my barometer.

'His name's Geoff Boycott,' I said. 'If he was here he could give you a quote.'

'Gotcha,' Hackett said. 'Lancashire and England. One of the greats – if you're into that paint-drying crap.'

I sensed Boycott's eyes watching.

'What do you want?' I repeated.

Hackett spread his legs.

'A quote. Anything. We need both sides of the story. Stuart and Elaine don't talk to us, which is probably in their best interests, so I thought their hired thugs might have something to say. First question: what do you think really happened to Christa?'

I glanced at Boycott but his face gave nothing away. If I'd had a cricket bat handy Hackett wouldn't have needed words.

'Here's a quote,' I said. 'Take a jump. You want me to lift the window a little more?'

'C'mon, Flynn,' Hackett said. 'Quit the politics. Give me your professional view. You know they did it.'

'Do me a favour,' I said. 'Close the door on your way out.'

'Flynn and Shaughnessy. The Eagle Eye Deeeee-tective Agency.' Hackett shook his head. 'Who thought that one up?'

I put my coffee down.

'Listen,' Hackett said, 'don't get me wrong. I'm just a grunt working for the gutter tabloids. The lowest of the low. I know it. But I'm not stupid. Your clients killed their daughter two years ago. That's not in doubt. Everything else is an act with you their latest attraction. So let's start there. Actor-to-actor, let's drop the bullshit. Give me a comment. Innocent or guilty or don't-give-a-shit. I can use any of those.'

'How about "Take a hike",' I said. 'Unless you want to tell me why you're really here.'

Hackett got up and walked across to my barometer.

'Pressure's up,' he observed. 'Thirty-one. Thirty-one what? Inches? What the hell's that in millibars? I hate these old units.'

He tapped the glass. Adjusted the marker.

'You're wasting your time,' I said. 'I've nothing to say. If you want a story just make something up like you usually do.'

'Let's see if I've got it right,' Hackett said. He was still messing about. I couldn't see him properly over the roll-top but there was nothing stealable back there.

'The Barbers say they want Christa found. They show you the Hoax Photo and say it's top priority. Write you a blank cheque. They don't care what you do for the money because they know it's a wild goose chase. So do you, but the blank cheque makes that one attractive bird to stalk. And the main point anyway is *not* to catch it. But the chase has to go somewhere. So where are you looking? What stones are you turning? Can we put out a hint that something's on the burner? Our readers know Elaine killed her daughter but they want to know what they're up to now.'

My ears pricked up. Hackett's "top priority" characterisation of the Barbers' briefing was damn close to the mark. Where did he get that? A lucky hit, extrapolating from the book? I thought about it. When I'd finished thinking I walked to the door and held it wide.

'If that's all you've come for,' I said, 'we're through.'

Hackett threw a frustrated grin and I saw his game. He'd been hoping to find us out and our receptionist in so he could pick up a few tid-bits on the sly. Clearly the guy didn't know Lucy. She'd give him the story, right enough – right along with her theories about the Kennedy assassination and the moon landings.

I jabbed my thumb.

'Out, Hackett. I've things to do.'

Hackett came over with his hands in his jeans pockets. 'What the hell have you got to do?' he said. 'All the Barbers want you to do is not-find anything. Sounds like not-work to me.'

'Like writing the not-news,' I said. 'What the hell brought you up here, anyway? Are the pubs closed?'

Hackett looked instinctively at his watch. Caught himself. Pulled up a sneer.

'Ex-Met,' he said. 'One of the smart guys. What happened when you made your move to the private sector? You leave your detective skills behind? Is evidence no longer evidence?'

I waited.

'Everything Stuart and Elaine said about that night has been torn to shreds,' he said. 'Their whole account is disputed by independent witnesses. So either the witnesses are lying or the Barbers are. What would your old police instinct be?'

I kept quiet. This was a conversation that wasn't going to happen. A funny version of my interview with Barry Bedford this morning.

Hackett shrugged. 'Have it your way, pal. But chew on this: the fantasy's about to end. *The Nation's* ready to expose your clients as liars. With a hundred per cent proof.' He grinned at me. 'We've a feature tomorrow called "Questions That Need To Be Answered". You'll find the questions interesting. Maybe you can fill in the answers.'

'Nothing's ever a hundred per cent certain,' I said, 'until it's checked by professionals. '

Hackett smiled. Chewed gum. 'Sure. Stick with that line! But that's a great quote. "Nothing's certain." That sums things up nicely.'

He turned and walked out. Fired a last salvo over his shoulder.

'Heed the warning, Flynn. If you believe the Barbers' fairy tales then you're stupider than I thought. And keep reading *The Nation*. You'll learn the truth.'

This from a guy who'd put Boycott in Lancashire. But I guess if *The Nation* applied the same journalistic standards across all its departments Hackett could handle the sports desk fine.

He paused to spit his gum into Lucy's waste bin as he passed. Left the door open.

I slammed it shut and went back to my office. Got my feet back onto the windowsill and returned to my thinking.

CHAPTER TWENTY
Question three

I came out of the shower next morning to find Arabel reading a tabloid at the breakfast table. She turned and held up a copy of *The Nation* like dirty washing.

I took a look. Swore. My phone rang.

'You seen it?' Shaughnessy said.

'Just now.'

Hackett had been as good as his word. The Barbers were back on the front page.

'We letting it ride?'

'Yeah,' I said. It was the weekend. Shaughnessy was calling from Portsmouth, preparing to cast off for a sail down the Channel with Jasmine. Hard to cancel on commitments like that. And I couldn't think what the hell we could do with this anyway so best to stick to my own commitments.

Shaughnessy rang off. I sat down to read the inside pages. Arabel chewed a croissant.

The story was front page but all the copy was inside on account of the screaming headline that grabbed all the space. Centred between a picture of the Barbers and a picture of Christa was Hackett's carefully considered clarion call:

GUILTY
AS
CHARGED

and the drop:

BARBER LIE NET CLOSING

I guess the headlines weren't Hackett's. *The Nation* had a sub-editor or tea lady for that. If Hackett wrote headlines the front page would have read **"Got The Bastards!"**.

Hackett's bombshell was in the form of two new witnesses who'd "exposed the lie in the Barbers' campaign of shame". I searched for names but *The Nation* were keeping them under wraps. All we had were Hackett's assurances that both were "credible and impartial sources" who had come forward "reluctantly" to share things they'd seen and heard – although he didn't explain why they'd not come forward reluctantly twenty-two months ago. But their accounts led *The Nation's* readers to ask some "searching questions" to which Hackett invited the Barbers' response.

The first thing readers wanted to know was what it was that Stuart had been loading into the back of their Fiat at nine p.m. on the evening Christa disappeared. Which was an interesting question: a sighting of Stuart and Elaine loading their car had been one of the old tales that had fallen apart when it turned out that the witness was nowhere near the site at the time. Now here was the same story, different witness, throwing the spanner right back into the Barbers' claim that they were out getting cash at that time. The new witness refuted the claim: the Barbers' car had been parked by the caravan at nine to let Stuart manhandle a bulky plastic sack into the hatch. *The Nation's* readers wanted to know what the hell was in that sack.

'You still on question one?' Arabel asked.

I nodded.

'Wait till you get to question three.'

The second question was based on another sighting. Whether this was the same witness wasn't made clear. What *The Nation's* readers wanted to know this time was what it was that had stung the Barbers into driving the Fiat away from the caravan site at "reckless speed" a few minutes after loading it up. You sensed the depravity building. Now we had *reckless* child-killers.

'You got to question three?'

I finished my coffee. Grinned at Arabel.

'Don't tell me – they're going to jump a red light.'

Arabel grinned right back in a way I didn't like. I looked for what *The Nation's* readers had for us in Question Three.

What they had was worse than a red light. What the readers wanted to know ("tell us or sue us!") is why Elaine Barber had concealed the fact that she "couldn't cope" with her daughter's tantrums, something another new witness had overheard in a "professional environment" just days before Christa disappeared. Which "professional environment" we were talking about was kept close to *The Nation's* chest, along with their wit's identity. I read the thing through. If there was anything behind this one then we had a problem, because the story lined up perfectly with the police theory that Elaine had snapped when Christa threw a screaming fit. That theory had come from neighbour Irene's account of hearing the screams inside the Barber caravan. But this was the first time someone had claimed to have heard Elaine admit she couldn't handle her daughter.

The claim put a slant on things, worked nicely with the sighting of the Barbers loading a sack into their car. Hackett had been pulling overtime on this one.

'It could have happened,' Arabel said. 'Even the best mothers can be driven over the edge.'

I concurred. And Elaine admitting she couldn't cope didn't sound good. I read on.

Found a final question.

This one hadn't registered with Arabel but it snagged my attention.

What *The Nation's* readers wanted to know this time was who the accomplice was who'd helped dispose of Christa's body – and was still conspiring with them today.

What the hell did Hackett have here? The police had torn the Barbers' story apart in the months after Christa disappeared but this was the first time I'd heard mention of an accomplice. Hackett claimed to have uncovered a conspiracy going back nearly two years, and he had the conspirator still scheming with the Barbers, talking to them on a regular basis. But where would he get stuff like that? I had a sudden hunch.

Arabel was still watching me. I scanned the rest of the story. Found what was behind her look. Hackett had wrapped up with another piece on the Barbers' "minders". His fishing trip to my office yesterday had paid off with a quote to bolster his fairy tale. Apparently the Barbers had set their minders onto the task of chasing down the famous "Hoax Photo" in a desperate smoke and mirrors charade to shore up their image as grieving victims, with any doubts quashed in their minders' heads by the "breathtaking fees" involved. I hadn't confirmed to Hackett one way or another whether we'd bought in to the photo, and I didn't recall discussing our charges, but the detail reinforced my hunch.

Despite the "breathtaking fees" it turned out that the minders were not wholly on the Barbers' side. Hackett finally got in his quote. My words, but with the context skewed to make a better story. Hackett recounted how he'd challenged the minders about their clients' innocence, then threw in my comment about "nothing is certain", which gave a nice answer to the wrong question. So now we had even the Barbers' team questioning their innocence.

I folded the paper. Grinned at Arabel. I open my mouth with one quote and Hackett has it gift-wrapped. I made a note to keep my mouth shut in future. Or keep a bat by my desk.

I went to grab my stuff. Put *The Nation* on hold. Rule one in reacting to tabloid firecrackers is don't react. Check first if there's any truth behind their headlines.

But *The Nation* had got one thing right: the Barbers had questions to answer.

CHAPTER TWENTY-ONE
You had to love the girl

I'd have made a handsome sight strolling down the street togged up in my cricket gear if it wasn't for the fact that Arabel had togged herself up in a short-skirted outfit that rendered me invisible. There's something about white cotton against gold-brown skin that messes with men's brains. I stayed cool; flipped the car keys; picked them up; got the car open.

Arabel connected a USB and we drove out of London with surround-sound Marley, sunshine, and Arabel's arm across my shoulders. The day should have felt good.

'You're thinking they did it.'

Arabel was yelling in my ear. I yelled back.

'Not on *The Nation's* say-so.'

'Gotta be something behind their story.'

'Sure there is. Hackett's a repository of knowledge. The bastard had Boycott playing for Lancashire.'

'Who's Boycott?'

I grinned at her. Arabel's roots were in the Windies. That wasn't going to work.

She squeezed my neck. 'Kidding, babe. Answer my question.'

'I can't answer your question.'

'But you're worried that *maybe* they did it. That your clients are dirty.'

'Sure. I don't like the idea of working for the wrong side. But that's not the problem.'

'I know, babe. The problem is that if Stuart and Elaine are lying then Christa's dead.'

'A pretty big downside.'

Arabel squirmed in her seat, folded her legs. Her legs were very foldable. 'Still not your fault, Flynn,' she said.

'Sit still,' I said. 'We're nearly off the road.'

She grinned wickedly. Worked her fingers. Squirmed a little more. The girl got off on risk. I concentrated on the wheel.

We cut round Guildford to a place called Tynford, a village with a three acre green right on the main street. The green was overlooked by a pub on one side and a pavilion on the other. There was seating on the pavilion veranda but Arabel opted for the pub, which opened early on match days. She left me to it and headed across to find a table with a view. Twenty pairs of eyes followed her. I sensed the temperature rising. Brian O'Connor, our captain, gave me leery.

'How about Arabel takes a few strolls during the home innings?' he said. 'We need the wickets.'

A guy with jowls and a boater, who was there to umpire, threw us a dirty look. 'If that woman moves before the visitors go in,' he said, 'I'm abandoning the match.'

O'Connor looked at me. That was an attractive option. An abandoned match would at least get us a share of the points. I was playing for Holmstead Common, a Berkshire village I'd only ever visited on match days. The age when cricket teams were recruited from within parish boundaries were long gone. Nowadays half the houses in Holmstead were holiday lets and the remainder plus adjoining farms couldn't raise a hatful of cricketers amongst them. Which is why Holmstead fielded a team of ringers from inside the Orbital, with a distinct bias towards Yorkshiremen that had got us the nickname "Little Yorks". Honour in the league said we were the side to beat. Beating Yorkshiremen was easier said than done but we had no illusions about today's chances. Tynford had five ex-county players in contention and it was going to take something special to pull this one off. The something special was supposed to be me. I'd never made first class cricket but then I'd never tried. In the helmet-clad era of post-Packer viciousness, chasing murderers had seemed more attractive.

Brian jollied the guys but threw me a worried frown. He knew the odds.

Tynford won the toss and went in to open. The green was pristine but the pitch had baked dry in the morning sun. By the afternoon we'd be batting on rock.

Roger Ellison was our specialist fast bowler. He gave Tynford a taster in the first over, kept their lead batsmen jumping. Got a breakthrough after just four balls. Their man hooked high to stay out of hospital and clipped the ball with the lower edge of his bat and I dived in from silly mid-on and took our first wicket. Two runs for one. Suddenly Tynford didn't seem so invincible. Clapping drifted across the green. A couple of cat-whistles. Arabel, still paying attention. It was good she caught my moment of glory because her attention span was almost up. Arabel came to cricket matches to read. I'd spotted a dog-eared Kafka in her bag. I wasn't much on literature but it seemed the guy had an edge over second-class cricket.

Tynford brought in their third man and picked up after that and we settled into a long slog to keep them within reach.

I backed out to square leg and settled into my own slog, trying to figure out how much the Barbers were keeping from us. I didn't buy Hackett's view that the whole thing was a sham but I was wondering whether some part of it was. Came back to the question of why we'd taken the job. Found I still had an answer to that one: we were in it for the chance we'd get to Christa. I guess that was a good enough reason.

I fielded on autopilot; sifted the signs that pointed to the Barbers, came to no conclusion bar a sense that things were shifting in the wrong direction.

Roger tossed me the ball and I snapped back to bowl four overs. Applied a nice combination of technique and frustration to my deliveries. The frustration seemed to work. I took two wickets for seven. The second had Tynford's captain yelling beamer but the umpire turned a deaf ear. The batsman threw me a vicious look as he walked. I shrugged. The ball seemed good to me. He just failed to anticipate a switch from spin to toss. And the ball would have been well below his neck if the bastard hadn't ducked. I heard no applause from the pub. Kafka had taken over.

My two wickets were the highlight of the morning. For the most part we were as effective as sponge hammers against the league leaders on their home turf. Tynford declared at a hundred and eighty with four overs to spare.

They'd laid on a spread that was heavy on fruit juice and cucumber sandwiches. I looked at Brian. It was going to take more than sunbeams to pull the one-eighty back. I grabbed a juice and checked my phone. A message waiting. Harry. I called back.

'We've ID'd the Astra guy,' he said.

I plugged my finger into my ear against the veranda babble.

Stepped down and walked into the shadows below the boards.

'Get this,' Harry said, 'he's one of Giannetti's.'

That raised my brows. George Giannetti operated a murky investigation firm from a Marylebone basement, servicing the end of the business unfettered by ethics or considerations of law. George was a guy who got things done, as quickly and dirtily as the client's cash demanded. Our paths had crossed from time to time, usually without an uplifting result.

'The driver's a guy called Brendan Martin,' Harry said. 'Freelance PI. I followed him to Giannetti's this morning. If this is Giannetti's operation its dirty.'

I agreed. 'You okay to stay with Stuart and Elaine?'

'Got them until Monday. Bernie's covering nights. They're staying home so I'm easy.'

'We'll talk tomorrow,' I said. I killed the line.

I snatched a couple of sandwiches and walked over the green.

Arabel had pushed Kafka aside in favour of a chicken salad with a side of fries. I eyed her plate and pinched fries when she wasn't paying attention. Fries go well on cucumber sandwiches.

'Great catch, babe,' Arabel said.

I grinned. The three hours since then had passed her by. She probably imagined I'd been taking wickets all morning. I finished my sandwiches; drank a shandy and left her to it. Holmstead went in to bat. I was fourth in. Our leading guys needed to build up thirty runs then I'd attack and see if I could get us within shouting distance. Within three overs we'd lost two wickets for ten and the plan was shot. Plan B was for Flynn to make up the missing twenty then carry on as planned with another half century. I walked out; faced into the sun; pulled my cap low. Nearly broke my wrist tamping the ground. For a moment the Barber thing went away. There's a focus you get when you're facing a fast bowler on a rock-hard pitch.

Focus is not the same as judgement. The ball screamed down the pitch, off and long but instead of blocking I went for broke. Attacked. The ball kicked in and up and survival instinct pulled my arm up to ricochet the thing right onto the wicket. I was walking before the bails hit the ground. The bowler was the guy I'd dismissed this morning. He threw a leer as I passed. A single pair of hands sent a desultory clapping across the green from the pub. Even a duck impressed Arabel. You had to love the girl.

I climbed onto the veranda and walked through a sea of grave faces. We were ten for three chasing a hundred and eighty not-out. It didn't need a crystal ball to figure where this was going. Brian O'Connor stared at me.

'Eddie! What the fuck?'

I shrugged.

'One of those days, Brian,' I said. 'Sorry, pal.'

~~~~~

I changed and pushed the kit into my bag. Pulled the fisherman's on and walked round the green. Arabel was cross-legged on a bench. She grinned.

'Neat, babe,' she said. 'I thought we'd be here all afternoon.'

I looked at her. 'The guy bowled a googly designed to kill,' I said. 'Maybe we should all start wearing helmets.'

'He's the guy you nearly decapitated this morning. At least he *had* a helmet.'

So she'd been watching after all. I grinned.

'The same guy. Just a couple of hours angrier. Give me a decent pitch and that kind of stuff isn't going to work. You know where the ball's going.'

'How's Brian taking it?'

Arabel knew damn well how he was taking it. 'Like the captain of the Titanic,' I said. 'Biding his time.'

A burst of "howzatts" came off the field with a chorus of cheers as another of our batsmen walked. The ship was going down faster than I thought.

I went inside and ordered pasty and mushy peas with another pint of shandy. Went to sit close to Arabel to catch the umbrella's shade. The heat was a sauna. My shirt was sticking to my back. Maybe the humidity hinted at change. I pulled out my phone and keyed the screen.

'Luce! How's it going?'

'Eddie! Is your match over already?'

'For me it is. I was out for a duck.'

'Ah, Eddie that's so unfair! Who wouldn't duck when someone's throwing a ball at their head. They should make allowances.'

Arabel was watching my face. I nodded as if I had a sensible conversation going.

'Anything?' I said.

'A bite!'

A newspaper rustled. *"'Reunited. Understood. Wait instruction."* They're there, Eddie!'

So our Christa Photo guy was continuing to talk. Turning up the pressure had worked.

'You talk to Angela?'

'She gave me an address. It's the East End pawn shop. The guy's using the same service as before. There's a phone number too. An unlisted mobile.'

'Maybe the guy's. We'll check it out. And if he's using the pawn shop to place the ads we'll get him.'

'Do you think he knows where Christa is?'

I swigged shandy. Emptied the glass.

'I don't know if anyone knows where Christa is,' I said.

CHAPTER TWENTY-TWO

If they're lying about that they're lying about everything

Sunday. A blank in the Barbers' promo schedule. An opportunity for a chat. I drove to Elstree first thing. Followed Harry Green onto the Barbers' forecourt. Bernie was leaning against the front door.

'Howd' it go?' he said.

'Fine,' I said. 'Good match.'

'Big innings?'

I looked at him. Bernie's eyes opened.

'Nay,' he said. 'Never a duck!'

'Had to happen some time,' I said. 'The pitch was concrete and they had a bowler with attitude.'

'Was he as good as me?'

'No, Bernie. I'm still alive.'

He nodded wisely. Bernie clung to the fantasy that he could have been a feared fast bowler. Didn't understand that you can't be feared if you're banned. All fast bowlers want respect, but most operate on the principle that it's wickets they're after. Bernie's theory was that if you exterminated the man then you'd get to the wicket. Probably taught the technique in the marines.

Bernie pushed himself off the wall and gave me a consoling pat on the shoulder; headed off home. Harry and I went in.

Elaine had fixed a spread. We sat down to Sunday breakfast like any happy family. Harry grabbed two boiled eggs and shelled them on his plate. I poured a coffee and we talked trivia for a while. At eight fifteen the doorbell rang and Elaine brought Sharon Larkin through in a waft of Chanel. She was wearing a halter top and form-fitting shorts; took a tour round the table to give us all a gander then settled on the chair next to me. She held out a cup. I topped it up. She thanked me, sweetly.

'What's the news, Eddie?' she said.

I looked at Elaine.

Elaine nodded. 'We keep Sharon informed.'

Harry and I exchanged looks. He took a last swig of tea and went out.

'I guess you know about the caravan,' I said.

Sharon sat forward. Her arm touched mine. 'Bowland called us. He says they made a real mess.'

'He's right.'

'We don't use the caravan,' Elaine said. 'It doesn't matter.'

'We should have sold it,' Stuart declared.

Elaine shook her head. 'When we get her back. I can't lose that last link until we have Christa safe.'

'What's your assessment, Eddie,' Sharon asked. She was looking into my eyes. 'Is it the guy who's been threatening us?' Her arm pressure increased. I shifted. Broke contact. Turned to the Barbers.

'It's a possibility,' I said. 'The spray messages had the same ring.'

I pulled my phone out and passed it to Stuart. He and Elaine inspected the snaps then passed the phone to Sharon. Her mouth turned down.

'This is horrible,' she said. 'But it's him. All that "Baby Killers" stuff. It's just like the letters.'

'The letters mostly say "Killer Couple",' I pointed out. 'That's not quite the same.'

'But not so different,' Sharon argued. 'This has to be the vigilante.'

'As I say – it's a possibility.'

'Did they leave any traces?' Sharon asked. She was still sitting close. The sun was well up and the kitchen was heating fast. I told them about the spray can top, the hardware store in Salisbury.

'That's a long way out,' Sharon said. 'Does it mean the guy lives out that way? Were the London postings meant to mislead us?'

'It's possible, assuming this is our hate-mail guy.'

'It is,' Sharon insisted. She angled her arm until it brushed mine again. 'The caravan is just his latest nasty move.'

I didn't argue.

'And you were almost on his heels, Eddie,' she continued. 'It feels like you're getting close to this maniac.'

It felt like Sharon was getting close to me. Now her leg was touching mine. Sharon Larkin had a thing about getting close to people.

'You said you needed to talk,' Stuart said.

I stood up and walked across to the open door.

'I guess you know why,' I said.

'The *Nation's* nonsense.'

'The story does throw up a few issues.'

Elaine sighed. 'Are you starting to believe the tabloids now?' she said.

I looked at her. 'I believe nothing without evidence,' I said. 'But I was hoping you could throw some light on their stories.'

'Hackett should be strung up, along with his lousy editor,' Stuart declared. 'They're running a vendetta, plain and simple.'

I didn't need him to tell me that. It didn't make Hackett wrong, though.

'What do you want to know, Eddie?' Elaine said.

'The first thing I need to be clear on is whether you really did have problems coping with Christa.'

She shook her head.

'There's nothing to that story. *The Nation* has it entirely wrong.'

'Wrong how? They've a witness heard you talking about being at your wit's end. You've always insisted that Christa's tantrums were not a factor but this witness seems to tell a different story.' I watched the garden. 'I'm not here to defend a witness *The Nation* doesn't name. But just tell me how they got it wrong.'

'We know who the witness is,' Elaine said. 'I can tell you exactly.'

I waited.

'Her name's Denise Walker. She was one of the kitchen staff at the Patricia Holland School where I taught. Denise was cautioned by the headmistress after she gave the police the same story eighteen months ago without checking her facts.'

'You think Hackett's information is from the police?'

'I'm sure that's where he got Denise's name. Perhaps he persuaded her to repeat her mixed-up story.'

'And what was the mix-up?'

'She heard me discussing a child at the school. And like anyone discussing a professional problem I might have used exaggerated language. But I never discussed Christa at work. Christa had no problems outside the normal range. Denise overheard something she didn't understand and twisted it into her own fantasy view.'

Sounded plausible. The school was on my tour schedule. I shifted topics.

'The story about you colluding with someone the night Christa disappeared, someone who's still with you. What's that about?' I walked back to the table.

'That one's stumped us,' Stuart said. 'We haven't a clue what Hackett's got hold of. Who is there to conspire with? There was no-one that night and there's no-one now.'

'Okay,' I said. 'Hackett didn't give us his source for that one either. But I'm wondering what makes him confident enough to put it out.'

I had a theory but I didn't mention it. When no-one replied I moved on.

'The thing about you loading something into the back of the Fiat,' I said. 'That's a puzzling claim.'

Stuart shook his head.

'A rehash of the old story,' he said. 'We loaded nothing into the car. We drove out to get the cash just like we said, with Christa asleep in the caravan. This stuff is fiction, Eddie. And *The Nation* doesn't give a single name.'

'I'm with you there,' I said. 'Anonymous witnesses don't impress me. But Hackett's not stupid. His "tell us or sue us" sounds pretty confident. Holding back witness IDs may be just his way of spinning the story out.'

'What can I say?' Stuart replied. 'This witness never came forward before. And they saw things that didn't happen.'

'If there was something – anything,' I said, 'it would be better if I knew.'

I looked at Elaine and caught an unguarded look. Distant, dark thoughts, like she was on a different track, this conversation just background.

She snapped back. 'Eddie, we need you to stay on our side,' she said. 'Forget Hackett's anonymous witnesses. If he ever brings them out we'll show you liars. All that happened that night was that someone took Christa.'

'I'm not taking anyone's side. You asked me to search for Christa and I'm doing it. Without prejudice.'

'But that doesn't mean swallowing everything Hackett puts out,' Stuart said.

'I swallow nothing,' I said, 'on either side. That means I check my stories.'

Elaine was watching. The look didn't come back but something you might call hostility lit her eyes. 'So what have you checked?' she asked.

I walked across and toyed with the espresso machine. Admired its stylish lines. The thing would look nice at Chase Street. Maybe even produce coffee. I flicked the controls. Turned back.

'I spoke to Barry Bedford. And to the dog handler.'

Stuart swore. 'Everyone knows their stories,' he said. 'The police were fixated on the evidence about the body in the car. But you know that they couldn't repeat the finding. Their expert was discredited.'

'Call it an ex-policeman's instinct,' I said, 'but I prefer to credit or discredit people myself.'

'Okay, Eddie,' Elaine said. 'Tell us: is Starr credited or discredited?'

I looked at her.

'I'm not saying his finding was valid but the guy is not discredited.'

More silence.

'Care to explain?' Stuart said.

'Exactly what I say. I can't vouch for what Peter Starr found in your car but the man himself is not discredited.'

'So you're saying that we really might have had Christa's body in the boot?' Stuart's jaw was rigid. All three of them were staring at me.

'The moment I believe you had your daughter's body in your car is the moment I stop searching for her,' I said. 'Right now I'm still looking.'

Three pairs of eyes stayed locked on me. The moment passed. Elaine changed tack.

'Are we anywhere with the photograph?'

'Your contact's talking to us through the *Reunited* ads. We'll have an ID within a couple of days.'

Finally the Barbers perked up. But it was Sharon who spoke first.

'Will this take us to where the photo was taken?'

'Eventually, yes.'

Elaine's eyes closed for a moment. 'That's good,' she said. 'The *Nation's* stories won't matter once you've tracked down the photo.'

'And what about the vigilante?' Sharon asked.

'Just the possible link to the guy who spray-painted the caravan.'

'At least we've got that.' Sharon got up to walk round the room.

Tucked her fingers into her shorts. There was a lightness to her step. 'Elaine, we're making progress,' she declared, 'even if Eddie's being cautious.' She spun round. Put her hands on her sister's shoulders. 'Imagine!' she said. 'We might be getting nearer to Christa.' She came back round and sat again. 'Eddie if you get Christa back we'll be forever in your debt.'

I sincerely hoped not. Eagle Eye worked on a thirty day settlement. I spotted Harry in the garden. He'd wandered round from the front of the house. I left the Barbers and went out.

'You were right,' he said. 'Someone's listening.'

So my hunch had been on target. The conversation with Hackett, then yesterday's stuff in *The Nation*, both pointed to things he shouldn't know. Eavesdropping at the Barber house would explain things. Harry had just swept the place. He took me back inside. Pointed silently to a mains extension lead and a broadband microfilter that were both more than they looked; lifted a table flap; had me feel under chimney breasts. We went out onto the forecourt.

'Nine bugs plus relay,' Harry said. 'UHF – illegal as hell. The relay records then transmits on request. Someone probably drives by every day or two for an upload.'

'So they know what Stuart and Elaine are saying.'

'Everything. Anyone they call. It's like the Leveson Inquiry never happened. If this is Hackett he's sticking his neck way out.'

He and everyone above him at *The Nation*. Leveson had shown that responsibility doesn't stop with the grunt who does the dirty work.

'Let's reel them in,' I said.

Harry smiled. 'I've faulted the relay. Whoever's listening has just gone deaf. I'll put a camera in there. If anyone turns up to fix the problem we'll have them.'

Sharon appeared through the front door and Harry nodded at me and went back in. I wasn't so quick. Sharon clamped my arm.

'Don't take Elaine too seriously,' she said. 'My sister's been under intolerable pressure. She just needs to know that someone's on her side.'

I recovered my arm. Checked the time.

'That's no problem,' I said, 'as long as she lets me do my job.'

'Of course she will. Do it all your way. We just need you to trace the photo. I hope to God it's Christa but even bad news might allow Elaine to move forward.'

Sharon was doing some moving forward herself. I side-stepped and turned to go back into the house.

'Hey!' Her hand was back on my arm. 'Is it early for lunch? I know a place.'

I looked at my watch again. 'It's nine thirty,' I said. 'I'd say that's early.'

Her smile stayed bright. 'Some other time,' she said. 'I think the two of us would get on fine.'

Sure. Until Arabel found us.

I drove out, leaving Harry to fix up his camera away from the Barbers' view. Better they didn't know about the bugs just yet, because I wasn't sure where this left us. If Hackett was listening in that would explain his inside info, including the "conspirator" story. The problem was, if he got that story from here then it meant that the Barbers were up to something, hiding something about their daughter's disappearance. And if the Barbers were lying about that they might be lying about everything.

CHAPTER TWENTY-THREE
Yorick wasn't so talkative

The Petticoat Lane car park was solid so I parked the Sprite at a dodgy NCP off Commercial Street and walked round. Sunday morning and fine weather had brought Londoners and tourists out alike to shed cash in the markets. They crammed the lanes and shouldered each other aside to get at the stalls and the boutiques behind that sported price tags to make Oxford Street whistle. Other Londoners drifted with the flow and relieved the visitors of their money by other means. Not that pickpockets scared me: I'd been here too often with Arabel to imagine I'd get out solvent.

I cut towards the remnants of the tenements that had once covered the area. The handful that had survived the blitz hunched defensively within the maze of utilitarian blocks and scrappy vertical visions of the sixties. Behind me the sparkling cliffs of global finance defined the new boundary of the East End more clearly than any map.

Lucy's classified-ad address brought me to a pawnbroker's window in a crumbling terrace that would have been downmarket in the old East End. A flaking brown fascia topped a dusty display window through which the detritus of unredeemed tuppenny loans glinted like archaeological finds. The only new paintwork near the place was the graffiti on the half-lowered security shutter, but the open door and gleaming alarm said that the business was operating. A window sign advertised payday loans, cheque-cashing and post office boxes, as well as something called administration services which apparently included the placing of classified ads for punters without cards.

I went in and walked an aisle of junk towards a display cabinet spotlighting the better stuff – smartphones and jewellery. An old guy watched me from behind a grille. McLellan, I guessed, the name in the *Evening Standard's* records. I poked around and tried to figure who'd buy an upright Hoover with a missing grip or a nineties-vintage notebook computer. I stopped at the display cabinet and keyed my phone. Inspected the contents while the call connected. Some of the stuff under the glass was pretty decent, at very decent prices. I might have been tempted if I didn't know it was nicked.

'Anything you like, officer?'

I glanced up. Seven years out of the force and it still showed. Maybe it was time to change my deodorant. The guy's undisguised hostility belied his question. I ignored him, checked out what looked like a brand new Nikon, yours for eighty-seven quid.

'Don't bother yourself,' the guy said. 'It's legit.'

I looked up again. He was small, shrivelled, seventy-plus, a liver-spotted face gaunt enough to have Yorick grabbing for the vitamin pills. My call picked up. A guy's voice. I hung up.

'Mistaken identity,' I said. 'I'm not a cop.'

'And that's a bleedin' budgerigar you're lookin' at. Go on! Gedartahere. I've no time for grass'oppers.'

Sixty years of ice in the voice. Legit? Sure, if he said so. But on the far, far side of the fence. I threw him a grin and turned to leave. Questions would only tip him off, and he'd already answered the one I had when his phone didn't ring. The number left with the *Standard* wasn't his. The person who'd just picked up was the one who'd come in here to place the ad, but I didn't see Yorick furnishing me with his name.

Alas.

~~~~~

Back at Battersea I went up to the loft and opened the skylight. The heat had dried the wood so it swung out easily for the first time. Too easily: I'd need buckets when the rain returned. The city's breath flowed in across hot slates. A jet whispered over the river. I grabbed my paints and pulled the easel out.

A dealer under Camden arches had offered seventy quid for one of my paintings a few years back, which implied that he was confident of flogging it for a couple of hundred. It was a landscape I'd worked up by the City Basin in Islington before the developers moved in. The derelict wilderness below the London skyline had disappeared soon after I was there but my impression of the old space had caught the attention of someone willing to pay two hundred smackers and the dealer came running for more. I played along. Upped the price. Found I had a paying hobby.

My current project was worked up from an idea that hit me in Abney Park, a cemetery at the top of Hackney that only a few Londoners know. The place is a maze of mouldering memorials and forgotten graves strangled by enough jungle to get Rousseau drooling. You can't quite see the City skyline from the spot due to the trees and rooftops of Hackney but artistic licence had thrown a backdrop of glass towers onto my canvas, sparkling above the green decay I'd encountered last autumn. The essay was legitimate, phoney skyline and all. As kosher as any of Rousseau's, anyhow: at least I'd kept the tigers out.

I fetched a jug of iced water and an electric fan and immersed myself in the painting for two hours before hunger sent me to the kitchen. I baked a chicken and ate the whole thing with chips and garden peas. Then I showered and pulled on fresh clothes and went out. The sun's power was waning but the air still flowed like syrup above the scorching pavement. I drove over the river, angled towards Paddington and parked behind Chase Street. Walked to the Podium.

The Podium had live jazz most nights but Sundays were slow. Sometimes a single set, sometimes just piped music. Barney promised a quartet at nine and took a fiver off me. I settled into a corner away from the early crowd and sifted priorities over a pint of Pride. By nine the crowd was up to thirty and a French outfit came on. A half-decent sax player but their stuff was derivative, lacking energy. Maybe the heat had got to them. Maybe their gig was old.

We needed to move forward with the Barber job. The vigilante was our priority but until he made a move we were stalled. So we'd use the lull to chase the Photo. I was still going with the assumption that it might be Christa but the more I tried to push Hackett's "Hoax" theory away the more it lit up inside my head. If the Barbers were fooling us there'd be a nice irony in using their money to bring justice for their daughter but the irony would be as satisfying as Australian lager. Sure, if the Barbers were fooling us we'd nail them, but the thought didn't have me hankering for Monday morning.

The set expired at twelve. Four beers had my eyes drooping. I walked back to Chase Street and grabbed my duffel from the car and went up.

I didn't bother with the stair lights. Climbed two storeys by feel.

Aimed the key from memory. As the key touched the metalwork the door swung inwards.

The Podium's fug cleared double quick. I stared into the blackness and strained my ears for something to explain why our offices were unlocked.

I eased the door wider. Scanned for any sense that someone was in there. Caught the tension of someone trying not to breathe. Or maybe it was street noise. I reached round for the switch with the hairs on my neck standing. Then a shadow detached itself from the blackness and came at me.

Something hit me on the side of the head, letting loose an explosion of stars that would have lit the place up if they'd been on the outside of my skull. I twisted and threw a defensive punch that connected with a shoulder as my attacker passed. Then he turned and the object that had hit me whistled back in. I ducked and the thing crashed into the door jamb. I came out of the crouch and turned, launched myself, low, head first into someone's abdomen, and the momentum took us both down the stairs.

The top flight isn't long but it's painful if you go down on your backside. I landed on top, which helped, but my attacker was still kicking and throwing punches as we hit the landing. I took half a dozen shots to my arms and shoulders and the guy pulled himself up on the banister. But I was up too. I threw a right and connected with the guy's jaw and he staggered backwards along the hallway. He regained his balance, sprinted for the lower flight and twisted to throw a final punch as I caught up at the turn. I saw it coming by the street light. Parried it and curled in a right that caught him hard in the abdomen. The guy let out a "whoof" and went backwards down the stairs. The lower flight's not so short. Twenty steps at least, which produced an impressive crash and the sound of splintering woodwork as the guy hit the deck. But he was resilient. He was up and yanking at the front door before I was half way down. When I hit the street the guy was already thirty yards away and shifting impressively for someone with a limp. A big man, darkish hair, flannel jacket.

I started after him then saw sense. I'd catch him but we'd be a quarter of a mile away. My head was spinning and I'd done something to my arm. A race through the streets didn't appeal. I stood and watched the intruder scarper round the end of Chase Street. When he'd gone I went back in and switched on the hallway lights.

The end banisters were splintered at the foot of the stairs. I jammed them into something like their original alignment and went up. The first landing had taken a few cracks to the wood and plasterwork too. Nothing too serious. We shared the hallway with Rook and Lye which probably meant we shared the insurance excess. The lawyers would let us know.

I climbed back to the top floor and retrieved the fire extinguisher that had nearly brained me. Checked for damage to the door. Nothing bar the extinguisher's dent in the jamb. So the guy was a professional at getting past locks. He just needed to improve his exit technique. But I guess he'd call it bad luck that the offices were used as a crash pad.

I checked the place over and found things undisturbed. We either had the world's tidiest burglar or the guy hadn't got started. I went for the latter. Our burglar had fled empty-handed.

I soothed the swelling on my head with a wet cloth. It would look like hell tomorrow but nothing was broken. It would be our acrobatic friend who'd be hitting the paracetamol in the morning. You don't go down two flights backwards without repercussions.

I crashed on the couch; let the adrenaline subside; listened to the Westway and late trains, police sirens. Each time I dozed though a neon sign lit up and shocked me back awake.

"Hoax Photo".

Eventually the trains stopped and the Westway quietened, but the sirens and the throbbing in my head continued for another hour before the neon flickered out and left me in peace.

CHAPTER TWENTY-FOUR
Bad-temper-land

I woke at seven, feeling like a punchbag; washed and shaved in Eagle Eye's tiny bathroom; pulled a change of clothes from the duffel and opened the windows to catch any breeze then went out for coffee. The damage downstairs looked worse in the light.

I walked towards Connie's. Dodged a Westminster Council cleaning cart parked on the pavement. Nodded to a guy with a brush. Got a hostile stare. Seemed word was out on our cancelled council payments.

Connie's shutters were still down so I walked the quarter mile to Westbourne Grove to savour the racket of diesels and airbrakes, horns, tempers venting. I grabbed a quick coffee and croissant at a café that serviced retailers and office early-birds then took the back streets home. Even the back streets were battlegrounds. A taxi U-turned in front of a passing motorcycle. The biker braked hard and rode alongside the cab, slapping the roof and yelling profanities. The cabby yelled back. Their voices echoed off the buildings until the two of them nearly rear-ended a double-parked car and the horns took over. Seven forty-five. Not yet hot but people were thinking ahead.

The Westminster Council guy had reached the end of Chase Street and met up with a pal for a fag. They inspected me as I passed. Vented smoke my way. I hit Connie's. Saw his shutters were up. If I'd waited five minutes I could have saved the tour through bad-temper-land.

I went up and flipped the sign. Went through to my office. Raked my chair back and contemplated the view. Picked up wondering where the Barber assignment was going. Just after eight a bike rumbled outside, and a minute later Shaughnessy poked his head in my door. Eyed the cut on my scalp.

'I thought I was imagining the mess downstairs,' he said.

'Not unless I'm imagining the gremlin trampolining in my head.'

I told him about our nocturnal visitor.

'Someone interested in the Barbers?'

'That's what I'm thinking.'

Shaughnessy thought it over. Filed it. Tilted his head towards the door. 'Gonna get a visit from Rook and Lye,' he predicted.

'I'll have Lucy fetch the china.'

Lucy came in on cue. Something had happened to her hair. It was snow white with red flashes. I would have said something but the outfit that went with it made hair-talk nugatory. A black chiffon miniskirt lured your gaze to where the screaming lilac diagonals of her tee shirt gave you instant dizzy spells. Lucy pushed clutter aside and perched herself and her outfit on my roll-top. I keep clutter there to stop perchers. I raised my eyebrows.

'Nothing,' she reported. *'The Nation's* taking a breather. Guys, you see that mess in the hall? It's like a car crash. And you look like you hit a bus too, Eddie.'

I told my tale again. Racked my chair forward. Lucy's legs were a safer view than her tee shirt. So *The Nation* had no exclusive to kick-start our day. We'd have felt like we were ahead if we weren't still reeling from last week's exclusives.

I summarised yesterday's chat with the Barbers. Shaughnessy pursed his lips. 'The witness claiming they loaded something into their car is coming in late.'

'Two years late. But we need to know what's behind it. If there's any truth in the new stories then the Barbers have a big problem.'

Shaughnessy agreed. 'If they disposed of something bulky from their caravan that night I'd not be looking for an abductor. When's Hackett going to identify his witnesses?'

'Once he's milked his exclusive. The police are probably breathing down his editor's neck but I don't see *The Nation* playing ball until they've got the full exposé out on their front page. They want sole credit when they sink Stuart and Elaine.'

'And they'll go with the exposé as soon as Hackett has his trump card.'

'Yeah,' I said. 'He wants the body.'

'The way they're building things up, maybe they're close.'

'That's the impression. But tracing a body two years after the event is not easy. Unless Hackett's picked up something from the house bugs to steer him.'

'We're still assuming the bugs are his?'

'We need to confirm it but the bastard knows things he shouldn't,' I said. 'You going to take a look?'

'I'm on it,' Shaughnessy said.

The Barbers were off to Birmingham with Harry. Their schedule would keep them out of town for a couple of nights. Maybe leave the coast clear for someone to call in and repair the surveillance kit. If someone showed up Shaughnessy would be waiting.

'How did they take your chat with Peter Starr?' he asked.

'They stuck to their guns: Starr's wrong; there was no body; end of discussion. The problem is, Starr's credible.'

Lucy mulled things over.

'You think they maybe did it?'

'I'm not convinced that they didn't.'

Shaughnessy concurred.

'We could be with the wrong people here,' he said.

That was the risk all along. But that was still all it was: a risk. For the moment I preferred to assume we were working for the good guys, that we might get Christa back. And until we had evidence to the contrary we'd keep moving on that track. The photograph was the key. We needed to reel our *Reunited* guy in.

'What did McLellan say?' Lucy asked.

I detailed my trip to the East End, my confirmation that our classifieds guy had placed the *Evening Standard* ad through McLellan's shop and left only his contact number. An untraceable PAYG. We'd identified unlisted numbers before but this guy would be wary. The photo was high stakes.

'I read about a trick for catching PAYGs,' Lucy said.

Shaughnessy and I looked at each other. Knowing Lucy's reading material, the trick probably involved ESP or Martian force fields. But the agency is nothing if not progressive. We listened to her scheme and exchanged a second look. The thing wasn't so crazy. Had to be a one in ten chance at least. We gave Lucy the nod to give it a try. Anything to move forward from the blank of two equally credible scenarios – the abduction-photo scenario and the body-in-the-car scenario. We needed to know which was real.

CHAPTER TWENTY-FIVE
Perspective from a cellar

I drove across Marylebone to a shabby street of three storey buildings with fossilised commercial fronts a million miles from Oxford Street. Bookies and takeaways, second-hand furniture stores, charity shops. Pavements littered with refuse sacks and discarded packing. Abandoned skips. Permit-only parking. I found a space between two vans and crossed to a shop sporting purple brickwork and window merchandise that would have been scandalous thirty years ago. Mannequins posed in raunchy lingerie and fetish outfits, surrounded by whips and cuffs and stuff that stumped my imagination. Flaking black letters promised "Adult Video" in lieu of a shop name. In the age of Anne Summers on every high street the place was a throwback: a door that never opened; customers you never saw. I went in but ignored the inner door. Walked a dingy hallway to a one-eighty turn onto stairs down to the cellar. The steps were dangerously steep, illuminated by a forty watt bulb that kept your feet in shadows. The carpet looked like salvage from the blitz.

A lower door opened into a low-ceilinged office with yellow fluorescents and a metal desk with an empty chair. Off to the side a second door was part open. I went through and found another desk topped by an electric fan and the soles of size fourteen boots below an open newspaper. Half-windows looked onto the street at pavement level. The glass had ventilators but the office was fugged with cigarette smoke.

'Busy, George?' I said.

The paper came down and a face like overcooked lasagne threw out a stare that wasn't over-friendly. George folded the paper but kept his feet on the desk and his fag in his mouth.

'Busy enough,' he said.

I peered up through the windows at passing feet and hubcaps, shadows crossing. You get a certain perspective from cellars, a good sense of the world going by.

'...seeing as you give a shit.'

I turned back. George was right. I didn't give a shit.

George Giannetti was in the same business but based on a different planet. Giannetti's firm was the type that had time to put its feet up. One where activity was infrequent but payments big. George was mostly a one-man operation but probably saw three times Eagle Eye's turnover – though the tax man might dispute that. If you wanted things done fast and quietly, things a legitimate firm wouldn't touch, you came to George.

We'd last met six months ago when some people we'd been investigating received a tip-off and hired Giannetti to stall our operation. Giannetti duly obliged. His interference cost us some expensive equipment and might have cost us our reputation if we hadn't cottoned on and closed his game down. His shenanigans would certainly have cost us our fee if our client hadn't discovered that the tip-off came from his own end. In the event we came out neutral. The fee got paid and our client shook hands and apologised. I had to dissuade Shaughnessy from paying Giannetti a visit though. Our liability insurance didn't cover building demolition. How do you demolish a basement anyway without disturbing the dirty mac brigade upstairs?

Now we had Giannetti in our hair again. The guy tailing the Barbers had come right to his door and so here we were. Another chance to socialise on the low side. Seemed Giannetti was in a socialising mood: he kept his paper down and his fag flapping.

'Saw the freak show, Eddie. Loved that flour-bomb. You should go into slapstick.'

I waited.

George grinned; stubbed his cigarette.

'Is this a social visit?' he asked. 'Or are you here to make trouble?'

'I'm good for either,' I said.

'Well, trouble I can do without,' he said. 'So say what you've come to say and get out.'

Not even a cup of tea. But Giannetti was not the guy for freebies. I got to the point.

'Who is it, George?'

Giannetti linked his hands across his stomach and tilted his chin. His face had taken so much sun it had turned to cracked copper. Only the eye sockets were natural and they were a kind of grey.

'Who are you working for?' I said.

142

Giannetti stretched a grin; raised his palms.

'Haven't a clue what you're talking about, Eddie.'

Sure he hadn't.

'We spotted you a week ago, George. We clocked Martin's car outside our building before we'd even signed the Barbers up. I want to know why you're following them around. And I want to know if you had someone call at our offices last night.'

Something that might have been genuine surprise shadowed Giannetti's smile. But with Giannetti nothing is genuine. I walked across and planted my fists on his desk.

'You might as well tell me, George. Martin is neutralised, so your tailing operation's over. But I want to know who's so interested in the Barbers.'

Giannetti pulled out a fresh pack of cigarettes. Took his time lighting up.

'Where did you hear this bullshit, Eddie?'

'We heard nothing. We followed Martin right to your door. You should tell him to get a quieter car. The Astra kind of stands out.'

Giannetti shrugged. 'Martin always was a flashy operator. But he's not working for me.'

I leaned closer. 'Bullshit.'

He threw a smirk and another shrug. 'Believe what you want,' he said.

'You saying Martin isn't one of your people?'

'Maybe he is, maybe he isn't. I've help on call whenever I need it. But I'm not tailing your clients, Eddie. Everything I want to know about the Killer Couple I get from the papers. And what I read doesn't make me want to get closer. But then,' he pulled the cigarette from his mouth, 'I guess you know about that.'

'We followed Martin right here,' I said. 'You think he was calling in upstairs?'

Giannetti took a drag; burned half the cigarette; raised his index finger. 'That's much more likely,' he said. 'They've got some good movies up there. Tell me what you like and I'll get you a discount. We've all got our peccadilloes.'

'Forget my peccadilloes. If Martin's not tailing the Barbers for you then who's he working for?'

'How the hell would I know? As if I give a shit. If that's all you've come for I've got things to do.'

I tried to figure whether Giannetti was being straight with me. Concluded he was. There was no reason why any of Giannetti's part-time helpers couldn't be moonlighting elsewhere. Maybe we'd followed Brendan Martin to the wrong door. And whatever he knew, Giannetti wasn't about to tell me. I'd got what I usually got with George, which was frustration and high blood pressure. Lung problems I could do without. I pushed myself off his desk and headed for the door. Told him I'd see him. We both hoped different.

'Hey, Flynn!'

I turned back.

'They did it,' he said.

I looked at him. Giannetti shrugged.

'They killed her!' he laughed. He pointed his fag. 'Don't tell me you're the only person on the planet who doesn't know that. Tell me you're not buying into the fantasy that you're going to rescue their kid.' He laughed some more. 'Jesus Christ! The Killer Couple did it! Live with it!'

I walked out. Climbed the stairs to reach air.

My phone rang.

Harry. Calling from the Virgin mid morning service to Birmingham, the first leg of the Barbers' two day tour. I asked him what was happening.

'They've got another letter,' Harry said. 'The guy's about to act.'

CHAPTER TWENTY-SIX
Mind the dog

Harry read the letter over the line. The message was as unsavoury as its predecessors. But this time we had a promise:

Enough talk! Time for a DEMONSTRATION!

Seemed our vigilante was gearing himself up for action. I thought about it. Didn't see him making a move while the Barbers were out of town. Unfamiliar territory and routine acted against him. The trouble would come when the Barbers arrived back in London. Harry concurred. I told him to hang tight. Keep his eyes skinned in case we were wrong.

I needed to take a look at *The Nation's* new witnesses – in particular, the one who'd seen the Barbers loading something into their car the night Christa disappeared.

The Nation had the wit. walking by the Orchard Grove on his way to the pub. The only pub near the site was the Saracen, and a lone person heading for it on a summer's evening was probably a local. Maybe someone at the pub would have ideas. I headed out of the city, back to the New Forest.

The Saracen's beer garden was busy but the inside was dead. Just two locals nattering over a lunchtime pint and a florid guy polishing taps. A girl rushed by loaded with plates for the garden. Lunch seemed like a good idea. I pulled the barman over and ordered a Shepherd Neame and meat and potato. Hung about while the order went through.

'Nice,' the barman said.

He nodded at a screen. Six CCTV frames, one of them featuring a Frogeye, parked up against the wall. Driving the Sprite has advantages beyond simple road tax exemption. As conversation openers only a Lamborghini does it better, but who wants to talk to a rich show-off? Poor show-offs are another matter.

'She's pretty cool,' I agreed.

In summer, with the hood down. Not quite so appealing on a rainy winter night, but you can't have everything.

'What's your other car?' the guy said.

'That's it,' I said.

The guy was impressed. Asked if I travelled much. Wondered about luggage. I explained that appearances were deceptive. There was plenty of space in the boot. Plenty for me, anyway. Weekends away with Arabel were a struggle since the car didn't have a tow hook.

'Passing through?'

He planted my beer and I handed over an agency card. Watched the guy's face turn less friendly. He put the card down on the wet surface.

'You after someone's husband? He's not here.'

I threw a grin. I'd followed husbands into plenty of places just like this; could describe more pub interiors than CAMRA. But publicans are the last people to cry foul over husbands sampling their hospitality with someone they shouldn't. Husbands on the razzle bring more dosh than husbands on the straight.

'I'm trying to solve a puzzle,' I said.

The barman still wasn't so friendly but he hung around. Who can resist a puzzle?

'There's a story in *The Nation*. About the Barbers.'

The guy watched me. He read the tabloids like everyone.

'They've a guy who saw something,' I said. 'A local. Maybe comes in here.'

The barman shook his head. 'Can't think who that would be.'

The bastard was being coy. He had ideas for sure. He was just being taciturn from habit.

I took a sip of the beer. It was cool and heady.

'Well that guy's my puzzle,' I said. 'Why would he come out with that information after all this time? It would be good to get his story.'

'Which paper are you working for?'

'None. Private client, connected to the case.'

A light bulb illuminated but the guy's mouth stayed shut even if his eyes widened. A second later he spotted a customer coming in and left me to it. I smiled at his departing back. Looked like I'd finally met the barman for whom taciturn trumped nosy.

My meat and potato came out and suddenly I was hungry. I ate fast at the bar, finished my pint and headed for the gents to freshen up.

I was sousing my head over the basin when the door opened behind me and the mirror reflected an old guy with sparse grey hair and stubbled cheeks, a heat-denying tweed jacket. One of the locals who'd been propping up the bar. I'd been figuring how to wangle my way into their conversation, but the guy beat me to it. He had his own opener.

'Another one stirring the muck.'

I reached for a paper towel.

'Muck needs stirring sometimes,' I replied.

'Like as not. Nowt to do with me, anyhow. The press can keep their scandals, especially when they come from a yark like Nesbit.'

'I'm not press,' I said.

'Press or summat,' the guy said. 'Y' can tell a mile off.'

I grinned through the mirror. Press and private investigators operate in similar circles. Where we differ is objectives. The investigator wants the truth, the tabloid wants a story.

'Harrogate,' I said. 'Right?'

I was watching. Saw his jaw drop. Suddenly he was on the alert.

'Near as meks na difference,' he said. "Owd' yer figure that?'

I turned; balled the towel; lobbed it into the bin.

'I was brought up in Wetherby.'

His eyes widened some more.

'Well beggar me! Yer don't talk like a Yorkshirem'n.'

'Who's Nesbit?' I asked.

'He's a silly bugger. So who *are* yer with?'

'Myself. Private detective.'

'Oh aye?' The fact didn't impress him any more than the thought that I was a hack. 'And yer sniffing around at this kiddie disappearance.'

'I'm with the family. The rags have been spinning stories and they need to know if there's any truth in them.'

Not wholly accurate. The Barbers knew the truth for sure.

The guy threw me a sour look.

'James Nesbit,' he said. 'That's the bugger's bin bletherin on. If you listen to him he saw every damn thing that 'appened.'

'He's the one talked to *The Nation*?'

'Aye. Nesbit would tell anyone anythin' if there wer' brass in it. Doesn't make it true, though.'

'I guess *The Nation* paid him a pretty penny,' I speculated.

'Well he wouldn't open his mouth for nowt! But them daft beggars 'ud swaller a pink elephant if you put drippin' on it.'

'He live round here?'

'More's our luck! Caravan by High Bank Farm.'

'Is that the Orchard Grove way?'

'Down past. On the bridle.'

'That's good,' I said. 'Maybe I'll pay him a visit.'

The old guy barked a laugh and turned to take a piss. 'You can visit all yer like. But y'll get no sense out of that mardy beggar.'

I tossed another paper towel and headed for the door.

'Gotta try,' I said.

'Don't tell him I sent yer,' the guy said.

I went out. He kept pissing.

~~~~~

The Orchard Grove was comatose in the dust haze. I parked by the site office and went into the shop. Its short aisles were crammed with a mish-mash of food and essential household stuff but a rack behind the door yielded a fifty-thou' Ordnance Survey with an age-faded cover. I hit the bell and a lethargic woman came out to ring up my purchase. I went out and opened the map at a table; spotted High Bank Farm half a mile down the bridle path.

I went out onto the path but turned away from the farm. Walked the length of the site behind its boundary hedge. Peered through at the Barbers' unit. Arrived at the stone posts that marked the access path to the bottom end of the site.

Interesting.

I retraced my steps and headed out between woods and spring barley. Ten minutes kicking dust got me to a metal gate. I pulled the lever and crossed a farmyard onto a metalled lane and looked across at a derelict farm worker's cottage sinking under foliage. Sooty holes for windows. Roof reduced to the stubs of charred joists. A barely visible track ran past the building to where the vegetation besieged an olive-green caravan that had been towed in a few decades back – maybe right after the house burned down. A couple more years and the caravan would be swallowed entirely, but the trodden path and overflowing wheelie bin said someone was still in residence. A transformer on a pole dropped a cable to service the caravan, and a TV aerial was hoisted twenty feet up. Radio sounds floated across the lane.

I looked round. No other caravan in sight. This was Nesbit. I crossed over and pushed my way up the path and squeezed past the bin towards the caravan's cinder block steps. I was three yards from them when I sensed movement, and out of nothing the day exploded into hell.

A furious yowling burst from the high grass to my right as something rushed in like an express train. I turned too late to avoid a ten stone mastiff that sprang at my jugular with a mess of foaming jaws. Adrenaline jackhammered me backwards in a survival reflex and my feet caught in the undergrowth and took me down over a metal crate. I rolled over and felt my trouser leg tear. The trouser leg wasn't the issue. The issue was death. I brought my arm up to fend off the jaws, but at the last moment the death-charge was checked as the dog was snapped back by a chain, inches short. It's jaw worked furiously, bathing me in slaver. It's hind feet scrabbled for traction as it performed a berserk acrobatic routine, crazed with frustration. I scrambled clear, wondering how many seconds I had before the chain gave way. I got myself up and backed further into the grass, eyeing the thing. A subjective view but I'd not have rated the chain to hold a poodle. And the thrashing tornado in front of me shared as much DNA with a poodle as a steam train does with a shopping trolley. I checked the caravan's open door to see if anyone was rushing out to handle the funeral arrangements but nothing moved.

My pulse stabilised at two hundred and gave me a chance to think. In or out? If I stayed in the undergrowth I could maybe reach the steps, depending on the chain's anchor point. If the mastiff had the steps covered then I was blocked. And if the chain broke then the fat lady would be running for a tree. I estimated angles, lengths, forces. Concluded that it was in for a penny and went for the door; trampled grass whilst the dog excavated a channel along the path. As we hit the caravan its chain fouled on a stabiliser post, holding it short. But not short enough to let me get at the steps. I went round and hopped directly onto the platform. Checked my trouser leg. A nine inch tear trailed frayed, bloody strands. The slacks were shot, maybe my leg.

The radio sounds continued through the open doorway but then there was movement inside and a shape materialised.

The guy was in his fifties; five-six; borderline obese; white tee shirt hanging over khaki shorts; sandals with no socks; a mottled face advertising dubious lifestyle choices. The face had a mixture of surprise and annoyance. Surprise at a visitor. Annoyance that the dog had been thwarted. The guy stood at the door and yelled at the mastiff to shut up and the noise ceased but the brute didn't have any appointments. It subsided below the steps and switched to a continuous growl, eyeing me for the return trip.

The man turned to me.

'Are you James Nesbit?' I said.

'Depends who you are.' His face wasn't getting any friendlier. He glanced at the dog, trying to work out how I'd got up his path. I looked too.

'I nearly had a problem there,' I said.

'He doesn't like people on his territory.'

I knew there'd be a reason. I stared at the guy, and my own face wasn't so friendly. Nesbit eyed me back; didn't seem worried that he'd almost had somebody mauled on his property; didn't seem the type to worry much about anything, including personal hygiene. A pungent smell hovered and his face sported two days of stubble. Fashionistos set their clippers to give the forty-eight-hour shadow. Nesbit got the same thing by not shaving.

'Maybe you should adjust the chain,' I said, quietly. 'Your dog would have got me if I'd not jumped off the path.' I looked pointedly at my slacks.

'He'd have got you if his chain hadn't tangled,' Nesbit replied. 'It's supposed to reach to the house.'

I looked at him, speechless; let the trouser thing go. Looked like the situation had nearly been a damn sight more serious than a visit to a seamstress. I wondered if the chain would stay tangled on my way back or did I need airlifting? Arrived at the conclusion that I didn't much like James Nesbit or his dog.

I pushed personal feelings aside.

'I've a couple of questions,' I said.

'What questions?'

'About what you told *The Nation* concerning the night Christa Barber disappeared.'

'I've said all I'm going to on that.'

'There's nothing else you remember?'

He shook his head. 'Nothing. Who the hell are you?'

'The name's Flynn. Maybe you've read my column in *The Times*?'

Nesbit looked blank.

'We're following up. Trying to understand what happened to the girl.'

'I'm not at liberty to talk. *The Nation* has an exclusive.'

'You mean they paid you?'

'No comment.'

I knew they'd paid him but if I judged Archie Hackett right we weren't talking lottery wins. Maybe just enough of a windfall to stir Nesbit's creativity.

'You walked past the site and saw the Barbers loading something into their car.'

He said nothing. Below the steps the mastiff's growl was working back up.

'I checked it out.' I tilted my head in the bridle path direction. 'There's hawthorn bushes along the site. They block the view. You'd have to be standing at the access path to see anything.'

Nesbit was shaking his head, talking over me.

'No comment.' Over and over. Just that. 'No comment.'

'The problem is, if you're walking up towards the pub you'd be looking in the wrong direction. The only way to see the Barbers' caravan would be to turn round and look back. Were you being nosy, James?'

'No comment,' Nesbit repeated. Then contradicted himself. 'Anything wrong with looking?'

'Nothing. If that's what you did.'

'No law against it, last I heard.'

'Sure,' I conceded. 'This isn't about whether someone's being nosy. The problem is that the Barbers' Fiat would have been parked on the other side of their Galaxy. So I've been trying to figure how you'd see something being lifted into it. You'd need to walk right onto the site, stand by their vehicles.'

'I saw what I saw,' Nesbit said. He threw a belligerent stare. 'Just like I told the *Nation*. I've nothing else to say.'

'Any reason you didn't speak up two years ago?'

But Nesbit had turned back into the shadows, leaving me standing. It was the end of our conversation unless I followed him into the caravan, which I wasn't going to.

'Mind the dog,' he called as he disappeared.

I looked at the mastiff, which triggered it. It leapt up and lunged against its chain; reverted to its demented yowling. Its teeth gnashed impressively.

It wasn't quite true that you couldn't see through the bridle way hedge. If you chose your spot, poked your head right in, took a few scratches, you'd get glimpses inside the site. But no detail. There was no way you'd see the Barbers lifting anything into the Fiat. But maybe Nesbit didn't know what was seeable and what wasn't. Maybe Hackett's cash had pulled up a memory that didn't exist. I looked round and wondered what Nesbit had spent his money on. Nothing outdoors. Perhaps he had some new gadgets inside. Or maybe he'd taken it all to the Saracen. Whatever the payoff, his story about seeing the Barbers loading their car was hokum.

I stepped off the platform and gave the mastiff a wide berth, and its chain held long enough to let me out onto the lane. I cut through the farm and headed back up the bridle path at a smart pace. The sun was savage on my neck and my shin hurt like holy hell.

I pictured Hackett fishing at the Saracen until he netted someone willing to spin a yarn to match the story he wanted. Maybe someone who'd remembered the old discredited story from the police investigation. But Hackett hadn't followed up. A simple walk down the path would have quashed Nesbit's tale. I also doubted that Hackett had ever visited James Nesbit's place, or met his dog. The thought of the mastiff leaping for Hackett's jugular had appeal, but more likely the dog would have recognised poisoned bait and stayed clear.

Back at the site I swallowed a cold drink under the shop awning and made a call. Set up an appointment.

So far I'd collected more contradiction than sense. All I had was a set of negatives. I needed to start turning up positives. Things I could believe in. A few needles of truth in a haystack of lies.

CHAPTER TWENTY-SEVEN
He was frightening, even at three years old

I pulled up on the forecourt of a nineteenth century Queen Anne house two miles from St Albans. The building had a revival-grandeur facade spoiled by the mess of twentieth century extensions and annexes sprouting from each side. I walked into an oak-panelled entrance hall and found a reception desk fronting a glass-partitioned admin area. Kids voices echoed from deep in the building. The receptionist led me to an office where a prim woman in her fifties stood to offer her hand and identify herself as Olivia Watts. Olivia asked how Elaine was. Didn't comment on my shredded trouser leg.

Elaine had worked two stints at the Patricia Holland Special Needs School, once before their first child, Grace, was born then a second stint the year before Christa arrived. Olivia Watts was the headmistress. She featured heavily as an ally in *Waiting For Christa*. I apologised for disrupting what I assumed was a tough schedule. Olivia waved it away.

'Elaine said you might want to speak to me,' she said. 'I'm just glad someone's still looking for Christa.'

'Well, we'd like to get her back if possible. We're just a little late getting involved.'

'You were with the Metropolitan Police. I suppose you'll be considering all possibilities.' Olivia's face reflected the possibilities she was thinking of.

'We're keeping an open mind. That's why I'm looking for family background. Things that are not in Elaine's book.'

'What would you say are the chances of Christa being alive?'

I smiled. 'What would you say?'

Waiting For Christa had painted Olivia as a firm optimist, but that was for public – and maybe Elaine's – consumption. Olivia was close to the family but I was hoping she'd also have a little distance. She considered my question.

'I'm not as confident as I was. I want to believe that their photograph is Christa but if it's not then I doubt if she's still with us.'

'How long have you known Elaine?'

'Nine years. She came to work here in 2002.'

'The work suited her?'

'Perfectly. You need special talents to manage our children. They each have their unique characteristics and some of them are difficult even for professionals. Elaine had the perfect combination of skills. She was a great teacher and a natural at handling children.'

'What about her plans for her own family?'

'They were trying when she joined us. We'd anticipated her taking maternity leave at some point.'

'But it took them a while.'

'Seven years at that point. Elaine was starting to worry. When Grace came along they were over the moon.'

I waited.

Olivia sighed. 'Grace's death nearly destroyed Elaine,' she said. 'We'd become close but even I couldn't get through to her. Cot death's a terrible thing. No cause or reason. If your child's ill at least you can prepare for the worst. But with SIDS you just go to wake up the child one day and she's gone. No warning, no goodbye.'

'And you struggled to help Elaine afterwards?'

'She'd withdrawn completely. I visited her as often as I could; suggested after a few months that we'd be ready if she wanted to return to work. Maybe continuing her job would help her to move on. But she wouldn't consider it. I suppose she felt that she needed to be Grace's grieving mother. If she returned to work it might be as if Grace had never existed.'

'She took a while to come out of it, they say.'

'Quite some time. Stuart and her sister supported her as best they could but they couldn't be with her the whole time. Luckily, Elaine had an *au pair* who'd been looking after Grace. She helped her for a while.'

I looked at her sharpish. A *what?*

'Elaine never mentioned an *au pair* living in the family,' I said.

'I don't suppose she thought it was relevant. The girl left them six or seven months before Christa was born. I don't think they've been in contact since.'

'But she was with them when they lost Grace? Did you ever meet her?'

'A few times. A girl called Melanie.'

'How did she strike you?'

'I wasn't keen, truth be told. She was only seventeen and a little immature even for that age. The product of a bad upbringing. She struck me as unstable, disturbed. There's no doubt she helped Elaine after Grace died but eventually they had to sack her for theft. A miserable affair. But she was gone long before Christa came along.'

I thought it through. The Barbers' book was effusive on the people who'd surrounded and supported the family through their two crises. Odd that an *au pair* who'd helped Elaine through their first tragedy didn't get a mention. And Olivia's "unstable" and "disturbed" didn't sound good. In the investigation business it's the missing detail you watch for. The dog that doesn't bark. I'd asked Stuart and Elaine for a briefing on *everyone* connected to the family. So they had a little explaining to do. I put it aside; switched back to the topic.

'Elaine eventually returned to work.'

'A year later. She called me one day and said she was ready. I was delighted. We were going through an expansion. The timing couldn't have been better.'

'Did she show the effects of losing Grace?'

'Not here. She threw herself into her work. You'd never know that she was suffering. But Stuart told me she was still prone to depression. He was hoping a second child might start to heal things but for a long time Elaine refused to try.'

'No cause was ever found for Grace's death?'

'It was classic SIDS. No reason that Grace should have stopped breathing. No cause.'

'Then Christa came along.'

'Unexpectedly. Elaine was seven months pregnant before she realised it.'

I raised an eyebrow.

'Women's bodies play these tricks,' Olivia explained. 'Sometimes you think you're pregnant and you're not. Sometimes you don't notice the signs until you're late term. Elaine had hardly showed with Grace and it was the same with Christa. I hadn't suspected anything until she came rushing in to spill the beans. Then I could see it – something I'd taken for a little excess weight. I was over the moon. It looked like Elaine's grieving might finally be over.'

'There were no problems with Christa?'

156

'None. Elaine had all kinds of gadgets checking on her while she slept. She didn't give herself a night out in a year. But Christa was fine. She got to two years old and the risk of Grace's tragedy repeating was gone.'

'What was Christa like?'

'A lovely child. Happy, affectionate, full of life. The opposite of the newspapers' descriptions of a child with uncontrollable tantrums. I could strangle those damn journalists. We deal with tantrums here – the ones sourced in abuse trauma – and believe me, that's a world away from any problem Christa had.'

'Are you saying there was nothing behind the stories?'

Olivia sighed. 'Christa could be a handful, occasionally. She was prone to the occasional temper tantrum but it was nothing out of the normal, certainly nothing Elaine couldn't handle.'

But I wondered whether Olivia had seen Christa's behaviour first hand or got it from Elaine. Maybe the problems were worse than Elaine revealed. I didn't like the coincidence of Irene Keenan hearing Christa screaming in the caravan that night, no matter how much the old lady herself had downplayed it.

Olivia read my mind.

'May I tell you a story?'

I smiled. People had been telling me stories all week.

'One of the children Elaine used to manage was a four-year-old called Brendan. He'd come to us from a traumatic infancy. He'd been brutalised and neglected for two years until he was removed from his family. His foster parents were struggling. They needed our day-care support for his behavioural problems – what you might call tantrums. But any comparison of Brendan's tantrums with Christa's would be comparing a hurricane to a rain shower. Progressing Brendan to the point where he could interact with people and other children was a long struggle. The boy could switch from being a beautiful child responding to love and attention to an uncontrollable fury at the drop of a hat. He couldn't cope with any threat to his security or breaks in his routine. And when he flew into one of his rages he was frightening, even at three years old. He made me think of a feral cat: all teeth and nails, hideous screaming. When he first came to us all we could do was contain his rages when they came on. At best it would take half an hour to bring him round and at worst he'd continue until he drove himself into a fit and we had to sedate him.

'Elaine took on Brendan's management and the sedation stopped. She'd be with him for an hour sometimes until he came down naturally and she brought his rages down month by month until he was quite manageable. Brendan had hung on to just one possession from his old life. A stuffed toy – a blue rabbit, if you can imagine it, called Benny. He clung to that rabbit as if to life itself. He lived, ate and slept with Benny close by. One of the most remarkable things Elaine achieved was that Brendan would trust her with the toy. She was the only person allowed to hold him.'

She sat back and sighed.

'We had another child at the time. A six-year-old called Fiona. She's still with us. A beautiful child, but she has a mean streak running through her that I doubt we'll ever sort out.

'One day Elaine left Fiona alone with Brendan for just two minutes whilst she checked her schedule. The first we knew that something was wrong was when Brendan started with the worst shrieking we'd ever heard. Elaine found him in the bathroom. Apparently Fiona had snatched Benny from him out of sheer mischief. She knew what the rabbit meant to him. I suppose she just wanted to play with fire. Then when Brendan chased her into the bathroom she became scared of what she'd unleashed. Even then she couldn't resist one last prank. She threw the rabbit into an un-flushed lavatory and fled. Benny finished up covered in faeces and that was more than Brendan could take. He had a fear of toilet activities. In his old home he'd been left in his own filth twenty hours a day and beaten whenever his mother discovered any new mess. So the sight of his toy rabbit covered in shit was intolerable. When Elaine saw the situation she pulled the rabbit out of the mess and hugged it to her to let Brendan see that Benny was okay. Ignored the filth covering her. Just hugged Benny and hugged Brendan. Then she washed Benny down and got him looking bright and blue again, all the while bringing Brendan back from his terror. Elaine was with him for forty-five minutes before he calmed down. I'd hate to think how anyone else would have coped.'

Olivia shook her head angrily.

'But according to the police and the press, when Elaine's own child had a twenty minute tantrum two years ago – something that wouldn't raise an eyebrow here – she couldn't cope. We're supposed to believe that she lost control and killed her own daughter.'

Olivia looked at me.

'That's simply not credible,' she said.

I said nothing. The idea didn't seem so credible to me when Olivia told it that way, but the police and the press hadn't pulled their assumptions out of thin air.

'The *Nation's* story about Elaine admitting she couldn't cope. That came from here?'

'I'm ashamed to say that it did. One of our kitchen staff overheard something she misunderstood and passed it on.'

'Denise Walker. She still with you?'

'Not since Saturday. We'd have appreciated it if she'd given us the chance to check her story two years ago before she went to the police, but what was done was done. We couldn't reprimand her for co-operating in a missing child investigation no matter how misguided her action. But when she spoke to *The Nation* last week I had no option but to give her notice.'

'Any problem if I talk to her?'

Olivia thought about employee confidentiality. Found a way.

'Her name's in the phone book. I'll ask my assistant to look up her address from there and not from our records. Keeps us technically correct but saves you the time. Though I don't think you'll hear anything new from her.'

Olivia's intercom chimed. She excused herself; asked for two more minutes and Denise Walker's address. I stood.

'One last thing,' I said. 'Elaine said you were with her the night the vigilante tried to run her down.'

'Yes. Though I've never been as sure as Elaine that it was deliberate. We were waiting between parked cars to cross the road. Elaine was just stepping out when a car swerved in. She jumped back and stumbled into me. Luckily the car turned away at the last moment, clipped a few wing mirrors and zoomed away – like you'd expect with a drunk driver. I suspect that's all it was.'

She walked me to the door. Shook my hand and hung onto it for her parting words.

'I don't know if Christa's still alive, Eddie, but take my word for it:

Elaine didn't kill her.'

I drove back to town, contrasting Olivia's sincerity with James Nesbit's calculated indifference. Decided that the scales had tipped a little the Barbers' way today. Then decided to leave the bleeding heart stuff until I knew for sure. That always works best.

CHAPTER TWENTY-EIGHT
Swingometer

I siphoned water from Shaughnessy's cooler and sat opposite him behind Harry's side of the partners desk. Got my feet up. Watched the ceiling.

Shaughnessy pushed his keyboard aside and eyed my boots. Then looked more carefully.

'What happened to the trousers?'

'Trouble with a dog.'

'A dog shredded them?'

'No. If the mutt had reached me I wouldn't be here. It was scrambling through the briar patch that did the damage.'

I gave him what I'd picked up, which was that at least some of the stuff against the Barbers was hot air. *The Nation's* latest witness and his dog gave the story of Stuart and Elaine loading their car that night the credibility of a fairy tale. And my talk with Olivia Watts had tilted the swingometer even further to the right. If Olivia's judgement was sound then the premise of the police case – that Elaine killed Christa over a tantrum – was not tenable. But I was starting to wonder about Stuart. None of the varying accounts of the affair pegged him as the guilty party but I couldn't help wondering if something else had happened in the caravan that night.

And now we had a new factor: the Barbers' *au pair* who'd lived with them through the trauma of their first child's death but was conspicuous by her absence from Elaine's book.

'They're hiding her,' Shaughnessy said.

'Yeah. I'll ask them why. And whatever the reason, I want to speak to the girl.'

I sat back; watched the ceiling; waited for Shaughnessy to tell me why he was not at the Barber house, waiting for our bug-repair man. Only one reason I could think of.

'We got a hit,' he confirmed.

'Someone turned up?'

'Someone we know.'

'Martin.'

Shaughnessy nodded. 'He arrived half an hour after they'd left. Went in through the damaged window like it was the tradesman's entrance. Substituted the relay.'

'We get him on camera?'

'I snapped him outside. Harry will upload the flash from the indoor cam. We've got him.'

'So Martin's been listening in to our clients. My money says he's feeding Hackett.'

I sipped water. Giannetti, Nesbit and Nesbit's dog, all in one day. I hadn't had a worse social life since I left Hendon. And tomorrow's diary now had Brendan Martin and Archie Hackett in the appointments list.

Shaughnessy's inkjet whined and spat paper. He handed me two sheets that Harry had emailed from Birmingham. A photograph of the "Time for a demonstration!" letter plus his analysis. I read the letter, trying to tease out something that was irritating my subconscious. Couldn't pin it down. Maybe the letter's tone. Less extreme than the previous mailing, despite its promise of action. Harry had picked up the same thing. On the technical side the letter had reverted to inkjet printing and a Gatwick postmark, a break with the westward drift of postal locations and spray can vandalism. Was this two writers or one guy travelling?

Shaughnessy and I kicked it around. Tracing the hate-mail was going to be slow and expensive. All squeezed on top of checking out the Barbers' background and chasing the Christa Photo.

We were still kicking when the outer door opened and a visitor came through. She was togged up in an outfit of screaming black-and-lilac, topped by wrap-around sunglasses wider than a bus windscreen. The effect you'd get if you crossed Ali-G with a psychedelic wasp. It was only the hair that gave things away.

'If you're in there, Lucy,' I said, 'come out with your hands up.'

My guess was on target. The shades were pushed up and Lucy blinked like a mole from its burrow. She grabbed a cup of water. Drained it. Perched herself on the desk.

'How's it going, fellas?'

Shaughnessy and I looked at each other.

'Just tell us, Luce.'

She smirked.

'You guys should be paying me detective rates.'

'You wouldn't like the conditions. And we probably couldn't afford you.'

'Good point. Talent you have to pay for.'

Which is why so many businesses operate without it.

'*Reunited*,' Lucy said. 'We've got him.'

'The thing worked?'

'Like in the book.'

She smirked some more. Her scheme had been a little over-dependent on petty greed but I guess that's how most scams work. Seemed this one had ferreted out our Christa Photo contact.

You can't place an ad in the *Standard* nowadays without handing over your ID along with your card details. Something our *Reunited* guy was reluctant to provide. So he'd placed the ad through McLellan's pawn shop but gave his real PAYG number. I guess he felt safe with that. He would have been, if he'd had the sense to stay clear when the newspaper texted him – via Lucy's phone – congratulating all *Prize Draw Finalists* in a previously unannounced *Evening Standard Classifieds Sweepstake*. The *Finalists* were instructed to show their faces at the *Standard's* Kensington sales desk by two p.m. to claim their share of a ten thousand pound prize.

You might think that someone setting up a two hundred K photo scam would pass on a ten K draw, but that would depend on whether the guy running the scam was the one placing the ad. Seemed he wasn't, because our *Reunited* guy turned up at the *Standard's* offices thirty minutes before the deadline.

Unfortunately, *Prize Draw Finalist* isn't the same as *Prize Draw Winner*. And the *Standard* doesn't have a sales desk. Our contestant was kicked out of the building without even a consolation voucher. What he did collect was a tail.

'He didn't spot you?' I said.

'I stayed incognito.' Lucy flipped her shades back down.

Shaughnessy and I exchanged looks.

'You followed him in those? How the hell did you see him?'

'They're not so bad once you adjust. Just the Tube was kinda tricky. I couldn't get my card in the slot.'

Our *Finalist* had probably anticipated a taxi ride home with a bottle of bubbly; had to settle instead for the Tube and Lucy on his tail.

The Tube isn't so user-friendly though if you're running blind. All those escalators and ticket slots. The real miracle was that Lucy hadn't fried herself on the tracks.

She kicked her heels. Raised the shades. Gave us an East End address right round the corner from McLellan's pawn shop, together with a name: Bill "Goat" Scully. Forty-something. Bad dress sense. Funny walk. Jumpy. Lucy had the details on a Post-it block. She peeled pages and handed them over as evidence.

'What do you mean "jumpy"?' I said. I'd be jumpy too if a lilac wasp was following me.

'Nervous. Like a tick. Twitch City. The guy spoke fast and could never sit still, like he was up to no good. I think Scully took the Christa Photo. That's why it's blurred.'

I liked her logic but I didn't see this guy as our photographer. The lousy quality was down to the need to get a quick snap, maybe from a passing car, probably with a software zoom.

'That's a terrific job, Luce,' I said. 'How did you get his name?'

'I followed him into the pub,' she said, 'and asked the barman. Scully's probably still there. He seemed to be in for a session.'

I had to admit it: Lucy's sleuthing techniques were sound. I'd have done the same, only I'd have worn a beard. I looked at Shaughnessy.

'I'll pick him up,' he said.

'Luce,' I said, 'remind me to give you a rise.'

'Wilco. Right after I've reminded you to pay me.'

But she seemed happy enough. She flipped the shades back down and slid off the desk and went back out into her twilit world. Shaughnessy followed her, heading for the East End.

I shut up shop and flipped the sign. Sensed progress. This Scully character was our link to whoever had snapped the Christa Photo. A week tops and we'd know where the snap was taken, know who the girl was. I'd have felt positive if I was confident it would be Christa.

CHAPTER TWENTY-NINE
How does the cat copy?

I was back in at eight a.m. next morning. Found Harry at his desk and Lucy working the filter machine. I sneaked my mug into the queue and went through. Harry pushed an envelope across and I read the latest hate-letter in the original.

Harry confirmed his analysis. 'There's more similarities than differences across the letters, but I still see two writers.'

'Two independent writers? Or two writers taking turns? Or one guy with up and down moods?'

'Hard to see any "up" here, Eddie. But I'm going with two writers. A copycat. But how does the cat copy? And why?'

'They've had access to the letters,' I said. 'Martin and company have been inside the Barbers' house and the police had the early ones. The leak's from one or the other. But as you say: why?'

I changed tack. 'How's our classifieds guy?'

Harry had taken over tailing Scully yesterday evening when he got in from Birmingham. He swivelled his seat.

'He's an odd bird,' he said. 'Sean tailed him round half the East End then I covered the rest. The guy's a socialiser but he didn't go near any family with a kid. And I didn't catch any talk about the photo. The main topic of the night was a box of sat-navs that needed shifting and a couple of horses that cost Scully a packet.'

'Horse racing at night?'

'It's big with the punters. The all-weather tracks operate until nine forty then they feed in the U.S.'

'Scully talk to anyone interesting?'

Harry grunted. 'The guy talked to everyone. Bookies, boozers, a dozen pawn shop operators and some dodgy characters up Bethnal Green. Finished up at a Chinese takeaway. The guy's a mixer. Just not with anyone who looks like his photo-scam buddy. The evening wasn't entirely wasted, though. I picked up a winner at Wolverhampton.'

I looked at him. Harry shrugged.

'It was a no-brainer. The second fave was up at five-to-one with nothing else in contention. Had to be worth a tenner.'

'Scully put his money down?'

'He took the hundred-to-one outsider. Guess he'd picked up a tip. The guy actually looked surprised when his nag fell. We're looking at a guy who likes long shots, Eddie.'

Lucy came through with drinks. Perched herself on Harry's desk. Harry grabbed his mug. 'I'll stay on Scully,' he said. 'If he's the messenger he's going to talk to someone.'

I agreed. Shaughnessy had headed to Birmingham to catch up with the Barber road show. Harry could keep tabs on Scully for a day or so whilst we gave him another prod. I briefed Lucy: we needed another classified. In this business you stay with winning ideas and I had one that I figured would turn the pressure up.

But there was someone else I needed to talk to. I made a call. Elaine answered.

'Your ex-*au pair*,' I said. 'Tell me about her.'

CHAPTER THIRTY
A cruise on the wrong ship

I circled round the back of Primrose Hill and coasted down a ramp to a parking area beneath a tower block. The basement was dark and deserted except for two burned-out cars. I reconsidered. Swung the wheel and climbed back to the light and left the Frogeye two streets away between a Merc and a Mazda – more attractive options to someone eyeing for new wheels. I walked back to the tower and pressed a button by a steel security door. No response. I hung around until two women exited, then stepped round them and took the lift to the eighteenth floor. The lift had a distinctive odour and a barely perceptible motion that screamed technical problem. Just before lunch we arrived at eighteen and shuddered to a halt. Then nothing for ten seconds. The first nine I was cool, was just reaching for the alarm button when the door scraped open. I exited and walked round the landing to a security grille guarding a door on the south side of the building. When I pressed the bell the inner door was opened by a black woman in her twenties. She had sturdy athletic limbs and a three-year-old clinging to her bare leg. The two of them looked me up and down through the grille.

What Elaine had told me, basically, was that they'd hired an *au pair* they knew nothing about. Elaine's only information on Melanie Brand had been the address in this tower where she'd been lodging with a friend when she applied for the post. That was it. No background checks, no references. I hadn't pressed Elaine on her recruiting practices. She wasn't paying for parenting advice. But despite her assurances that their old *au pair* was irrelevant to Christa's disappearance I wasn't paying her for advice either. I needed to see first hand that this "unstable" and "disturbed" addition to the Barber family had nothing to do with what happened. I gave the woman behind the grille my name and asked if she knew Melanie.

The woman's face took on a cautious look. The kid stayed cool.

'What you after, hon?'

'Just a chat with her.' I grinned down at the kid. The girl had her mother's broad good looks. And her mother's vibes: she gave me narrow-eyed.

'Melanie's not in trouble,' I said, 'but it would be good to talk to her.'

'Whyd' ya come here? Mel don't live here.'

'This is the only address I have. I take it you're Davina.' I gave her harmless charmer.

HC didn't impress. The woman asked where I'd got that piece of information.

'She *is* Davina,' the little girl yelled, her hostility eclipsed by the need to keep records straight.

Davina cuffed the child. 'Shut yer mouth, Florence Anita, before someone drives a bus through it.'

I grinned down at the kid but she'd reverted to a no-nonsense stare. The information exchange had been a pure formality.

'Mister,' Davina said, 'I don't know nothin' about Mel. You've come to the wrong place.' She stood back, and Florence Anita grabbed the door ready to slam it.

I held out my arms. 'Well, I'm kinda stuck, Davina. You're my only hope.' I said it quick because the door was closing fast, propelled by the kid. Davina's hand reached out and stopped it. Florence Anita kept pushing.

'Why you lookin'?'

'I'm working for the Barbers. Trying to find their child. I'm hoping Melanie might give me some insights into the family.'

Davina wasn't greatly impressed by the information but I saw curiosity kick in. She stooped to prise Florence Anita's fingers off the door. The kid put up a fight. We were there a while before the door was open enough to let Davina out to unlock the grill and I ran the gauntlet of a ferocious stare from Florence Anita and went in. Davina led me down a hallway. I sensed someone stirring behind a half-open bedroom door. Davina yelled as we passed.

'Karl, get up you lazy bastard, we've got a visitor!'

Smart woman. Warning us both.

The flat was tidy but jaded. Frayed carpets and faded furniture. But a view over London you'd pay a million for. I wondered how long Camden Council would hold out before turning the building over to the developers.

Davina waved at a chair. 'Siddown, Mister. Tell me why you're lookin' for Mel.'

I stayed standing. Offered my hand and my name.

She shook my hand without enthusiasm then leaned against the wall and jabbed the tips of her fingers into her shorts. Florence Anita jumped onto the sofa to use it as a trampoline.

I explained that I was looking into the Barbers' background. Needed to talk to people who'd been close to them.

Davina had been struggling with something. Suddenly it clicked. She laughed. 'You're the geezer in the jacket,' she said.

The jacket was in the dry cleaners but I got her drift.

She tossed her head and laughed. 'Well, hon, you took a cruise on the wrong ship there.'

I waited.

'The Barbers are goin' down,' she said. 'It's the Titanic all over. And there'll be no tears from me. I'm sorry Eddie Flynn, but I don't like your clients one little bit.'

'Sorry Eddie Flynn!' Florence Anita yelled. Her acrobatics had built almost to my height. I frowned at her but that only provoked things. 'Sorry, Freddie Lynn!' she yelled over and over. She didn't seem very sorry until Davina leaned over and cuffed her again and told her to stop her mouth.

'I see you've read the papers,' I said. 'But I'm not sure I'd place much faith in what's there.'

'No, hon, I put my faith in common sense. And your clients are getting into deeper shit every day. You tellin' me there's nothin' behind what *The Nation's* saying? You think your clients are gonna come up smelling of roses?'

'Why don't you like them?'

'Because of how they treated Mel. Kicked her out when they'd no more use for her. Left her without a roof over her head.'

'How long have you known Melanie?'

'Since 2004. She was up from Southampton, livin' on the street. We met on the Market. I've a stall: old jewellery and stuff but I got some phones and MP3s too. Mel wanted to sell a couple of Nokias.' She laughed. 'The girl was on a loser there! The Nokias were more bleedin' antique than my jewellery. I couldn't give her anything for 'em. I've no room for stuff that don't sell.'

'But you became friends with her?'

'Yeah. She came back, desperate for cash. I told her no again but she was stuck for a roof so I offered her a room 'ere while she got herself sorted. Ten quid a week, which is absolute charity. But she had a few part-time jobs so I always got my tenner and we hit it off.'

'How long did she stay?'

'Three or four months. Until she went to the Barbers.'

'You say the Barbers didn't treat her right?'

Davina shrugged. 'So-so at first, except for bugger all in wages. I'd give my kid more spending money than that. Then after all the help Mel gave Elaine after their cot death baby they kicked her out on the street. A pretty shitty way to say thanks.'

'Pretty shitty!' Florence Anita yelled. She was back to jumping. I gave her another frown for the bad language, which encouraged her to try the phrase a few more times and cap it off with a forwards bounce that slammed her into my chest. I grabbed her and lowered her to the floor where she climbed back onto the sofa and re-launched herself. I sensed a losing game. Next time she hit me I carried her across to look at the view. The City towers shimmered above the silver of the Thames, a panorama that would have stretched to Kent without the haze.

'Florence Anita, you get the hell off the man,' Davina yelled, which got Florence's arms locked tight round my neck.

'Did you see Melanie much after she left the Barbers?' I asked. Talking wasn't easy due to choking.

'Just the odd time. She stayed here the night they threw her out, but it was kind of difficult. Karl was with me by then and three's a crowd.'

'When was this?' I was waiting for Florence Anita's grip to loosen so I could ditch her beyond leaping distance. Davina finally came to the rescue. Pulled the kid gently from me. I got a whiff of musky fragrance; a flash in her eyes.

'She likes you,' Davina confided. I felt my heart warm, the way it does when someone effuses about the dog that's humping your leg. Maybe I'd misinterpreted that mastiff's intentions yesterday.

'It was the end of '06,' Davina said. 'Mel turned up at the stall soaked through. The Barbers had put her on the street. She kipped on the couch the one night then was off.'

'You know where?'

'Back to Southampton. She talked about checkin' in at the YMCA. We bumped into each other on Oxford Street a coupla years later but we didn't hardly talk. Just a minute in the rain. That's the last I saw of her.'

Florence Anita was struggling in Davina's arms. She put her down and the kid headed straight for the sofa and began her trampolining. I grinned at her from the safety of distance. The kid realised I was out of range and reverted to yelling 'Sorry Eddie!' until Davina yelled back at her to bladdy well shaddap.

'So you've not seen Melanie since 2006?'

'Long time,' Davina concurred. 'We was close for a while. I always wondered what happened to her. So how about tellin' me exactly why you're after her. I don't like geezers chasing friends of mine, even if I like you.'

'I like you! I like you!' The parrot had a new theme.

I liked Davina too. A lot more than I liked the look of the slob who'd just appeared in the doorway. Karl was a white guy, ten years older, going to seed in the way heavy drinking and a fondness for the funny stuff expedite. His face was a patchwork of bad living. Hair styled to match. Voice surprisingly deep. He pulled Florence Anita off the sofa and swung her round.

'Hiya, Chucky-Duck,' he said.

He swung her again and turned to Davina and the kid pulled herself free and came to play under the window.

'Wazzup?' the guy asked.

'Nothin', Karl. Just some stuff about an old friend.'

He nodded at me.

I wasn't looking for an audience. I explained that I was an investigator; didn't expand on it.

Karl shrugged, aimed his growl back at Davina. 'What we doing with investigators? You owe money Dav?'

'Just helping with an old friend,' Davina repeated.

'Okay,' he said. 'You ready to go?'

'In a sec.'

'Soon as you can.' He looked at his watch.

Davina gave me a look that said we needed to wrap this up. Florence Anita quit messing about and held her arms up. I turned and looked at Davina and Karl, and the atmosphere thickened until

171

Davina strode across and picked the child up.

'Why are you looking for Mel?' she asked again.

'I'm taking another look into Christa's disappearance,' I said. 'The family's background might be relevant to that, and Melanie was part of their household for eighteen months.'

'Old history,' Davina said. 'Mel was long gone before Christa was born. Doubt she's anything to say on the matter.'

'You say you knew her pretty well?'

'As much as anyone could, with Mel.'

Karl flopped onto the sofa. 'Who's this Mel?' he said. 'Someone I know?'

'Nah,' Davina said. 'She was here one night. You were pissed.'

Karl shook his head. 'Don't remember,' he said. 'What's she up to?'

'We don't know,' Davina said. 'The man's looking for her.'

He looked up at me. 'Got what you want?'

I tried to stay nice. 'More or less,' I said. 'I won't keep you a minute.'

The guy locked eyes for a moment then heaved himself back off the sofa. 'Okey doke,' he said. 'We're out of here in two minutes, Dav. Get your shit together.'

Davina looked at me and shrugged. Walked me to the door with Florence Anita. I walked slowly.

'I heard Melanie was highly strung. Was there something in her background?'

Davina laughed.

'You got that right, hon! She came from a right old family, know what I mean? Abuse City and all that. Mel hated the lot of them except her stepsister.' She glanced back into the flat. Karl had disappeared into the bathroom.

'Mel was bloody mixed up,' she said. 'No other word for it. But she was a good mate. We got on. She could have stayed here after the Barbers but it wouldn't have worked with Lurch in residence.' She tilted her head meaningfully.

'Lurch!' screamed Florence Anita. Davina shushed her.

'Mixed up how?'

'Mister, when you come from one of those fucked-up families you're mixed up in every way. I dunno exactly what went on down there in Southampton but it wasn't no idyllic childhood.'

'How did it show?'

'Mel was emotional. Ups and downs. Temperamental. She played the boys. Liked to tease. It was friggin' embarrassin' being out with her sometimes. Dressed to kill and leadin' the boys a dance. She even brought one or two back here, but mostly she liked to have a good time then ditch the sods. Good luck with that I say! Most geezers round here you wouldn't prod with a pitchfork. But Mel got off on building them up an' then dropping them. She was a bitch that way. Boys and drink. Them were 'er weaknesses. She liked to live dangerous. I just hope it worked out for her. She was a mate.'

'You saw her only once after she'd gone back to Southampton?'

'Just the once. Didn't really speak. I asked what she was up to and she said this and that. Casual jobs in London. Bit of work in Southampton. I asked if she was doin' any more *au pair-ing* and she bloody laughed. Told me that's the last thing she'd do. Worked like a slave then chucked out on her arse. She hated those Barbers.'

A rumbling from the bathroom became a yell for Davina to get her own arse in gear. She reached to open the door. I walked out.

'Sorry Eddie!' Florence Anita said. This time she actually looked it. A little like that mastiff when the chain pulled it up. But the kid was okay. Her mother was fine.

Melanie Brand. Unstable. Temperamental. Risk-taker. Gone long before Christa disappeared. But for someone who'd been close to the Barbers and their previous child I didn't like all those adjectives. Hard to see how she might be connected but harder still to dismiss her.

I needed to track her down.

CHAPTER THIRTY-ONE
Flaming duck

I headed towards the M1. Checked my rear view. No change: I still had a tail. Brendan Martin's white Astra had been behind me since I left Chase Street. Seemed the guy had a new assignment this morning.

The weather came on the radio, animated talk about Western Atlantic lows. The man gave it a week then we could stop moaning about the heat and get back to bitching about the rain. Right now, stalled in aircon jet-blast under a vicious sun a little rain didn't seem such a bad idea. The traffic rolled and stopped for twenty minutes before it cleared a three-car shunt and started moving. I turned onto the motorway. Fifteen minutes got me to Chiswell Green. I exited and scanned my A-Z. Found my way to a street of 30's semis, a house halfway down with flaking brown paintwork and a garden that was tidy but dead. I parked and walked up the path and rang the bell, and the door opened on a dark interior and a matching face.

She was a lean woman. Early sixties. Stringy hair. The dour look of the religious who rate piety above charity. I didn't doubt Olivia Watts' judgement but I needed to hear Denise Walker's story from her own lips. Unlike friend Nesbit yesterday I didn't see canteen staff at Elaine's old school as procurers of fantasy for cash. The face that looked out from the gloom, though, threw up a new possibility. If anyone looked right for telling tales from spite it was Denise.

I smiled. Apologised for disturbing her empty day, then truly disturbed it by asking about Elaine Barber.

Denise's eyes contracted to pinpricks. She stepped forward to see me better.

'Who are you? The press?'

'I'm working with the Barbers,' I said. I handed her a card. 'We're trying to help them but we need to know if they're being truthful with us.' I gave her the confidential tone of a double glazing rep when he gets you to agree that you really need triple. 'Truth be told,' I said, 'we keep hearing that Elaine Barber is guilty as sin.'

Denise pursed her lips. 'I've said all I intend to about that woman,' she said. 'And if you're mixed up with them you're as bad as they are. Don't come bothering me again.'

The door started to swing shut. I sensed my double glazing sincerity falling on stony ground. Denise Walker's house had never had double glazing and never would. I wondered how many reps were buried in her back garden. I thought fast; spoke through the closing gap.

'Elaine hasn't fooled you,' I said. 'You know she did it.'

The gap opened again. The face hovered in the shadows.

'Elaine never did fool me. She can twist her words as much as she likes but I heard what I heard.'

'Just like it was.'

Denise's eyes hardened.

'She couldn't cope. She was at her wits end. She killed her baby. Goodbye.'

'But she didn't mention Christa by name.'

The words stopped her. This was the question that mattered and I threw it out without dressing. Denise's hostile glare didn't change.

'That bitch took my job,' she said. 'I hope she rots in hell.'

The door slammed shut.

No sale.

~~~~~

I took the A roads back to town; passed the Watford crematorium then jumped cars, took a few turnings. Just past the schools I put my foot down and sprinted a quarter of a mile then braked hard and turned into a side road that took me into an avenue of pre-war semis. A hundred yards down I hit a junction and spun the wheel to drive back parallel to my route then turned again and took a street back to the main road, completing the circle. The exit onto the main road was closed to vehicles by a line of bollards. Closed to modern vehicles, that is. I squeezed the Frogeye through with millimetres to spare and regained the main road; put my foot down and raced round the circuit again. Thirty seconds later I was back in the closed-exit street. I braked and angled the car across the road to block the white Astra that was backing towards me from the dead end.

The Astra's wheels locked and it halted three yards from the

Frogeye. I got out. Strolled over and put my arm on its roof. The face in the open window matched Harry Green's photo except that Harry's snap didn't have the bruising you get from a fist in the face and a tumble down stairs. This was the guy who'd rushed me in the dark two nights back.

'Martin,' I said, 'you're through.'

Brendan Martin worked gum and stared from behind mirror shades. The shades partly hid the damage but what I saw looked nasty. The Astra's aircon was going full blast.

'Mind moving your car?' Martin said. Still cool, but his logic was kind of shaky.

'What's the point?' I said. 'You have to stay with me anyway.'

His shades reflected my face against the sky. My own shades were darker patches in the reflection. I repeated the news.

'You're through. The job's terminated.'

Martin lifted his lip. Carried on chewing.

I slapped the car.

'Send in your bill,' I said. 'Then disappear. I don't like being followed around. I don't like people breaking into my office either. So we'd better not meet again.'

'Is that a threat, Flynn?' The shades held steady.

'Don't be stupid, Brendan. If we wanted to threaten you we'd talk about housebreaking and bugs. We've got you right on camera.'

A sweat bead crawled from beneath Martin's shades. Aircon can only handle so much.

'Move your fucking car,' he repeated.

'Sure. You okay to find your way back or should I drive slow?'

I stared him out. A pointless exercise between guys wearing shades. Then I slapped the Astra again. 'If you want your surveillance gear check eBay,' I said. 'Just watch for snipers.'

I walked back to the car. Made a slow three-point turn and circled back to the main road.

Martin could put in his bill or not. He was about to get his cards anyway.

~~~~~

It took me an hour to work down to Wapping. I parked in a narrow permit-only street behind the Times complex and walked down to Tobacco Dock. Located *The Nation's* offices in a ten storey lozenge-shaped building that had sprung up on waste ground opposite the walls. *The Nation* didn't have the scale of News International. A foyer plaque located them on just the three lowest floors. I didn't get much co-operation on any of the floors but I persevered until I extracted what I needed then went back out and drove to a corner pub huddled under Blackfriars Bridge. The interior was glitz, wooden friezes and marble slabs, mirrors. The place was busy with the late-late-lunch crowd. I nosed around and spotted a table in an alcove occupied by three guys and a woman. The table was littered with empty glasses. I walked over and joined them. The group looked at me as I sat down.

'Ah, fuck a flaming duck,' one of them groaned.

The other three looked at the flaming duck for an explanation. Hackett was still wearing his ancient leather jacket, oblivious to the heat's effect on body odour. The guy's mess of hair put me in mind of Dylan Thomas but Thomas had never aspired to the poetry that graced the pages of *The Nation*. Hackett's late-late-lunch pals looked a little more together, but you couldn't ignore the seedy air of a table full of empties in the middle of the afternoon.

'Another afternoon's graft in the Pulitzer business?' I flipped my fisherman's off; fanned my face.

One of Hackett's cronies answered for him: the female reporter I'd seen at Kestrel. Late twenties, swept-back blonde hair, too-pale face and red Chanel cat eye spectacles that screamed TV anchor ambition. I could have warned her: on-the-job training with Hackett wasn't the route to Sky News.

'Pulitzers don't apply in Britain,' she said.

I kept my grin. 'Damn!' I said. 'And how does that make you feel?'

The three looked at Hackett to see how they felt. Hackett was good for it. 'Get this, girls and boys!' he said. 'We've been fingered by the Barbers' private eye. This is one of the big dicks they're swinging round town.'

My smile held, even if my fists bunched up under the table.

'Let me introduce London's hottest detective: Mr Edward Flynn!' Hackett flapped a hand with alcohol-assisted finesse. 'Eddie's team is hot on the trail of Christa Barber. Expects to dig her up any time now.'

His audience chuckled him up. Hackett was a wheeze in the right crowd. I wasn't here for the wheeze. I chilled my smile.

'If I'm not intruding in your schedule, Archie, it would be good to have a chat.'

Hackett sprawled back and clasped his hands behind his head.

'My schedule's full. Let me give you a call.'

I waited.

'You're not a half-bad detective,' he mused. 'How did you find me?'

'Followed the smell of booze,' one of his buddies said. A thin guy, angular head, slitted eyes. Wit for brains.

'It was pretty easy, Archie,' I told him. 'I asked your boss.'

Hackett's smile tightened.

'I guess Natasha hasn't any hard evidence that you spend the day loafing in the boozer, but I'd find it worrying that she was on target with her guesswork. Even more that she was happy to share it with a guy off the street.'

'I pull my weight,' Hackett said. 'Natasha's happy with the results.'

He had a point. Hackett had the Barber story, and the Barber story was paying *The Nation's* bills. The rag's circulation had been on a bear trend for a decade before they fired up their anti-Barber campaign. But Hackett's editor hadn't given me the impression that she was enamoured with her star reporter in any wider sense. When the wheels came off the Barber bandwagon Hackett had better have something else up his sleeve or he'd have a hell of a lot more time to spend in the pub. And Hackett's editor would be a good deal less happy if she knew about the bugs at the Barber house. Unless she already did.

'We need a chat,' I repeated. 'In private.'

'Some other time, pal.'

I turned my grin back on, real unfriendly; shook my head.

'Better now,' I said. 'This is sensitive.'

I don't know how much Hackett had drunk. Even the hardened boozer isn't thinking straight when he thinks he's being clever. That's why he missed the nuance of the word "sensitive". He opened his hands to invite me to talk. 'We're all friends here,' he declared.

TV Anchorwoman pursed her lips and opened her eyes wide

behind her designer specs. A little too wide. There were a few empty glasses crowding her own side of the table.

'Don't worry, Eddie' she confided, 'we won't tell. There's nothing about Archie could shock us.'

I didn't know if she was being patronising or crafty, sensing dirt. I'd time for neither.

'Sweetheart,' I said, 'drink up and leave. Archie won't want you to hear what I'm going to say, no matter what he thinks, because then he'd have to spend the next decade kissing your arse to keep you quiet. And he knows that the good buddy act doesn't hold up once the chance of a scoop pops up.' I smiled at her. 'What you don't hear today can't hurt him tomorrow.'

'Ah, come on, Eddie,' Hackett said. 'You're bullshitting. Have a drink. Preferably at another table.'

His buddies chortled it up some more. The guy was a wheeze. But my tee shirt was sticking to my back and my palms were clammy and I just wanted the hell out.

'Fine, let's do it here. I guess your buddies are all in the business. Might appreciate some juicy post-Leveson dirt. And there's no-one more willing to rake up a newspaper's indiscretions than a fellow rag, hey? Is *The Nation* ready for that spotlight, Archie?'

I saw Hackett finally get it. He threw a puzzled look – but not puzzled enough. He knew I'd got something. I clarified things.

'I talked to Martin. We know what he was up to. And we've solid proof he was working for you. So now's your last chance, Archie. Tell your buddies to drink up and get lost or have them hear stuff that's gonna give them a crisis of conscience when they rat you out.'

Hackett came fully alert as a sense of danger penetrated his booze-addled brain. He knew I wasn't squeezing him over Martin tailing the Barbers. He knew it was about the bugs. His expression rattled around, testing scenarios, found the only survivable one. He held up his hands and shrugged at his drinking cronies.

'Okay, friends,' he said, 'the detective seems to have got some actual dirt here. It appears that I do need that private conversation. Time to get back to work.'

'Come on, Archie,' Anchorwoman pleaded. 'There's no dirt we haven't heard before.'

But that was the point. The dirt they'd heard the last couple of years was now very toxic dirt. Toxic enough for Archie to drop his act. He jabbed at his watch and flapped his cronies away. They got up reluctantly and went off to wherever their wage packets lived. Hackett finished his drink, pushed the empty across the table then invited me to spill the beans.

'I've talked to Martin. Your spy game is over.'

'What spy game? Who's Martin?'

'Don't waste my time, Archie. We've got Martin on video servicing the bugs at the Barbers' house. He's been caught cold.'

Hackett shrugged.

'Not guilty,' he said. 'You won't find a connection to me.'

'Wrong. You've been too clever with your stories, Archie. You've put out details that could only come from the bugs.'

'Circumstantial,' Hackett said. 'You won't prove any link.'

'We won't have to. The Met have a team dedicated to Leveson sweep-up. We give them Martin and he'll take you down with him. The Met would love to bag a few more editors and proprietors and they'll squeeze Martin until he caves. You're shot, Hackett.'

The bar's fug was giving me a headache. The air was unbreathable. Hackett hung on to his sneer but his eyes were testing the options. He'd known the risks of going with the eavesdropping and he'd taken the gamble, probably without his editor knowing. But the gamble had depended on Martin not being caught. He should have pulled him out as soon as the Barbers hired private investigators but I guess the scoop came first. Hackett had rolled the dice once too often.

'Okay,' he said. 'We'll pull back on the Barbers. I already have what I need.'

'Legally or illegally?'

He laughed. 'The fuck's it matter? We've got them, Flynn. You think the police are gonna chase me when *The Nation* hands them the Killer Couple on a plate?'

His confidence was returning. Hackett was still gambling that he could pull this one off with the big splash. I wondered what the hell he'd got to give him that confidence. Had to be more than the dodgy witnesses he'd dug up this last week. He spotted my thoughts and sat forward.

'I'm almost home, Eddie,' he said. He leaned further and his jacket creaked. 'The Barbers are screwing you over, pal.'

I said nothing.

'We've ID'd their accomplice. The one who's been with them from the start. We know what happened that night. We've solved the case. And the issue of a few bugs isn't gonna make a ripple once we've dropped that bombshell. So worry about your clients, not me. And make sure to pick up your copies of *The Nation* next week. Live and learn, my friend.'

He slid himself off his stool and walked out.

I sat there for a couple of minutes, breathing the fug, then got the hell out.

CHAPTER THIRTY-TWO
You got a human tragedy

Lucy wasn't around but she'd left a note confirming that the new ad was in the *Standard*.

Watching Scully wasn't enough. We needed him talking to whoever was behind the Christa Photo. If Lucy's new message worked he'd be doing just that. Very soon.

I shut up shop. Drove to the Barbers'. Found the forecourt cluttered with cars including a Merc I could have done without.

Bernie let me in. Briefed me. The out-of-town jaunt had gone smoothly. A couple of hecklers in Leicester, but Bernie and Shaughnessy had stayed clear. No sign of our vigilante. Not that we were about to relax. That promise of action in his last letter didn't sound like an idle threat. The Barbers were in the kitchen, preparing tea. Owen Jagger was perched at their breakfast bar with a coke, looking fresh and ready to go, his coif up like the winner in a topiary competition.

'Eddie!' he yelled: 'How's it going?'

I gave him something non-committal and settled myself at the main table. Jagger had to have an appointment somewhere. I could wait.

'That was a good tour,' Jagger declared. 'We get more friggin' interest out in the sticks than in London. What is it with the media in this town?'

Shaughnessy was leaning against a unit, watching the cooking. He caught my glance and lifted his jacket off a chair. Pulled a handful of bugs from the pocket. Martin's surveillance kit. Shaughnessy had cleaned the place as soon as they got back. He'd already briefed Stuart and Elaine.

'So where are we Eddie?' Jagger asked. 'Who are the reprobates who wrecked the caravan?'

'We're following leads,' I said. Fourteen years of Met training wasn't wasted on me.

'We need to find these people,' Jagger said. 'You get a human tragedy and what's the response? Lynch mobs and opportunists!

'Bout time we strung the *parasites* up for a change, hey Eddie?'

I didn't know if Jagger was throwing rhetoric or expected me to rush out for rope. Luckily his name wasn't on our contract. No-one else spoke, though, which encouraged him: 'What leads we got, Eddie? Come on, spill the beans.'

Elaine planted a bowl of rice on the table and pulled a wok off the flames; started dishing stir-fry. Everyone gathered round. Stuart fetched a couple of wine bottles that had been breathing on the side. Bernie, Sean and I shook our heads. Water was fine. Jagger stayed at the breakfast bar.

'You've ID'd the *Reunited* person,' Elaine said when we were seated.

'A guy called Bill Scully. Lives in the East End. We're watching him now.'

'Do we know how he's connected to the photo?' asked Stuart.

'My guess: he's doing the footwork for whoever's behind it.'

'Has he been in contact with any family?'

'No. But whoever snapped your photo wasn't close to the girl's family. It was an opportunist thing. And Scully's peripheral to it all.'

'Christa,' Elaine said: 'The girl in the photo.'

I didn't take her up on it. 'We'll get to whoever took the photo,' I said. 'But worst case, you'd still be looking at handing over cash for whatever information he has.'

'The cash doesn't matter,' Stuart said, 'as long as it gets us to Christa.'

'That's ALL that matters,' Jagger affirmed. 'Getting the baby back. So we can put this tragedy behind us.'

The guy was spouting nonsense. If we found Christa safe then there'd *been* no tragedy. But Jagger had a good grasp on his rhetoric. "Tragedy" was his meal ticket and despite his proclamations he wasn't in a hurry to see that ticket expire.

The stir-fry was good. The chilled water was good. It took a while to clear our plates but Jagger was still hanging on when Stuart stood to clear up. Seemed he wasn't shifting until he'd heard what I'd come to say. In the end Stuart opened up the discussion.

'We're wondering why you asked about our *au pair*.'

'I'm wondering why you've never mentioned her in your book or your media pieces?'

'There was no reason to. Melanie had nothing to do with Christa's disappearance.'

'That's a big assumption.'

'No assumption at all,' Elaine said. 'She left us long before Christa was born. Never knew her. And we've had no contact since. She's irrelevant, Eddie. We've no right to invade her privacy.'

'Let's look at that,' I said. 'Your friend Olivia told me that she left only six or seven months before the birth. That's not so long.'

'I don't recall how many months it was,' Elaine said. 'But Melanie never met Christa.'

'She left under a cloud. What was that about?'

'She took some money,' Stuart said. 'We had to let her go. But that was two and a half years before Christa was taken.'

'Hey, Eddie,' Jagger said. 'What's with the inquisition? Who the hell's this Melanie? She something to do with the baby? Geddaway!'

I watched the Barbers. 'I need to see the whole picture,' I said. 'And that includes your family background – before and after Christa's disappearance.'

'Christa's abduction wasn't related to the family,' Stuart pointed out. 'A stranger took her.'

'We're keeping an open mind on that,' Shaughnessy said, 'until we've ruled out everybody remotely involved with you.'

'Including the two of us?' Elaine asked.

'Let's stay with Melanie,' I said. 'She was close to you for two years, then left with a grudge not long before Christa was born. I can't ignore that.'

'I see what you mean, but you're wasting your time.'

'And I heard that Melanie had emotional problems.'

'She'd had a difficult upbringing. She'd left home at sixteen.'

'Anything show in her behaviour?'

'We sensed that she had things bottled up,' Elaine said. 'She could be intense. Had this thing about ownership, even with her work. Once you'd given her a responsibility she clung on to it; didn't brook interference. And she could be moody sometimes.'

'Olivia used the word "unstable".'

'I think she misread the intensity of Melanie's moods. She only met her a couple of times.'

'So – no instability?'

'No. Just moods.'

'Where was her family home?'

'Southampton.'

'We didn't probe her background,' Stuart said. 'When we advertised for an *au pair* Melanie was the first person we interviewed. We liked her and made a judgement.'

'All you had was her friend's address in Camden?'

'We made a judgement,' Elaine repeated.

'And you had no contact after she left? No forwarding address?'

'She didn't leave any. I repeat: Melanie's not part of this.'

I finished my water and went to the sink for a refill.

'Melanie was with you when Grace died,' I noted.

The two were quiet for a moment.

'What's that got to do with it?' Stuart said.

'I assume Melanie looked after Grace?'

'That was her main duty.'

'Were you aware of Melanie's emotional problems at that time?'

Elaine pushed her wine glass away. 'Eddie, I don't know where you're going with this. What's your point?'

'No point. I'm just keeping an open mind on anyone involved with your family. Maybe a stranger did take Christa but the point is that we don't know it. And we won't get to Christa by closing our eyes.'

'But I still don't see the point in chasing Melanie. She was gone long before Christa's abduction.'

'The woman you saw the night Christa disappeared: you put her at about twenty. That would make her Melanie's age. No chance it was her?'

'Absolutely none. And it would hardly make sense that an *au pair* we'd not seen for two and a half years would take our daughter.'

I swigged water. Put my glass down. 'Fact is,' I said, 'the stranger-abduction theory bothers me. You were away from the caravan for just forty minutes and yet your Mystery Woman chanced to walk to the site, knew to select your caravan and happened to find an unlocked door with a child left alone inside. We're stretching probabilities with that scenario.'

'We assume she'd been watching us and just got lucky when she checked the caravan. But however it happened, it was a stranger.'

I let it go. Racked Melanie Brand up to the top of my talk-to list.

Stuart finished stacking the plates and lifted ice cream from the freezer. Shaughnessy and I passed. Bernie held out a pudding bowl. I left them to it and took a walk in the garden for a breath of air. The sun was on the horizon and the air tasted good. Then Jagger came out behind me.

His cream cotton suit flashed orange in the sunset. He'd ditched the tie and splayed his shirt collar. He walked across and lit up a Savannah to foul the atmosphere.

'Eddie,' he sighed, 'we need to take it easy.'

He waved the cigar. 'Elaine. Stuart. They've been through a lot.'

'What's the problem, Owen?'

'This inquisition stuff. It sounds like you're investigating *them*. How's that gonna get us to Christa?'

'I don't know. The family background might have nothing to do with what happened. When I confirm that I'll stop looking.'

'Am I understanding you? You' think that Stuart and Elaine brought this *au pair* girl into their family without checking her out? Made enemies of her? That she came back to take Christa? You think they caused it all?'

'I don't know what happened,' I said.

'Don't' you think Stuart and Elaine would know if this girl had been anywhere near them?' Jagger pulled the Savannah from his mouth and cocked his head.

'I'm looking at all possibilities,' I said. 'You see a problem with that, Owen?'

Jagger stabbed the Savannah back in his teeth. 'Not for me to say, Eddie. *They* hired you. But if it was me I'd tell you to keep your nose out.'

I gave him a grin with teeth of my own. 'Like you say, Owen. Not for you to say. Not for them, either, if they want Christa found.'

'Ah, *c'mon,'* Jagger said. He glanced over his shoulder and hunched forward. 'We know the search is a fool's errand. Christa's not gonna turn up. We all know that, for Chrissakes!'

'Not according to the book you're promoting.'

'Hey – Stuart and Elaine believe Christa's out there and God bless 'em! Must be hell what they're going through! But there's no reason the rest of us can't be objective. Stuart and Elaine are never going to give up but the rest of the world needs to stay with reality. Christa's gone and we all know it.'

186

'Let's find where the photo was taken. Then we'll have a better idea.'

'Jesus, Eddie! When you clear up the photo thing all we'll know for sure is that the girl in the picture *isn't* Christa. All your friggin' investigation will have done is steal their last hope. You'll take their money and hand them something that kills them.'

I smiled. More teeth. 'Are we into ethics, Owen? You don't like the idea of someone scrabbling for the Barbers' dosh? I can lend you a mirror if you want to debate that one.'

'Hey, I do what I do! I make a living! Ethics doesn't come into it any more than for a bus driver.'

'At least a bus driver gets you where you want to go.'

'You saying I've not got the Barbers anywhere? How do you think they made their money? How far do you think their story would have gone without *professional* help?'

'Maybe money isn't the point. Maybe they just want their child back.'

'And you think you're going to give them that? Don't make me laugh, Eddie.'

I walked back towards the house. I'd had enough of the Savannah's stink. But Jagger came after me.

'All this running around, digging up this Melanie character,' he said. 'Chasing after the Hoax Photo. All it's doing is muddying the waters. The Barbers need to concentrate on their campaign. Make the sales. I'm gonna talk to them. Tell them you need to pull back from the detective stuff and concentrate on keeping them safe.'

When we got to the door he shut up. I went in and nodded goodbye to Stuart and Elaine. Shaughnessy was ready for the off too. We left them to it and were just walking into the hallway when a crash sounded from a room up ahead. Glass breaking, the whump of something exploding, the smell of burning. I ran through and opened a door onto smoke and flames. A second later the sounds were repeated from the front drawing room and Shaughnessy and Bernie went tearing past. The house was under attack.

CHAPTER THIRTY-THREE
They didn't see or didn't care

Flames were spreading on the carpet below the smashed lights of a leaded window. A chair was burning. I jumped the flames. Hung my weight on a curtain. It came down in a spray of fittings. I flung it over the carpet and smothered the flames but the chair was going up a treat. Old. No retardant coating. Acrid fumes stung my eyes. I grabbed cushions and beat at it, yelled for backup. Stuart came in with a fire extinguisher. Chemical. I pulled the pin and attacked the chair. Then Shaughnessy was at my side, grabbing the extinguisher from me.

'I've got it!' he said.

I sprinted out of the front door towards the side gate – a twenty-yard detour versus vaulting the electric gates. The detour cost me five seconds on top of the thirty since the Molotovs came through the windows. When I hit the road I saw a figure sprinting and took off after him. There was still a chance unless the bastard's stamina was better than his getaway planning.

Turned out the getaway plan was better than it appeared. The guy needed stamina only for the hundred yards to where his car was parked on the verge, pointing east. He dived in and accelerated away while I was still fifty yards back. In the movies you keep running, stay on the car's bumper for a couple of miles until it finally sneaks ahead. I kept running but in the opposite direction. Back at the house the gates were swinging open and Shaughnessy was hoisting the Yamaha off its stand.

'Silver 911 cabriolet,' I yelled and Shaughnessy was gone.

The lump hammer that had punched through the leaded glass was abandoned on the gravel. The guy had swung it twice, smashed the lights in two windows and heaved the Molotovs in. Crude but effective.

Jagger scuttled out of the front door, Savannah askew, face a picture of wide-eyed schlock.

'This isn't supposed to happen, Eddie!' he yelled. 'This is what I was talking about! You're here to protect the family.'

I didn't have time. I ran back in. The house stank of burnt fabric. A vicious haze stung my eyes. Bernie had pulled the windows open and was laying damp sheets over the burned patches. The Molotov had been more successful in the front room due to the curtains catching. Scorch marks and smoke blackened half the ceiling and Bernie had used a water extinguisher which added to the mess. Elaine and Stuart were in there looking stunned.

'Christ,' Stuart said. 'If we'd not been home the house would have burned down.'

'Either they were unlucky or wanted you here,' I said. 'Maybe the aim was to make a point rather than raze the building.'

There'd been a few cases in the last decade of point-making through arson. Most of them had finished with dead bodies.

My phone chirped. Shaughnessy. Wind-torn voice.

'He got to the A1. Could have gone any way. I'm taking the Twenty-Five.'

'Got it.'

Jagger was still standing on the step as Bernie and I sprinted out. The Porsche had beaten Shaughnessy to the main road which opened a spaghetti-load of escape routes. When a quarry disappears in an unknown direction it's pretty much a losing deck, but sometimes you can get a result. We called it the "fan". You cover each route out from where you last had them. Drive a mile or two out. Look for witnesses – pedestrians, cyclists, parked-up drivers. If you get nothing you take the next route. It's a race against time. Potential witnesses are evaporating. If you're lucky you get a hit on your first or second guess and you've a new starting point. The fan kicks in again and you chase the routes from the new base. The thing depends on guesswork being more right than wrong because those witnesses are evaporating fast. With a little luck you stay in your quarry's slipstream, maybe get a sense of the direction they call home. Best case, the witnesses keep pointing the finger and you chase the quarry all the way there. The best result comes in about one in fifty times. So I'd heard: I'd never chased fifty getaway cars.

Bernie and I raced east out of Elstree. At least I did. Bernie's Land Rover had a top speed of about fifty. I left him in my rear-view and flicked the Frogeye past traffic, chasing Shaughnessy's wheels.

Shaughnessy had gone north at the roundabout to get onto the

M25. If the guy was our hate-mail source then our best indications were that he was from south of the Thames. A clockwise detour round the Orbital would get him there, clear of the city and its rush hour residue. But if you're looking over your shoulder you might go for the less obvious, disappear into the maze of routes that ran down through the city. I took the most likely, crossed the roundabout and drove east towards Barnet. Bernie would go south.

I put my foot down along a mile of lane that felt rural but had houses instead of fields behind the hedgerows. Ignored a turn that ran towards Bernie's territory. Slowed and hit traffic as the properties began to cluster into North London suburbia. I scanned the pavements, hit the brakes and pulled into a bus shelter under a leafy hedge. Two elderly women were waiting. The shelter was doing nothing to keep the setting sun off them and they were hot and vexed and hadn't spotted a sports car passing which might mean nothing. If the guy was thinking straight the Porsche would be moving sedately. Wouldn't catch the attention of pensioners whose bus is late. I hopped back in and drove on. Ignored unlikely turnings, roads going nowhere. Our guy wouldn't take them unless he knew the area. The houses got smaller, moved closer to the main road and down into the sub-two-million bracket. Closed in further until a cottage stood right on the road. A contractor's flatbed was parked on the pavement and a couple of guys were loading up. I stopped. Got a hit. They'd clocked the Porsche two minutes back. Our vigilante had headed into Barnet. We had a new base for the fan.

I made hands-free calls, pulled Shaughnessy and Bernie in towards my route. I'd take the main road out from the town. They'd backtrack the other options. Traffic thinned momentarily and I covered a deserted section at sixty, skidded round a complicated mini-roundabout and landed in a mess of roadworks on the main drag. I cursed and crawled the last quarter of a mile to the centre. If our quarry had come in this way he'd have been crawling too but if he'd taken another route I was losing time. The roadworks filtered me through a patchwork of business premises, churches and public buildings. No pedestrians about. I cleared the works and hit the high street. Turned south towards London.

A small crowd was pushing onto a bus up ahead but no-one was going to hold back to answer questions. I skipped past and drove towards the next stop where a middle aged couple were watching the bus approach. I pulled in. Got dirty looks. They were scared I'd divert the bus right past. I made it quick. Their answers were quicker. They either didn't see or didn't care or didn't know a Porsche from a Punto. I spotted two guys loafing outside a bookies a hundred yards on. Hit the gas. One of the loafers was definite that no Porsche had passed. The other wasn't sure. I sensed the route cooling. I put my foot down for one last leg. Passed the station, drove under the bridge. Found a taxi parked for a pick-up. The cabby said there'd been no Porsche and that settled it. I called the others. Shaughnessy was still backtracking into Barnet centre and Bernie was driving east along the North Circular to intercept the route in from East Finchley. I drove back to the centre and pulled over, flicked through my A-Z. Tried to picture it. Three main routes out from here. Mine had been a blank and Bernie and Shaughnessy were backtracking the others. Where was the guy?

Shaughnessy's Yamaha U-turned across the traffic and pulled up beside me on the double-yellows. He flicked up his visor. Shook his head.

All three routes nixed. The Porsche had evaporated. Maybe it had turned off into the side streets. If he knew the geography our arsonist would have a hundred ways to get off the main drag and sneak away, but why would he do that if there's no-one in his rear-view?

I studied the A-Z again. Thought about a guy hyped up, making quick decisions. Saw it. Yelled at Shaughnessy to follow and drove back the way I'd come in, through the roadworks. I crossed the mini-roundabout, continued for three hundred yards then U-turned and rolled back in. As I hit the roundabout this time I saw what our Porsche guy had seen: the road into the centre blocked by the mess of roadworks. Maybe the sight forced a quick decision. He'd steered left, diverted back towards the M25.

I doglegged the roundabout complex and followed the road half a mile through new housing and residential blocks with Shaughnessy tailing me. We passed a couple of lads standing round a Nissan outside a library. Shaughnessy peeled off to talk to them while I hit a junction two hundred yards on. I took the right and hit the road Shaughnessy had come in on, slowed, undecided, just as

Shaughnessy's call came through.

'We've got a hit. These guys clocked the Porsche.'

Turned out the boys had a reason to. They'd been picking up in front of the building when the Porsche came through fast, tried to squeeze between them and a bus and clipped their wing mirror. Neither boy had a number but they'd watched the Porsche turn left at the junction. I backtracked and Shaughnessy joined me to follow the road out.

We were heading back towards Elstree. The guy should have been moving the other way but maybe the scrape with the Nissan had unnerved him. I pulled over and checked the A-Z again. Saw it: if the guy was thinking half-straight he'd have corrected himself up ahead, taken a turning onto a road called Dancers Hill. The road paralleled the Orbital to the next junction. If he'd joined the Twenty-Five there the Porsche would have been swallowed in the traffic. Still, nothing lost by following.

I turned down Dancers Hill. The low sun threw the Yamaha's shadow ahead of me through a mile of unspoilt countryside alive with birdsong and Orbital hiss. We came out at a farmhouse and a cluster of houses and a place I knew: a tiny car showroom owned by Alfie Cotter, the vintage dealer who'd sold me my first Frogeye. I still dropped in from time to time to see what gems Alfie had on show behind his windows. All his stock was locked safely indoors but Alfie had cameras alongside the road, up on poles, a pair at each entrance. One of each pair was lined up along the road. I pulled over. The west-facing one was looking right into the sun so anything it had caught would be washed out, but the east-facing one might get us the Porsche's rear end, maybe a plate number. Alfie was closed up for the night but we'd squeeze him tomorrow for his CCTV recording.

I grinned up at Shaughnessy. His visor stared back but his head nodded. If Alfie's cameras had snapped a Porsche passing we'd have a plate number, and the Barbers' vigilante would have just lost his anonymity.

CHAPTER THIRTY-FOUR
Sue us if your disagree

I got to the office at eight thirty next morning. Lucy had the coffee on, the windows open and a cute smile for my new plan to combat the heat. I planted an electric fan on the drinks table by her desk. Ducked to find a socket.

'Wow, Eddie,' she said, 'you're a gentleman.'

I smiled back. Continued setting up. The reception area ran from front to rear, street window to washroom door. Shaughnessy's and my offices opened off to one side. If both our windows and doors were open the fan could get an airflow going via reception. I aligned the fan and switched it on and Lucy's face dropped. The blast wasn't going near her desk. I spotted a sneaky look; knew I'd have to watch her.

Shaughnessy and Harry came in.

We went through to their office. Lucy brought drinks through and settled on Shaughnessy's desk with an open tabloid.

'Well, Eddie, you said Hackett was about to spill the beans.'

'What's he got?'

'It's not good.'

I'd already figured that. She gave us the summary.

'They know who disposed of Christa's body.'

I raised my eyebrows. Harry slurped his tea. Shaughnessy sipped water.

'And apparently this same – quote-unquote – conspirator is still helping Stuart and Elaine. Hackett doesn't say what with.'

I felt the same unease I'd felt when Hackett made his promise at Blackfriars. At the time I'd put it down to the air in the place.

'Any names?'

'No. But he's thrown out a challenge. He says the Barbers killed Christa. He's inviting them to sue *The Nation* if they disagree.'

We'd sanitised Hackett's bugs but I guess the damage had already been done. He'd already fished out what he needed. And the real problem was that whatever he'd picked up from his eavesdropping was something the Barbers were keeping from us. Hackett was running rings round us whilst our clients played coy. Maybe we should have left his bugs in place. Listened in ourselves.

If some of the accusations against the Barbers were less than watertight it didn't hide the frays in their own story. We had witnesses who said they did it, witnesses who said they didn't, witnesses telling lies, people close to the family they'd forgotten to tell us about. And a guy baiting Stuart and Elaine over a photo he claimed was Christa. Not to mention the lunatic trying to burn their house down.

'We've been assuming that this vigilante is just a fruitcake,' Harry said. 'But maybe he's got something on the Barbers.'

'Yeah,' I said. 'Maybe he has.'

'I'll see what the CCTV picked up,' Shaughnessy said. 'The sooner we get the guy off the street the better.'

I looked at Lucy.

'You place the ad?'

'It ran yesterday,' she said. 'Do you think Scully will bite?'

Harry planted his teacup. 'If he does,' he said, 'I'll be on him.' He grabbed his keys. 'Let's see how the bastard spends his day.'

He went out.

I finished my coffee. Mopped my brow. Shaughnessy's room was stifling. The fan was making no difference.

CHAPTER THIRTY-FIVE
You bet she had a grudge

The Southampton YMCA was based in an old town house on the main road in. The building was decorated with a facade of latticed windows and an imposing entrance portico you could admire but not reach due to railings that channelled traffic straight past towards the city centre. I was forced almost to the parks before I managed to backtrack behind the place.

Melanie Brand's friend Davina had her staying at a hostel in the city after she left the Barbers. The YMCA was as good a place as any to start looking.

Inside, a receptionist with an eye patch and neck-tattoo confirmed that there was no Melanie Brand currently resident and declined to tell me whether there ever had been. My story about searching on behalf of a former employer – with the implication that there was a job waiting – didn't move him. YMCAs are not secretive but they protect records like any hotel. Maybe Melanie had stayed here, maybe not. The guy gave me a list of seven registered hostels in the area and wished me luck.

I bought a local A-Z and marked out a route. Covered two city-centre hostels on foot without result; retrieved the car for the wider tour. First stop, another YMCA west of the Common. Same result as the first: no Melanie Brand currently resident, no other info offered.

I followed the road out past the container port and over the river to a hostel called the Meadow Road on a street that had not seen a meadow for a century. The hostel was three houses knocked into one in a twenties terrace, fronted by a tiny garden with decorative street railings. Inside, a tiny cubbyhole served as a reception, *sans* receptionist. I opened a lounge door and found two women watching daytime TV. One was nursing an infant. The other told me to ring a bell. I did. Either the bell wasn't working or the receptionist's hearing was off because nobody came. I stood around for a couple of minutes before the woman I'd spoken to came out and offered to go and see. She was a blonde girl in her early twenties with a broad freckled face.

She returned with a stout woman called Marge who shook her head. No Melanie Brand resident. I asked if Melanie had ever lived here but Marge gave me the same answer as the YMCAs. The hostel didn't give out residents' information.

'I'm just looking for a contact address,' I explained.

'We don't release forwarding addresses unless the guest requests it,' she told me.

I asked if there was any way she could pass on a message but Marge explained that that wouldn't make sense unless she confirmed that Melanie had stayed there, which she wasn't at liberty to do. 'We try to be flexible,' she apologised, 'but some of our guests prefer to keep their circumstances quiet. Some are vulnerable.' She looked me over. 'Your best bet is to keep asking around. She may be in another hostel. If she's moved into private accommodation you won't find her.'

She was wrong. We'd find her. It would just take time. I still didn't know whether Melanie had anything to tell us but the grudge-thing said we needed to find out. The grudge suggested that if the girl knew any dark secrets about the Barbers she might be happy to talk.

I thanked Marge and headed out. Was about to drive off when the blonde girl came out onto the pavement and hesitated, hands jabbed into her shorts pockets. She was tall, looked good in denim. I killed the engine.

'Going into town?' she asked.

My A-Z was pointing me north but I could swing back to the centre without too much damage. I reached across and opened the door. It took her a while to get all her limbs in but eventually she figured it out. She strapped in and we drove out onto the bypass, back towards Southampton.

'Nice car.'

I grinned at her. Impractical cars. Impractical men. Irresistible.

'You were asking about Mel,' she said.

My thoughts snapped back.

I repeated my spiel about looking on behalf of a former employer.

The girl turned, elbow on the seat-back.

'What kind of employer?'

'A family. Four or five years back. Do you know Melanie?'

'I did. But the only family she ever worked for was the Barber family. And it can't be them looking for her.'

'Why not?'

'Because they threw her out. I doubt if they're offering her another job.'

I grinned; changed gear; skipped past a container truck.

'You've got me,' I said. 'I'm not here about a job offer.'

'So why are you looking for her?'

'It's a long story,' I said. 'My name's Eddie.'

'Louise. Why are you looking?'

I explained that I was looking into what had happened to Christa, and how the Barber family background might be relevant. Mentioned my chat with Melanie's friend Davina, the fact that Melanie had left the Barbers with a grudge – something Louise had just confirmed.

'You're investigating Christa? Do you think she's alive?'

I watched the traffic. 'Do you know where Melanie is?'

'No. I've not seen her for three years.'

'How well did you know her?'

'Pretty well. We met at the YM six years ago. Got to be good friends.'

'That was before she went to work for the Barbers?'

'Yes. She was only in the YM for two weeks but we kept in touch.'

'Where did she go?'

'London. Worked at a takeaway in Kensington but jacked that in when the guy started coming on to her. Then the Barbers took her on.'

'Where did she go when she left *them?*'

'Dunno. But she came down here one weekend and we had a night out. She talked about staying but then was off again.'

We crested a flyover in three lanes of heavy traffic. Gantry cranes worked the road-rail terminal off to our right. Louise had to yell above the din, one of the disadvantages of being roofless. Another disadvantage is that when the traffic stopped the aircon was off. And the sun was hot as hell. The traffic slowed, stalled and shifted. We filtered right towards the centre.

'When did you next see Melanie?'

'She came back in the spring of 2007. Stayed with us at the YMCA until May. Never got a job though. She had other things on her mind.'

'And after that?'

'London again. Then she reappeared a few months later but the YM was full. I wanted to get out of the dump anyway so we both got in at Meadow Road. Mel was there with me for the best part of a year. Picked up a few jobs.'

'That was three years ago? Where did she go after that?'

'She never told me. She went off one day and that was it. No contact address. No calls. I guess she'll get in touch in her own time.'

I glanced across. Saw pain. Began to sense a dead end. I tried another tack.

'Melanie was with the Barbers when they lost their first child. Did she ever talk about that?'

'Yeah. That shook her up. She was attached to that baby. She stayed on afterwards and helped Elaine to pull through.'

'So she got on with Elaine?'

'Yeah, until they threw her out.'

An artic was hogging the outside lane. I spotted a chance and danced left, skimmed past at wheel hub height. Reached clear air.

'I hear Melanie's temperamental,' I said. 'Plays around a little.'

Louise agreed. 'Mel can party with the best of them. We'd be out all night most weekends.'

'Drugs?'

'Nothing hard.'

'Staying out late must have clashed with her job at the Barbers if she chased that lifestyle there.'

'It did clash. Mel had nights off but I don't think they liked her staying out.'

'She played the boys?'

'She had fun. Nothing wrong with that.'

'Any relationships?'

'Plenty. They usually lasted a week. Sometimes just a night.'

'Would you say she was temperamental?'

She thought about it. 'She could be a bit off with people if they got on the wrong side of her. It never gave me any problem.'

'What kind of thing got on her wrong side?'

Louise shrugged. 'Mostly if she didn't get her own way. Or if the boys tried to get the upper hand. She'd had bad experiences when she was a kid.'

We slowed for lights by a glass complex near the old docks.

'Here's fine,' Louise said.

The lights changed. I turned off the main drag, found myself heading towards a multi storey. Swung round a mini-roundabout and pulled up on double yellows outside a striated shoebox that announced itself as a Premier Inn.

'Melanie had a grudge after the Barbers threw her out,' I said. 'Right?'

Louise fiddled with the door handle. 'You bet she had a grudge. After all she'd done for them.'

'Some problem with missing money?'

Louise gave up with the door and turned to look at me. Her face was silhouetted against the sky but for the first time anger came through.

'That's what they told you?'

I pulled my shades off.

'Was there something else?'

'Something else?' Louise laughed. 'Sure there was something else! The Barbers threw Mel out because she was pregnant.'

CHAPTER THIRTY-SIX
It's what I do

A million things went through my mind. Louise went back to fighting the door.

'Louise,' I said, 'I need more.'

She got the door open. Checked her watch.

'Gotta rush,' she said. 'I probably shouldn't have told you all this. I'm not sure I want people chasing Mel, especially the Barbers.'

I killed the engine.

'Sure, I'm working for the Barbers,' I said, 'but they're not chasing Melanie. I am. I want to hear her views on the family. And I'll find her. It's what I do. But if you have something that would speed things up I'm keen to hear it. So here's the deal: when I catch up with her I'll drop you a line. Then it will be up to the two of you whether you get together. Help me out, Louise.'

She extracted herself; turned and sat on the wing. Looked down at me.

'I don't know what else there is.'

'Just give me a couple of minutes. Tell me about Melanie getting pregnant.'

Louise twisted. Stretched her arm along the windscreen.

'I'd guess it was the usual thing,' she said.

'She didn't say who?'

'I doubt if she knew. Just a one-night-stand gone wrong. Mel didn't realise until she was two or three months gone. But she decided she'd better inform the Barbers. Big mistake. They threw her out.'

'Did she consider terminating the pregnancy?'

'Sure. She was hot and cold the whole time. One moment she'd be scared to death about what was happening, wanted it to go away, the next she was talking about how a kid might work out. In the end she went back to London to stay with friends. Tell the truth, I was glad to see her go, let someone else deal with that shit.'

'But she came back in the middle of the next year. Did she have her child with her?'

Louise shook her head. 'She'd had a miscarriage. After all that worrying. Maybe the stress did it. Perhaps her body followed her real wishes.'

'How did she react to losing the child?'

'She was down. I don't know if it was because she'd lost the baby or just the shock of seeing where her lifestyle was taking her. She was back clubbing, playing the field but she wasn't the same.'

Two youths sauntered past, caps-backward, pants sagging. One of them threw a wolf-whistle. Louise held her hand high, gave them the bird.

'What did you know about Melanie's family?'

'Just the bits she told me. And based on those I wouldn't want to know them. They live on the Barton Estate over the river.'

She stretched further along the windscreen. 'The estate's a dump, mister. And Mel's family fitted right in. A dysfunctional case study. Mel's mum was an alcoholic, and her stepfather and -brother were evil sods. The stepfather liked to slap her mum about after he'd had a few. Later on he found a better hobby with Mel herself. She told me the bastard was abusing her before she was ten years old. And by the time she was twelve his son had joined in – a piece of dirt called Craig. Fifteen years old. Mel had nowhere to hide. She had an older stepsister – Craig's twin – who tried to protect her but I don't think she could. And the stepsister pissed off as soon as she turned sixteen so Mel was on her own for three years. You could see where some of her attitude came from – the way she played the boys then left them high and dry. I tried to steer her away from it, but she couldn't throw off those years of abuse. Made me shudder. While the rest of us were out with our mates after school Mel was in a room with her stepfather or Craig.'

'Her mother didn't intervene?'

'She couldn't. Her husband would have just given her a slapping. From what Mel told me her mum just retreated to the pub next door to spend her social. Ignored what was happening back in the house.'

The story was familiar. My Met job had taken me to a dozen scenes where the ultimate detritus of dysfunctional families was lying cold on a floor. And for every cold body there were a hundred still walking but dead inside.

Louise's detail was bringing the Barbers' *au pair* into focus but whether any of it was relevant to Christa's disappearance I didn't know. Only Melanie could tell me that. I promised Louise that I'd put her in touch if I found her friend. She shrugged. Pushed herself off the car. Walked away.

CHAPTER THIRTY-SEVEN
Celeb job. Big money

Back in Paddington I grabbed a table outside Connie's. He came out double-quick, wiping his hands.

'Eddie!' he yelled. 'What I get you?'

'What's on?'

'Special – Lamb kofte on pitta.'

'Sounds good.'

'Is *very* good! I see you in paper, Eddie. Make Chase Street proud. Hobnobbing the celebs.'

'Just a job, Connie,' I said.

'But *celeb* job! Big money!'

I looked at him. Saw where this was going. The bastard was after his arrears.

'Plenty big, Connie,' I said. 'It's a fine job. Very profitable.'

His face lit up.

'So now we get square up,' he said. 'The slate is wipe clean.' He threw his arms wide in a gesture grand enough to clear the national debt.

'You're top of the list, Connie. I'll send Lucy round next week.'

He gave me a contented sigh and urged a glass of wine to celebrate his new-found prosperity. I stayed with mineral water but doubled up on the kofte, and Connie went away to rack up the tab by another twenty-three quid.

The koftes came. They were good. I took my time, shaded by the umbrella, watched people pass. A few were heading for our building, though they weren't looking for private investigators. Seemed our litigation friends were doing a roaring trade. Their corporal punishment commercials were going out every hour on the London stations and the money-tap was running. Or maybe today's crowd were sunstroke victims. Rook and Lye were just the people to find a culprit. If the heatwave persisted, God had better get a lawyer and he'd better be good.

My phone rang.

Harry.

'Scully's just read the *Standard*.'

'Any reaction?'

'Zilch. The guy's sticking to his routine. We're in the bookies.'

'Stay on him. He'll talk to someone.'

I was confident about that. Lucy's ad was designed to jiggle the carrot *hard* and make it clear that the opportunity had a limited shelf life:

REUNITED

Please expedite.
Can't hold assets.
Final opportunity to complete.

The assets we were talking about were two hundred grand. That sort of carrot would help most people focus.

I finished my lunch and walked up to the building with my gut busting from my greed. Pushed past Rook and Lye's overflow in the vestibule – a problem Eagle Eye never faced. Upstairs, Shaughnessy was perched on Lucy's desk, flipping through paperwork. He looked up

'We've got our vigilante,' he said. 'The Porsche drove out through Dancers Hill like you figured.'

My dealer friend had been happy to let Sean trawl through the recordings. He handed me two CCTV prints. The first was from the camera pointing into the sun and was a burned out glare. The other was from the camera looking the other way and was a perfect shot of an empty road. Shaughnessy grinned.

'There's something that might be a small car coming out of the sun on the first camera,' he said, 'but the timing was out on the second one. The cameras record at a quarter hertz. The vehicle raced right past us.'

He touched a distant dot in the second picture that might have been a Porsche or might have been a horse. But it was the washed-out frame had caught Shaughnessy's eye.

'It's the right time and the car's small,' he said. 'Moving fast enough to beat the second camera. And when we enhance it we get the first five characters of the plate.'

He handed me another sheet. The enhanced car was still just a shape but the plate's first five characters were readable. Five were enough.

'Is Roger on it?' We were squeezing our DVLA contact hard this week.

'Already done,' Shaughnessy said. 'He ran a training demo. Pulled up twenty matching plates and guess how many were silver Porsches?'

I guessed.

'One vehicle,' Shaughnessy confirmed. 'Registered to a guy named Paul Tyndall. Address on Dartford Marshes.'

Interesting. Dartford would tie in with the eastern border of our hate-mail postal area.

'He's our vigilante,' Shaughnessy said.

I looked at the car streaking towards us from the arson attack. If Shaughnessy was right this was the guy who'd had the Barbers looking over their shoulders for the last year. We'd expected a long slog to get to him but he'd given himself away with the clumsy attack. The tide was about to turn for our vigilante friend.

'I'll head over. Take a look,' Shaughnessy said. He left us to it and went out.

~~~~~

Lucy had some paperwork of her own: she'd done a trawl through the Barber history, looking at dates, extrapolating missing ones. She handed me an A4 summary and headed out to her afternoon job.

I took the stuff through to my office along with the electric fan. Fished out my desktop flipchart and sketched in Lucy's dates; added what I'd picked up on Melanie Brand.

Then I sat down and looked at what I had. The flipchart flapped in the fan blast. I went backwards and forwards through the timeline: Melanie joining the Barbers to look after their first child; staying on after the infant died, helping Elaine get her life back together; a year later, pregnant, thrown out of the Barber house seven months before the birth of their own second child, Christa; Melanie living briefly in Southampton then dropping out of sight before returning to Southampton, childless, unstable, bitter; fading finally into the unknown a year before Christa Barber disappeared. I needed to know about that year. I needed to talk to Melanie.

I switched off the fan and let the flipchart settle. Locked up. Headed back to Battersea.

~~~~~

I had a couple of hours to kill. I filled a water jug and went up to the attic to work on my Abney Park painting, attacked the composition with deft touches that barely stayed ahead of my nerve and got the Rousseau tone down to a more derelict impression that finally caught what I'd felt when I visited the cemetery last year. At seven thirty I stood back. The next touch would make or break the thing. Something was still missing but I didn't know what. I showered and went to collect Arabel.

We had seats waiting at Scott Ronnie's – Arabel's mixed-up name for the place – and ate expensive chicken salads in the dark, listening to a five-piece ensemble doing some kind of 70's jazz-funk revival. Talking is tricky at Scott's. I shifted my chair. Got closer to Arabel. She was wearing a lime mini dress that defied the gloom and hinted at long legs. She figured I was getting fresh; leaned against me. I pressed in, got to her ear.

'Your St Mungo's friends,' I said, 'I guess they've got contacts?'

Arabel un-leaned. Her eyes flashed.

'What are you after, Flynn?'

'You know I wouldn't ask...' I said.

She waited.

'The Barbers' *au pair*. I need to talk to her.'

Arabel watched me, trying to figure where this was going. I explained what I'd found. Gave her the picture of an unstable and rootless young woman drifting across the south between no places she called home. 'Last known location was the Meadow Road hostel in Southampton. I need to know where she went after that.'

'You dragging me into this?'

'I'm thinking someone at St Mungo's might talk to the Meadow Road people. They'd probably give you the information if you explained.'

'Explained what?'

'How Melanie might be vulnerable. That we need to talk to her. That's pretty close to the truth.'

'Not close enough. It wouldn't be me talking to her. And you don't know that she needs help.'

'Who talks to her is not the issue. Melanie's been running all her life. And her time with the Barbers didn't work out well. I think it would be good for her to tell her side of that story. The Meadow Road could put me in touch with her.'

'Maybe. If that was your real purpose. But you want to find out if Melanie is linked to Christa's disappearance. That's not the same.'

I held up my hands. 'Whoa, 'Bel. That's getting ahead. I just want to talk to her about Stuart and Elaine. And if there's something bad in there it might be the chance for her to draw a line under things. I'd put her back in touch with her friend, at least.'

Arabel shook her head. 'I don't know, Flynn. I don't think we could say it was all in Melanie's interest. There's privileges and responsibilities our organisations share, people to protect. I don't want to cross a line. I know you need to talk to this girl, and I know you'd try to help her. But I'm not sure you should be asking me to be part of it.'

'Think about it, 'Bel,' I said. 'Whatever you decide is fine. But you should trust me.'

'I will think about it,' she agreed. 'And I do trust you. More than you do.'

~~~~~

By the time we got in I was dead on my feet. I crashed on the bed whilst Arabel showered. Went out like a light. Came to with the pressure of her straddling me. She was barely a shadow but the heat from her body told me she was there. I sensed her leaning towards me, her face floating above mine.

I reached up but she grabbed my wrists, held them away.

'I've got a friend,' she said. 'She's involved with a couple of women's refuges here in town. The Meadow Road would talk to her.'

I tried to close my hands on her hips to convey my gratitude but her grip tightened.

'I'm taking you on trust, Flynn,' she said. 'This had better work out for Melanie or I'm not gonna be happy.'

'I'm just going to have a chat with her,' I insisted. 'If she tells me to take a hike then that's the end of it. If she's hiding I won't blow her cover.'

The last thing I wanted was to threaten Melanie Brand. Everything we knew told us that life had already dished enough poison onto this girl's plate.

Of course, there was a possibility that Melanie *was* involved in Christa's disappearance, in which case it wasn't so clear whose interests would be uppermost. But I didn't mention that.

CHAPTER THIRTY-EIGHT
The trick is not to ask

Arabel got back to me mid morning.

'My friend talked to Meadow Road.'

'They have an address?'

She hesitated. I pressed the ear plug.

'Flynn, this had better not hurt Melanie.'

'Bel,' I said, 'I don't know how she fits in but if I talk to her I'll try to help. Nothing goes further unless she agrees.'

Assuming she was an innocent party. If Melanie was involved in Christa's disappearance then our talk would be a long one.

'Okay, Flynn, you've had your warning. Here's the address.'

~~~~~

Arabel's information took me to a council estate near Eastleigh, north of Southampton. I exited the motorway and followed my A-Z into a grey-brick housing development served by blanched tarmac avenues pitted with potholes. I parked outside a semi on the crest of a rise and climbed steps through a sloping front garden. Kids' voices yelled from behind the house. I rang the bell and watched the street. Deserted. The only sign of life was a car twenty yards up, bonnet raised, radio blaring, no-one tinkering. The asthmatic breath of the motorway drifted across the fields. The estate looked beaten by the heat.

I turned to face a woman who'd opened the door. Mid thirties, housework clothes, rubber bands in her hair. Talk-radio played behind her. She was too old to be Melanie. I asked if she knew anyone by that name.

She shook her head. Wondered if I had the right address. 'She moved here three years ago,' I told her.

'That was before me,' the woman said. 'I've been in two years.'

'Any idea who the previous tenants were?'

'Never met them. I just got this place when the council list came up.'

Not good news. Squeezing Melanie's details from a council database was not going to be easy. Then the woman's face brightened. 'Just a sec,' she said. She disappeared back into the house. The radio jabbered on. The sun burned my neck. When the woman reappeared she handed me a slip of paper.

'I'd forgotten I had it. The last tenants left a mail-forwarding address but nothing ever turned up.'

I looked at the paper. A surname: Duggan. Forwarding address in Chatham, Kent. Maybe Duggan was a friend of Melanie's. I smiled my thanks. Trawled for more.

'How about your neighbours? Were they here back then?'

'Maureen was.' The woman tilted her head towards the adjoining semi. 'The other side are new.'

I thanked her again and said I'd call next door, but she stopped me.

'Maureen had a fall,' she said. 'She's in a nursing home.'

'That's tricky,' I said. I looked at the slip of paper again. 'I really could do with talking to someone who knew Melanie. Do you think Maureen would remember?'

'They were neighbours,' she said. 'I suppose she would.'

I waited. The trick is not to ask. Ask nosy questions and you get a brush-off. Tell them you've a problem and they'll help you solve it.

'If you want to give it a try,' the woman said, 'she's in the Oakdeane.'

She gave me directions and a smile that knocked a decade off her face. 'I don't know how co-operative she'll be,' she said.

'Is she ill? Confused?'

Her smile now could be mistaken for mischief.

'I saw her last week. Her faculties were as good as ever.'

Then she clamped her mouth. I thanked her.

'Like the car,' she said. She seemed the good type so I took her down the steps and gave her a tour. Pointed out the little idiosyncrasies that make the Sprite so interesting to drive – the ones that wouldn't pass modern regulations. She particularly liked the boot that didn't open.

'Structural integrity,' I informed her. 'The boot's part of the body shell. Needs the strength, since there's no real chassis. It was also cheaper to manufacture that way, like with the door handles.'

210

She looked. Saw there weren't any. Laughed in amazement.

'I never knew they had remote locking in the fifties!' she said.

I grinned and reached down to operate the remote locking. Jumped in.

'Life was simpler then,' I said.

I tooted the horn and left her smiling.

~~~~~

The Oakdeane Nursing Home was back in Eastleigh. A uniformed orderly met me and confirmed that Maureen was a resident. He said she'd be delighted to see her nephew. Not today, though: she'd just finished lunch and had settled in for her afternoon nap which usually lasted three hours. I told him I'd be back; asked how my aunt was.

He smiled. 'The same as always, sir.' We grinned at each other like I knew what the hell he was talking about and I let myself out through the security door and headed for Chatham.

The mail-forwarding address was a cul-de-sac off a dual carriageway near the town centre. A terrace of flaking two-up-two-downs ran fifty yards up one side of the street to where a detached house stood for sale in a leftover space beneath a railway embankment. The building broadcast neglect. Cracked walls, flaking window frames, moss-covered roof, rampant vegetation that had crumbled the tarmac'd front garden and sealed the garage doors. Even the estate agent's board sprouting from a pile of refuse bags was rotting.

A bloke appeared in the end-of-terrace doorway, fag in hand. He watched as I parked. I called across to ask if the house was tenanted. He returned a stare and a stream of smoke.

I walked over and rang the door bell. No answer. I walked round to the back. A rear garden, waist-high in weeds, the vegetation broken only by an abandoned clothes carousel at its centre and a greenhouse leaning drunkenly against the railway fence. The place was going to need a little creativity for the estate agent's listing. I pushed across to the garage but found no way back to the street: the gap between the garage and house was barely two feet and was jammed with bin bags and a discarded mattress and a mess of coloured plastic like a kid's inflatable pool. I walked the long way back. Pushed open the letter box. Three envelopes on the floor inside. If the place was empty you'd expect either a heap or nothing. I returned to the car. Neighbourhood Watch was still in his doorway, observing me with the superiority of the idle. I made a three-point turn and drove out.

~~~~~

Back at Paddington the office was deserted. I grabbed a cup of water from Shaughnessy's cooler and went into my office. Set the fan to max. Swivelled my chair and got my feet onto the windowsill. Watched the Westway. On the far side, up on the tower block, the semaphore guy was back. His flag drifted languidly from side to side signalling something. I watched for a while and wondered whether the Barbers' *au pair* was relevant to our search. Came to no conclusion.

The outer door opened and Harry came through. He looked like he'd been jogging in a sauna. His shirt was sticking and his hair was plastered. He subsided into one of my club chairs with a sigh and stretched his legs way out; clasped his hands over his belly.

'Scully made his move,' he said.

I swigged water. Waited.

'The guy's like a rat in a maze.'

'Where did the maze end up?'

Harry grinned across. 'You're gonna love this, Eddie.'

Thought so.

'The bastard took the number seven bus. Got off on Du Cane Road. That's as far as I could follow without a pass.'

I put the water down.

Harry stretched his toes. 'Yeah,' he said, 'Scully's talking to someone in The Scrubs.'

Harry's smile was the one investigators use when things go the way they expect. The smile on mine was one of disbelief.

'Someone in Wormwood Scrubs is behind the Photo?'

Harry was watching his feet. I turned back to the window. The flag guy had disappeared. Just an empty balcony. Maybe he'd been trying to warn me. I picked up my cup and went out for a refill. Came back and leaned against the roll-top.

'That's a whole different thing,' I said.

'Different for sure,' Harry said. 'Who the hell's Scully talking to in jail?'

That one I could maybe answer. I grabbed the phone. Made a call and spoke to a receptionist; deflected refusals and assured her that her boss would be okay to talk to me. I repeated my name and she put me on hold. Ten seconds later the line was picked up.

'Eddie! How are you?'

'Great, Charlie. How's the lumbago?'

'How long have you got?'

'Question withdrawn. I'm due home tonight.'

There was a long laugh from the other end. I hit speakerphone and it rattled round the room. 'Charlie, I've got Harry Green here.'

'Harry? How is the old sod?'

'Still wearing those jackets.'

The laugh repeated. Harry's smile stayed.

'I need a favour,' I said.

'Well I knew damn well you weren't interested in my health, Eddie. What's up?'

'You got a visitor this morning. Name of Bill Scully. It would be useful to know whose name was on his VO.'

'Good as done. Let me get back.'

I killed the call. Flopped into the Miller. If anyone could tell me whom Scully had visited at The Scrubs it was the prison governor.

Charlie Stuart had once held the same post at Whitemoor which had the reputation back then as the toughest Cat. A in Britain. Our paths crossed when I was in the Met, chasing a two-man hit team working for a South London gang, and accidentally stumbled into a situation. I'd followed the villains way off territory to Hatfield where I spotted them forcing their way into a house, grabbing the woman who'd opened the door. I laid low and put in a few calls. Discovered I was in the middle of a caper to spring the gang's top man from Whitemoor. The woman and kids at the house turned out to be the prison governor's family. Charlie was sweating behind his desk up at the jail faced with the choice between letting a dangerous criminal loose or losing his family. No choice, really, and the villains' clockwork schedule was tight enough to make sure the thing would have come off – if it wasn't for a Met detective camped by chance right outside Charlie's house.

The Whitemoor staff already had the villain out on the football pitch watching a helicopter touch down when Charlie got the call to say that his family were safe. The call was routed from my mobile. I was inside his house trying to calm a terrified woman and kids, with their two assailants sprawled on the kitchen floor.

My call messed up the villain's travel arrangements. The helicopter never got back off the ground and our disappointed vacationer was escorted back to his cell and another ten years scanning the travel brochures.

Charlie Stuart called in to see me three months later. Not about the thwarted jailbreak. What mattered to Charlie was what we'd found out later – a detail he'd never told his wife. Once the villain was up in the air things were scheduled to take a nasty turn – because his thugs had been briefed to kill Charlie's wife and kids to make a point.

Charlie moved closer to home after that. Took a posting at The Scrubs. Whenever Met business put me inside his walls I called in for coffee. Charlie's increasingly protracted lumbago stories weren't to be taken lightly but I knew that if I ever ended up behind bars myself Charlie would see me right. I'd be in a cell with my own Jacuzzi and cricket nets. He'd lent me a hand a couple of times while I was still in the job but this was the first outside favour I'd asked. The phone rang five minutes after I'd rung off. Seemed favours were still on the plate.

'Care to tell me what this is about?' Charlie said.

'Better later,' I said, 'when I know.'

'Fine. But I'm intrigued. Because I've got Scully on a VO for an old friend of yours.'

This was a figure of speech. I had no friends in Wormwood Scrubs. When Charlie got me that Jacuzzi he'd also need to put in a private army so I could sleep at night.

'Who is it?' I asked.

'Hayes.'

I sat up.

'Yeah,' Charlie said. 'Hammer Hayes. One of our finest. Anything else you need?'

'A refresher,' I said. 'I didn't know Richard was back inside.'

I'd helped send Hayes down nine years ago for GBH. He should have been out by now assuming he'd behaved himself. But I guess his good behaviour didn't follow him to the outside world.

'He was sent back down a year ago,' Charlie said. 'You want me to send the full facts and figures?'

I gave him my email and he promised me the info by morning.

I planted my phone on the desk. Harry was watching me.

I sat back. Racked the Miller to thirty degrees. Put Harry in the picture. Hayes was one of the Dean gang that had once crossed swords with the Richardsons themselves and nowadays had pretty much a free run south of the Thames. Hayes was Marcus Dean's enforcer. His job was to keep people in order or put them permanently out of business. His speciality was his artistry with the instrument that got him his moniker. When we raided his house in '01 we found a display cabinet with twenty-three hammers on show, ranging from lumps to ball-peens. Word was that the tools made it into the cabinet only once they'd proven their worth. You looked through the glass and saw twenty-three broken or dead bodies. The most frightening item in there was a little pin-hammer. The thing weighed about two ounces, a kiddie's toy amongst the ten kilogram lumps. The thing had your imagination running riot trying to figure how it earned its place. It was something we never found out.

What we did find out was enough to send Hayes down for eight years. We linked him to attacks on two witnesses who'd been scheduled to testify against Marcus Dean. One of the wits was dead, the other in intensive care. In the end we couldn't tie Hayes to the killing but the intensive care guy's DNA was in the rubber grip of one of Hayes' claw hammers. Seemed Hayes had got careless with his cleaning.

I was out of the force soon after that, and losing contact with the likes of Hayes was one of the plusses of my early retirement. Now, out of the blue, here he was, somehow connected with the Barbers, and it made no sense at all. Hayes operated in a different world from our clients. How the hell was he linked to Christa's disappearance?

~~~~~

Shaughnessy came in. We heard his inkjet spitting and two minutes later he slid a photo onto my roll-top. A man I didn't know with a woman I didn't know standing outside a house I didn't know.

Shaughnessy flopped into the chair next to Harry.

'Tyndall,' he said.

The Porsche driver who'd torched the Barbers' house.

'That's his bolt-hole on Dartford Marshes. The middle of nowhere. The guy owns a bodyshop on the industrial park over the river.'

'Who's the woman?'

'Girlfriend or wife, I guess. I'll keep digging.'

I looked at the photo. Tyndall didn't look the type to write letters but he did look the type to torch your house. His face had a cast that fitted the vigilante role nicely. Maybe the pair of them were in on it. Was the woman the writer? He the enforcer?

And who the hell were they?

216

CHAPTER FORTY

The girl with the jet black hair

I picked up a sandwich at Connie's then drove back to Chatham; parked a couple of streets away and crossed an overgrown recreation area that bordered the cul-de-sac. Found cover beside a storage hut opposite the end house. The street was deserted. I ate my sandwich and waited.

Getting to the vigilante was good. If we could confirm that the couple were just random nutcases then that side of the job could be wrapped up. They'd be out of business and talking to the police by next week. And if they weren't random, if there was a reason they were chasing the Barbers, we'd soon know it. My interest now was this house.

The cul-de-sac stayed quiet as time crawled through mid afternoon. Trains clattered on the embankment. A dog ran across the street. Then a kid came up from the main road, kicking a can. He was seven or eight years old, grey flannel shorts, shirt askew, rucksack dragging behind. He walked head-down, concentrating on his footwork. When he reached the end house he booted the can into touch and pushed himself up onto the low wall; sat kicking his heels in the sun.

Fifteen minutes later another group came up. A woman and two girls. One was a toddler, two years old, the other was maybe four, chattering as she skipped and pirouetted around them. I grabbed my Leica and snapped telephotos. The woman was in her late twenties, shortish, straw hair unkempt from a heavy day. They turned into the end house and the boy slid from the wall and followed them in.

Two minutes later the kids were out from round the back of the building. The boy and older girl messed about and batted each other with plastic swords until they fell out and reverted to insults. The toddler strung along for a while then found alternative distraction under a rubbish-strewn bush.

The woman was too old to be Melanie. So maybe she was Duggan, the name on the forwarding address. Maybe Melanie had been her friend or lodger back at Eastleigh. If so, had she moved here with the woman or gone her separate way? I magnified my snaps; looked at the four-year-old. Searched for anything recognisable in her features. Came to no conclusion. The boy and toddler had their mother's blond hair. The girl had a jet black mane, almost unnaturally dark.

I waited by the shed as the rush hour cranked up on the main road. The kids played around the house, oblivious to traffic, trains and private investigators. Just before six they were called in for tea. No sign of anyone returning from work or anyone else living in the house. A woman and dog were wandering my way so I walked back through the recreation area to a spot on the main road. Watched the cul-de-sac for another hour in dust and fumes. Only three people walked up the street. None went to the end house.

The sun had dropped behind the roofs but the temperature was still way up and I was out of water. I hung on for one last hour but didn't spot any father figure arriving home, and no sign of anyone who might be Melanie. The two kids came back out to play in the distance until their mother called them in at eight. I watched the girl with the jet black hair chase after her brother and disappear.

I walked to the car and headed back to London.

CHAPTER FORTY-ONE
The chainsaw's throwing teeth

I was back in the Chatham cul-de-sac early next morning. Watched
the house for two hours without any sign of a young woman heading
out for work or returning from night shift. Nothing to suggest that
Melanie was living there. At eight fifteen the family came out and I
followed their early morning routine. The woman despatched the
kids to school and nursery then took the bus to a waitressing job in
the town centre. The family were so ordinary you'd never see them. I
resisted the urge to jump to conclusions about the four-year-old. I'd
come here looking for Melanie, not Christa. There were plenty of
four-year-olds, and plenty with the blonde hair that would match the
Barbers' daughter, unlike this girl's jet black locks. I couldn't shake
the impression that there was a passing resemblance to Christa but
was it anything more than that?

I walked to the river. Leaned on the railings and watched the tide
running. Called Harry and got him digging through the Land
Registry records for the house owner. If he was a landlord maybe
he'd know something about his tenants. Harry said he'd take a look.
Following Scully wasn't going to deliver anything further.

I agreed. Time to drop Scully and concentrate on Tyndall and the
woman.

I called Shaughnessy. He was outside Tyndall's bodyshop by
Dartford Marshes.

'I've dug around,' he said. 'The guy's got a history: busts for
fencing and dealing. Small-time stuff, but he's been at it since he was
a kid. I'm guessing the bodyshop isn't entirely legit. There's nothing
that links him to Stuart and Elaine, though. And nothing to suggest
he's the vigilante type. The guy's just a down-at-heel hustler.'

'The driving force could be the woman.'

'That's my guess. She's next on my list.'

'Let's keep Tyndall in our sights. Make sure he doesn't get near
Stuart and Elaine.'

'Got it.'

I filled Sean in on my Chatham family, the possible link to the

Barbers' *au pair*. He asked about the four-year-old.

'She's the right age,' I agreed. 'But the black hair's odd. Doesn't match Christa's but doesn't match the woman's or the other kids' either. We need to know more before we can rule them out.'

I rang off; got an incoming call.

A Met detective called Zach Finch.

'You get that jacket cleaned?' he said.

Zach was my old buddy from the job. He'd been in the force since they chucked him out of school and was still a detective sergeant by virtue of three decades of declined promotion offers. Every murder I'd cleared I'd had Zach at my shoulder. I almost had him at my shoulder too when my career jumped the rails. Zach had been a raging bull, all set to throw in the towel himself and grab early retirement. I talked him out of it; painted a picture of life behind a shopping trolley, tailing his wife through Tesco's. Zach reconsidered. Stayed in the job. We still helped each other out occasionally. Seemed Zach had been reading the papers.

'My jacket's in the cleaners,' I said.

'Egg and flour are hell,' he warned. 'Lucky it wasn't paint.'

'That's how I felt when the stuff hit me.'

A rasping wheeze came down the line. I waited before making my pitch.

'I need an update on a villain.'

I'd have Charlie Stuart's e-mail later this morning, but Zach could give me an up-front on Hammer Hayes' recent activities. He made surprised sounds when I mentioned the name.

'The bastard's inside, where he belongs,' Zach said. 'All The Hammer's collecting now is plastic cutlery.'

'That's what I heard. How'd it go down?'

I heard a rattle like a chainsaw throwing teeth.

'Beautifully. It was Andy Morecroft's from Seven. Hayes was up on extortion and GBH. He'd knocked over a club in Bermondsey who'd declined the Deans' protection. Put its owner in a coma. But he made the mistake of going in right after closing time so there were three witnesses. Club staff. Hayes duly nobbled them, leaving Andy with only circumstantial evidence and Hayes figured he was in a turkey shoot. A walk-in-walk-out trial. What he didn't know was that one of the wits was a grass of Andy's. Andy gave the guy a choice:

take the stand against Hayes and disappear safely or have us leak the fact that he'd been talking to us for years. The wit decided that co-operation was the better health option.' Zach laughed. 'Hayes never saw it coming. Turned up at court with a smile and a wave. Went out in cuffs.'

'This was a year ago?'

'May last year. Went down for five. Don't tell me you've got him mixed up with the Barbers.'

'It's looking that way.' I explained about the Christa Photo. How the classifieds ads communication had dried up in May last year. An unexpected trip to jail might explain that. Perhaps Hayes' scheme was forcibly put on hold. But the thought of missing the jackpot must have eaten away at him during those long nights in the cells: maybe he'd made arrangements to take the thing forward. Maybe the resumed *Reunited* ads were his.

'You think he knows where the kid is?' Zach asked.

'Hell if I know. But seeing Hayes linked to the photo doesn't give me a good feeling.'

Zach went quiet a moment.

'You think the kid's dead?'

I went quiet too.

'I'll have a better idea when I find out what's behind the photo,' I said. I promised Zach we'd get together and hung up.

Zach's information gelled with Hayes being the source of the Christa Photo, which wasn't good news. The criminal element increased the odds that the photo was a money-grabbing scam, a dead end. And the Barbers might be willing to risk two hundred K on the photo but I didn't like the idea of finishing up high and dry after the payoff. I needed to get a sense of whether the photo was Christa before any cash changed hands.

I thought about it.

Opted for legal advice.

CHAPTER FORTY-TWO
Legal bloom

London's a lawyers' town. From the heights of its glass towers to its gold-flecked pavements and the limitless opportunities of its derelict corners, wherever greed makes its home, litigation tags along. Few areas of human endeavour deny their lawyers' cut but big finance and rampant cash forge the honey-pot of them all.

If enterprise is the city's mind then litigation is its lifeblood, and its heart is the legal army that toils ceaselessly on behalf of the denizens, helping them grab and keep and hide vast quantities of cash. And always, with every heartbeat, a percentage haemorrhages.

Law envelopes the city like stratified fog. Bespoke-tailored lawyers sit at attention in City boardrooms; bewigged QCs confer in law court chambers; shabby, beat-down solicitors wear out the steps of the magistrates' courts and down on the streets legal shops bloom as litigation fever spreads like super-resilient MRSA, oiled by endless TV ads and Yellow Page saturation.

In the lowest layer of all, deep and shadowed, organised crime is the paymaster and opportunity truly soars. Far below the radar, doors on unfashionable streets conceal sharp-suited vultures getting quietly rich off clientele with things to hide and prosecutions to dodge and limitless cash to do it with.

John Capper's heavily-acronymed name was up on a door next to a mini cab office just up from the Grand at Clapham Junction. The plate was plain, like the door. Capper's firm didn't run Yellow Pages ads and were only ever on TV to deliver statements from courthouse steps. Last I knew, Capper had a single partner and a half-dozen solicitors and fee-earners to facilitate the legal affairs of the higher echelons of South London crime. But his receptionist wasn't the one I remembered. I guess she'd aged beyond the thirty barrier. The current girl had five years to run and gave me a pretty smile and a nice view of her legs as she told me that Mr Capper was busy this morning. I offered to wait and perched myself in one of their easy chairs. Capper's offices were small but quality. No threadbare carpet or ceiling patches in here. The quality stopped with the décor, though. Capper's clients brought their own bouquet. One of them was sitting two seats away, a ferrety guy whose glitzy shirt and blazer couldn't hide the fact that he was sweating. The guy made an act of not seeing me as he killed time flicking the pages of an old *Fortune 500* that he wouldn't have known from *The Dandy*.

The receptionist made a brief call then flashed me a knowing smile and waved through a couple of guys who'd come up the stairs behind me in heat-denying black suits. They disappeared into an associate's office. A while later a guy in an open-necked shirt wearing a bunch of gold and an air that said he didn't wait for anyone came in and strode straight through to the partner's door with just a nod and a wink at our girl. Twenty minutes passed. Ferret riffled his *Fortune 500* in furious bursts, like he'd been waiting awhile. He kept eyeing Capper's door. The big guy was running late.

Just on forty minutes there was a burst of laughter and the door opened to eject a man in a striped suit and open-necked shirt. He strode out with a salute and a leer at the receptionist. Her console flashed. She looked up to call Ferret through, but I was already up and inside Capper's door before the words got out. I closed the door behind me.

John Capper had the pale bland face and immaculate dress of a city chairman, though he draped a little more gold than would seem right for the boardroom. His bespoke navy suit was crease-perfect at two-fifteen in the afternoon. Maybe he had a rail full of them in the little washroom annexed to his office. Maybe this was his two o'clock suit. The suit and perfectly parted hair were a front, though. The guy and I went back.

He looked surprised when I came in, since he'd instructed his receptionist to keep me on hold for a couple of hours. He went through the act of checking a blank legal pad then leaned over and called ground control to ask if they'd got the appointments mixed up. Ground control confirmed that Mr Ferret was still waiting.

Capper smiled at me. Started to say something. But the smile and the words froze when I planted my backside on his desk. He pulled it together, kept his annoyance out of his voice.

'Eddie,' he said, 'how are you? I'm sorry – just a couple of appointments then I'm all yours.'

'I'm in a hurry, John. How about pushing your appointments back a couple of minutes.'

Capper stood. Raised his hands.

'Hell, Eddie, you know how it is. This job gets crazier every day. I'm up to my ears. Let Suzanne get you a coffee. White with sugar, right?'

'Give your client the coffee. He needs it.'

I pushed my backside further onto his desk so he knew I was here to stay unless he had the desk carried out. Capper's phoney smile died. He walked out and spoke to his receptionist. Came back. Closed the door and sat down.

'I'd like to say this was a pleasure, Flynn, but you'd know I was lying.'

'You're a lawyer, John. You're always lying.'

'Fine. Let's cut the knife-work. What do you want?'

He brushed imaginary fluff. Crossed his legs. He'd have leaned forward to intimidate me if I wasn't up on his desk.

'Is my memory right?' I said. 'Didn't you have more time for me in the old days?'

Capper's face cracked a smile. 'Your memory's perfect,' he said. 'But this isn't the old days, unless they've taken you back onto the force.'

Touché.

I slid off the desk and went to peer at the photo gallery on his wall. I'd seen it before but I could never stop admiring the gall of a guy who puts himself on display with people scrambling to stay out of the penal system. But "Caper" Capper had gall a-plenty. His admiration for his celebrity villains was sincere. Understandable, since they fed his bank account faster than any legit punters ever could.

My memory about Capper's hospitality was clear. The bastard had always been hospitable as hell when the Metropolitan Police came calling. But my memory also logged the fact that he'd never missed an opportunity to shaft us once our backs were turned.

'You still Hammer Hayes' brief, John?'

I turned and caught his stare.

'*Richard* is still in my client portfolio. Yes.'

'Good.' I turned back to the wall. 'I need you to get in touch with him. Arrange a visit.'

'Why would I do that?' Capper asked.

I was looking at a new picture, pegged up dead centre, pride of place in Capper's gallery. I was looking but suddenly I was not believing.

'You're kidding,' I said. 'Is this for real? You're hanging out with the Archbishop of Canterbury? Has the guy switched sides?'

Capper threw an angry silence. I kept staring at the photograph, waiting for it to make sense.

The picture had Capper at a table laid out for fine dining. He was seated in a group of four. But it was the guy in black standing by Capper's shoulder who'd caught my eye. Either someone had been busy with photo-processing software or Capper was hobnobbing with the higher echelons of the Church of England nowadays. Then something clicked: the face next to Capper. I dug out a name and laughed. Good and loud.

'It's Jackie Jackson you're with,' I said. 'Let me guess: Jack's been laundering through the charities and got himself invited to a bash. You're just a hanger-on. It's Jackie the photographer's interested in – getting him on record as a model citizen.' I laughed again. 'I'll bet the Church of England doesn't know where Jackie's dosh comes from though. Hey, John?'

I turned again. Capper was glaring. Pretence dropped.

'The reason you need to arrange a visit to Hayes,' I said, 'is that I've urgent business to talk through with him.'

'Take a hike. I'm not his errand boy.'

'Come on, John. You're the guy with the big red telephone. Your firm's on his visitors list which means you're the quickest way in. That makes you the errand boy whether you like it or not. Unless you fancy your chances when Hayes finds he's missed something he should have known about.'

'I don't control Richard's list. He says who goes in. Send him a message. You'll be cleared through in a couple of weeks.'

'I can't wait. Put me down as one of your team.'

'No deal, Flynn. That's an abuse of the system. If you want to see Richard you'll go in like every other civilian.'

I sighed. Walked over. Pressed my knuckles onto his desk.

'Here's the dilemma,' I said. 'I've got something that Hayes needs to know right now. I could go through the channels and get a message to him in a week or two, but then he'd call you and ask why there was a delay that left him seriously in the shit. Are you happy to discuss screw-ups with The Hammer, John?'

Capper turned up his lip and flicked his hand, but the image of an unhappy Hayes took hold in his head.

'Fine. I'll call him,' he said. 'Richard can decide. So what do I tell him that's going to have him panting to have you in there?'

'Say I'm interested in a photo sale. Want to discuss spanners.'

'What the hell does that mean?'

I planted a card on his desk.

'Tell him,' I said.

I walked out. Winked at Capper's receptionist. She tried to smile but uncertainty messed it up. Ferret gave me daggers. I went out into the street to find my car. Three buses roared by in convoy and threw hot grit in my eyes.

CHAPTER FORTY-THREE
Wrong option

Sunday morning, six a.m. I drove out of London for a last look at the Chatham house. I wasn't going to find Melanie there but I needed to talk to the woman. Find out if she was Duggan and whether she knew where Melanie was. Harry had ID'd the property owner. A landlord as we'd guessed, but he wasn't home to talk about his tenants. Plan B was the direct approach. Talk to them myself. I decided on one last look before I barged in, see if anything new came up. I was still intrigued by the four-year-old.

The house was quiet until nine a.m. when the girl came out to push a toy stroller up and down the street. Thirty minutes later Neighbourhood Watch appeared on his end-of-terrace step to cast an invisible demarcation line. The girl contracted her theatre of operations. Stayed clear. Then the woman came out with the other kids, picked up the four-year-old and they all headed off. I followed, glad of the break. That's the investigation business: observing the ordinary, taking careful notes.

> *9:48 a.m. ... family head to park*
> *10:59 a.m. ... family returns / kids on street*
> *11:06 a.m. ... woman leaves, walks to convenience store*
> *11:22 a.m. ... woman returns with shopping*
> *11:30 a.m. ... attackers jump her*

They came out of nowhere as she cut through a pedestrian tunnel under the railway. She was carrying two plastic carriers and texting one-handed, thirty yards ahead of me, a silhouette at the tunnel exit, one moment alone, the next sandwiched between two youths.

It took me a moment to tune in. Deserted Sunday streets aren't prime mugging territory and mothers returning from the convenience store are not prime targets. I guess it was the smartphone. Her assailants were two white youths in regulation hoods. I saw the woman drop her bags, and the glint of sunlight on steel, the stance of the figures, said they were talking with knives.

One of them reached to grab at the woman's phone and I saw her react, take a swing at his face, but then she was pinned back against the wall with a knife against her neck and resistance stopped. The fingers slid the handbag from her shoulder. The phone was eased from her hand.

The woman had pluck. They were home and dry, turning to run, when she made a grab at her bag and got her fingers round the strap. For a moment there was a tug of war then the guy swung a fist and planted her on the ground, which settled the argument. Her assailants turned and made off.

Chose the wrong direction. Came back through the tunnel.

I was still ten yards out, moving fast, when they saw me. Surprise crossed the punks' faces. They made a quick decision: opted for heads down, hustle past, imagine I hadn't seen them. Pretend that the pink shoulder bag they were carrying was routine male adornment and that their hands were in their pockets only from the cold. If they could have pretended that the guy in front of them wasn't blocking the tunnel they'd have been fine. If they'd been smart enough to turn and run the other way they'd have been fine. But they chose the wrong option and kept moving and when I blocked them they chose wrong again. Pulled the knives back out. Stood their ground with the smirks of punks used to handling people. I smirked back.

The pair were squeezed from the same mould. Twentyish, marginal education, wrong kind of friends, too many movies, too many hours at kick-ass computer games. Schoolyard bullies, not yet seasoned by a spell in the slammer. The only distinction between the two of them was that one had edged a couple of feet nearer and was pointing a knife my way with his arm outstretched in that funny way you see in the movies. Funny but not effective: a straight arm is at a tactical disadvantage. No further reach unless the body behind it moves. No coil to unleash a slash or a thrust.

I stepped left, twisted right and brought my right hand down to clamp Hoody One's wrist while I reached for his elbow. By the time Hoody Two moved up in support Hoody One's knife was on the floor and his shoulder was dislocated. With a dislocated shoulder you go wherever you're led. Or pushed. In this case, backwards into Hoody Two. Hoody One went down and Hoody Two tried to stay upright but a fist to the side of his head took his balance and he went down too. They were tangled together and yelling stuff about my parentage, which you also see in the movies. At least they'd got something useful there.

I retrieved the knives and bent the blades with my foot in the angle of the wall, creased them one way and then the other. If our thugs straightened them a little they'd be like those Arabian Knights with their wavy daggers. Until then the knives had no assault value. I retrieved the woman's bag and phone and walked through to the far end of the tunnel. The woman was pale and trembling but her eyes were focused. She thanked me and cursed the thugs. I heard them picking themselves up behind me.

I squatted to get her shopping back into the bags. Her eyes were still on her attackers. A bruise was reddening on her cheek.

'Don't worry about them,' I said, 'they're going the other way.' I took her arm and eased her out onto the road. She was still thanking me but mostly she was trying to hold back the tears.

'Far to go?' I asked.

'Just down the road.'

'Need a hand?'

'I'm fine.' She tried to take the shopping bags but her balance went, nearly dropping her to the pavement. That fist in the face. I reached to steady her. Gave her a grin.

'Need a second opinion?'

Give her credit, she tried to grin back. 'I suppose that's answered your question,' she said. 'Perhaps this isn't the time to pass up a Good Samaritan offer.'

The Good Samaritan held his grin and took her arm to see that she didn't dive for the pavement again. I wouldn't have wanted her to take that smack in the face for anything, but this was an opportunity too good to pass. I'd needed a way in to talk to this woman. Now I had it. 'My name's Eddie,' I said.

'Clare.'

'Which way, Clare?'

I'm good at subterfuge.

She gestured and we set off along the road. Reached the cul-de-sac and walked along the terrace.

The kids were playing in the front yard. They stopped at the sight off their mother's bruised face and the stranger gripping her arm. I grinned at them.

This was it unless Clare thought to invite me in. I pulled out my fisherman's and fanned my face in a show theatrical enough to put me on stage. Luckily, a sense of gratitude, or maybe just the effect of the blow, took my act over Clare's head. She offered me a drink.

I looked at my watch as if the question was in doubt then shrugged. Said that would be fine. We went in, kids and all.

No amount of housekeeping could hide the fact that the house was in need of serious work but the inside was liveable. Better than many. The kids followed us into the kitchen-diner and the boy asked what happened. I smiled at them and searched the features of the four-year-old girl, looking for anything of Christa.

'I had a fall,' Clare said. 'This nice man has helped me home.'

A fall was credible, but the kids weren't convinced. Their mother arriving home supported on some guy's arm was weird. The boy persisted with a demand to know *how* his mother had fallen. He needed to get to the bottom of this. He turned his glare on me. I held my smile and kept quiet.

Clare poured me a glass of lemonade and the ice was broken as the kids swarmed round the bottle. They put the issue of their mother's mishap on ice for a moment.

'Nice house,' I said.

Clare shrugged. 'Not my idea of home,' she said, 'but beggars can't be choosers.'

'Temporary?'

'I wish.'

A nice lead into a conversation about her tenure, which was what I was after. But the lead was lost in a flurry of re-thinking triggered when I spotted a family photo. Clare and a guy I took to be her husband. Two kids: one was the boy aged around four at the time. The other was a year-old girl with jet black hair. Features not yet developed into the four-year-old watching me, but there was no doubt it was her. Her hair matched the man's.

I threw a querying look. Clare read the question.

'My husband,' she said. 'He died two years ago. Before our youngest was born.'

So the dark-haired girl had been with them since she was an infant.

She was not the Barbers' daughter.

I switched back to my original interest – the possibility that Melanie Brand had moved here two years ago from Eastleigh. I gave Clare my regrets about her husband and asked if they'd lived here before he died.

Clare shook her head. 'God, no. We had a nice house. I couldn't keep it though. We moved here eleven months ago.'

I sipped lemonade. Nodded sympathetically as the link to Melanie evaporated: if Melanie was ever at this house then she was gone before this family arrived.

My sympathy was genuine. Things had gone wrong in this woman's life – the very worst things – and I was prying in business that was none of mine. Clare was coping, keeping it together in this dingy backwater, never imagining that she'd had a private investigator sat in the bushes for two days ready to get her tangled up in an affair that had no more relevance for her than the Queen's birthday. For a moment I was right down there with our hoody friends.

Maybe not quite down there. As I turned for the door Clare stepped forward and planted a kiss and thanked me for reminding her that there were people who cared. I flicked on my fisherman's and winked at the kids and walked back to the car.

Despite my reservations, I'd been speculating about the dark-haired girl, wondering if we were about to prove the Barbers right, to find Christa alive and well. But if Christa *was* alive she wasn't living on this street. Reality swung back hard to remind me that in cases like this you rarely saw happy endings.

I'd come here to find Melanie, hoping she'd have something to say, but if she was ever at Chatham she was long gone. Maybe the landlord, when I found him, would have a forwarding address but I didn't hold much hope. The state of the house didn't suggest a landlord who kept records.

I still wanted to hear what Melanie had to say about her former employees. But a discomfort gnawing away at my gut said that all the chasing around outside Christa's family might be pointless. Maybe the affair was all inside, after all.

Two weeks in and the possibility that our clients were lying to us was as real as ever.

CHAPTER FORTY-FOUR
Technicolour graffiti

The heat slowed time. The drive back to London was a purgatory of tortured rubber and shimmering refractions. I flicked the radio on. The weather woman gave us three days. A low was racing towards the Scilly Isles. The heatwave was on borrowed time. I pulled my 'phones on. Pushed in the USB and turned Charlie Parker up loud. His squeals warped the hot air. I ditched the 'phones. Stayed with the traffic noise.

Arabel was working. I had places to go but no energy to take me there. I peeled off and crossed the Thames by Tower Bridge. Drove up into Hackney and parked in a stub road off Stoke Newington High Street to walk across to the Abney Park gates.

I entered the cemetery and trudged the cobbled main avenue busy with Sunday walkers parading under the scrutiny of dodgy youths lurking amongst the monuments. Came out at the chapel squatting at the cemetery's dead centre, staring at the modern world through blinded windows. The corrugated sheets that had replaced the stained glass had accrued their own technicolour graffiti in the final whiplash that left the place cowed and rotting, hunched down with its memories. I continued past the war memorial to a forgotten corner. Sat on a toppled obelisk opposite a cracked headstone that was the centrepiece of my painting. The headstone was canted away from the monstrous urn-topped monument beside it like a mugger's victim, but its quartz blazed with a light and energy that said the tenant below was not accepting his fate lightly. The inscription read 1855.

I tried to figure out what was missing in my painting. Spotted something new: a porcelain vase, standing bright and shiny on the base; a half-dozen wilting roses throwing a slash of red across the riot of greenery.

A century and a half and someone was still coming...

I pulled a copy of the Christa Photo from my pocket. Searched for the thing I was missing. The blurred figure of the girl was turning, reaching to someone just off-camera. Her hair was blonde and her face was bright in the sun, but the focus and camera shake lost all detail. You sensed you were seeing someone but you weren't. However strong their convictions, the Barbers were simply making the photo fit.

The girl's surroundings were a mish-mash: a splash of bright colour in the foreground, green and white slashes behind her. But something was bugging me in the picture. I looked for it but the longer I stared the less I saw.

I gave up. Called Bernie. Everything quiet at the Barber house. A day off to hide from the press. Harry reported similar tranquillity. Paul Tyndall had emerged mid morning to a lazy Sunday: a couple of pubs, more drink than was legal for driving a Porsche; a game of pool; a late lunch; a drift home. Harry would hang on at the Dartford cottage until late evening, see what gave.

I killed the call and returned to watching my headstone until the solitude was broken by an old derelict who worked his way out of the trees and stood on the path to stare at me, curious about a lone guy sitting around doing nothing – as if Abney Park wasn't full of them. He followed my gaze; looked at the grave; looked at me.

I pulled up a grin.

'Price of a fag?' he said.

The price of a fag was six-eighty, unless you knew someone who sold singles. A cold drink back in Chatham had cleaned me out but I checked anyway, found a pound coin and three twenty-pence pieces. I held them up and the guy came over, eyeing me like I was out to rob him. He took the money without comment but by the time he'd turned away he'd counted it.

'Miserable git,' he growled.

He walked back towards the trees. Swung his foot at the vase. Toppled it into the weeds. The roses scattered.

I stood and gathered them up. Relocated the vase. A magpie hopped through the branches and watched me. It gave me the same dirty look as the old guy, then took off in search of something to steal.

~~~~~

I set up the easel and inspected the painting. The brushwork from two days ago had worked. I'd captured what I was looking for: the patch of pristine wilderness in the centre of London. And now I had the missing element: I painted in the vase, toppled and cracked, a single red rose lying across the grave. Ninety minutes later I stepped back and saw that the thing was finished. I rinsed my brushes.

I drove up to the Podium for a single pint and a dodgy sandwich. Sat through the first set. Found no inspiration. At ten I packed in. Drove home for an early night.

Things were about to crack open. The Barber case was a tangle of rubber bands pulled tight. Once one snapped the whole mess would fly apart and we'd see it all.

I went up. Stood watching the street. Pulled the Christa Photo out again but what was hidden stayed hidden. I gave up and hit the sack.

CHAPTER FORTY-FIVE
Nuke

I slept badly, disturbed in the small hours by sirens and possibilities. When I woke the sky was bright and Monday morning was in full flow outside my window.

I went through to the kitchen and loaded the machine with Buckaroo coffee which works on the same principle as defibrillators to get the body into action. I swigged a cupful, crunched toast, told myself I was awake.

I drove to Paddington and went up to the office. Turned the sign. Lifted the sash in my room and reclined the Miller, swivelled it to face the window. Trains were running four deep below the building and the Westway was in full flood across the tracks. London Town: open for business and rushing some place I'd never discovered.

The outer door opened and Lucy came in. She wore a cool blue snazzy outfit with a skirt that minimised on material. After a moment I stopped noticing the skirt. I was looking at Lucy's face. It was the look she usually reserved for the council bill.

'What's up, Luce?'

She held out a folded newspaper in a way that gave me a bad feeling.

'Have you not read it?' she said.

I shook my head.

'Wow, Eddie.'

She opened *The Nation's* front page so I could read the headline. When I did I looked up at her and gritted my teeth.

Hackett had promised a bomb. He just hadn't warned us it would be a nuke.

CHAPTER FORTY-SIX
Truth, facts and horror

A photo and eighty point headline took up the front page, leaving room for just two tiny paragraphs of copy. I turned to the inside page to see where things went. When I finished I folded the paper and laid it on my desk. Racked the Miller back and swung my feet onto the windowsill. Lucy leaned against my roll-top and watched me.

Shaughnessy and Harry arrived and came in to see what all the quiet was about. Lucy passed the tabloid round. Harry snorted. Shaughnessy looked at me.

'We need to talk to them,' he said.

The paper came back and I read it again. As bombshells went, Hackett was as good as his word.

The photo showed a meadow sloping to a cluster of beech trees. In the foreground close under the trees the shadows of the low sun accentuated a shallow mound in the earth. Above the picture the headline screamed:

SAD CHRISTA'S
FINAL HOME

with a sub-head:

AND THEY'RE **STILL** OUT SIGNING BOOKS!

The by-line had Hackett's name and a few lines of the story before a CONTINUED OVERLEAF showed the way for readers who weren't sure.

Overleaf, *The Nation* shouted about Truth and Facts. First of which was that the Barbers had killed their daughter. This was common knowledge, but now we had the full horrific details. *The Nation* revealed that Elaine had snapped during her daughter's tantrum that infamous night and had throttled her in a moment of madness; or had thrown her across the caravan; or smothered her with a pillow; or very possibly drowned her in her bath. *The Nation* gave us astonishingly detailed accounts of each scenario, considering that all but one had to be fiction.

They had other new stuff. They'd identified a person who'd conspired with the Barbers to cover up the killing, and they'd followed the conspiracy all the way to the present and the spot where Sad Christa had been lying in the earth for twenty-two months. Finally, *The Nation* trumpeted, the truth behind the sordid affair could be revealed. They yelled for the Barbers to come clean.

By the end of the fourth page it was clear that *The Nation* was not actually revealing very much. Somewhere amongst all the trumpetry a touch of coy had crept in. The rag declined to name the conspirator or identify the grave's location, pending "internal consultation and legal advice", meaning that they were going to string this out for as long as they could. After the "consultation" though both *The Nation's* readers and the police were promised ringside seats for the show-and-tell.

I stared at the picture of the earth mound. Considered where this left us.

If *The Nation* was on target then Hammer Hayes' photo had just been sidelined. Because the girl in the photo for sure wasn't Christa. That wild goose was roadkill.

And it pushed our vigilante guy back into the spectators' stand too. If *The Nation* could deliver on their claims then the "Killer Couple" would soon be beyond the reach of hate-mail and arsonists.

If Hackett was right we all could pack up and go home.

I rotated the Miller; transferred my feet to the roll-top; grinned at the team.

Hackett had got there ahead of us, just as he'd promised. But he'd got one thing wrong. He'd told me I knew nothing.

But I knew where he'd found "Sad Christa".

~~~~~

I made a call.

'They just read it,' Bernie said.

'What's the reaction?'

'Shaken. Elaine's cursing the rag to high heaven. She says *The Nation's* fantasising. But they're nervous as hell, pal.'

'Are they still going with their schedule?'

'Yeah. We're out at ten. They say they're not letting Hackett derail them.'

'They realise they're going to get unwelcome attention today?'

'They say they'll face it.'

'Need extra hands?'

'I'm not sure,' Bernie said. 'We're not here to keep the press off them, right? I'm just worried it might get chaotic. Have we got this Tyndall guy under control?'

'Sean's with him. If he comes near the Barbers he'll feel a tap on his shoulder.'

'Then I'm fine,' Bernie said. 'Let's see how it goes.'

'Is Stuart or Elaine there?'

Bernie went to find them and handed his phone over.

'The thing's bullshit, Eddie,' Stuart said.

'Good. You can explain that statement in more detail when I get there. I already made it clear that I'm not happy spectating from the sideline.'

'It's bullshit,' Stuart repeated. 'We're talking to our solicitor today.'

'Fine. But right now I'm more concerned about things that Hackett knows that I don't.'

'Eddie, we've told you everything. We can't disprove Hackett's fantasies. You just need to trace the photo. When we find Christa all Hackett's bullshit theories will evaporate.'

'We're working on that,' I said. 'But we're going to sit down and talk anyway. Thirty minutes.'

'Sure. We'll be here.'

But Stuart sounded nervous, just like Bernie said.

CHAPTER FORTY-SEVEN
That was a touch untimely

There were four of us round the table. Me, Bernie, Stuart and Elaine. I watched the Barbers while I breathed the aroma of burnt fabrics. Told myself I wasn't in a bad mood.

The Barbers weren't in great spirits either. Their phone had been off the hook since *The Nation's* splash, and their gate was besieged by a press mob. The couple were tense as hell.

'We need to get things straight,' I said. I stood and went to open the garden door to breathe air that didn't stink. 'You've asked us to find Christa. When we do that we'll get to the truth, whichever way it lies.'

I turned. Elaine was wearing white slacks and a black tee shirt, and her hair was freshly washed but her eyes were tired. Stuart didn't look too good for the new week either.

'What can we say,' he said. '*The Nation's* spouting fantasy. Just stay focused on the photograph, Eddie.'

His eyes held mine with the intensity I'd seen that first day in Shaughnessy's office. Signals passed between us but I didn't know what they meant.

'Let's go back to the start,' I said. 'How did you come to be raising Melanie Brand's daughter as your own?'

I watched them freeze. Bernie was frozen too but that was his natural stance. I waited but the Barbers seemed unable to get back into the conversation so I turned back to the garden. Saw movement through the gaps in the bottom fence. The press, crawling into every hole. I thought about directional mikes. Closed the door and turned. Elaine's hands were unsteady on the table top.

'So you know,' she said. 'There was always a chance you'd find out.'

I went to the sink. Ran the tap. Splashed cold water on my face.

'That and other things,' I said. 'What I don't know is why you're hiding these things from us. You want us to find Christa but you're sending us out with our hands tied. That's a problem. I don't like being played.' I dabbed my face.

'Believe me, Eddie, we're not playing you,' Stuart said. 'Christa's our daughter in every meaningful sense. And we want her back.'

'So how does hiding the fact that she's someone else's child help me? You didn't think it was relevant that Christa has a natural mother running around out there?'

'Melanie had nothing to do with Christa's disappearance,' Elaine said.

'Take me through it: what's the basis of that assumption?'

Stuart shrugged. 'It wouldn't make sense. Melanie never wanted Christa. She was glad to hand her over to us and she'd been out of our lives for two years. She never came near the Orchard Grove.'

'How did the adoption come about?'

'It's not complicated,' Elaine said. 'Just a case of two people who wanted a baby, and a teenage girl who did not.'

Stuart took up the story.

'Melanie came to work for us when Grace was eight months old. She didn't have much in the way of references or previous experience but she was open about her situation. She was sixteen; had left home because of family problems; was desperate for a job and a roof. And Grace took an instant liking to her so we took her on. Probably against common sense.'

'She carried out her duties,' Elaine said. 'Was good with Grace. Helped me after Grace died. I suppose we were uneasy when she stayed out at night but there were no hard and fast rules. It was just a little unsettling, the hours she kept and the way she dressed. Made us wonder if she was forward with the boys.'

'But you knew nothing specific about her background? Her history or behaviour? The company she kept?'

'She was a teenager. It was her own affair. We just hinted that she should be extra quiet when she came in. I suppose what we meant was that we'd rather she was in at a more reasonable hour, but we didn't confront her with it.'

'How did losing Grace affect her?'

'She was devastated just like us,' Stuart said. 'So much so that there was no question of terminating her employment. So she stayed and helped Elaine pull through.'

'When did you learn that she was pregnant?'

'When she was two months gone,' Elaine said. 'She came home one day and broke the news.'

'So you threw her out.'

Stuart shook his head. 'We were sympathetic; told her she could stay on.'

'But we had to be clear that she couldn't remain for her full term,' Elaine said. 'At the end of the day we weren't her family. It wouldn't have been appropriate for her to be with us for the birth.'

'Did she talk about terminating the pregnancy?'

'She made a couple of comments that implied she was struggling over what to do. But it wasn't our business. We just offered support. Told her to take her time, make her decisions.'

'What about the father?'

'Melanie wouldn't discuss him,' Stuart said. 'She didn't want the boy involved.'

I thought of Louise Ryan's story. Melanie playing the boys. I guess when the game finally went wrong Melanie's instinct would have been to run from the trap she'd been baiting.

'So why did she leave?'

'We don't know. Three days after we'd discussed things she left without warning. No notice, no goodbyes.'

'But you told people you'd sacked her for theft.'

'She actually did take some money. Mostly just back-pay but it was a little more than she was owed. So our story wasn't far from the truth.'

'And you don't know where she went?'

Elaine stood and came across to stare out of the window. 'She'd mentioned the possibility of going to stay with friends. That's all we knew.'

The kitchen was heating up. Elaine re-opened the door. I didn't mention directional mikes – it was take a risk or stew.

'So how did you come to adopt Christa?'

'Melanie came back,' Stuart said. 'She turned up six months later, still pregnant and desperate, looking for a roof. She'd put off the decision on ending the pregnancy until it was too late. Elaine and I offered her a bed for the night and said we'd help her find somewhere to stay. That was all we could do. But then I had a thought: Elaine and I were still desperate to start a family. We'd waited six years for Grace to come along, and after her death Elaine wasn't initially inclined to try again.'

Elaine leaned back against the unit beside me, arms crossed, head down.

'We'd started trying around the time Melanie left,' Stuart continued. 'But by the next spring nothing had happened. We pictured it being another six years. Now here was Melanie with a problem she couldn't solve, but maybe a solution to ours.'

'I took some convincing,' Elaine said. 'But what it came down to was that after all the waiting and uncertainty we might be able to start a family again. No child should ever be unwanted and Melanie certainly didn't want hers. If we adopted her baby from the start then she'd be as much ours as any child could be. In the end I agreed with Stuart. We put the proposition to Melanie.'

'And she agreed?'

'She bit our hands off. She was terrified at the thought of being a mother. We offered her a home whilst her pregnancy came to term, promised to bring in a doctor if there were complications, and offered her ten thousand pounds to set her up afterwards, start her life again; rent a flat, get a job. The only condition was that she was to have no further contact with the baby.'

'And that's how it worked out?'

'She stayed two days after Christa was born then I dropped her at the station,' Stuart said. 'We never heard from her again.'

I walked across. Sat down. Grinned at Bernie. His face gave nothing. He'd come in on a security gig and found himself playing an extra in *Home and Away*.

'Did you ever wonder what happened to her?'

'Of course we did,' Elaine said. 'We're not the heartless fiends the press make out. But breaking off contact was for the best – on both sides.' Sudden concern came into her voice. 'Have you talked to her?'

I shook my head. 'Not even close. I've an address two, maybe three, years behind. Even her friends have lost track. Melanie's still drifting. But I can't rule out her involvement in Christa's disappearance. I need to talk to her.'

But they were both shaking their heads. 'If Melanie had been near the caravan that night we'd have noticed,' Elaine said. 'And if we thought she was involved we'd have had the police searching for her from the start.'

'Let's be clear, Eddie,' Stuart said. 'We don't want it to come out that Christa isn't our natural daughter. You can see the problems that would bring. That's why we've kept Melanie out of it. And unless we find something that points to her being involved we want to stay with that approach. Let's leave the girl alone.'

I smiled. 'Has Owen Jagger been bending your ear?'

'Owen doesn't know about this,' Stuart said. 'But yes, he's talked to us. He thinks you're focusing too much on our family. And maybe you are.'

'If you're not happy with what we're doing,' I said, 'just yell out.'

A head-shake. 'Let's just concentrate on finding where Christa's photograph was taken. That's our priority.'

'So tell me what's happening. Why have we got the paparazzi outside your gate this morning?'

'Hackett's pissing in the wind,' Stuart said. 'He's pulled together scraps he doesn't understand and patched them into a make-believe scoop.'

'But he's pretty specific. He says you killed Christa, and he claims to have proof. He's inviting you to sue him. Are you going to do that?'

'Find Christa,' Elaine said. 'Let's see where Hackett's proof is then.'

'That front page – "Christa's Final Home" – do you recognise the location?'

'Hell, no!' Stuart said. 'How would we? If Hackett's so sure let him take the police to the spot. What are they going to do? Start digging?'

That's exactly what they'd do. The prospect didn't seem to concern the Barbers, though, so it was something else they were tense about. But then we were sitting in a half-burned house surrounded by a baying tabloid pack.

'Okay, *The Nation* has it wrong. They've concocted stuff about you based on misinterpretations of things they've seen or heard. But they've got a location and they say that Christa is buried there. Are you ready to face the possibility that they might be right?'

The two of them paled. Elaine walked back to the table, tight-lipped.

'They're wrong,' she said. 'Christa's alive.'

I stayed quiet.

'Just find where her photograph was taken,' she said. 'That will answer all the questions.'

'Are you any further with that?' Stuart asked.

'We're making progress. Does the name Hayes mean anything to you?'

The Barbers' blank expressions gave me the answer.

I pulled the photo of Tyndall and his girlfriend from my pocket. A touch untimely, since the Barbers had just told me to quit chasing Melanie Brand, but I wanted to know whether we'd already found her. Who'd be more upset about Christa's supposed death than her natural mother? Maybe upset enough to want to hurt them; burn down their house. Maybe Melanie was the woman with Tyndall.

Elaine took the photo and they scrutinised it without so much as a flicker of recognition. Both looked at me.

I decided this wasn't the time for explanations. Pushed the photo back into my pocket and said I'd see them later. Nodded to Bernie. Then as I turned to throw a parting salute I caught a look on Elaine's face. Just the briefest impression but I couldn't miss the void behind her eyes. A depthless fury of secrets and despair.

CHAPTER FORTY-EIGHT
A nice spot to dig

I eased out through the paparazzi, ignoring a barrage of questions. They'd clocked me as one of the Barbers' minders. Assumed I knew something. A beefy guy planted his palms on the Frogeye's wing and yelled for a comment. I kept the car rolling and eased him away but a couple of frustrated slaps hit the bodywork as I waited for traffic. I put my foot down and cursed the bastards.

I drove towards the city. Reviewed what I had.

Christa as Melanie Brand's child had been a certainty. Too many coincidences to be otherwise. Melanie's pregnancy fit the timescale too neatly and explained Olivia Watts' story of Elaine's surprise announcement – eight months gone and barely anything showing. Now we knew why. I guess the "barely anything" had been a little padding, added to give a sufficient hint of pregnancy when Elaine broke the news without raising questions about why no-one had noticed earlier.

The Barbers' confirmation put Melanie firmly in centre-picture. I could buy their story that she'd been happy to hand over her child but that didn't mean that she'd stayed happy. I pictured Melanie in one of two roles: a mother who'd snatched her child back or a mother looking for vengeance. But the Barbers' lack of reaction to the Dartford snap suggested that Melanie wasn't the woman with our vigilante. That left the first theory – that she'd taken Christa. Despite the Barbers' dismissal of the idea, I wasn't ready to count the girl out. I needed to talk to her.

I'd almost been ready to explain the Dartford photo, break the news that we'd caught up with their vigilante, but something had held me back. I wanted to know first whether we really were just dealing with a random nutcase or whether there was a link between Tyndall and the Barbers, one that Stuart and Elaine were hiding.

The priority now was to get to Christa, or the truth about her. For that we needed to locate both the photo and Melanie Brand and see if either pointed towards the missing girl.

If *The Nation* was on target, of course, then it was all too late.

~~~~~

I parked beside the old coach house and walked across to Damien Larkin's house. Knocked on his door again. Same result as last time.

I crossed the gardens and walked out onto the meadow; followed it down to the copse. A pair of swifts tracked me with a frenetic routine of climbs and turns through the stultifying air.

At the bottom, where the hedgerows intersected at an angle under the trees, I found the scene captured in *The Nation's* "Sad Christa" photo. The beech trees overhanging the hedge, the sloping meadow, the same indistinct mound right in front of me. Not that the mound was anything special. The meadow was mottled with them, features you wouldn't give a second glance to. I guess that Hackett had just selected one at random and snapped away. An ominous mound makes a nice composition when you're yelling about dead bodies. But the location was as good as any on Larkin's land. Remote from the road and tree-covered. A nice spot to dig unobserved. I pictured it, the way I used to picture the scenes of the unimaginable and unspeakable when I'd been in the job. Half sensed a shadow on the place. Put it down to imagination.

CHAPTER FORTY-NINE
Heatstroke in hell

Maureen Parker was awake this time. They'd seated her in a rear conservatory where the sun and glass had stoked up a temperature fit to floor steel workers. A couple of electric fans were throttled like aero engines but produced no effect outside their slipstream. I was sweating before the orderly had finished his introduction.

Maureen screwed up her face in a little drama of trying to remember where a nephew had suddenly popped up from. She knew damn well she had no nephew but she wasn't to be deprived of her moment: I guess she didn't get many visitors to cold-shoulder. The orderly grinned at me and headed somewhere cooler.

I gave Maureen my real name and my real occupation. At the word *investigator* her prune look intensified into the expression of someone witnessing the horrors of hell. I sat down and inched into a fan's airflow.

'I don't know any nephew called Eddie,' Maureen declared, ignoring my introduction and staying with the original issue. She spoke of *Eddie* as if he was a third party. I'd have put it down to dementia if I hadn't seen the glint in her eyes. The old bird was simply enjoying being obtuse. We could have gone on with the little play – Maureen was in hog heaven defending her family tree – but I was on limited time before heatstroke floored me. I leaned in to short-circuit the show.

'I'm here about your old neighbours,' I said.

I'd figured Maureen out. Seen the spite behind her eyes. She was the kind who always had something to say about neighbours and I threw them in like chum to the sharks.

The bait worked. Maureen quit her family tree. Her cold eyes locked onto me. The old bird looked frail in the depths of her chair but something about her made you think of nettles. Her white hair fluttered in the fan blast.

'Disgusting people,' she said.

I waited.

'It used to be respectable types living round here,' she amplified.

'Nowadays, you don't know who'll move in.'

'I'm looking for a young woman. Melanie Brand. Was she one of your neighbours?'

She shook her head impatiently. Melanie's name meant nothing to her. She didn't want to talk about *nothing*.

'Were they a couple?' I tried.

That opened Maureen's eyes.

'"Couple"? That's hardly the term I'd use.' She glared at me. 'Lesbians! That's what they were! Disgusting pair.'

I guess Maureen was endlessly disgusted by the detritus of her overworked imagination. Melanie as a lesbian was a surprise though, although it wouldn't be the first time a gay woman had hidden a dark bitterness under the cover of promiscuity with the boys. Not that I was taking Maureen's word for it. We'd been talking for two minutes and I already felt like I'd known the old bird for years and trusted her no more than if I had. I threw Melanie's name in again to see if Maureen had missed her cue. Still got no reaction. Did the old bird not know her neighbours' names? I switched back to her line of interest.

'Your neighbours were having a relationship?'

'They were lesbians! I don't call that a relationship.'

I waited.

She pursed her lips. 'The way the two of them acted. Living together like that. Kissing each other right on the doorstep. Not a bit of decency between them.'

'Did you know their names?'

'Of course I did! You think I don't know my neighbours? Not the younger one, though.'

'What about the older one?'

Maureen threw me a sly look.

'What's it to you?'

I put concern in my face. 'The one called Melanie may be in some trouble.'

'I didn't know any Melanie.'

The orderly reappeared and asked if he could bring a cuppa. I declined. Maureen's 'about time!' indicated acceptance. The orderly threw a neutral smile and went off.

So Maureen could ID only one of her neighbours. Was Melanie

the other person living there or was she just using the address for the Meadow Road's records? It was beginning to look like a long shot but I leaned across and showed Maureen the Dartford snap. The Barbers had denied that the woman with Tyndall was Melanie but there was no harm in a second opinion. And when Maureen held the photo an inch from her face her prune look sharpened.

'She's one of them?' I asked.

Maureen gripped the photo like she was holding the woman's life in her claws. I waited. Wondered if the Barbers had told me porkies. If so, their act had fooled me, but Maureen's was better. You can't fake disgust. Maureen knew Tyndall's partner.

'Which one is it?' I asked.

Maureen stared at the photo long enough to dredge up a little more disgust.

'It's her – Heather Duggan.'

I smiled and took the photo back.

Not Melanie. But Maureen had just put the woman who'd lived at Melanie's last contact address – who'd maybe had a relationship with her – with the Barbers' vigilante.

The First Rule of the investigation business says there's no such thing as coincidence. Christa's natural mother was linked to the people persecuting the Barbers as "baby killers" and that put her right at the centre of the affair. The Barbers' *au pair* had just racked up to top priority.

My tee shirt was soaking. I thanked Maureen and left her to her repulsions. Walked through into the main building. The temperature dropped twenty degrees.

I drove away chewing over a new problem.

If Melanie was linked to the "baby killers" campaign then she must believe that her daughter was dead.

I'd find Melanie, but she wouldn't get me to Christa.

CHAPTER FIFTY
Strike the band

Tuesday morning. Eight a.m. I sipped cold water at Shaughnessy's window whilst Lucy read us *The Nation's* latest offering. I heard nothing new in the copy, although Hackett's smoke and mirrors hid the fact nicely. His promised revelations – names and places – weren't to be rushed. This was all about timing.

'Thursday,' I said.

Lucy and Shaughnessy looked at me.

'The splash is Thursday. They'll build things up this week, maximise the circulation. But they won't leave it too late. *The Nation* wants a couple of days to bask in the fall-out. They're not about to hand over to the Sundays for that. So they'll strike the band tomorrow, Wednesday, reveal most of their story but hold back the names and places until Thursday.'

'I heard their circulation's up half a mill.,' Lucy said. 'Everyone wants to know where Christa's buried.'

'How are the Barbers taking it?' Shaughnessy said.

I described yesterday's chat. The Barbers' denial of the *Nation's* story but the two of them nervous as hell. I also described what I'd dug out on Melanie, how Christa's natural mother was linked to our Dartford vigilantes. Lucy's eyes popped. She'd have her nose in *The Nation* for damn sure this week.

The connection between Christa's natural mother and the "Baby Killer" vigilantes was worrying, though. Didn't point to the child being safe and well.

But if the Barbers had killed Christa, why were they so intent on tracking down the photo? Bluff? Tracking the photo, of course, now depended on a chin-wag with a professional thug banged up in Wormwood Scrubs.

But the new issue was the other photo – the one on *The Nation's* front page tagged as Christa's grave.

'We need to close this off,' I said.

'I'll dig on Hayes,' Shaughnessy said. 'See if there's anything connects him with the Barbers.'

If Hayes' brief came through I'd talk to the guy directly, but he wasn't going to dictate his biography over our bread and onions. The stuff I needed was the stuff he wouldn't be telling me — maybe something Shaughnessy could pull in.

Harry was out watching Tyndall. We were keeping the bastard in our sights until the thing was cleared up. Guilty or innocent, the Barbers had hired us to protect them. Right now they were on a train heading for Manchester. Returning to London tomorrow via Sheffield. Bernie could handle their tour solo as long as we kept Tyndall away from them.

My new priority was a chat with Elaine's black-sheep brother Damien about why the press were on his land. I was about to head out when my phone rang.

John Capper. Hayes' brief.

'Richard will see you this morning,' he said. 'I've pegged a solicitor's conference at ten thirty. You're on the list. Meet me at The Scrubs.'

CHAPTER FIFTY-ONE
Shark thing

Wormwood Scrubs prison is a stone's throw from Paddington. I took the Westway and came off at White City; found a parking spot thirty yards from the gates and walked down Du Cane under the shade of budding plane trees. Turned in towards the iconic gate turrets set in the twenty-foot walls over which the Victorian buildings have been glowering since the 1880s. Imagine chimney stacks, picture the corner turrets on each wing as a nod to gothic, and you're looking at the archetypal satanic mill – one with a doorway set to swallow you whole. But there were no looms chattering behind these walls. Just thirteen hundred remand and medium-risk Cat B prisoners, serving their time. Hammer Hayes wasn't my idea of Cat B material but I guess the bastard must have learned to toe the line – at least inside the system.

A new Visitors' Centre was being decked out on the street but the entrance was taped over. I walked round to the old building and found John Capper sweating in a sharp suit. I had a light summer jacket over my tee shirt to suggest arrival from a desk, but appearances weren't the thing. Capper had me on his brief's list and as long as my ID matched I was in. Capper nodded a sour hello and we went through.

We bypassed the ticket queue. Solicitors' privilege. I dropped my phone and keys into a locker and we were escorted straight to security. We walked through a metal detector and uniformed staff checked ID and patted us down; peered into Capper's briefcase. I filled in a form and we were taken through to the visits room which was as depressing as when I'd last seen it. Capper pushed my form into the letterbox and we waited for them to bring Hayes up.

We sat for five minutes. Capper kept quiet, nervous about coming here with a ringer. He needn't have worried: a warden came through and told us that Hayes wanted to see only Flynn. Seemed this was a conversation best kept from legal ears. Capper threw a relieved smirk and waved me through.

I went in and sat on a blue seat at a wooden table. A minute later

Hayes came through and sat on the other side of the table. His chair was red. The prison service has these systems.

Hayes gave me a slow, intense look to get us off on the right tack. I'd last seen him right after the jury verdict nine years ago and he'd given me the same look then. Now here he was, on the wrong side of the table once again. Two in a row would make you think of a guy getting careless. But Zach's info pointed to simple bad luck. Hayes wasn't the type to serve time. My own collar should have been his first and last.

The stints inside hadn't done Hayes any favours. He looked midsixties, though he was a decade younger. Fifties is when men are strongest and meanest and Hammer Hayes was in his prime. He wasn't the biggest guy I ever saw but he was the nastiest. You looked into his eyes and knew it.

I threw a grin and let the silence drag. Looked round the tiny room. Grinned some more.

'Still living the high-life Richard?'

Hayes stayed with his stare.

'Detective Inspector.' He rolled the words out with slow emphasis. 'Long time no see.'

I shrugged. 'Seems like yesterday. But I guess time drags inside.'

'I get by,' Hayes said. 'And I keep in touch. Heard you'd got the boot a while back. Very gratified to hear it. I've pictured you many times in your new line of work, serving those notices and chasing fellows with their peckers out. Gives me a bloody good laugh, Detective Inspector.'

He sat back and folded his arms.

'But this visit,' he said, 'is a surprise. Has me wondering what you're up to, Flynn. Surely you're not still trying to play the big league. That would make you a very silly boy.'

The baby talk was meant to intimidate. Villains have this thing about keeping conversation at the schoolyard level. They get it off TV.

'Richard,' I said, 'I'm on this side of the table and you're on that side. Let's dispense with the career advice.'

His face darkened. 'Last time our paths crossed,' he said, 'was official business. I could let that go. But my brief would have me believe you're now messing in my personal affairs. I can't believe you'd be so foolish, Inspector.'

He was sticking to this "Inspector" thing like he'd have me running out in tears. But he was six years too late. That world was gone and mostly forgotten. And people like Hammer Hayes were the reason I didn't miss it.

Pre-amble over, Hayes waited, arms folded.

'We know about your scam,' I explained. 'We're working for the Barbers. Looking at the Christa Photo. Caught a funny whiff and here I am.'

'I wish I knew what you were talking about.'

'Well I think you do know, Richard. Or you'd better. Otherwise I won't be able to help.'

Hayes stayed cool but he was watching me like he was ready to launch himself across the table. If he did I'd be ready.

'What puzzles me,' I said, 'is why you're involved in something like this. Hoax photo scams seem a little downmarket for you. Although,' I leaned forward, 'I guess two hundred K isn't *so* far down.'

Hayes ignored the bait. 'I read the papers,' he said. 'Your dry cleaning bill must be hell, Inspector.'

'Swings and roundabouts,' I said. 'Higher cleaning bills but less to scrape off my boots.'

Hayes unfolded his arms. Clasped his hands on the table. Leaned forward himself.

'Stick to looking tough around your clients, Flynn. Keep out of the other stuff.'

'The other stuff is what my clients are paying me for.'

'Then you'd be better reviewing your involvement with them.'

'Why would I do that? The pay's good. And I'm getting results.'

Hayes' stare stayed neutral. Whatever was churning in his head wasn't on display. But he leaned further. Almost nose-to-nose. Tapped a finger on the table.

'Get out of my business, Flynn,' he said. 'You're not protected by your filth colleagues now. You don't have an army backing you up.'

'I never did have,' I said. I gave him a moment to refresh his memory. Got back to the subject. 'We know the photo scam's yours. And we know you want it to go down smoothly. Maybe we can be of mutual benefit.'

Hayes shook his head. 'We're not discussing my affairs, Flynn. The

254

only question is whether you're going to give me a problem.'

It was difficult to see what kind of problem I could be if Hayes wasn't involved with the photo but I didn't pursue it. The bastard was running the scam, all right. And we both knew he'd not be revealing the photo's location to anyone until he had the two hundred K in his hand. But I wasn't here for that. I just wanted to know whether the snap was genuine.

'I can bring the deal off,' I said. 'I've got the Barbers prepped and ready to pay. Your problem is how to get the money without attracting attention. Especially if the photo's a hoax, which is my guess. Either way, I can oil the wheels.'

Hayes smiled. Leaned back, away from me.

'No deal, Flynn. I don't work with filth. Ex- or otherwise. I don't know what you thought you were back then, but you're nothing now. Neither us nor them. You're just the guy in the middle in the dirty mac. And someday I'm going to return this visit.'

Not in the near future. The bastard would be inside for a couple more years at least. Which was why he needed to close the photo scam business from inside. He had his machinery ready to roll, someone he trusted ready to handle the photo payoff and had his tracks covered so the caper could never be traced back to him. Only now it had been traced. I was here as proof. I saw it in his eyes: Hayes was wondering if his scheme was about to get derailed. Something to consider in those long evenings in his cell.

'Have it your way,' I said. 'Go it alone. The Barbers are keen to know about the photo but they don't want to be ripped off. They're looking for a steer on whether to pay up. Maybe I'll caution against it.'

That finally got through. Hayes' head lowered. His shoulders came up.

'Do anything to block this and I'll have you put down,' he said. 'And give your clients a message from me: the snapshot's genuine. They can pay up and get their kid back or I'll have them dancing after my shirt tails for the next ten years. I might even send more photos. And some of them might not be so nice. Steer your clients with *that*, Flynn.'

Then he stood and walked out.

I sat in the blue chair and thought about it. Hayes' threats didn't worry me. If he came after me he'd get as good as he gave. I was focusing on his words. Sensed a ring of truth. With *The Nation* about to torpedo the Barbers and prove that Christa was dead, Hayes should have been sweating that his photo scam was on the slab.

But he was not sweating. So maybe the photo was genuine. But if something had happened to Christa in the twelve months since Hayes took his snap would he know about that?

CHAPTER FIFTY-TWO
Camper van City

If Hayes' photo *was* Christa then it meant she'd been abducted as the Barbers claimed. So why did the *Nation* have her buried on Damien Larkin's land? I took the Westway out of London and headed back to Devizes.

I found Larkin Campers on a decaying business park on the outskirts of the town. The dealership was open but un-staffed. I walked across a compound crammed with jaded camper vans to a door marked SALES in a low brick building, went in and waited a moment then lifted the flap at a counter and went through to the back office.

The guy sitting in the big leather swivel behind the boss's desk wasn't surprised to see me. He wasn't friendly, either.

I introduced myself for the sake of formality. Explained my business.

'I guess we both recognise the location of *The Nation's* "Sad Christa" photograph,' I said.

Elaine's brother pointed his pen. 'The thing's bullshit,' he said. 'I don't know where that rag got their crazy ideas. I've nothing the hell to do with this.'

'*The Nation* disagrees. They think you've got Christa buried on your land.'

'Bullshit,' he repeated. 'I'd nothing to do with what happened to Christa.'

'No smoke without fire, they say.'

Damien slapped down the pen. Pushed himself back. 'Who's side are you on, Flynn? My sister's or that newspaper's?'

I thought it through.

'I'm on Christa's side,' I said.

'No! You're not! Because if you were you'd be out looking for her instead of chasing tabloid rumours.'

'I'm looking wherever seems relevant. Care to explain how *The Nation* ended up on your land?'

A head-shake. Fast. Furious.

'That hack came in here two weeks ago with his questions and insinuations. The rags have always left me out of this before. Whatever Elaine and Stuart did is their own affair. Only now *The Nation* is trying to suck me in. But it's pure fantasy. I'm not involved. Never was. So: leave me the hell out of it!'

'Whatever they did? What does that mean?'

'Nothing! Whatever the hell happened. I know no more than you, Flynn. That's what I told that jerk from *The Nation*. But the bastard went right out of here and ran all over my property and now they're claiming my back yard's a cemetery. When they release the location I'm gonna have every news-louse and cop on the planet crawling over my land!'

I shrugged. 'If there's nothing to hide, no harm. They'll refill the holes.'

Damien nearly came over his desk. 'Sod the holes! The police aren't going to stop at the meadow. They're going to tear the house apart. This place, too. My computer and god-knows-what. They're going to come in here with warrants.'

I leaned against the wall. 'So what's the problem? You say you're not involved with your niece's disappearance. What's the issue? Are they going to find something if they dig up your field and check through your house?'

He looked at me a moment then hammered his fist onto the desk. His pen jumped onto the floor.

'Yes, they're going to find things,' he yelled. 'The last thing I want is the cops digging through my affairs. We've all got stuff to hide. But it's nothing to do with Christa. I know no more about her than you do!'

'Hackett seems confident. He's telling people to sue him. Are you going to sue him?'

'How the hell do I sue *The Nation* when the police are prosecuting me for something else?'

'So what are you hiding? You cheating on your tax? Got some kiddie-porn on your computer?'

'Jesus!' Damien said. 'Get out of here, Flynn! You're as bad as the news guys. I hope one day your life gets turned over. See how you like it.'

I stayed put.

258

'I'm not interested in anything that's not related to Christa,' I said. 'I just want to know what you know about the affair.'

'And I'm not interested in your damned questions,' he answered. 'I'm through with this bullshit. *The Nation* publishes their latest fiction and Elaine's own investigators turn up here. I'm going to call her. Tell her she needs to be clearer about what she's paying you for!'

I pushed myself off the wall. Ambled over. Draped a leg over his desk. Leaned in.

'Stay cool, Damien. I'm just doing my job. If you've nothing to give me on what happened to your niece then I'm out of your hair. Christa's all I'm interested in.'

Damien coughed out a laugh. 'Well then, Flynn, you've had a wasted trip. Because I know nothing. Absolutely nothing. *Capisci?*'

'Yeah,' I said. I looked round the office. A mess of cracked plasterboard and girlie calendars featuring last decade's camper van models. 'Maybe you can help with one thing, though. The day after Christa disappeared you visited the caravan site. But your sister Sharon wasn't exactly flattering about your contribution. I hear you weren't known for helping out and Sharon didn't seem very complimentary about the help you did give. So I'm wondering why you turned up so quickly next day?'

For a second Damien struggled to grasp the question. Then he broke into a laugh. A big, loud, ugly thing.

'Why I turned up so quickly?' he said. 'I *turned up* because sister Sharon was screaming down the phone that I'd better get my arse over there pronto to look after Elaine. It was Sharon who dragged me down there. I wouldn't have gone near the place. It wasn't my kid who'd gone missing and there wasn't a damned thing I could do to help. '

'So what *did* you do?'

'Nothing! I got sucked into a shit-storm. What was I supposed to do? Pull on my SCUBA gear and jump in the river? They stuck me with holding Elaine's hand, trying to keep her from going over the edge whilst everyone was out searching. That bitch Sharon can keep her opinions to herself.'

'How long were you with Elaine?'

'Forever! That afternoon. All next night.'

He slumped and ran his hand through his hair; massaged his eyes.

Looked at me.

'Elaine's okay,' he said. 'She's always been decent to me. But I haven't spent more than the odd hour with her since we were kids. How the hell was I supposed to comfort her when she'd just had her kid stolen? God damn it, I never even sent Christa birthday cards! That night was the longest of my life.'

An electric fan rasped across the silence. Then Damien smashed his fist onto the desk again. Paperwork jumped. The pen stayed on the floor.

'Dammit!' he said. 'Get lost, Flynn. And if I see you snooping round my land – working for Elaine or not – I'll get my shotgun.'

I said nothing. Saw a coronary lurking down the road. I slid my backside off his desk and walked out.

I headed home wondering if Hackett had found his way to Devizes based on misreading something his dirty tricks had picked up. Damien Larkin struck me as the kind of guy to be hiding plenty of things, but I didn't see buried bodies amongst them.

That's when the Christa Photo popped into my head. Out of nowhere I saw it: the thing I'd missed in the blurred image. I accelerated onto the M4 and put my foot down. When I looked at the speedo I was over the ton and near to parting with my fisherman's. I lifted my foot and got back to the legal limit and raced towards the shimmering horizon.

CHAPTER FIFTY-THREE
A touch of shake

I followed the Orbital to Chatham; drove towards the centre and turned into the cul-de-sac. It was mid afternoon. No-one home at the house.

I walked round the building to the refuse-choked space between the garage and the house and pulled out the bike frame and mattress to get at the mess underneath. Freed the coloured plastic I'd spotted last week. Yellow, deep blue, red. I heaved it loose in a stampede of bugs. The plastic was tough, heavy duty. I unfolded it and deciphered a toddler's inflatable slide. I dragged it across the garden to the far side of the house; dropped it on the wilderness that had once been a lawn and fought my way back into the undergrowth to pull the clothes carousel from its hole. I flipped the carousel upside down and used it to prop up the plastic in an approximation of the way it might stand when inflated. The thing was a shapeless mess but the colours were set up at a representative height. It was good enough. I wasn't going to blow the damned thing up. Then I walked onto the road and turned to snap a few pictures with my phone zoom set high. Added a touch of shake. Then I found shade and checked the results. I'd snapped eight pictures. Seven were a meaningless mess. The last was almost focused, just the hint of blur from my deliberate shaking. It had caught the propped-up plastic down at the right hand corner of the frame, and if you imagined the colours expanded, imagined a kid's inflated slide, if you looked at the blur of the leaning greenhouse in the background and the hint of wooden slats against the railway embankment, then you might imagine the figure of a young girl, side-on, right there in the middle of it all, and it would match as near as made no difference.

I'd located the Christa Photo.

CHAPTER FIFTY-FOUR
Aspirations rarely work

I dragged the plastic slide back and jammed it in with the rest of the debris. Went round to the street and leaned against the Frogeye's wing to think.

We'd been chasing two different things. The vigilante and the Christa Photo.

Turned out that this house was common to both of them.

Coincidences don't work for me. The Christa Photo was taken at a house where Heather Duggan once lived. So the house was linked to both the vigilante and Melanie Brand, Christa's mother.

Which meant the little girl was Christa for sure.

That took me right back to yesterday's conundrum: if Melanie or Heather had taken Christa why were they threatening the Barbers? Why were they accusing them of killing her?

I looked at the house. Tried to picture it a year ago, the little girl playing in the garden. I turned a slow three-sixty; took in the whole dingy street; pictured the child holding someone's hand as they walked down from the main road. Whose hand was it? And why had the whole thing – photo and threats – spiralled in to Heather Duggan and Paul Tyndall?

I still needed to get to Melanie but the couple at the cottage on Dartford Marshes were the real centre. Was Melanie with them? Maybe even Christa?

The door in the end-of-terrace opened. Neighbourhood Watch came out with his fag. Gave me the eye again to let me know he was on to me. He was still eyeing me as I drove out.

~~~~~

There's no good route in from Chatham. I fought traffic for ninety minutes as the rush hour congealed. By Paddington I was whacked. I trudged up the stairs and printed off my phone snap. Walked through to Shaughnessy's office and planted it in front of him. Grabbed a cup of water and flopped into his easy chair.

'The Chatham house,' I said. 'I've been sat outside it for four days and hadn't see it.'

Shaughnessy was quiet. He rooted out a copy of the Christa Photo and laid it next to my snap. Looked at me.

'She was there.'

He came to the main question. 'Is she still alive? Or are we a year too late?'

'She was being cared for when the photo was taken. There's a chance she's still okay.'

'So what's the vigilante stuff?'

'That worries me.'

Shaughnessy continued scrutinising the photos. Fired the next question.

'Is there someone else at the Dartford house with Tyndall and Heather?'

'That's what I'm thinking.'

Shaughnessy raised his eyebrows. 'Be great to find Christa safe and well – unless your name's Hackett.'

'Yeah. Turning the kid up would kind of wreck his splash.'

Maybe *The Nation* really had misinterpreted their illegal eavesdropping, as the Barbers claimed. Maybe their story was about to fizzle. But I knew better than to depend on it. I asked Shaughnessy how his research was going.

'I've got some of Hayes' activities before he went down but nothing that connects to the Barbers. People haven't exactly been queuing to talk to me. I've still a few lines out, some people to talk to tomorrow. A few quid might oil their memories if they've more greed than sense. Be nice if Hayes becomes irrelevant, though. If we find Christa his scam's history.'

My phone rang. I picked up. Stood and walked over to the window.

Elaine's voice over the sound of a train. On their way to Sheffield with Bernie and Jagger. They had a launch event tomorrow morning then a rush back to London for an afternoon TV slot. Elaine asked for an update.

I still wasn't ready to talk about their vigilante, but locating the photo was their core focus. So I told her we'd traced it. Had the location. Were connecting it to names and places.

I heard an intake of breath, a sound like crying. Stuart's voice came on.

'Eddie, what's happened?'

I repeated the information. 'We're nearly there,' I said, 'but we need to be cautious. The photo's a year old.'

Stuart hissed and swore. I listened to him passing the news on to Bernie and Jagger. Then he came back.

'Where?'

'The photo location is a house in Chatham. And a woman who was there at the time is the one I showed you a couple of days ago with the guy in that photo. They live in a cottage on Dartford Marshes. We've not spotted a child there but we've ID'd the couple. We'll know more tomorrow: with any luck we might be moving towards Christa even if she's not with them.'

'But she might be?'

'Yes.'

He swore again. More words spoken behind the hiss of the train. Then Elaine came back on the line and asked more questions. I described the location of the cottage.

'We'll come back,' she said.

'No. Give us time. We don't know how things stand. If we're getting near to Christa we don't want to take risks.'

Elaine tried to argue but I was firm. Insisted they continue their Sheffield thing. We'd talk tomorrow when they got back to town. Elaine was reluctant but in the end she agreed. Then her voice recovered its strength.

'This makes the situation clearer, Eddie,' she said. She handed me back to Stuart.

'Eddie, let's talk tomorrow, discuss the next step. Meantime, let's put things on hold. As long as Bernie's with us the vigilante guy's not a threat, and once Christa's back his game's finished. No more of this "Killer Couple" nonsense.'

I waited a moment. Didn't mention that we'd already got their vigilante and that he – or they – *were* the people at Dartford. I chose my words carefully.

'We haven't found Christa,' I said. 'We've still to confirm that it's her in the photo. And we've not seen a child at Dartford. We need to keep all lines open for a few days. We're nearly there, Stuart. Let's not relax now.'

'I hear what you say, Eddie, but I disagree. You've traced the photograph, and we *know* it's her. So let's decide how to approach these Dartford people. If there's any further investigation needed you can advise us.'

I thought about it.

'Fine,' I said. 'Your decision. We'll talk tomorrow.'

I killed the call. Shaughnessy looked at me.

'They want us to put on the brakes,' I said.

'Too early,' Shaughnessy said. 'Until we've tied everything together we risk losing the trail.'

'Why do they want us off the job?' I asked. 'How can a few more days hurt?'

Shaughnessy pushed the photos aside. 'It's as if they don't want us to uncover anything else,' he said. 'But it's hard to see what they're afraid of. If we find Christa they're in the clear. No more "Baby Killer" stuff. What are we missing?'

That was the question. And until we knew the answer we'd continue looking. We wouldn't back off until we had Christa safe or proved that she wasn't saveable. And I wasn't looking for the Barbers' approval. I stared out of Shaughnessy's window. Watched the street.

'Gonna be a busy day tomorrow,' I said. 'Best scenario: we might get to her.'

Shaughnessy coughed behind me. I shut up. I've learned not to talk about best scenarios. Aspirations rarely work in this business. I turned and threw a grin that was mostly fear. Knowing our luck a golden spanner was heading for the works right now.

Sure: we were nearly there. But we still hadn't a clue what was happening.

~~~~~

I called Bernie's number. The phone rang for twenty seconds which included the ten it took him to walk along the railway carriage and take the call in private.

When he picked up I detailed the one-sided conversation he'd just overheard. Asked about the mood.

'You've stuck a twig in the nest, pal,' Bernie said. 'Stuart and Elaine are hopping. Guess I understand, if you're getting near Christa.'

'I don't know how near we are. We've still too many unknowns. But we need the Barbers to stay out of the way. They're going to change their minds tonight and decide to come straight back to town. Don't let them do that.'

'I'm on it,' Bernie said. 'And you've got Jagger's support – he wants tomorrow to run according to plan. He's fantasising about breaking the news that we're close to finding Christa right there on their afternoon TV thing. He wants to wrong-foot the press. Get *The Nation* on the defensive.'

'We can't let him do that. That will tip off whoever has Christa. Talk to him. Make him understand. He can launch his bombshells when we actually have Christa – if we ever do.'

'Got it. I'll threaten to break his arms if he lets this out of the bag.'

'Tell him you'll mess up his hair,' I said. 'That'll work better. But talk to Stuart and Elaine. They need to understand that if we spook whoever has Christa then they'll run. Tell them they'll be looking for another firm if that happens.'

'Done, pal.'

I cut the line.

'We've got two days,' Shaughnessy said. 'Once *The Nation* sets off its fireworks the wraps will come off the whole thing. I can't see the Barbers keeping quiet if they're being chased by a posse.'

I left the window. Flopped back into the chair.

'There's one thing stumps me,' I said. 'How did a professional villain come to be taking that photo? How did he know about Christa or where to find her? I can't help thinking that if the wrong people get wind of where we are then we really could lose her.'

'You think Hayes is involved beyond the photo scam?'

'No. His profit is in revealing where Christa is. But there are too many unknowns. I get the feeling someone's about to break and run. We need to look hard tomorrow, get the Hayes connection and make sure Tyndall and his girlfriend don't make a move we don't know about.'

'I'll get the connection,' Shaughnessy promised. 'Harry can cover the cottage. You still going for Melanie?'

'I'll take a last dig. Something tells me she can answer all our questions.'

~~~~~

I picked Arabel up as she came off shift. We shopped fast then she showered while I worked in the kitchen. My mind hadn't been focused at the supermarket. I had ingredients for eighty per cent of ten dishes. Opted for a surprise dish, the main surprised party being the chef. I fired up the pressure cooker and boiled up lamb that had been intended for a terrine, then chilled the top back off and threw in vegetables; nuked a couple of jackets and rushed for a shower.

The quick stew worked well with chilled beer and an open window. Arabel's a slim girl but her stomach capacity would have a tyrannosaurus gossiping. I kept up with her through the simple fact of having eaten nothing since breakfast.

I told her about Chatham. She interrupted her eating to compare my snapshot with the Barbers' book jacket and her eyes opened wide. I explained how the Chatham house linked Christa to Heather Duggan, Paul Tyndall's girlfriend. And how Heather and Melanie Brand had once lived together – maybe had a relationship a while back. Arabel was suitably impressed. More so when I explained that Melanie Brand was Christa's mother.

When she'd finished being impressed she thought it through.

'You think Melanie was involved in Christa's disappearance?'

'It's a possibility, though I don't see it.'

'It would be great if you found Christa, babe. But you need to watch you don't steamroller Melanie in the process. Forcing her into the limelight might not help her.'

'I'll keep her out of it, best I can.'

'And if you can't?'

'At least I can give her some warning.'

'What happens if she took Christa?'

'There's nothing that suggests she did. She didn't want Christa, remember?'

'Maybe she changed her mind.'

'Sure,' I said. 'I can't rule her out. But I'm not seeing her as the abductor, despite the connections. I'm still missing something.'

We left the washing-up stacked and walked over to the park to counteract some of the calories. Found the weather changing. Gusts tugged at us as we walked down to the Pagoda. The lights were coming on. Arabel gripped my hand and strode fast; didn't say much until we got back to the Sun Gate and were waiting for traffic.

'Think you'll close the case this week, Flynn?' she asked.

'Yeah. I just don't know what we're going to find. Or what *The Nation* might drop on us. But it will be over by Friday.'

We crossed the road. Walked up the street. Arabel stopped at the gate.

'Make sure that Melanie doesn't get hurt,' she said. 'I don't want to think *I* helped if things turn out bad.'

I held the gate open; said nothing. I had no control over how things would turn out.

CHAPTER FIFTY-FIVE
Step-shit in the brambles

The Meadow Lane's forwarding address had given me a connection between Melanie and Heather Duggan, the woman mixed up in the vigilante stuff at Dartford, but it hadn't got me to Melanie. The only other route to the Barbers' ex-*au pair* was her family. Not a great possibility from what Melanie's friend had told me but it was all I had. I headed out to Southampton mid morning. Called Lucy hands-free for an update on *The Nation's* latest front page.

'You were right, Eddie. The main splash is tomorrow. They're going to name the culprits and tell us where Christa is buried.'

Maybe I was wasting my time chasing Melanie. Maybe I should just take a subscription to *The Nation*. Invoice the Barbers at sixty pence a day. I killed the line. Flicked on the radio.

LBC were running a weather update, describing torrential rain over Dorset like it was a new phenomenon. The storm would hit London by mid afternoon. The guy warned of three inches. The sky ahead of me was murk. I kept my foot down and raced towards a hazy prospect.

According to her friend Louise, Melanie's old family home was located next to a pub on a housing estate east of Southampton. My A-Z guided me to a wall of bunker-like dwellings guarding the northern boundary of the estate. I cut through a gap and drove between tower blocks into a wilderness of council semis blighted by cracked rendering and ugly porches. The roads weaved and crossed, doubled back and traversed grassy spaces to meet up in dreary plazas of boarded-up shops. The fifties developer had a vision of green lawns and curving pathways, but five decades of tyre tracks had re-mapped the open grass with bare-earth shortcuts to convenient parking. I quartered the labyrinth for ten minutes using the tower blocks as a compass. The mounting breeze raised dust devils. Plastic bags skittered along the road.

I finally spotted the sterile architecture of a fifties' pub at a junction on the south side of the estate. The sign had come down but its name was memorialised in faded lettering across the building's facade. *The Curzon*. A soulless name for a soulless drinking hole. Louise's information said that the run-down house next door was Melanie Brand's childhood home. I parked. Lifted my shades. The house was a disaster even by the estate's apocalyptic standards. It squatted behind drawn curtains, its front face a mosaic of rotted rendering. Slabs of fallen masonry lay amongst the rampant weeds in the front garden and a detached downspout angled out in a drunken salute. I sensed a council out of maintenance funds. Or maybe the house had been one of Mrs Thatcher's right-to-buy sell-offs. Whatever the buyer had paid back in the eighties, the house was worth less now. The front gate was jammed half-open by a decade's untended undergrowth. I squeezed through and pressed the door bell. Nothing. I rapped on the woodwork. Same result. Tried the window. Knocked as hard as I dared. Wondered if I'd driven ninety minutes for nothing. A dog barked up the street. The heat burned my soles.

Then movement within. The lock clicked and a man's face appeared, sporting three days' stubble; unkempt straw hair; bad teeth, worse breath. A tracksuit top hung free from a massive gut. A lifestyle thing.

I asked if this was the Brand house.

He said no.

I'd taken him for sixty-plus. Re-calculated, factoring in personal neglect. Came out at forty-five.

'I'm looking for Melanie Brand,' I said. 'Did she live here?'

His face signalled that she might have done but he didn't seem interested in putting the concept into words.

I repeated my enquiry. Put in a little more volume. Leaned forward, like there was only one way we were going with this. The guy gave it some thought.

'She's not here,' he said.

Maybe she'd popped out to the local Spar. Maybe she'd not been here for five years. The answer wasn't too specific. I smiled, thanked the guy and pushed past him into the hallway. The action woke him up. He came after me and yelled at me to steady on and what the hell I was doing?

'I need some information,' I said. 'Is anyone else home?'

The hallway was a mess of scattered coats and trainers. A bicycle was propped against the wall, minus its chain which was oiling the carpet. The place stank of Indian takeaways and beer. I hoped to hell someone else *was* home because I didn't want to talk to this guy. Even if he'd been articulate and clean he wouldn't have been my choice for a natter because this had to be Melanie's stepfather, the guy who'd been diddling her since she was a kid.

'Who's home?' I repeated.

He glanced up the stairs. 'Wendy,' he said.

'Melanie's mother?'

'Yeah.'

'Mind calling her?' I went and closed the front door so we were clear. The hallway darkened.

The man eyed me; pulled up a little belligerence. 'How about telling me what you're after.'

'Just a chat.'

He tried to find an answer. Gave up. Yelled up the stairs. It took a couple more to shake Wendy loose but she finally appeared dressed in a tracksuit top and Union Jack shorts. She came down, tilting her head.

'Feller to see you,' the guy said.

I pushed open the lounge door. Went in where we could talk without me being in such close proximity to the guy. The room was dark behind its drawn curtains and stank like an army of takeaways had died in there. I flicked the light on. Illuminated cartons and cans lying where they'd fallen.

Wendy came in and stood by the door. She sported a smaller version of her husband's gut. Flabby rolls for arms.

'Mrs Brand?'

The dim light illuminated bags under her eyes, the loose yellow skin of someone who's stopped caring.

'Not any more. I was remarried.'

'I'm looking for Melanie,' I said. I explained who I was. Didn't say why I was looking, and Wendy didn't ask.

'Melanie's not lived here since way back,' she said.

'Never comes home?'

She shook her head. 'Not in years. Ungrateful sod.'

From what her friend had told me Melanie had plenty to be ungrateful about. I didn't see her rushing back at every opportunity. I wasn't going to find her here but I needed some sort of contact. I asked, but Wendy shook her head again.

'We never hear nothing from her. She doesn't care if we're alive or dead.'

'No Christmas cards?'

Wendy laughed, the wheeze of a heavy smoker.

'Has she any friends round here?'

'Who are you?' Wendy said. 'The police? What's she done?'

I guess my introduction had gone over her head.

'Does Melanie have friends?' I repeated.

'No she doesn't have any friends. No-one I know about.' Wendy gripped the door. 'And if you find her you can tell her to keep clear. That girl was nothing but trouble.'

The guy had slid into the room behind her. He watched from over her shoulder. I breathed shallowly.

'Can't help, mister,' he apologised. 'Melanie flew the nest years ago.'

'Flew your ruddy nest, you mean,' said Wendy.

'Bugger off!' the guy said but I spotted a smile. One that made me want to leave. I was choking on this stink for nothing: Melanie's family weren't going to give me anything. The thing had been a long shot. The two of them watched me, old soaks, aged by sloth. But ten years ago the guy must have been pretty unpleasant to live with. I pictured a young girl growing up here.

'Thanks for your help.' I said.

They stood back as I pulled the door wide and walked into the hallway. Then someone came trotting down the stairs and blocked my path. A youth. Mean. Muscled. A younger version of Wendy's husband. He wore a Saints' shirt over khaki knee-length shorts, black trainers, no socks. Melanie's stepbrother, Craig. The guy who'd shared her with his father. He eyed me over and asked what was up. 'Selling insurance, mate?' he asked.

I kept a straight face. 'I doubt if you're insurable,' I said. I waited for him to shift but he folded his arms and asked Wendy and her husband again what was up.

'He's after Melanie,' Wendy said.

'Oh aye?' Craig smiled at me. 'Why's that?'

'Know where she is?'

'No.' He held his smirk.

'Then we're through,' I said.

I made to squeeze past but he stepped to block my way. I was still on my shallow-breathing routine. I asked him if he'd mind moving.

He grinned and moved just enough for me to squeeze past, and it was only because I turned away from him that I spotted a photo hanging in the gloom.

I stopped.

The picture was a faded family snap taken round the Christmas table. I guess even dysfunctional families get out the crackers and funny hats once a year. The remarkable thing was that anyone had thought to hang the picture. Maybe it had been the mood of the moment. Looking at the group you could almost mistake them for normal. Wendy was a couple of stones lighter and considerably neater; ditto her husband. Next to him a younger version of the slob beside me was glaring at the photographer. But it was the two other figures who caught my attention, two girls seated side by side. The one mimicking Craig's glare had to be Melanie. She was in her early teens, dark-haired, pretty if she lost the frown. The figure next to her with the forced smile I already knew: Paul Tyndall's girlfriend, Heather Duggan, the woman Melanie had been living with when they had Maureen Parker as a neighbour.

Not lesbians.

Stepsisters.

That was Melanie's connection to Tyndall and Heather. She'd gone to live with her stepsister when she was desperate for a roof. I turned and asked Wendy about the photograph and she confirmed my identification.

It was the first picture of Melanie I'd seen. Or maybe the second. Because the face was eerily similar to the original rough photofit the Barbers released two days after Christa disappeared. Their Mystery Woman. The polished version in their book was missing those intense eyes, was barely a likeness at all. Was the first photofit the real Mystery Woman?

'Mind if I take a copy?' I asked.

Craig chipped in behind me.

'You like pictures of little girls?'

I lifted the frame. Turned to look at him

'It won't take a second. I just need some light.'

The youth shook his head. Sheer awkwardness. It gave him a kick.

'Teenies your thing then?' he persisted.

I was out of chuckles myself.

'If they ever are,' I said, 'I'll give you a call. You and your dad.'

The smirk vanished.

I made to push towards the light at the back of the house but the slob's fingers grabbed my arm. I turned.

'You've got three seconds,' I said, 'before I break them.'

His grin came back but he let go. Not totally stupid.

'Okay, mister,' he said. He tilted his head towards the rear. 'Away we go.'

The kitchen let me out into the blinding light of a back garden jungle. An old patio table stood at a slant that had just the right angle for holding the photo. As I put the frame down I sensed the movement I'd been expecting and turned, moved aside quick. Not quick enough to avoid the slob's foot. He had powerful legs and chunky trainers and the kick slid across my thigh like a wrecking ball. Hurt like hell but the guy was clumsy rather than skilled. His technique was fine for the occasional Saturday afternoon ruck down at St Mary's but he'd never picked up real fighting skills. I snatched his foot before it got back to earth and levered it up, locked the knee with my forearm and pulled him forwards, away from anything grabbable. He came hopping after me into the undergrowth. I kept the foot up at chest height and there wasn't much he could do. A nasty-looking patch of brambles lurked half way down the garden and I rotated him so his back was to the mess. His arms were flailing.

'Your only warning,' I said.

I pushed hard and got him hopping backwards and then heaved like hell and he went down into the thicket. The thorns ripped skin and tee shirt alike and he started yelling blue murder. I walked back to the table and took the photo from the frame and laid it on the tilted surface. Wendy and her husband watched from the back door as their step-shit struggled to free himself from the brambles. It would take a while unless he wanted to lose skin.

I zoomed my phone. Held my breath and pressed the button. Checked the result. Passable.

Behind me Melanie's stepbrother was almost free. I left the photo on the table and avoided the stink by going round the outside of the house.

My thigh was burning as I hopped back into the car. I comforted myself by imagining what falling into those brambles must have felt like. I fired up the engine just as Craig ran out of the house. He was too late. I reversed to the junction and skidded away.

The link between Melanie and Heather Duggan was now solid, which confirmed Melanie's connection to the Chatham house and therefore to the child in the Christa Photo. Further proof that the child was Christa. Had Melanie lived in Chatham with her? Was she living at Dartford now? Was Christa? One thing was certain: the whole revolved around Heather and Melanie.

What I still couldn't figure was why Heather or Melanie was persecuting the Barbers as "Baby Killers".

Which brought me back to the fact that the Christa Photo was over a year old. What had happened since then?

CHAPTER FIFTY-SIX
You can't un-see...

I headed back to where it all started. A call came in from Shaughnessy.

'Hayes and Tyndall are second cousins.'

Bingo. The connection. Simple chance hadn't put Hayes outside a property linked to Tyndall. I thumbed the indicator; skipped past a lorry.

'Are they close?'

'Not close, not strangers. An acquaintance has them meeting at occasional get-togethers – weddings and the like.'

'So if Tyndall was involved with Christa word might get to Hayes.'

'Hayes is the type to keep his ear to the ground. My guess is he heard a whisper that Tyndall had the girl at Chatham. Sensed an opportunity. Tyndall's not in Hayes' firm, so no loyalty issues. Hayes saw the chance of an easy buck and decided to sell his cousin out.'

I passed Lyndhurst. A strengthening breeze dropped the temperature ten degrees. I was driving towards a wall of cloud that cascaded from a high pristine white through dirty yellows to an evil black base.

I concurred with Shaughnessy. A professional hoodlum wasn't going to think twice about shafting his petty-crime cousin. And two hundred thou' is a nice incentive. I briefed him on the other family link: Melanie and Heather. Things were starting to tie up, even if all we were getting was a knot. We just needed to keep the Barbers clear and quiet for two more days whilst we unravelled it – assuming there was anything left to unravel after *The Nation* ran their splash tomorrow.

'Are you with Tyndall?'

Shaughnessy had taken over from Harry, who was on his way to cover the Barbers when they arrived back in town.

'I'm on his tail now. I'll stay close until we know which way things are going.'

I disconnected and drove on towards the Orchard Grove with my photo of Melanie. Forget the Barbers' assurances that she hadn't been near the place: I wanted to know whether anyone at the site recognised her picture.

I called Bernie, confirmed the Barbers' schedule.

'We're just in at St Pancras, pal. We'll be at the house in forty-five. Harry's taking over for their TV thing.'

'Tell Stuart and Elaine to hang on until I get there,' I said.

We were going to have a serious talk.

~~~~~

I turned past the derelict barrier. Rolled through the trees to the caravan site and pulled up outside the office. A blast of wind set the tree tops swaying like inverted brooms. Birds darted across the funny light. People were busy round the caravans, stacking chairs and folding awnings. Inside the office the lights were on and a radio was playing an afternoon show.

Bob Bowland was sitting at his desk, tapping at a keyboard. He came to attention with a gleam in his eyes. He'd read the papers. The Barber show was live again and like everyone else he was waiting to see what would come up from the table when *The Nation* pulled the lever. He nodded. Smiled.

'Help you?'

I smiled back. The Christa circus was a promised treat – as long as it stayed clear of Bob's site this time. As long as I didn't tell him he had a body under his floorboards.

'Just tidying up,' I said. 'Trying to clear a few things before the papers jump on top of us.'

'Hell of a thing.'

I held the smile. Bowland knew that the Barber ship was going down. Maybe I could give him a view from the bridge. But I had less of a view than he assumed: I'd been running around in the engine room when the deck started canting. I pulled out my phone and showed him the picture of Melanie and Heather.

'It's a long time ago, but maybe you remember one of the faces.'

Bowland pulled on reading glasses and got the picture close. His eyes flicked between the two girls.

'The one on the left,' I hinted.

But he shook his head.

'Is this the conspirator?'

My smile held. Seemed we all had tickets to *The Nation's* mystery tour.

'I'll take a walk round if it's no trouble,' I said. 'Check with one or two others.'

'Be my guest,' Bowland said.

There was a flash. A rumble like tipped rubble rattled the windows.

'Hell of a blow coming in,' Bowland said. His eyes were on the window. 'They say we're going to get six inches.'

It had been three just an hour back. I guess Bob had a more creative forecaster. But I could see his concern. The Orchard Grove was barely three feet above the river. His bookings weren't going to multiply if half the caravans were floating in mid-Channel by morning.

Another rumble. Longer, louder. I left Bowland and walked down the site.

The Smiths were folding a sunshade and stashing things under their deck. The guy called his wife over to look at the photo. They both shook their heads.

'We didn't notice anyone that day,' Reg said. 'Were these two involved?'

'The one on the left might have been. She's a little younger in this picture but you'd probably recognise her.'

They both looked again but recognition eluded them. A fat raindrop hit my neck. I turned to see the cloud breaking over us like a twenty thousand foot tsunami.

'The satellite's already gone,' Reg said. 'We'll be missing *Neighbours* if it doesn't clear.'

They hustled into their caravan to worry. I looked at the Barber unit, hunched on its deck, indifferent to the weather. The bloodwork still covered the windows. It was hard to imagine that the place had ever been just a happy holiday home. The unit brooded in the yellow light like a mean dog.

I walked across to Irene Keenan's.

She came out, wiping her hands on her apron; had a smile for me but shook her head when I asked her to think back to the day Christa disappeared. Like the Smiths, she'd gone through it a million times. She hadn't spotted anything out of the ordinary until the alarm was raised. I held my phone up anyway and she fingered her glasses to take a look.

Her gaze lingered – then locked.

'Oh my goodness!' she said.

She looked at me in dismay; angled the phone towards me. Her shaking finger tapped the screen.

'This one,' she said. 'Who's she?'

The figure she was touching was Melanie Brand, the girl the Barbers claimed had been nowhere near the Orchard Grove. I looked at Irene.

'You saw her here?'

'Yes!'

'Before Christa disappeared?'

Lightning flashed off her glasses. She shook her head.

'Oh no,' she said. 'She wasn't here that night.'

But she looked like she was about to weep.

'Tell me,' I said.

~~~~~

I walked fast to the site office. A raindrop smacked my face. Then another. Hard. My call connected.

'Luce,' I said, 'we've got a problem.'

'Wow, Eddie! I already paid the electricity.'

The electricity blinded me with a searing flash. A second later hell's drums toppled and the ground shook.

'It's not the utilities this time,' I said. 'Have you got the vigilante letters handy?'

'Right on your desk.'

'Grab 'em. Read 'em out.'

The raindrops were coming fast and hard, streaking down like silver bullets. People were starting to run. I reached the shop awning. Lucy came back.

'Go through them in order,' I said.

She read all seven. By the time she'd finished the rain had turned to hail that threatened to split the awning and I could hardly hear her. I yelled for her to hang tight. Cut the line. Stared down the site at the distant blur that was the Barber caravan. Asked myself how the hell I'd missed it.

It was like one of those Rorschach things. Once you saw the shape in the random mess it stood out a mile. You couldn't un-see it. I thought about Hackett and his *Nation* story. The guy had used all the wrong deductions but he'd come damn close to the right conclusion. I stepped out from the awning's protection and jumped into the Frogeye. No time to clip the hood on. I'd be outpacing the storm anyway. I needed to get to the Barbers – fast.

I drove five minutes in the deluge before I broke out ahead of the storm front and put my foot down towards London. Lightning strobed in my rear-view. Blackness chased me. My phone rang as I hit the M25. I picked up, hands-free. Harry: over at the Barber house ready for their afternoon gig.

'She's gone.'

I was moving onto the slip for the Orbital north. The words jolted me with a premonition.

'Where?'

'Stuart says she's heading to Dartford. Said she couldn't wait. She took the Galaxy ten minutes ago. Jagger's having fits over his TV schedule.'

One-up to premonitions. The news was as bad as it gets.

'Didn't Stuart try to stop her?'

'Not hard enough. They were out front arguing and then Stuart came back to tell me she'd split.

'What did he say?'

'She's going for Christa.'

'We don't know Christa's there! I thought they agreed to hang fire until we'd talked.'

'Sounds like she's going with the odds,' Harry said. 'Stuart says she's been talking about nothing but rescuing Christa since yesterday.'

'We need to stop her,' I said. 'Stay with Stuart.'

I hit Shaughnessy's code. He was with Tyndall. If they were at his bodyshop he could be at the cottage in two minutes. When Elaine showed up he'd be waiting.

Turned out he wouldn't. Shaughnessy gave me news I didn't want to hear.

'I'm outside a wreckers in Swindon,' he said. 'Tyndall's here with his flatbed scavenging an old Citroen.'

Swindon! Shaughnessy was further away than I was! I cursed again and thumbed the indicator; skidded into the southbound slip just as the divider came up, left traffic standing on the curve. I brought Shaughnessy up to speed, told him where Elaine was going.

'Holy smoke!' he said. 'I'll see you there.'

The slip merged with the Orbital and I accelerated between artics and hogged the outside lane.

Elaine was on the same road but diametrically opposite me on the far side of London. She had a ten minute start and there was no way I was going to beat her to Dartford. The best I could do was arrive at her heels. I kept my foot down through the variable limits. My direction was taking me back towards the storm front. Five minutes later I was in it and the rain came on like nobody's business. I flicked the lights back on and floored the pedal, raced south through the deluge.

"Bad as it gets" had just got worse. I'd misjudged things. Should have told Bernie and Harry to keep the Barbers at Elstree by whatever means. Now Elaine was going to turn up alone at Dartford, and if she ran into Heather Duggan there was going to be only one outcome. A bad one.

CHAPTER FIFTY-SEVEN
The knives come out

Just past the M23 the traffic was stalled by an outside lane shunt. The rain was bouncing off the road so hard the surface was invisible. I eased the Frogeye over and drove five hundred yards on a flooded hard shoulder; cleared the blockage and floored the pedal.

Day had turned to night. The sky rippled with lightning and was dumping a deluge that would have Noah grabbing for his wellies. The inside of the Frogeye was turning into a swimming pool. Water was actually accumulating on the floor. I wondered if my insurance covered flood damage. If I stopped to put up the hood I'd lose five minutes. I kept going.

I left the Orbital on the tunnel approach and streaked west towards Crayford, pushing hard through spray and oncoming headlights. I hit a roundabout by the river and aquaplaned round it then put my foot to the floor for a dicey half mile of narrow lanes across marshy grazing land. Shaughnessy's description had me searching for a track feeding an isolated farm cottage. The track appeared, unmarked and barely visible through the screen. I hit the brakes, corrected a slide and pointed the Frogeye down towards the river. Spotted the cottage – and the Barbers' Galaxy, parked askew outside it, driver's door open as if Elaine had sprinted in. Beyond the Galaxy, another car. A black Renault Clio.

I hit the horn. Kept my thumb pressed. The racket of the storm smothered the sound. I jumped out and sprinted for the house.

The front door was wide open and rain was pooling on the tiles inside. I yelled Elaine's name. Heard a scream and a crash from the back of the house. I ran down the hallway and burst into a kitchen. It was a large room, extended by knocking the old parlour through; a centrepiece table in varnished oak; wooden units; old appliances. The scream repeated and I saw Elaine Barber, down on the floor in the corner to my left. On the far side of the table was a wild-eyed Heather Duggan, clutching a kitchen knife.

Elaine yelled my name and scrabbled backwards towards me, rolled onto her knees. Her hands clawed my soaked trousers. 'She's trying to kill me!' she sobbed.

Heather stayed behind the table, unsure who the hell I was. Finally found her own voice and yelled back. Thunder burst over the house like an artillery barrage. 'She's crazy,' Heather shouted. 'She's the one trying to kill me!'

I stepped over Elaine and walked round the table. Heather backed away, pointing the knife.

'Take it easy,' I said, but Heather gripped the handle until her knuckles showed white. She shook her head, yelled at me to get the hell back.

Behind me Elaine was yelling at me to watch the knife. The two of them were screaming at each other and screaming at me. Pure pandemonium. A minute later, though, and it would have been worse.

Heather was waving the knife at me and sobbing that we'd come to kill her. I took another step. Feinted then moved sharpish and grabbed her wrist. Got her fingers open and eased the implement out. Heather's body stiffened with fright.

'It's okay,' I said. 'Let's go and sit down.'

But Heather was staring at something behind me. Mouthing words that wouldn't come.

I turned just in time to meet a kitchen knife coming down towards my neck. But kitchen knives move in big arcs. You have to take a swing or a lunge. All too slow when the target is expecting it. I leaned sideways and caught Elaine's arm as it arced through, lifted it high and got her off balance then tapped her feet from under her. As she went down I released the knife and jabbed it into the rack along with the one I'd taken from Heather. Then I reached up and slid the rack onto a cupboard top, pushed it well back. Any more tricks, they'd need a ladder.

Elaine was still sobbing something about Heather trying to kill us, which hadn't the same ring now she'd just gone for my jugular herself.

I looked down at her: 'It's all over, Elaine,' I said. 'It's not going to happen.'

I reached down and helped her to her feet, pulled a chair out and sat her down. Heather stayed by the window.

'Let's all calm down,' I said. 'No more tricks.'

I pulled my phone out and went to stand with Heather. She was shaking with shock.

Before the call connected the kitchen door moved and a head peered fearfully in. A little girl. Four years old. Confusion on her face.

Elaine screamed and jumped from her chair. Squatted down and grabbed the child in a bear-hug. She was sobbing Christa's name as she pulled the girl to her chest. The sobs turned to weeping as she clung onto the child for dear life. Beside me, Heather started to move forward but I grabbed her arm – hard.

I made the call. Watched Elaine weeping, repeating Christa's name over and over. Brushing her hands endlessly through the girl's hair. But the child just stared at Heather and stared at me and looked lost.

CHAPTER FIFTY-EIGHT
It's all under control, fellas

I'd just moved our gathering to the front parlour when a motorbike coughed outside and Shaughnessy came in. The rain was easing. Daylight returning. Thunder rumbled in the distance.

Elaine was sitting on the sofa clutching Christa at her knees. The child stood bemused, watching Heather. Heather was slumped in a chair, face in her hands. I was standing by the fireplace in an expanding puddle. Shaughnessy looked at me then at Elaine. Elaine appealed to him.

'She was going to kill me!'

'Then you wouldn't have been able to kill me,' I pointed out.

Elaine closed her eyes. 'Eddie. I'm so sorry. It was a moment of madness. I thought you were on her side.'

I shot Shaughnessy a grin.

'We know the truth, Elaine,' Shaughnessy said.

Elaine's eyes opened again.

'You saw her, Eddie! She had the knife!'

'But if they fingerprint it they'll find yours there, since you were holding it when I barged in. You just reacted quick. Slid it across the table. And Heather grabbed it. What else would she do, seeing as you were about to kill her?'

Shaughnessy went out and found bath towels. Tossed them across. I pressed them against my slacks and tee shirt. Got a couple of gallons out. I wasn't much dryer but I was a hell of a lot lighter. I tossed the towels. Said: 'We know everything, Elaine.'

Elaine shook her head. Christa turned in her arms and checked us all out.

'You killed Melanie Brand,' I said.

The light flared in Elaine's eyes, then it went out. She slumped. Pulled Christa closer.

'She was trying to take my baby,' she whispered. 'It was self-defence.'

Heather's head came up.

'Not your baby,' she spat. 'My sister's baby.'

Elaine returned a look to turn milk.

'Bitch!' she hissed. 'You caused all of this. It was you who incited Melanie to try to take Christa back.'

We were setting up for another ding-dong. I considered getting the knives back down but heard sirens in the distance. Better if everyone stayed alive to tell their tale.

I left Shaughnessy with Elaine and took Heather through to the little sitting room on the far side of the hallway. She sat down and answered a few questions, confirmed a few theories.

The sirens worked their way over the marshes. Vehicles pulled up. Feet came running and two Kent Police officers barged in. Sixteen minutes after my emergency call. Impressive. But I guess it's not everyday that the call comes in to say that the country's biggest soap is entering its finale.

More boots. More uniforms. A sergeant and a female constable. The sergeant listened to what I had to say then called base and went to talk to Elaine. Assigned Christa to the policewoman's care. Elaine tried to resist but the policewoman coaxed her hands open, offered to get Christa a drink. Led the child away.

Twenty minutes later two Kent CID men arrived. The one in charge was a DI called Lomack. He got himself briefed then confined me and Shaughnessy to the kitchen while he chatted to Elaine. Their talk was brief. He arrested her on suspicion of murder then went to talk to Heather. I heard him place Heather under arrest for the abduction of Christa, then he came back to the kitchen with his partner. Shaughnessy and I were watching Christa eating Coco Pops on the policewoman's knee. Lomack looked at them. Then at us.

'I've heard about you two,' he said. 'You shot those guys in Sussex.'

I smiled. 'It was only one guy,' I said. Shaughnessy didn't smile. Lomack let it go. Tilted his head towards the front rooms.

'Well you've pulled a good-'un here, chaps. Nicked your own client.' He gave the two of us a bright look.

I held the smile. Shaughnessy held the stare. 'They paid up front,' I said. 'We're covered.'

Lomack's eyes stayed bright. 'Give us your card,' he said. 'If my wife ever decides to check me out she can have your number.' He looked at his partner and they had a good laugh. When the laughs were done he told me and Shaughnessy to start talking.

~~~~~

It didn't take long. We gave him the basics to underpin his two arrests. Lomack had territorial issues. The Christa affair wasn't his but Elaine's attempted killing had been right here in Dartford. I agreed to talk to whichever force took up the baton. Lomack said he was through and Shaughnessy and I walked out of the house.

A mob was trotting up the track, news people, jostling past the police vehicles. It had only been an hour and fifteen but word was out. A leak from my second call, most likely – the one to Stuart. He was on his way over with Jagger who I guess had made some hasty calls. If something big was happening he didn't want it to go down out of the public eye. The camera guys swarmed up. More vehicles were manoeuvring out on the road.

Shaughnessy and I stayed clear and waited for Stuart to arrive. Call it professional courtesy. We wouldn't be doing any further business once he'd spoken to the police. I squatted to feel the Frogeye's floor. The carpet was sodden but most of the water had drained out. Must be a leak somewhere. I figured the car would be okay if it didn't blow a fuse when I pressed the starter. A yell from the mob snapped me back.

'Flynn! What the hell's happening?'

I turned. Hackett was stumbling across. Unlikely that Jagger had included him on his call list but I guess the grapevine spreads wide. Hackett gestured at the police vehicles, wide-eyed. The cops hadn't been due into this until *The Nation's* splash tomorrow. I grinned.

'She's inside,' I said.

'Who? Who the hell's inside?' Hackett's cronies had caught up and were yelling similar questions but Hackett was the one with the most riding on this. I stretched my grin. Gave him the news.

'Christa's in there,' I said.

'No way!' Hackett said. 'She's dead. I've got proof.'

The journalists were crowding, all babbling at once.

'It's your story that's dead, Archie,' I said. 'Better get on the blower. Tell them to work up a new front page for tomorrow.'

Hackett realised I was serious. A vision of his career nose-diving flashed across his thoughts. Then his journalistic instincts kicked in and he yelled at me along with the others to tell him what was happening.

'Talk to the police,' I said, 'or make something up.'

'They're here,' Shaughnessy said.

I looked and saw Harry Green marching up the track with Stuart at his side and Jagger puffing along ten yards back. They pushed through and Stuart looked at me like nothing made sense. But it did make sense. Perfect sense.

'She's inside,' I said. 'Go say hello to your daughter, Stuart.'

The mob surged with him towards the cottage. One of the uniforms barred the door but I yelled across that Stuart was family and the policeman let Harry escort him through.

Jagger arrived, flapping his arms at the press who had questions he couldn't answer.

'Give me two minutes, fellas,' he wheezed. 'I'll have something for you.' He came trotting over.

It was going to take more than two minutes to get his head round the new situation. He looked at me then Shaughnessy then me again. We walked him away from the din.

'What's happening with Elaine?' Jagger asked.

'She's under arrest,' I said, 'for killing her *au pair*.'

'Her what? What damned *au pair*? What have you pulled off here, Flynn?'

'The truth,' I said. 'You always suspected that Elaine had killed Christa, Owen. Well you weren't too far off. She'd killed someone, at least.'

'What the hell are you saying?' He was dancing. Suit creased. Looked like hell. Not as bad as me, of course, since his car had a top, but it was lucky that Jagger no longer needed to show up for his TV slot. The only TV screens featuring his clients from now on would be their cell-block monitors. Jagger's eyes were popping.

'What have you done Flynn? Have you let something out without clearing it with the family?'

'I told you, Owen: Elaine killed Melanie, her *au pair*. That's what the whole thing has been about. We don't need your permission to report a murder.'

'Holy shit, Flynn! Elaine's no goddamn murderer! Tell me you're kidding! Tell me you haven't just shopped your own damn client!'

I sort of grinned.

'No kidding, Owen. Elaine killed Melanie two years ago, the night Christa disappeared.'

Jagger spun a three-sixty. Looked for a way out. Locked onto the press mob. Turned back.

'Tell me! I gotta talk to them!'

'We just did,' Shaughnessy said. 'You'll need to work Elaine's prison timetable into your schedule from now on.'

'The baby!' Jagger rasped. 'What happened to the baby? Did Elaine kill her too?'

I shook my head.

'Christa's inside the house. She's fine. I guess that's some consolation.'

'Alive?' His eyes were popping like the buttons on his Armani. 'The baby's *alive?*'

'Just like you've always told us, Owen.'

But his golden goose was dead. The Barber circus had just crashed the buffers. His milch cow had wandered off into the sunset – unless Owen was going to squeeze a new bio from Elaine. *"Waiting For Parole"*.

Jagger squeezed his eyes tight. Mashed his fists into them. 'You really did it!' he gasped. 'This is for real! You've shafted your own clients.' His fists came away and Shaughnessy and I looked at him then Shaughnessy pulled on his helmet and walked to the Yamaha.

'Tomorrow,' he said.

The press mob suddenly swarmed round the cottage door. People were coming out. Uniformed officers first, leading Elaine and Heather. Then the two CID guys. Behind them, Stuart and Harry. The press yelled questions, fired their cameras. Lomack raised an arm. Walked to the side and held up his hands for quiet. The press surged, giving the others a chance to get to their cars and almost allowing the policewoman to sneak out with Christa. But a camera guy clocked the child and Lomack's statement was broadcast to thin air. The press stampeded back and closed in around Christa. The uniforms intervened and opened up a path and the policewoman got the child to the patrol car through a storm of flash photography.

I climbed into the Frogeye and waited for a path to clear. Spotted

Jagger staring as the patrol car moved away. Then he launched himself towards the mob, arms flapping.

'It's all under control, fellas,' he yelled. 'Press release, eight p.m. The baby's back! We told you we'd get her! Eight p.m. at Kestrel. Don't miss the scoop!'

The patrol car disappeared down the track and the press fell back to surround Jagger. I heard him yelling as I drove past.

Hackett was standing back from the mob. He watched me drive by with the look you see when redundancy slips are going out. If my guess was right, someone else would be working up *The Nation's* leader tomorrow. It would be the Barber story, of course, but a different one from the one they'd promised.

And no exclusive.

CHAPTER FIFTY-NINE
Gonna have difficulty selling that one

The rain came back as I drove in. I pulled over at Shooters Hill and dragged the frame out. Snapped the hood into place. Slid the windows open and flicked on the radio.

The news was an extended weather forecast; an inch and a half in London; floods in the West Country; more storms racing across the Atlantic. A changeable period was in the offing, temperatures below normal for May. I'd thought temperatures-below-normal *was* normal. Give it three days and no-one would remember the heat. Then the station cut into a breaking story from Dartford. I killed the radio.

I got lucky and parked outside my apartment, skipped up the stairs. My sodden clothes were chilling me.

Arabel had finished early and we were due to go out. I found her in the lounge watching the news. They'd TV got cameras outside the cottage; a guy doing his piece. Arabel turned.

'Hey, babe.' She looked at my wet clobber and I waited for the mothering instinct to kick in. Maybe she'd think of a way to warm me up. But she turned back to the TV. Stayed seated on the sofa arm.

'They're saying you found Christa,' she said. 'But Elaine's been charged in connection with the disappearance of her natural mother. Is that Melanie?'

'We found Christa,' I confirmed. 'But it didn't come out so well for Melanie. She's dead.'

'Elaine?'

'Killed her two years ago.'

Arabel's eye's closed. 'Poor girl. Not a single break!'

When her eyes opened she threw me a puzzled look.

'They're saying Melanie was related to the vigilante.'

'They were stepsisters.'

'So you were chasing Melanie because you thought she had either taken Christa or was in with the vigilante? You didn't tell me that.'

'I didn't know it. Not until this morning. I guess it was always a possibility that Melanie was behind the hate-mail – or that she had

Christa. But it turned out to be neither.'

Arabel muted the TV. She still hadn't mentioned my soaked clothes. She stood to face me.

'Flynn, you told me that if you found Melanie it would be in her own interest. That's why I helped you. But if she'd been sending hate-mail and was involved in the attacks you'd have had to turn her in. The same if she'd had Christa. They'd probably have put her in jail either way. That's not why I gave you that address, dammit! '

'You can't be jailed for abducting your own child, 'Bel.'

'But you can for the vigilante acts, which was one of your scenarios. And if Melanie had taken Christa they probably wouldn't have let her keep her. You must have known Melanie might get hurt.'

'Yeah,' I admitted. 'Guilty. I knew there was a chance of that. I was just playing the odds: my best guess was that if we found Melanie it would be the best thing for her, whichever way it came out. You can't go through life hiding.'

'Some women do. The ones who stay out of sight at places like the Meadow Road. They're the women my friend deals with, Flynn. Now I've gotta tell her that we used her information to chase someone who needed protecting. I'm gonna have difficulty selling that one, babe.'

I held up my hands.

'What can I say? I made a judgement. I thought we could help Melanie. Turned out no-one could help her.' I sighed again. 'Let me get showered. We'll grab some food and I'll tell you the rest. It's not good but you need to hear it.'

But Arabel shook her head.

'Some other time, babe. Been a long shift. Home sounds good right now.'

'We're not going out?'

She looked at me.

'You need to get out of those clothes.'

She turned and walked towards the door.

'I'd run you home,' I said, 'but the car's kind of damp inside.'

'No problem. A bus will do. Get yourself dried off, babe, before you get a chill.'

She walked out and closed the door.

292

It felt like I'd already got the chill.

Arabel was right. I'd hoped there was some way it would come out good for Melanie but I'd not been convinced. I'd started out believing she could help; finished up seeing her as the key to the whole thing. I'd needed to get to her, even if that meant digging up something that might hurt her. Hell! I wish that's how it had turned out. Anything was better than having her lying cold under Damien Larkin's meadow for the last two years.

I threw my clothes into the basket and stood under a hot shower for thirty minutes. Came out as cold as I went in. Thought how we'd had the perfect end to this job. Usually you get winners and losers. This time we'd hit the jackpot. Everyone was a loser. Especially Melanie and Christa.

CHAPTER SIXTY
Au pair slaughter

I sprinted up Chase Street through torrential rain. Ran in past Rook and Lye's door. No queue blocking the vestibule today. I guess the quest for culpability didn't extend to the punters getting their feet wet. The anticipated visit from our legal friends hadn't materialised but there was new woodwork on the stairs and a demand note somewhere on its way.

The top landing rumbled with the sound of rain on slate, and a bucket was catching drips in the reception area. The bucket was by the wall opposite where the ceiling patch resided on my own side. Maybe the leak had migrated. Lucy was at her desk with the papers.

'Wow, Eddie,' she said.

I grunted and went through; found a biscuit tin catching water in my room. The leak hadn't shifted, just expanded.

I hung my jacket. Grabbed a coffee and invited Lucy through to the front office. Shaughnessy was at his desk. Harry was slumped in an easy chair. I slumped beside him. Drank. The coffee was good. I stopped shivering.

'We're just wondering where to send the report,' Shaughnessy said. 'I guess Holloway allows mail.'

I grinned. 'There's nothing we can tell the Barbers that they didn't already know. And their retainer was good to Tuesday when they pulled us off the job so they don't owe us anything.'

Lucy sat at the partners desk and planted a heap of tabloids.

'It's front page in all of them,' she reported. '*The Nation's* interesting.' She handed a copy over.

All credit to the rag – the story might have changed but the theme hadn't. A picture of Melanie Brand under the headline: *"They Slaughtered Their Au Pair"* and a rogue's gallery off to the side: Elaine, Stuart and Sharon. They'd dug deep, found snaps with scowls that made Hindley and Brady look cheerful.

I scanned the story but ignored the bait of the sub-head which pointed us onward *"Christa alive and well – Barber lie exposed. Pages 2, 3, 4, 9 and 14"*. People were going to be late for work this morning.

Shaughnessy stood and walked to the window. Watched the rain.

'She almost pulled it off,' he said.

I tossed the tabloid back. 'Yeah. Elaine nearly got to Heather. But her plan was already shot. If she'd reached her last Friday she'd have had a chance. But by yesterday her self-defence story wasn't going to hold.'

'Not that she didn't try to sort out that problem,' Shaughnessy said.

'I can't *believe* Elaine tried to kill you,' Lucy said.

I grinned. 'Customer feedback isn't all it's cracked up to be,' I told her. 'But there wasn't much risk. It would take more than a madwoman with a kitchen knife.'

'How did you figure it out? Why were you so keen on getting to Melanie?'

'Because she was in the middle of it and the Barbers were too intent on steering us away. I figured that whatever Melanie had to say would be worth hearing.'

I sipped coffee. 'We were always hot and cold on them,' I said. 'Either Christa was abducted or they killed her. The evidence supported either possibility at first. The problem was, in the end it supported neither.'

I planted the coffee. Joined Shaughnessy at the window. Umbrellas flapped up and down the street. The space where the Astra had baked in the heat two weeks ago was empty.

That's what it had come down to. Two solutions that didn't work.

'Melanie's family photo was the last nail in the coffin,' I said. 'It meant that neither explanation made sense – because Melanie matched the Barbers' Mystery Woman, and she shouldn't have.'

'She shouldn't?'

'If the Barbers killed Christa then their Mystery Woman was a fabrication, a fictitious abductor. But why would they make her look like Melanie in their first photofit? The last thing they wanted was to have Melanie dragged in. It wasn't going to help their case if it came out that they weren't Christa's parents.

'On the other hand, if Christa really was abducted by a Mystery Woman then it was a hell of a coincidence that she looked like Melanie – unless that's who she was. But if Melanie had taken Christa why would the Barbers deny that they'd seen her? The fastest way to get Christa back would have been to identify her. Innocent or guilty: neither explanation made sense once we knew that Melanie matched the Barbers' photofit.'

I left the window. Leaned on the partners desk.

'That was our problem,' I said. 'Neither scenario worked.'

'But if the Barbers weren't innocent or guilty,' Lucy said, 'what was the solution?'

'Both. They were innocent *and* guilty. They didn't kill Christa but they did kill Melanie. Elaine killed her the evening Christa disappeared. They'd left Christa in the caravan to drive to a meeting that Melanie had forced on them to demand access to her. The meeting turned into a disaster that left Melanie dead. But finding Christa gone when they got back to the caravan was an even bigger disaster: Stuart and Elaine could only assume that Melanie had snatched her and hidden her before coming to meet them. Hence their Mystery Woman. Time was critical. They were desperate for any sightings of Melanie that might help locate Christa. But they couldn't reveal Melanie's identity because Elaine had just killed her.'

'The Mystery Woman detail snared them,' Harry said. 'It didn't get the police to Christa, but it left Stuart and Elaine with the risk that Melanie would be identified during the investigation, which they needed to avoid. So they updated their description. The second photofit was sufficiently altered to ensure that no-one would connect it to Melanie.'

'The clue to the whole thing was in the hate-mail,' I said. 'We were right about there being two writers. Subtle style differences, a different printer. What we missed was the big thing.'

'You spotted it when I read the letters yesterday?' Lucy said.

'Yeah. Something in the letters had been off from the start but I hadn't picked it up. Then I talked to Irene Keenan yesterday and it changed everything. And when you read out the letters it was clear as day. The original letters denounced the Barbers as killers but didn't say whom they'd killed. The copycat was more specific: they called the Barbers "baby-killers". That was the difference. The phoney letters were sent to obscure the meaning of the vigilante's hate-mail, which was about the Barbers killing Melanie. The vigilante was Heather, assisted by Paul Tyndall.'

'So what did Irene tell you?' asked Lucy.

'Something that gave a reason why Melanie might be dead. We

were thinking she was involved somehow – maybe as Christa's abductor, maybe as the vigilante. But all the signs in the last few days suggested that Christa was alive. So what was Hackett's *Sad Christa* stuff? He must have had some reason to think Christa was buried on Damien Larkin's land. Maybe he'd got his story half right. Maybe someone *was* buried there. Melanie crossed my mind but at first I dismissed her. We knew she was Christa's mother and I could picture her coming back to reclaim Christa or to squeeze money from the Barbers but I couldn't see Elaine or Stuart killing her over that. Elaine's a focused woman but nothing we'd heard about her suggested that she'd ever solve a problem by killing in cold blood.'

The rain had stopped. Sunlight flared off the rooftops and lit the room. Shaughnessy lifted the sash and a cool breeze ruffled paperwork. London breathed outside. The sound of dripping continued in the back rooms.

'Melanie did come back,' Shaughnessy said. 'She was living with Heather two years ago. Got a notion about reclaiming her daughter but maybe wasn't sure she could handle it; not sure she wanted it. By herself she'd not have acted. It took Heather to goad her into action.'

'Then the two stepsisters spotted Elaine in Lyndhurst,' I said. 'Heather pressed Melanie to confront the Barbers and demand access to Christa and in the end Melanie acted. Called Stuart and insisted that they meet her at the Saracen. That's why the Barbers left Christa that night. But when they did meet up the Barbers persuaded Melanie to slow down, give everyone time to think. Melanie was broke. Money was mentioned. The Barbers drove her into Lyndhurst to get cash to buy breathing space.

'Melanie squeezing them for cash was still no reason to kill her, of course. It was only when Irene Keenan talked to me yesterday that I saw how it happened. That's when I knew Melanie was dead.'

'What did Irene know?' Lucy was wide-eyed. Not everything was in her damn tabloids.

'Irene hadn't recognised the Mystery Woman photofits but she did recognise Melanie's photo,' I said. 'But not because she'd seen her the day Christa disappeared. She'd seen her more than two years before – before Christa was born. It turns out that Stuart was having the occasional weekend at the caravan with his seventeen year old *au pair*. Stuart had started taking Melanie there when things were strained between him and Elaine after they lost Grace. Seems he found his own comfort elsewhere. Irene had spotted them a couple of times. That's why she was uncomfortable talking about Stuart. She knew things about the family she wished she didn't.'

'And Elaine found out?' Lucy's eyes were widening by the second.

'At the worst time, in the worst way. It all happened that night. The two of them were waiting in the car whilst Stuart walked to the cash machine. They got into an argument about Christa, and Melanie was provoked into spilling her biggest secret: Elaine knew Christa was Melanie's daughter, of course, but now Melanie threw the rest in her face. Revealed that Stuart was the father. I guess Elaine's world came crashing down. For a moment she just lost it. Ironically, Melanie had just given Elaine a solid basis to keep Christa. If Stuart was the real father and Melanie had abandoned Christa then the Barbers were going to keep her for sure. But custody of her daughter became the least of Melanie's worries. Elaine saw red, made a grab for her, maybe got a scarf round her neck. Rage gives people unnatural strength. It was probably over within two minutes, and Stuart returned to find Melanie dead in their car. Then they drove back to the Orchard Grove and the nightmare got worse.'

'Because Christa was gone,' said Lucy.

'And the Barbers jumped to the wrong conclusion. It wasn't Melanie who'd taken her. Melanie and Heather had been waiting in the car near the site when the meeting was set up. They watched the Barbers drive past on their way to the Saracen and Melanie followed on foot. Seems she wanted to meet them alone. But once she'd gone Heather acted on impulse and drove onto the site to check out the Barber caravan, perhaps to get a sight of her step-niece. And when she found the door open she just went in and took her.'

'And no-one saw her?'

'Irene Keenan saw her – or rather her car. It's a black Renault Clio, not so different to the Barbers' Fiat. Irene swore that she saw the Barbers' car at their caravan when they claimed to be out, but what Irene saw was Heather's Renault. Irene's eyesight is sharp. It's her model-recognition that's shot. But it would take a second look for most people to tell a Punto from a Clio, front-on.'

'What about the other inconsistencies,' Lucy asked. 'Their whole account that night was contradicted.'

Shaughnessy sat back down at his desk. 'All part of the problem when you put a story together on the fly,' he said. 'Apart from Irene's car-recognition error the discrepancies with the Barbers' account that night were real. The Smiths did see Stuart poke his nose in at the Saracen – he was checking to see if Melanie was in there since she was late meeting them. And they really did see Stuart searching round the site in the initial panic, because the Barbers' first assumption was that Christa had just wandered out of the caravan by herself. Once they'd changed their minds – deduced that Melanie had taken her – Stuart grabbed the car and drove round the area looking for a parked vehicle in which Christa might have been left. But he found nothing. Could only assume that Christa was hidden somewhere in the area and that the only person who knew where was dead on his back seat. So now they needed the police to organise a search but they needed to hide the car first.'

'The dog handler was right,' Lucy said. 'They did have a body in their car. Just not Christa's.'

I went out to check the biscuit tin. It was full. The drips had slowed but the rain was coming back. We needed to get our landlord up on the roof. Threaten to sue him for flood damage. We'd do that once we were up to date on the rent. I emptied the tin and went back. Grinned at Lucy. Flopped back into the easy chair.

'The body in the car was spot on. My talk with Peter Starr told me that. Had me wondering whether the Barbers really had killed Christa.'

'That was tricky – disposing of Melanie's body in the middle of the search.'

'They had help. Elaine phoned Sharon, told her everything, and Sharon came through: knew where to take the body. The family estate at Devizes – remote and large enough to ensure that Melanie would never be found.'

'So Damien was part of it?'

I shook my head. 'Damien's involvement was all in *The Nation's* mind. Hackett's misinterpretation of one-sided phone conversations at the Barbers' house. Hackett knew that someone was working with the Barbers and I guess the Devizes location must have come up in the conversations. He put two and two together and got the wrong answer.'

'But Damien turned up at the Orchard Grove,' Lucy said. 'Sharon told you that.'

'Her mistake,' I grinned. 'It's always the detail that gets you when you're fibbing. Damien sounded suspicious as hell at first. You always look at family members when there's kids missing. But Sharon shouldn't have made Damien sound so useless, because that contradicted his apparent initiative in turning up to help. Damien cleared that up yesterday: he turned up because Sharon pressured him. And she did that because she wanted him away from Devizes so that she and Stuart could bury Melanie.'

Harry grinned. 'They got Melanie's body away under everyone's noses. It might have turned out all right if she had actually taken Christa. Christa would have been found somewhere nearby and no-one would ever have connected Melanie to the affair. She would have simply disappeared without anyone knowing or caring.'

'But Christa wasn't found,' I said, 'and the whole thing kicked off – the phoney appeals, the website, the book. It was phoney because after a week the Barbers were sure that Christa had died alone, undiscovered.'

'No wonder they were so distraught,' Lucy said. 'Imagine thinking that Christa was dying somewhere and that they'd caused it. Imagine what Elaine was feeling about Stuart and his stupid affair with Melanie.'

'I guess the feelings would have been a little mixed,' I said. 'If it wasn't for Stuart's stupid affair they wouldn't have had Christa in the first place.'

'Wow!' Lucy agreed. 'A real tangled web. But bringing out their book was cynical.'

'Sure there was a cynical side, but it was also a continuation of the act. They had to keep playing along with the abduction story even though they thought Christa was dead. They were locked into the thing – *The Sun* serialisation, the website, everything. But maybe the book was cathartic too. In Elaine's mind maybe everything happened just as they claimed. Perhaps she half-hoped that Christa *had* been abducted by a stranger and not by Melanie, and that if they persisted, carried on with their appeals, maybe they'd get her back. Maybe she just couldn't bear to admit that it was over.'

'Then they got the photo,' Lucy said.

'First they got the hate-mail. That was Heather, living with the consequences of what she'd caused. *She'd* pressured Melanie into going after the Barbers. She'd got Melanie killed and left herself holding Christa. And now Christa tied her. She couldn't go to the police with accusations without being exposed as Christa's abductor. So Heather expressed her rage in the hate-mail and shanghaied her dodgy boyfriend into those stupid attacks. The problem was that Tyndall had a dodgy relative who got the whisper of something up and saw a quick profit. Snapped the photo at Chatham. When the photo surfaced Tyndall and Heather fled the house – never imagining that the photographer was family and could track them down any time. But in the end it was the hate-mail that was Heather's downfall. Because the combination of the letters and photo told the Barbers that Melanie didn't take Christa.'

'Heather should have kept a lid on it,' Harry said. 'When you're bringing up a stolen kid you're not in a position to point a finger.'

I agreed. 'I doubt if Stuart and Elaine paid too much attention to the letters at first – they had plenty of hate-mail coming in – but when the photo appeared the Barbers recalled something they'd read in one of them. Something I spotted when you read the letters to me yesterday, Luce. The second letter had some funny words: *"you've fooled everyone, but I know what cold-blooded monsters you are"*. That stuff about fooling everyone. What did that mean? Everyone believed that the Barbers killed Christa. So why would their vigilante talk about them *fooling* anyone? And something else: the theory was that Elaine killed Christa when she snapped during Christa's tantrum. So what did "cold-blooded" mean? Then the Christa Photo turned up and the Barbers saw their daughter alive and well and interpreted those words in a new light. Finally realised that the writer was accusing them of killing Melanie. But the only way their hate-mailer could have known about *that* was if they'd been there themselves that night. And suddenly Stuart and Elaine knew why Christa hadn't been found: Melanie had had an accomplice. The accomplice had taken Christa.'

'So they held up their book to get the photo in,' Lucy said.

'When the photo arrived their whole find-Christa campaign became real,' Harry said. 'But they were trapped along with the abductor in a Devil's snare.'

301

I sat back, grinned. 'The abductor wasn't in any position to expose them over Melanie's killing, and the Barbers couldn't expose the abductor without being accused in turn of killing Melanie. Stuart and Elaine had a dilemma. Then everything went on hold because Hammer Hayes, the guy who'd snapped the photo, took a trip to jail himself. When the classified ads stopped they lost their route to Christa.'

'What made them start again?' Lucy asked. 'Why did they come to us?'

'That was Hayes becoming active again,' Shaughnessy said. 'They'd waited through a year of silence for the Christa Photo source to continue the negotiations. That was a mistake. They should have brought investigators in as soon as the communications dried up but they had things to hide and were locked into the idea that this guy would eventually talk to them again. But when the classified messages did restart they knew they couldn't risk losing contact again. They had to chase the guy fast. Pay him off if necessary. So they brought us in and took the risk that we'd link Christa's abductor to the vigilante. If we did that it would open up some dangerous questions.'

Lucy shook her head. 'But they knew that Christa's abductor was the vigilante, that it would all come out.'

I stood. Went back to the window. Watched the rain coming on harder. The breeze was icy under the sash.

'That was the Barbers' problem: they knew that Christa's abductor could put Elaine in jail for Melanie's death. So they had to set everything up. Sharon sent her own version of the threat-letters that were supposed to throw us off track. Copied the style of the real ones down to the last detail but with two differences: she posted them to the west to shift the centre of gravity away from where the real ones originated; and she put in the critical detail about "baby killers" so no-one would ever interpret the original letters as being about Melanie's death. Then when we located Christa, Elaine's plan was to go charging in and silence the abductor before they could expose her as Melanie's killer. A self-defence killing would sound credible.'

'What Elaine didn't realise yesterday,' Harry said, 'was that we'd already linked the abductor to Melanie. Elaine's plan was in tatters before she went rushing off to Dartford.'

'What about Grace,' Lucy said. 'Did Melanie have anything to do with that?'

'Grace died a natural death,' I said. 'No-one to blame.'

The rain burst on ferociously. Gusted under the sash. I slammed it closed. Lucy went out to change the bucket. Harry heaved himself from his chair and headed for the door.

'Call me when you've anything on,' he said.

Lucy excused herself too.

'I've gotta give my uncle a couple of extra days at the shop,' she said. 'I'll start on our bills next Monday.'

'Tell Umberto hello,' I said. 'And paying bills sounds good. Our coffers are as loaded as they'll ever be.'

Shaughnessy locked his desk. Sighed.

'Business beckons,' he said. 'I got a call. Some guy's wife is trying to poison him. He wants me to take a look.'

I raised my eyebrows. 'If he asks you to sample the food check our insurance policy.'

He threw a grin. Pulled on his jacket.

'I'll do that, Eddie,' he promised.

He walked out. I went through to my office.

CHAPTER SIXTY-ONE
Clean-up

I emptied the biscuit tin and set it back under the drip. Shifted the inkjet further along the cabinet out of harm's way. Cracked the window six inches. Angled my Herman Miller and got my feet onto the sill. Listened to the rain.

The hiss of traffic drifted over the Great Western lines, intermittent horns, short and businesslike. The heat's fury had gone.

The storm front had moved out over the North Sea leaving an ashen sky weeping endless rain. My eye caught a movement up on the Westway tower. I focused beyond the rain-streaked glass. Saw the flag, abandoned on the railings fifteen floors up, fluttering in the breeze, delivering its own semaphore.

I mulled things over. Concluded that we could rack this one up as a success. We'd been commissioned to get a result. Warned the clients they might not like it. Duly delivered. And we found Christa Barber and dug out the truth despite the clients' best efforts. If I ignored the fact that it almost ended in disaster I could say we'd done okay.

I watched the flag for a while but couldn't decipher any message. The thing had as much meaning as anything in this town. I picked up my phone and keyed Arabel's code. Got voicemail.

"Bel. Just checking in.'

I gave it another ten minutes then decided I'd better take a look at the unanswered messages Lucy had been stacking up for two weeks. Our next job would seem kind of quiet but maybe that wasn't a bad thing. And we needed to get back to regular business. Eagle Eye weren't going to survive on Shaughnessy's food-tasting jape. Not all of us, anyway.

I was reaching for the stack of Post-its when I heard feet on the stairs. The outer door opened. Footsteps hesitated by the bucket outside then a face appeared in my doorway.

He was wearing the same rumpled suit as last time.

I waved him in.

'Welcome to Eagle Eye, Barry,' I said.

The biscuit tin at his feet caught his attention. His head tilted to the ceiling.

'It's not much,' I said, 'but we're operational.'

He didn't look convinced. He eyed my club chairs. Lowered his weight carefully into one of them. Looked at me.

DCS Barry Bedford. The guy running the Christa Barber case. In town on clean-up business.

He sat back gingerly and put a curl on his lips.

'So, Flynn,' he said, 'here we are.'

I swivelled the Miller and racked it upright.

'Here we are,' I said. 'Like I told you: our firm was up to it. But I guess you've checked us out by now.'

He tilted his head.

'We've had a long chat with the Met.'

I shrugged. 'We got Christa,' I said.

He pursed his lips. For the first time there was something half friendly in his eyes.

'Yes, Flynn. Not a bad job. So...' he looked at me and worked hard at holding the friendly look, 'call this a courtesy visit. We appreciate what you did. Especially the turning-in bit.'

'I told you,' I said. 'We don't protect clients if they turn out dirty. Same as the old days.'

'That's why I'm here,' Bedford said. 'I checked out about the "old days". The Met's got a tradition of cultivating coppers who are too close to the bad guys. They told me you weren't one of those. That's why I called: to say I know it.'

He looked at me and pushed out a wheezing chuckle. 'From what the Met says, the Barbers were on the rocks the moment they hired you.'

Bedford was a biggish guy. His wheeze rattled around. At the end of it I was grinning myself. I thought he'd finished but then a laugh burst out unfettered as he looked round the room. Opened his arms.

'They just didn't tell me you lived in such a shit-hole!'

I held my grin. 'You should see us in winter,' I said.

Bedford shook his head. 'No,' he said. 'I'm not going to do that.'

We let it ride.

'Has it reverted to Hampshire?'

'Yes. The case is still mine and I've taken SIO on Melanie Brand's death too, so Stuart's with us in Southampton. Elaine's still talking to Kent about yesterday's circus but she'll be joining us tomorrow.'

'You've confirmed that Melanie's dead?'

'Pretty much. Stuart was out with us at six. There's a team with excavators on Larkin's land. We'll have her out by lunchtime. I'm on my way to Elstree to get the Barbers' house secure. We're going after everyone involved in this, on both sides of the fence. The Met are charging Heather with the abduction and Tyndall with attempted murder and arson. And the Leveson team is having a party.'

'Hackett,' I said.

'Hackett and his poxy editor and their poxy proprietor. They were tapping the Barbers' phones whilst the rest of the country was watching the *News Of The World* fall-out.' He shook his head. 'They just don't learn, these people. Hackett's editor is making surprised sounds but the bitch knew exactly what the guy was up to. *The Nation's* going to *be* the next big story.'

He looked at me a moment. Pursed his lips.

'There's a whole bunch of people you've smoked out of the woodwork, Flynn, so I'm not here to complain. I assume that the Met will want your firm's co-operation on the house bugs.'

'We'll give them what they need,' I said. 'What about Christa?'

The one we'd not discussed. I didn't see her coming out of this in such good shape. I could still see the confusion in her face as the policewoman led her away. By now the confusion would have fermented into fear, the need for her mother. Probably she was asking for Heather when she was coaxed off to sleep last night.

Bedford sighed. Heaved himself out of the chair. Visit over.

'Not my department,' he said. 'God knows what will happen to the poor blighter. She's not going back to Heather, that's for sure. I understand there's other family somewhere.'

I pictured the house on the Barton estate. When Social Services poked their nose in that door they'd run screaming.

Bedford was itching to get going. Stood watching my biscuit tin filling, fishing for parting words. Then he turned quick and held out his hand. I stood to shake it. He nodded once and went out. The outer door closed behind him.

I emptied the tin into the bathroom sink. Swivelled my Miller back to the window and pictured Bedford driving in through the Barbers' gate, sniffing the charcoal smell of the empty house. He'd been after the couple for two years but I doubt if he was feeling good this morning.

I grabbed my phone and hit Arabel's code again. The call went to unavailable. The rain on the window beat a staccato refrain to the timpani of steady drips hitting my biscuit tin.

THE END

ACKNOWLEDGEMENTS

A novel appears in print only after the scrutiny of many eyes has helped polish out the flaws spat from the author's word processor. Thanks firstly to my wife, Odette, who read the first very rough draft and confirmed that it was on track; then to Sallyanne Sweeney of Mulcahy Associates for her detailed critical feedback at the early stage. For his independent critique of the mature draft, and offer of support with a review, thanks to author Kerry Donovan.

I delved into my extensive reference library wherever a little research was needed, and Richard Saferstein's *Criminalistics* and Kate Wall's *Special Needs and Early Years* both proved invaluable. The internet, of course, is a marvellous repository of information on every subject of interest to a crime writer, and I've used this resource extensively. London locations are depicted based both on visits during the course of writing the novel and from older memories: the burned out cars in the parking basement beneath the tower block are real, and Flynn's reaction, in heading smartly back to the light, uncannily matches my own when confronted with the same situation two decades ago.

Any errors of fact and location are the responsibility of the author, who has, nevertheless, written a work of fiction. The bad behaviour of the tabloid press, as we all know, is pure fantasy.

BEHIND CLOSED DOORS

Family feuds, booze and bad company. Teenager Rebecca Slater's walk on the wild side has taken a downward spiral. And now she's disappeared.

But her family don't seem to have noticed. Wealthy, private, dysfunctional, the Slaters deny that their daughter is missing – even as they block all attempts by Rebecca's friends to contact her.

So the friends contact a private investigator.

Eddie Flynn is good at finding people. And he's good at spotting lies. It doesn't take him long to see through the Slaters' denials. So he digs around, and isn't too surprised when some unpleasant people come scuttling out of the cracks in the Slaters' perfect world.

But for these people the teenager's disappearance is part of a plan. One that's too important to be threatened by an investigator with more persistence than sense. So it's time for the investigator to disappear...

Winner of the **Northern Crime 2012** award, *Behind Closed Doors* has been acclaimed for its departure from the norm for British crime fiction...

Donovan refreshingly breaks [the tradition] with remarkable success
Cuckoo Review

Eddie Flynn is part Philip Marlowe, part Eddie Gumshoe, a likeable wisecracking guy but with a temper when roused ... humour ... violent confrontations ... well recommended.
eurocrime

www.michaeldonovancrime.com

COLD CALL
Michael Donovan

In the black of night the intruder breaks into the victim's house armed with a knife and garrotte. Her body is found thirty hours later, a mass of stab wounds, a deadly laceration round her neck.

Is this the Diceman, killing again after seven years lying low? Or does London have a copycat killer?

P.I. Eddie Flynn has been out of that world since his failed hunt for the Diceman let the killer go free and cost him his job in the Metropolitan Police.

Now, with the new killer on the rampage a bizarre phone call from his dead victim drags Flynn right back to centre stage and a new hunt. But this killer – copycat or not – takes a P.I.'s interference personally.

So now he has a new focus for his madness.

"Chilling ... crafted with style...
wild nightmarish scenes."
Bookpleasures

"Masterful... If you haven't been
introduced to Eddie Flynn yet, be prepared"
Red City Review

www.michaeldonovancrime.com

Made in United States
Orlando, FL
03 December 2024

54815785R00193